HER
RIVAL

BOOKS BY EMMA TALLON

EMMA TALLON

HER RIVAL

bookouture

Published by Bookouture in 2021

An imprint of Storyfire Ltd.
Carmelite House
50 Victoria Embankment
London EC4Y 0DZ

www.bookouture.com

ISBN: 978-1-80019-338-3
eBook ISBN: 978-1-80019-337-6

This book is a work of fiction. Names, characters, businesses,
organizations, places and events other than those clearly in the
public domain, are either the product of the author's imagination
or are used fictitiously. Any resemblance to actual persons, living or
dead, events or locales is entirely coincidental.

For my beautiful children. Every beat of your hearts serves to motivate me a little more, each and every day. I love you so much more than words can describe.

PROLOGUE

'We should leave,' he said with a note of warning.

'Shut up,' she ordered, her eyes shining in the darkness as the flames crept out and up the sides of the burning building. 'I don't want to miss this.'

She wondered if the flames had reached them yet, up there, trapped in the office. She wondered whether they had screamed and fought against them, looking for a way out. She wondered if they'd managed to get downstairs only to realise that all possible escape routes had been blocked.

Her smile grew wider as she pictured it, as she savoured the thought in her mind as one might savour the most cherished memories of the things they loved.

Finally, she wondered whether it would be the smoke or the fire itself that would kill them, as they realised in their last few seconds that they were going to die there, and that it had been her who'd ended their sad little lives.

The flames grew and climbed the walls, and then the ear-splitting sound of glass shattering cracked through the air like a gun as the windows all exploded outwards in a glittering, beautiful display of destruction.

CHAPTER ONE

Two weeks earlier

The doorbell chimed just as Cath lifted her freshly poured mug to her mouth and the tea spilled down the front of her cream top.

'Oh, for God's sake. I only bought this yesterday.' She tutted and attempted to rub the beige stain away.

'Who's that?' Scarlet's voice wafted down the stairs.

'Dunno,' Cath answered, annoyed. 'But if it's your aunt Lil forgetting her key again that's caused me to ruin me new top, you'll be bailing me out for murder, I tell ya…'

She opened the door and her eyes flew wide open. 'Oh! Officer. That was a joke,' she said quickly.

The second officer standing slightly behind hid a grin, but the one holding her gaze did not, raising his eyebrow with a cool look of disdain. 'Mrs Drew.' He greeted her curtly. 'May we come in?'

Cath planted her fist on her hip. 'That depends. What's it about?'

'We just need to ask your daughter a few more questions about her relationship with Jasper Snow,' he replied, not put off at all by her blunt response.

Cath felt her blood run cold at the mention of Jasper's name but was careful to show no reaction.

'Why?' she asked. 'She's already been down the station countless times to talk to you lot.' She frowned and visibly bristled as the annoyance in her tone grew. 'I mean, what could you possibly *still* want with her, eh? That bastard killed Ronan – my husband, her *dad*. Why are you making us relive that?'

'We only need five minutes,' he pressed, undeterred. 'We just want to confirm a few things.'

'Unless you've got a warrant you can piss off,' Cath retorted. 'She's been through enough. In fact, I might have to have a few words with the superintendent about this constant harassment. It's a flipping joke.'

'It's OK, Mum.' Scarlet appeared and pulled the door open wide. 'Better here than having to drag myself down to the station again.'

Cath sighed and stepped back, allowing them room to walk in. It was true. Even if she did get them off Scarlet's back now, they'd only return later on.

She glared at them. 'I'd offer you a drink,' she said in a loud voice, 'but to be honest I don't want to.' Without bothering to wait for any response, she walked off to the kitchen.

They might be all powerful when it came to the law, but this was *her* house, her territory, and Old Bill was the enemy in their world. There was no point pretending she held any respect for them now. They knew who she was. She'd covered Ronan's back enough times over their twenty years together. She'd been questioned and interrogated and even arrested once or twice in the earlier days, when they'd tried to get her husband through her. But they never had. She'd never faltered and never shown fear. All they'd ever got from her was the metaphorical middle finger, time and again. And that wasn't going to stop now, just because Ronan was gone.

Picking up her tea, Cath leaned over the kitchen island and strained to listen to what was going on. They were asking Scarlet the same questions again, about the night Jasper had died. She listened as her daughter calmly reeled off the cover story they'd come up with.

Why were they still rehashing this? Were they just trying to trip her up, hoping she might mess up her story? Cath shivered.

That night haunted her dreams. She still remembered the feel of the gun in her hand and the sensation of protective fear and anger that had coursed through her veins as he'd run towards her baby, a knife in his hand. It had all gone a bit hazy then. All thought and reason had slipped from her mind, and all she'd been able to think about was stopping him. He'd already taken Ronan from them. She couldn't allow him to take Scarlet too. She'd shot him from across the room, stopping him in his tracks. And she'd felt nothing but relief as the bullet hit.

She hadn't killed him though. That had been Scarlet. She wasn't actually sure what had shocked her more – the fact she'd shot a man in the leg, or the fact that her own daughter had so calmly taken the gun from her hands and shot him in the head, finishing the job.

That had been the day Cath had realised Scarlet was truly a Drew. She'd been born a Drew and had been raised knowing what they did her whole life. But for years Cath had been convinced that Scarlet would break away, forge a new path. She'd even had a place all set at university. But in the end, she had followed in the footsteps of Ronan and his sister Lily. Fierce and powerful, Scarlet was a smart and incredibly deadly creature of the underworld. And it was in that moment, as she pulled the trigger and ended Jasper's life, that Cath had finally realised it.

Lily and her sons had sorted the body, putting it in the river along with a suicide note in the pocket, explaining that he'd taken his own life because he was so consumed with guilt from killing Ronan. It all would have been so cut and dried had it not been for the bullet hole in his leg. The bullet *she* had put there.

Her gaze slipped up towards the fridge as guilt flooded through her and the stress that weighed on her shoulders caused a familiar tug of longing. A glass of wine would really take the edge off.

Except it was barely half past eight in the morning. And she had promised Scarlet she wouldn't slip back into using alcohol as a crutch, the way she had after Ronan had died. She rubbed her face and picked up what was left of her tea instead.

Eventually, the conversation in the next room came to a close. She waited whilst the officers were shown out, then Scarlet walked in and sighed heavily, before sitting on a breakfast bar stool.

'Well?' Cath asked, worried.

'Nothing new,' Scarlet replied. 'All the same questions. Where I was, what time we were all at Lil's until, what we ate and drank…' She trailed off.

Cath bit her bottom lip. 'They're trying to trip you up,' she said. 'Find a hole in our story.'

'I know. And they haven't so far, but what if they do?' She turned her serious grey-blue eyes towards her mother. 'What then? They ain't dropping it, Mum. They know something's up, even if they can't prove it.'

'They won't,' Cath replied, her tone much stronger than she really felt. 'They have nothing, Scarlet. Look at me,' she demanded. She held her gaze. 'There is no evidence that you killed him, that this wasn't exactly what it was packaged as. The bullet in the leg is unfortunate, but it can be explained. He had a misfire.' She spread her arms to the sides and shrugged. 'It happens. The pressure is on right now, yes. But they'll have to drop it soon. They might smell something fishy but they ain't caught a cod yet. Christ, they haven't even found a flake of tinned tuna.'

Scarlet exhaled. 'Maybe you're right.'

'Of course I am,' Cath responded, not missing a beat. 'I didn't help keep your dad out of prison all these years to have *you* fall at the first hurdle. Not that I'm exactly thrilled that you're jumping these particular hurdles,' she added with a grumble.

'Yet here we are,' Scarlet replied. She stood up, ending the conversation as Cath had known she would. She hated it when

Cath brought up the subject of her life choices. 'Hopefully you're right and they all move on soon.'

'They will. Just hang in there, keep your wits sharp and they'll be gone soon,' Cath said with a tone of certainty.

Scarlet shot her a smile, then went upstairs to continue getting ready for the day.

As Cath watched her retreating form, she felt a chill settle into her bones. She'd put on a brave face for Scarlet's sake, but in reality she was terrified. They *knew*. They didn't have evidence yet, but they knew. They wouldn't keep hounding them otherwise. The question wasn't whether or not they suspected the Drews' involvement in Jasper's death anymore. The question was, with no evidence, would they give up and mark it as a cold case? Or would they keep hounding them one by one until eventually someone slipped up?

CHAPTER TWO

Scarlet stepped out of the sleek black Mercedes that used to belong to her father, pushed the door shut and walked with purpose towards the factory, her family's main legitimate business, with a spring in her high-heeled step. She swept her thick raven hair back over her shoulder and straightened the smart suit jacket she wore over her fitted black dress.

Cillian, one of her older twin cousins, fell into step beside her as she entered the building. With the same pale skin, dark hair and striking looks, it was clear the handsome pair were related. Their Irish blood ran strong in their veins, though they'd both been born and raised in London.

Flicking away the toothpick he'd been chewing to assuage his nicotine cravings, Cillian undid his own suit jacket and reached into the inner pocket. He pulled out a phone and handed it to Scarlet. 'Here's your new burner. Main numbers are already programmed in.'

'Thanks.' She took it and slipped it into her handbag without looking at it. It was standard practice to swap out their phones – both the handsets and the SIMs – regularly. It made it harder for the police to trace them.

They moved quickly through the busy factory floor, ignoring the loud repetitive sounds of the heavy machinery and the shouts between the workers. As they mounted the stairs, Scarlet looked up towards the two offices overlooked the factory floor and saw her Aunt Lily standing at the window of one, watching them with one arm folded across her middle and the other holding a cigarette up in the air. Her stance was tense, more so than usual, she noticed. They entered as Lily sat down behind the desk at the far side of the room.

'You're late,' Lily stated in a calm, smooth tone.

'It couldn't be helped,' Scarlet immediately replied, not fooled by the casual way the words were delivered.

Lily had no need for menace or volume when it came to those who knew her. She was the head of this firm, and all who worked for her knew where the line was drawn. She ran a tight ship with a firm hand, and lateness was not tolerated without a bloody good excuse.

Scarlet sat down opposite her aunt at the desk. 'I had a call from Sandra,' she continued, her lips pressing together in a grim line.

'Oh?' Lily's forehead puckered into a frown and she took another drag of her cigarette, tapping it lightly on the ashtray as she blew the smoke back out. 'Why the hell is she calling you?'

'She's got the clap,' Scarlet replied. 'And not only that, she's given it to one of our regulars. Dimitri.'

'For fuck's sake,' Lily exclaimed, sitting back in her chair and raising her eyes to the heavens. 'Oh, the *stupid* girl,' she groaned. She shook her head. 'OK. That still don't explain why she called you though,' she added.

'I think she thought I was a soft touch,' Scarlet responded. 'She asked me if I'd help her sort it out and keep it from you.'

'Rookie error,' Cillian replied, sitting down in the chair next to her. 'That's going to cost us big time. When word gets out, we're going to get very quiet.' He sighed and eyed his mother's cigarette wistfully. It had only been a few weeks since he'd given up but the cravings didn't seem to be easing.

'We're going to have to do some damage control. When did she tell Dimitri?' Lily asked.

'He told her he had it. She knew *she* did but only found out after she'd been with him. She'd hoped she hadn't passed it on.'

'And she admitted she had it to him?' Lily asked, her deep brown gaze boring into her niece intently.

'No,' Scarlet said with a shake of the head. 'She denied it, but he wasn't buying it.'

'OK. You need to go back and tell her she's out,' she instructed Scarlet. 'I want her packed and out of the penthouse tonight. And Cillian, organise a party for all our regulars, everyone on the top list. We'll foot the expense, make a big show of gratitude for their ongoing business.' She took another deep drag and continued as she exhaled the smoke. 'We'll need to tell the other girls the score, make sure they're ready with reassurances.'

The handful of high-end escorts they ran for big-spending clients was usually a low-maintenance, high-yield business. It was also one of their few legitimate businesses, despite its darker roots. Lily had never touted their sex acts, only their time as social companions, which was extremely expensive, but all perfectly legal and above board. What the girls then did and offered behind closed doors was their own business.

Whilst they stayed out of it though, they made it clear they had to stick to certain standards. In passing on an STI, Sandra had broken their most sacred rule, and there was no going back from that. The rules were simple, but they were finite.

'No problem,' Scarlet agreed. 'I'll pop back in a bit; I just need to make a few calls first.' She shifted in her seat. 'There's something else I wanted to discuss if we have time?'

Lily glanced at her watch. 'We have a few minutes. What's up?'

'I think I've found premises that would work perfectly for the new laundry.' Her eyes gleamed as she imparted this news.

'The hairdresser's?' Lily asked, tilting her head to the side as she studied her niece.

'Yes.'

The family had been struggling to launder the amount of money they were currently making for some time. They'd had a few ideas but none that they could all agree would work – until now. Scarlet's idea to run dummy chairs through a new hairdresser's would solve all their problems.

'OK, where?' Lily sat back and waited with interest.

'Not far from the escort penthouse actually. It's right next to Snaresbrook Tube station, couple of doors down. It's empty but *was* a hairdresser's, so it's actually already laid out pretty well,' she replied.

Lily's gaze narrowed as she tried to place it. 'The one next to the dry cleaner's?'

'That's the one.'

'It's closed down? I wonder why.'

'Who knows? If it's down to not enough passing trade though, that's even better,' Scarlet said. 'The less custom we get, the more we can launder.' She shrugged.

'OK.' Lily nodded. 'Send me the details. I'll see if I can get us a viewing at some point today.'

'Great, will do.' Scarlet stood, followed by Cillian. It was clear Lily was busy, and they had things to be getting on with too.

'Take these.' Lily handed over several thick brown packets full of money. 'That's the chip shop, the pizza place and the café down the Eric and Treby. And while you're there' – she turned her sharp gaze to her son – 'speak to Chain about that truckload of goods coming in next week. It's a bigger haul than we thought. There will be too much for the markets.'

'Will do,' Cillian said with a nod.

He picked up two of the packets and slipped them into his inner jacket pockets. Scarlet grabbed the last one and put it in her handbag, following Cillian with a smile down the metal stairs to the factory floor.

Her smile swiftly faded though as they reached the exit and she clocked the patrol car parked up across the street. Her hand tightened around her handbag. Why were they there? Were they watching her now, as well as dragging her in for questioning every five minutes? Her whole body tensed as the men within looked over.

'Ignore them, Scar,' Cillian said quietly. 'They ain't here for you.'

Suddenly, they moved forward and drove off down the road, the traffic moving once more. She breathed out in relief as they disappeared, but the feeling of tension remained. She pulled a grim face. That patrol might not have been here for her, but that wasn't to say they had forgotten about her. Because whether she liked it or not, she still held their attention. Which meant she had to watch her back more carefully than ever.

CHAPTER THREE

Scarlet and Cillian pulled up outside one of the high-rises on the Eric and Treby estate. Dark moody clouds blended into the weathered grey building as Scarlet lifted her gaze upwards. The summer had been fast disappearing over the last few days with a spate of angry storms, and it appeared that another was threatening.

She stepped out of the car and lowered her eyes, casting them around warily to assess her surroundings. There was little sound in the air – children's chatter from the game of ball they were playing on a nearby patch of grass, the distant hum of a busy road somewhere behind them and the dull thudding of music playing inside one of the flats.

Cillian glanced up to the sky with a frown.

'Yes,' Scarlet said, reading his thoughts. 'Let's get done and out of here.' She eyed the small group of men in one of the alleyways. 'Why don't you take the café and chip shop; I'll pop in on Chain and do the pizza place.'

'You sure?' Cillian asked.

'Yeah.' Scarlet hoisted her handbag into the crook of her arm more securely. 'It's fine.'

She'd become a regular face around the estate and the gangs all knew exactly who she was, but this would be the first time she'd entered such a dangerous part of it without one of her cousins. As relaxed as the place appeared to be, the reality was very different. The kids playing ball were watchers for the gangs, reporting on all the comings and goings of outsiders. The men standing casually in the alley were blooded-in members of a ruthless gang run by a man most of them only knew by the name of Chain – his choice of weapon. Every one of them had a concealed weapon and would use it without hesitation if an unspoken law of the estate was violated. But Scarlet was a Drew. She was higher up the underworld food chain and controlled a lot of the work that was pushed their way. She could command their respect – so long as she offered them hers in return.

Cillian glanced up at the heavy clouds once more and straightened his jacket. 'I'll see you back here.'

Scarlet nodded and made her way over to the alleyway with her head held high. She reached the entrance and slowed, knowing she needed permission to step any further. She eyed one of the men leaning against the wall, watching her. 'Can you let Chain know I'm here to see him?'

'He ain't expecting visitors today,' came a low voice from the back.

'No,' Scarlet replied sharply, making eye contact. 'But he'll see me anyway.' She raised her eyebrows and waited. After a couple of seconds, the man she'd first addressed pushed himself off the wall and nodded for her to wait, then disappeared through the alley.

Turning away, Scarlet pulled out her phone and began replying to a text from a friend.

Eventually he returned. 'He'll see you in the shop,' he said.

'Thank you.' Scarlet offered him a smile as she passed, the invisible borderline at the edge of the alley having been relaxed to allow her entrance.

She made her way swiftly through, then crossed the square to the small shop filled with an eclectic assortment of electrical goods. She walked carefully down the narrow aisle towards the counter at the back, avoiding the precariously balanced items stacked on the shelves. No one was behind the counter, but as she reached it, the door behind opened and Chain entered, wearing nothing but a pair of tracksuit bottoms.

Scarlet couldn't help but notice the large defined muscles rippling through his torso as her gaze was instinctively drawn down. Suddenly realising she was staring, she looked away and heard Chain's low rumbling chuckle.

'What's the matter, Miss Drew, never seen a man before?' he asked, amused, his Jamaican roots curling through his predominantly East End accent.

'I just wasn't expecting this to be such an informal meeting,' she responded in good humour.

'I wasn't expecting to be having a meeting at all,' he replied, leaning over the counter and settling his gaze on her.

The way his sharp brown eyes held hers, like a predator waiting to see which way his prey would run, should have set her on edge. Indeed it did, to a degree. But she was used to him now and knew to ignore the things that would unsettle most people. He was a dangerous person, but then again, so was she.

'We've got a big load coming in next week, all high street. There's going to be a lot of overflow, so we'll bring some this way,' she said.

'How much and when?' he asked, standing and stretching his back.

'We're not entirely sure but likely around the same amount as last time. We'll drop either Friday or Saturday depending on how long it takes to sort our end.'

Chain nodded. 'OK. We'll be ready.'

The sound of a sudden downpour hitting the pavement outside caught Scarlet's attention and she turned to look with a curse. Sure enough, as she stared down the long narrow shop towards the door, she could see that darkness had swallowed up the outside world, the rain falling hard and fast. Somewhere in the distance thunder rumbled.

'Oh dear,' Chain said with a low laugh. 'Looks like you're caught in here with me for a while.' His eyes glinted mockingly and he leaned over the counter, lacing his fingers together.

'What, because of that?' she asked, pointing outside and letting a smile of amusement curl her lips upwards. 'I quite like a bit of rain,' she said, watching him. 'It washes away the sins. The blood, the bullets, the lives I've cut short…'

'So the rumours are true then,' he said. A statement, rather than a question. He looked her up and down and nodded. 'Here.' He reached under the counter and pulled out a small umbrella.

Scarlet stepped forward and took it. 'Thanks.' She retreated down the narrow aisle towards the door.

'You know, I wouldn't be so eager to wash those sins away, Scarlet Drew,' Chain's voice followed after her. 'Our sins have a way of protecting us, in this place.'

She smiled as she opened the door and stepped out into the storm. 'If only they could protect us everywhere.'

CHAPTER FOUR

Connor handed over a ten-pound note to the guy in the coffee truck and waved away the change, then picked up the two cups he'd just purchased and walked back over to his twin brother. He handed Cillian one of the cups and took a sip from his own.

'Argh, shit!' he cursed and put his hand to his mouth as the scalding liquid burned his tongue.

'Well, if you won't wait,' Cillian responded, shaking his head.

Connor just glared at him. 'Come on, let's get on before the heavens reopen.'

They were at the Roman Road market. They owned a number of the stalls and sold a mixture of legal and not-so-legal goods. Some of the money from the stolen goods could be laundered through the stalls themselves, but most of it had to be taken elsewhere. The market inspectors were hot on the paperwork and there had been more spot checks than they'd liked in the past couple of years.

They set forth into the throng of people busy shopping and headed towards their first stall. A pretty petite blonde grinned at them both as they approached.

'Hey, guys, how's tricks?' she asked, her blue eyes sparkling as they lingered on Cillian's face.

'Oh, you know.' Connor's gaze flickered between her and his brother. 'They're good.' The pretty blonde didn't bother looking back at him as she nodded in response. Cillian was looking away, seemingly unaware of his admirer. 'Right, well. We have to shoot, so if you've got the wedge?' He gave her a questioning look as she finally turned back to him.

'Oh, yeah. 'Course.' She grinned and pulled it out of a bag underneath the small counter. 'Here. It's been a good week.' Her gaze slid back to Cillian.

'Next week will be an even better one,' Connor replied as he stuffed the packet of money into his inner jacket pocket. He gave the area a cursory sweep in case anyone was watching, but nobody was. 'We've got a large load coming in – you can take your pick.'

'Nice.' She grinned again, but as her gaze slipped back to his brother, it turned slightly wistful.

'Ain't we, Cillian?' Connor said a bit louder, pulling him into the conversation.

'Hm?' Cillian finally turned around. 'Oh, yeah. Big load.' He pulled up his sleeve and checked his watch. 'We need to get on,' he said to Connor.

'Have a good week then, yeah?' said the girl as Cillian began to walk off. He raised his hand without turning back around.

Connor caught up and fell into step, glancing back at the stall. The girl was talking to another customer, but her disappointment remained visible. 'What was that about?' he asked.

'What?' Cillian asked.

'That, back there. She's got it bad for you, you know.' He laughed.

'Yeah, I know,' Cillian replied.

'Well, what you waiting for?' Connor asked. 'She's a hot little thing.'

'She ain't my type,' Cillian answered, his tone bored.

Connor frowned. 'You love blondes,' he replied. 'And she's at least an eight.' He glanced back. 'Make that a nine actually.'

'You go for her then,' he replied with a shrug.

'She ain't into me,' Connor responded. For some reason that neither of them had yet been able to fathom, despite the fact that they were identical twins with the same haircut, the same suits, even the same shoes, women only ever seemed to be attracted to one or the other of them.

'She just seems like she'd be a bit' – Cillian pulled a face – 'I don't know… vanilla.'

'Vanilla?' Connor waited for him to elaborate.

'Yeah, like, in the bedroom. She looks nice, don't get me wrong. But she looks a bit *too* nice for my liking.' He pulled a toothpick out of his pocket and began to chew on it. 'Do you know what I mean?'

Connor glanced back again. 'No. I don't get it. I reckon she'd be a lot of fun.'

Cillian twisted his lips. 'I can just tell she ain't what I'm looking for.' He flipped the toothpick around with his tongue and Connor frowned.

'Fuck's sake, would you just start smoking again?' he said. 'I can't tell you how many of those fucking toothpicks I keep finding around. They're doing my nut in. You know I sat on one the other day. Full-on pierced my arse. My *arse*, Cillian. My arse was much safer when you smoked.'

Cillian ignored this and lifted his hand to his neck. He rubbed it and rolled his head with a grimace.

'What's up?' Connor asked.

'Dunno,' Cillian replied irritably. 'Woke up like this a couple of days ago but it just ain't getting better.'

They'd reached the next stall.

'Maybe you should get a massage,' Connor suggested.

Cillian snorted with a frown. 'I don't have time for that shit. Plus, what do they really do anyway? Rub a few oils in and pray for miracles? Nah, it'll be alright.'

The stallholder finished up with his customer and turned to face them. 'Alright?' he said cheerfully.

'Hey, Phil, how's it going?' Cillian replied.

'Yeah, good. I couldn't help but overhear,' he said cautiously. 'My wife's niece does massage and she's actually really good.'

'Nah, I'm good, mate, don't worry—' Cillian started to protest.

'No, honestly,' Phil pressed. 'She don't do all that namby-pamby relaxing stuff – she hammers you hard. Don't give no mercy. Not even if you beg for it.' He chuckled. 'But I'll tell you what, once she lets you up, it's like you've been given a new spine. A bruised one,' he added, 'but you don't mind that.'

He reached into the bag where he kept all his receipts and papers and pulled out a business card. 'Here.' He offered it to Cillian. 'This is her. Belinda, her name is. Give her a go, son. She'll sort that neck out.'

'Thanks, I'll think about it.' Cillian pulled a tight smile and slipped the card in his pocket.

Connor looked up at the clouds. Once again the darker edges were beginning to close in. It seemed no matter where they went, the storm was unavoidable today. As he stared at the sky, he couldn't shake the sudden feeling that it was a bad omen. A warning of dark times to come.

CHAPTER FIVE

Lily stared out of the factory windows at the rain as it pelted down, unseeing, her mind warring with other things. It had been weeks since she had last seen her daughter Ruby, and a seed of unease had been growing in the pit of her stomach. It wasn't that it was unusual for Ruby to disappear for weeks at a time – or even months sometimes. She was a law unto herself, a self-destructive hurricane who pushed against authority, and in particular her family, as a habit. But usually Lily was able to get through to her phone if she kept ringing, even if it was only for a few seconds to check Ruby was alright. For weeks now though, her phone had been going straight to voicemail, and on top of that, she'd missed her own uncle's funeral. Ruby was routinely flaky and didn't take part in family events as a rule, but she'd loved Ronan. She would have wanted to be at the funeral to say goodbye, of that Lily was certain.

She sighed unhappily and crossed her arms over her chest. Something was wrong; she could feel it.

The office door opened and she turned to see Scarlet approaching, holding a pile of papers.

'Here they are, all printed off,' she said eagerly.

'Let me see.' Lily held her hand out and Scarlet passed them over. She scanned the documents, checking all the points they had discussed with the estate agent were in there, then nodded in approval. 'OK.' She looked up at Scarlet. 'You're definitely sure about this?' she asked, one last time.

'One hundred per cent,' Scarlet replied, not missing a beat.

'You know you'll be managing it? This venture will be entirely *your* responsibility,' she warned.

'I'm looking forward to it,' Scarlet admitted frankly. 'It will be good to make my own mark.'

Lily nodded. She could understand that. Scarlet was the newest member of the firm and, although she was already a valuable asset, still felt she had a lot to prove. She was young, only eighteen, and had jumped into the firm at a time of complete chaos.

When Ronan had been murdered, it had upended all of their lives. Lily had mourned a brother, but the firm had also lost one of its heads. Scarlet had joined them as both she and the firm were reeling from the loss, and all the while Scarlet was also mourning for her father. She was always meant to join when she had, but now she was starting out in their world without Ronan there to guide her. Despite it all though, she'd risen to the challenge and ploughed forward with her head held high and her heart in the game.

'Have you spoken to Natalie?' Lily asked. Natalie was Scarlet's best friend, who would be managing the hairdresser's day to day. She was new to the firm but not entirely new to the life. Her father, Ronnie Baker, had done some heavy work for them in the past, when they'd needed extra hands. Lily knew he'd have taught her how to keep her mouth shut.

'I told her we were looking at premises and she's ready to go at a moment's notice,' Scarlet replied. 'I'm meeting her for a drink tomorrow, so I'll tell her then.' She grinned.

The place they'd visited earlier that afternoon had been ideal. It had been a little tired on the inside, but after some successful negotiation on the rent, Lily had given Scarlet the go-ahead to proceed.

'These all look fine.' She passed the contract back to Scarlet. 'Go ahead and sign. Put the costs for the premises through the books, but for the rest, whatever you need to spend on refitting and restocking, use cash as much as you can.'

'Yeah, 'course.' Scarlet took the papers and scanned them over once more herself. 'We can use the chairs and that. They seemed in good nick. But there's still a lot to pay out for.'

'Make up some fake invoices for anything you use that's there. I reckon new chairs could be worth a few hundred quid each. How many are we having in there, ten?' Lily asked.

'Ten or twelve.'

'There you go then. There's your first load of washing.' She gave Scarlet a smile. 'New mirrors too. You can ramp up some big invoices with the refit.'

Scarlet nodded then pushed her dark hair back over her shoulder and walked out of the office. 'I'll get this sorted, then I'll head over to give Sandra the news.'

Lily looked grim as Scarlet reminded her of the damage control she still had to arrange. 'See that she's out tonight,' she warned. 'They know the rules. There ain't no leeway.'

'Got it.' Scarlet disappeared and the office door closed behind her.

Lily wandered back over to the window, putting her hands into the small of her back as she stretched it out. The rain was hammering down relentlessly now. Was Ruby staring at the rain too? Was she *in it*, soaking wet and freezing cold, trying to find a dry place to go? Lily closed her eyes for a moment.

Suddenly, her patience snapped and her eyes reopened with a look of steely determination. This had gone on long enough. First thing tomorrow she was going to Ruby's last known whereabouts and would start asking some questions. And whether people liked it or not, she was finally going to get some answers.

CHAPTER SIX

Scarlet stared up at the tall block of flats with a grim expression. When Sandra had called her earlier, she'd been looking for help, seeking mercy, but there was no mercy in their world. She exhaled heavily and marched into the building, stepping into the lift in the plush entrance hall and pressing the button that would take her up to the penthouse.

It wasn't that she didn't sympathise with the woman. Sandra had been one of their best girls, a favourite with many high-profile regulars. With natural blonde hair, high cheekbones and a winning smile, paired with a slender figure and full breasts, she wasn't hard to sell. But this was what made it all worse. Their income was going to take a big hit now, and their reputation most likely would as well. These girls were supposed to be clean, the best of the best. They were upmarket escorts, the diamonds of the sex market. But diamonds shouldn't pass on the clap after a night of passion. Diamonds were supposed to be pure, flawless. That was why clients paid so much.

Scarlet stepped out of the lift and into the opulent apartment, looking around the large, open-plan lounge, then up to the balcony above, for any signs of life. The penthouse was on two floors, with a glass wall offering wide, sweeping views of the city. The five bedrooms housed their five top escorts, and the living area was used to entertain clients before going out, or before retiring upstairs.

A door opened somewhere above her and Sandra's head popped over the balcony. 'Oh, thank God you're here,' she breathed with almost tangible relief. 'I know you said to leave it with you, but I didn't really know what you meant.' She flew down the stairs to the lounge where Scarlet stood. 'Have you figured out what we're going to do?' She crossed her arms and lifted one hand to her face, chewing worriedly on one manicured nail as she waited for an answer.

Scarlet shook her head sadly. 'Sandra, there is no figuring this out. I'm sorry.'

Sandra's face fell and she dropped it into her hands with a pitiful groan. 'Oh Jesus,' she whimpered. She looked up and grabbed Scarlet's arm, her eyes pleading. 'There has to be something I can do, some way I can make this up. What – what if I worked for free for a while?' Her expression turned hopeful. 'I'd have to wait until the drugs clear this up, of course, but then I could work for free until Lily feels like whatever's been lost has been earned back. What do you think? Would she go for that, do you think?'

Scarlet gently pulled her arm out of Sandra's grasp. 'You know the rules, and you know my aunt. There's no room for negotiation. She wants you out tonight.'

'Tonight?' Sandra wailed.

Two of the other girls came out of their rooms and watched the scene in silence. Scarlet's heart went out to Sandra, but she knew there was nothing she could do.

'I didn't even know when he came round,' Sandra cried. 'I swear, I had no idea; you have to believe me.' Tears began to fall down her face and Scarlet looked away.

'I do believe you, Sandra, but this was still a colossal fuck-up and the rules are the rules,' she said firmly. 'You have to be out tonight, and Lily is going to work on damage control so that we don't lose the faith of our other clients.' This last comment was for the benefit of the other girls.

'I can't believe this.' She put her hands to her face again as she began to cry full throttle. 'I've lived and worked here for three years. I've never once made a mistake.'

'I know,' Scarlet said quietly. 'Where will you go? Have you got family in the city?'

'No,' Sandra replied. 'I don't have any family; I was a foster kid until I aged out. And when I came to London I started working here straight off, so this is all I know.'

Scarlet made a snap decision. 'I'll give you an extra week's pay in lieu of notice, so that should tide you over for a bit.' They paid the girls well, so if Sandra was careful she'd be OK for a time. 'That should give you some time to find another position.'

The devastation on Sandra's face became a look of doubtful uncertainty. Scarlet turned to the window with a hidden grimace. Most escort businesses were not as exclusive as theirs, and being sent out into that world with no protection was like being thrown to the wolves. Not that this was Scarlet's problem. She wasn't responsible for the other woman. But for some reason Scarlet still felt as though she was.

'Look.' She turned back towards her. 'I don't have any leads for you; I don't know any other escort firms. And to be honest,' she added, 'I wouldn't exactly be able to give you the best reference considering the reason for ousting you.' Sandra hung her head. 'But if you wanted straight work, I can offer you a job. It's not as well paid as this,' she warned as Sandra's expression turned to one of hope. 'And it doesn't come with lodgings. But it's a job, and if you want it, it's yours.'

'What is it?' Sandra asked warily.

'I'm opening a hair salon down the street. I have a manager in place, but she'll need an assistant. It won't be very glam. You'll be running round doing all sorts. Making coffees, sweeping hair, arranging bookings, answering the phone—'

'Yes,' Sandra blurted out quickly, cutting her off. 'Please. I'd like to take you up on that.' She clung to the offer like it was a life raft.

'OK. Well…' She walked over to the large open-plan kitchen area and found a notepad and pen. 'This is the address.' She wrote it down and ripped the page out, handing it to Sandra. 'It's just down the road, near Snaresbrook station.'

Sandra frowned. 'Oh, yeah, I know it.'

'Be there at midday, the day after tomorrow.' She glanced up at the other girls, still silently watching the exchange. 'Connor will be in touch with you guys about damage control.'

Returning her gaze to Sandra, she saw the sadness in the woman's face as she looked around her home of three years. She closed her heart off and locked her jaw.

'You need to be out tonight,' she repeated, giving Sandra a long serious look. 'Get packed and find a place to lodge until you find somewhere more permanent.'

Sandra nodded. 'Yeah, OK. And thanks' – she gave Scarlet a small smile – 'for the job.'

'At least it's something until you find your feet,' Scarlet replied. She didn't imagine Sandra would stay for very long.

Walking back out of the flat, she pressed the button to call the lift and tried to shake off the sudden tiredness which threatened to take over. It had been a long day, but it wasn't over yet. She had a lot of planning and research to do before she could open this hairdresser's. For this to work, it needed to be run as professionally as possible. And she needed it to work.

Her jaw locked into a hard line once more as the lift doors opened. She'd do whatever it took. Because this was her chance to show the world that she was capable. It was her chance to show the whole underworld, her chance to show her aunt, and if she allowed herself to be honest for a moment, it was also her chance to show herself.

CHAPTER SEVEN

Lily walked down the dank alleyway with caution, trying to ignore the fetid stench that lingered in the air. Her heels clipped out a sharp rhythm in the silence as she drew ever closer to Ruby's last known residence. The third-floor flat was not one Lily had set her up in; Ruby had found it on her own. Lily would never have chosen this as a place for her only daughter to live. But she knew why Ruby had chosen it. This building was smack bang in the middle of all the local dealers. Ruby wouldn't have cared that her neighbours mainly consisted of junkies and deadbeats. Instead, she would have relished the fact that her next dose of heroin was never more than a few feet from her door, and that no one around was in a position to judge her for her poor life choices.

She marched determinedly to the front door and pushed it open. Breathing through her mouth to avoid the pungent aroma of urine in the hallway, she hurried up the stairwell to the third floor. A couple of thin, dirty children played on the floor of the first hallway she reached and she stepped around them gravely. Where were the parents? Why were they so filthy and unkempt? She allowed herself a small growl under her breath as she continued climbing.

She'd had even less than these people when she'd been left to raise Ronan, little more than a child herself. But Ronan had never looked as dirty as those two. It didn't cost much to keep clean.

She pushed on up the stairs. As the reminder of her brother settled, the familiar stab of grief shot through her, and she swallowed the lump that rose in her throat with difficulty. Those days were long gone now. Another life. And Ronan was long gone too. Right now she had to focus on the people who were still there, who still needed her. And she felt strongly that Ruby needed her now, more than ever.

Lily reached the third floor and stood for a couple of seconds, catching her breath. There were no lifts in these buildings. They were cheap, crappy structures thrown up by the council at the least cost possible, to house those who they had nowhere else for. Lily shook her head. How had Ruby ended up here?

She walked down the hall until she reached Ruby's door. Lifting her hand, she rapped loudly and waited. There was no sound within.

Lily looked up and down the empty hallway. About to turn away, she paused and tried the handle. To her surprise the door was unlocked. Her eyebrows shot up under the unruly blonde curls that had fallen forward over her forehead. She pushed these back with one hand and opened the door, looking in warily before entering.

It was as empty as she'd thought it would be. She stepped into the main room of the flat, leaving the front door ajar, and looked around.

The place was a state. There wasn't much in the way of furniture – an old, faded sofa and a cheap coffee table that had seen better days. Next, Lily inspected the kitchen. The hob looked unused, though the sides were filthy. She frowned as she caught sight of a few Rizlas and some tobacco dust. Ruby didn't smoke, so these were not hers.

She walked through to the bedroom and sat on the unmade bed, looking around the room for clues. Aside from a few old clothes at the bottom of the open wardrobe, this room was as devoid of life as the lounge had been.

The old springs in the mattress groaned as she stood back up and entered the bathroom. A sponge lay in the bath by the plughole. Lily leaned over and picked it up, squeezing it in her fist. It was bone dry and brittle. Ruby hadn't been here for a while. No one had, it seemed.

She decided to knock on the next-door neighbour's door. The walls were thin in places like these. Even if they didn't know where Ruby had gone, they might have overheard something that could help.

She knocked loudly and waited. The sounds of children squabbling and a TV blaring came through the door, but this was swiftly silenced with an urgent whisper.

After a minute or two, she leaned her head towards the door crack and began to speak as loudly as she could without shouting.

'I can hear you in there,' she started. 'Listen, I just want to ask a few questions. I ain't a copper or anything; I'm just looking for the young woman who lived next door.'

The silence stretched on and she bit her bottom lip. One of the children began to speak and she heard someone shush them.

'It's my daughter,' she continued. 'The girl next door, she's my daughter.'

There was a sound as though someone was moving closer to the door. Her hopes rose.

'I haven't seen or been able to get hold of her for a while.'

The door opened and a tired, scruffy-looking woman peered out warily. 'She was a right rude cow, that one,' she said sourly.

Lily bit back the retort that was trying to push its way out. Usually, she would immediately defend her children against comments like that, even Ruby, difficult as the girl was. But she still needed information. She forced a tight smile.

'I was just wondering if you might have seen her? Or if she's left information about where she might have gone?'

The woman peered up and down the hall and lowered her voice. 'Look, I don't know where Ruby went, but I'm pretty sure she won't be back. She left in a hurry, and not long after, some men came and took up camp in her place. Stayed there for days at a time; kept coming and going. Nasty bastards they were.'

Lily's insides began to turn cold and she balled one hand into a fist by her side.

'I don't know who they were but they weren't good people. She owed them money – I heard them talking about it a few times. It was a fair whack, by the sounds of it too. They still come by from time to time, just in case she comes back, I guess. One was 'ere just the other day.'

'Did they ask you about her?' Lily asked.

'They asked everyone on this floor, but like everyone else, I didn't know nothing. Other than the odd argument with one of us when her parties were too loud, Ruby kept to herself.'

'When did she leave?' Lily asked.

'Oh, this was two or three months ago now. I'm surprised they haven't relet her flat yet, to be honest.'

'And these parties you said she had,' Lily pressed. 'Did you ever go to them? Meet any of her friends or anything?'

The woman gave her a withering look. 'I don't associate with smack 'eads, love,' she said scathingly. 'And to be honest, I was glad to see the back of 'er, so my kids don't grow up anywhere near her either.'

With that she retreated and slammed the door shut.

Lily slowly backed away and made her way down the stairwell. She'd been right to worry about Ruby – it seemed she was in far deeper trouble than Lily had imagined. She kicked herself for not looking into this all sooner. Ruby was always running into trouble. In fact, she full-on chased it. But this wasn't her usual level of trouble; this was something far worse. Something she'd run from and hidden from everyone around her. Why hadn't she come to her mother for help? Lily would have bailed her out – Ruby knew that.

She stepped out into the sunshine and wrapped her hands around her car keys as the neighbour's words played over and over in her head. What the hell had Ruby got herself into?

CHAPTER EIGHT

Natalie walked into the pub and was almost knocked sideways by a group of men as they cheered a goal in the match they were watching. 'Oi, watch it!' she complained, scowling and straightening her bag. She saw Scarlet waving from across the crowded space and made a beeline for the table.

'Christ, it's been a day and a bleedin' half, it really has, I tell ya!'

'Yeah?' Scarlet asked.

'Yeah. I tell you what, I'm this close' – she put her fingers together in front of her face – 'to putting a dose of arsenic in my bitch of a boss's tea.'

'Really?' Scarlet couldn't help but grin. 'Got some arsenic ready and waiting in your pocket, have ya?'

'Well, no.' Natalie pulled out her purse. 'But if I did…' She twisted in her seat and glanced at the bar with a tut of annoyance. 'Hell, we ain't going to get through *that* queue before the end of me lunchbreak,' she muttered.

'That's OK, I already got the drinks in,' Scarlet replied.

Natalie turned back to the empty table with a confused frown. 'Eh?'

Her grin widening, Scarlet reached under the table and pulled up the ice bucket and bottle of champagne she'd been hiding.

'Ohhh!' Natalie's face lit up. 'What's the occasion?'

Scarlet produced two glasses with a flourish and reached for the bottle. 'It's finally happening, Nat,' she said as she popped the cork.

There was a cheer from the group of lads watching football, before they returned their attention to the game.

'I signed the papers for the premises yesterday and I pick up the keys tomorrow. As of now, I am the proud owner of one hairdressing salon.' Her grey-blue eyes twinkled with excitement as she saw her words register with her friend.

Natalie's eyes lit up and her whole face creased into an ecstatic smile. 'That is the best news I've heard all day!' she exclaimed. 'All week – all year!'

Scarlet laughed and poured them each a glass of the chilled champagne. 'I'm glad it's cheered you up.'

'What happens now? When will you want me to start?' she asked eagerly.

'As soon as you can,' Scarlet answered, passing Natalie's glass to her. 'I'm going to get cracking as soon as I get the keys. No point hanging around. Cheers.' She held her glass up and clinked it against Natalie's.

'Cheers.' They both took a deep sip of the bubbly liquid.

'What's your notice period?' Scarlet asked.

'Hang on.' Natalie held her finger up and reached into her bag for her phone. She dialled a number and took another sip of her champagne as she waited for it to be answered.

'Hi, Mandy? It's Nat… Yeah, I know… Yeah… Let me just stop you there, Mandy, because I'm not actually gonna be able to make it back today. Why? Well, Mandy, the thing is, my mate's just opened a salon and she wants me to manage it. From now.' She sat up and her tone changed from placid to hard. 'So you can stick your shitty job up your flat, lifeless backside, you miserable old bat. Oh,' she exclaimed, 'and by the way, your husband's shagging the nanny. Has been for months. All the best, hun!'

She ended the call, placed her phone back into her bag and turned back to Scarlet with a grin. 'I've wanted to do that since me first day,' she said.

Scarlet snorted with laughter and almost choked on her drink. 'Christ, Nat! Is her husband really shagging the nanny?'

Natalie shrugged. 'Who knows? Probably. But either way, it'll make for an interesting conversation at their house tonight.'

'Oh, Nat, you're wicked,' Scarlet said, lifting her hand to her mouth to try and cover her mirth.

'She had it coming to her,' Nat replied, pulling a face. 'She's an 'orrible cow. Do you know, she makes all of us do an extra half day a week unpaid? Talks to all the staff like shit and screams in your face something rotten out the back for the slightest thing.' She took another sip. '*And* she keeps two thirds of our tips,' she added.

'Well, you don't have to worry about any of that from now on,' Scarlet said firmly. 'As of tomorrow you'll be running things. Everyone can keep their tips, no one has to work for free and you can be happy. Now for the hard work.' She pulled a face and took another sip from her glass.

'Now for the hard work,' Nat repeated, with gusto. 'I'm looking forward to it. I already have a load of ideas to run through with you. I was thinking that we could offer an introductory deal to get clients in the door – maybe twenty-five per cent off their first visit and ten per cent off the next if they recommend a friend?' She lifted an eyebrow enquiringly. 'What do you reckon? I know it sounds a lot, but if it gets people coming in—'

'It's a great idea and we'll definitely look at it, but remember, the aim isn't to fill our books to capacity.' She pushed her long dark hair back behind her ear and leaned forward so she could lower her voice. 'We'll only be hiring out half the chairs. The rest will be running under fake books. This will be one of your jobs,' she said seriously. 'You'll need to create a bank of fake customers. And you'll have to keep track of them somehow without making it obvious to anyone else. Because the stylists we hire will be in the dark. The fewer people who know what we're really running, the safer we'll be.' She studied Natalie's expression critically. 'You understand how deep you're getting in here, don't you?'

Natalie wouldn't be joining the firm all in; she wouldn't be privy to anything else they had going on. But she would still be crossing the threshold into their world, and she would still be responsible for hiding their secrets. And once she started, she'd be just as guilty as the rest of them, if the shit were to hit the fan.

'I do,' Natalie replied hurriedly. 'I completely understand. And I'm completely on board with it all. You can trust me – you know that.'

'I do know that,' Scarlet replied, glancing around to recheck that no one nearby was in hearing distance. 'Which is why I offered you this job. It's also why Lil allowed me to bring you in,' she added. She paused and refilled both their glasses. 'But it goes deeper than that.' She glanced up at her friend. 'If we get looked into by anyone, an auditor, the police…' She paused to let what she was saying sink in. 'Do you understand what's expected of you?' She waited.

'I think so,' Natalie said slowly with a small frown. 'I mean, keep my mouth shut and maintain our story, right?'

'Right. But if things go south and you get arrested, you'll also be expected to protect the rest of us.' Scarlet twisted the stem of her glass with her fingers. 'This world we live in, it's harsh. I know you know a lot of the rules from your dad, but it's one thing knowing them and another thing entirely to live up to them. Do you think, in all honesty, that if you got arrested and they put pressure on you to roll on us, that you'd keep quiet?'

'Of course I would,' Natalie responded strongly, her frown deepening. 'I can't believe you even asked me that.'

'What if you were facing a sentence?' Scarlet stared at her levelly. It was a hard question to be faced with but one that needed to be asked, old friends or not. There was too much at stake to tiptoe around it. And Lily had insisted she ask it before they went any further. 'What if you were faced with the choice of a ten-year stretch or your freedom if you handed over my name. What then?'

Natalie shook her head. 'Scar, I know what I'm doing. I know that the risk is why you're paying me double what I was getting before. I ain't stupid. I understand danger money, and I know the score.' The corners of her mouth turned up in a bitter half-smile. 'It don't pay to stay legitimate in this world anymore. So I choose to take the other road. Risks and all.'

Scarlet nodded and took a deep drink from her glass.

'You'll need to keep these ghost chairs full,' she said eventually, taking the conversation back to practicalities. 'Booking in their clients at around the same pace the real chairs are getting booked so it doesn't look suspect.'

Natalie nodded and sat up straighter. 'I can do that.'

'Once a week we'll meet and you can let me know how much you've been able to push through, then I'll arrange to have the cash brought over,' Scarlet continued.

'And how much will you want me to put on the fake books?' Natalie asked.

Scarlet's clear grey-blue eyes held Natalie's across the table. 'As much as you can,' she said. 'It isn't going to be a trickle of spare change coming through this place. It's going to be a lot of money. A lot of money indeed.'

CHAPTER NINE

Cillian looked up at the building in front of him and then back down to the card in his hand. This was definitely the right place. His eyes rested on her logo plaque in the front window, alongside those of the other businesses within. He scrunched up his face and turned around. What was he doing here?

As he began to walk away, a window opened above and a voice travelled down. 'Oi! Cillian, isn't it?'

He paused and turned back, immediately regretting giving himself away. 'Alright?' he said awkwardly, staring up at the woman leaning out of the first-floor window. Her shoulder-length blonde hair fell forward like a curtain and shadowed her face, but he still caught the friendly grin.

'Come on then,' she ordered in a no-nonsense tone. 'I'll let you in.'

She disappeared and Cillian let out a groan of annoyance. Why had he let Connor convince him to book the appointment? He glanced down the road. He really did have better things to do than piss around on some bed having a snooze and a back rub. The front door opened quicker than he'd anticipated though, dashing his hopes of a quick getaway. He automatically turned towards the sound and flinched as a spasm of pain shot through his neck once more.

'Ouch, that don't look much fun,' she said, looking him up and down critically. 'How'd you do that then?'

She was shorter than he'd imagined. Five foot two or three at best, with big blue eyes, a wide smile and wearing a low-cut work tunic that flattered her tidy waist and the ample assets above.

'Woke up this way,' he admitted, slowly walking back towards her.

She pursed her lips. 'I'm not surprised with how uptight you are.'

'What?' He frowned. Was she insulting him?

'The way you're walking,' she explained. 'You're so stiff. I bet your back's tighter than Scrooge himself.'

'Oh, I see.' He reached the door and studied the tiny woman. She didn't look like she could beat her way out of a paper bag, let alone beat the issues out of his back.

He waited for her to check him out, the way most women did when he was this close, but instead she seemed to be staring intently at his shoulder. Her gaze travelled down his torso and she circled around to the side of him. He grinned, amused, and was about to make a joke when she reached forward and pressed hard into the base of his back with two fingers.

'Argh!' He bent sideways and shifted away from her in shock at the pain her touch had triggered.

'Hm, yes, I thought so,' she said, more to herself than to him.

'What the fuck was that?' he asked, staring at her with a wary frown.

'Your back,' she replied. 'The issues in your lower back have pulled the muscles taut right to the top. That's why your neck has pulled like that so easily.' She turned and took the steps back into the building. 'Come on. Clock's ticking.'

Bemused, Cillian followed her into the building and up the stairs to a small office that had been decked out as a therapy room.

'Get undressed down to your boxers and lie face down on the bed. I'll be back in a minute.' She left and closed the door.

With a shrug, Cillian did as he'd been asked and waited. After a couple of minutes she walked back in. With his face resting in the hole at the top of the table, all he could see were her feet as she nipped around the room getting ready. Some calming music came on and the smell of lavender permeated the air. Cillian rolled his eyes. This was going to be a waste of his time.

She began to rub oil into his back and he resigned himself to an hour of doing nothing. 'Belinda, isn't it?' he asked as she pushed further down his back.

'Billie,' she corrected. 'Only me family call me Belinda, and usually only when I'm in trouble.'

'You get in trouble a lot then?' Cillian asked with a grin, turning to look at her.

She pressed on his back, forcing him back down. 'Keep still,' she ordered.

Cillian sighed. 'If you insist, though I don't really see much point. If my back's fucked, then my back's fu— Argh!' He cried out in pain.

Billie had been rubbing the same area over and over in a fast circular motion, but as he spoke she'd asserted some controlled pressure and pulled the muscle down hard. 'Oh really,' she admonished. 'I've had girls who moan less than you.'

'Have you fuck!' he retorted.

Billie gave a low throaty chuckle. 'Now stay still, seriously. I need to work on this muscle.' He groaned as she began to dig in harder. 'It hurts now, but if you can take it, I promise you'll leave here a new man.'

'I can take anything,' Cillian claimed, sounding more confident than he felt.

'Sure you can,' Billie replied, her smile curling into her tone.

Cillian forced himself to breathe through the pain as Billie ground his back for the next hour, only letting out an occasional grunt when she pushed him to the very edge of his limits. To his surprise, she was a lot stronger than he'd given her credit for, and whilst her efforts were sometimes difficult to withstand, he could already feel moments of relief as she broke down the tension that was knotted throughout his back.

All too soon his hour was up.

'I'll leave you to get dressed. Sit up slowly, take your time. When you're ready, meet me outside,' she said.

Cillian sat up feeling dazed and battered, yet somehow rejuvenated at the same time. He shook his head, trying to get rid of the calm fog that had settled in. To his surprise, his neck no longer hurt at all. He twisted it from side to side, amazed. 'Well, I'll be damned,' he muttered.

He got dressed and straightened himself up in the mirror, before joining Billie in the hallway. She handed him a bottle of water.

'Here,' she said. 'Drink this on your way to wherever you're headed next. I've moved a lot of toxins around your body; you'll need to flush them out.'

They walked down the hall and the stairs together and Cillian shot her a curious glance. 'I think you enjoyed that,' he said. 'I reckon you take a sadistic pleasure in torturing people.'

Billie stopped on the last few steps and a grin crept over her face as he reached the door and turned around. 'Me?' A devious twinkle appeared in her eye. 'Maybe I do. Maybe pushing those pressure points and making big bad men cry out is how I get my kicks. Who knows?' She gave him a wink before turning and walking back up the stairs. 'And maybe you enjoy *being* tortured. Now there's a thought. Bye, Cillian.' She turned a corner and was gone.

Cillian stood staring up the empty stairwell with a wry smile on his face. 'Maybe,' he muttered, a seed of genuine interest in the woman beginning to take root.

CHAPTER TEN

Lily took another deep drag from her cigarette as she looked down at the man on his knees before her. They were standing on a small terrace outside one of the fire escapes at the rear of the factory, most often used by workers for cigarette breaks. As there were no cameras, it was also somewhere she could conduct some of her less palatable business. George and Andy, two of her most trusted men, stood either side of the kneeling man, a hand on each shoulder holding him down, looking fierce.

'Let's run through this once more, shall we, Jay?' Lily said in a low deadly voice. 'Just so I completely understand the situation. You were *aware* that the pub is under our protection, and you were *aware* that it's a no-sell zone – and *I'm* aware that *you're* aware of all this, because I gave you a warning only two weeks ago. Do you remember that?' She paused but as he went to respond she cut him off. 'I remember it very clearly. I remember warning you that if you went near that pub again for anything more than a quiet pint, there would be consequences.'

'Lily, look…' he started.

'It's Ms Drew to you,' she said sharply. She took another deep drag of her cigarette and exhaled briskly. 'So, we were all aware of what was what, and yet you still decided it was a good idea to rock up there last night with a bag full of product.' Her voice grew harder and angrier. 'And what's more, when the landlord reminded you of your place in the pecking order, *you* threatened *him*.' She looked up at Andy and George in disbelief. 'Can you believe that?'

she asked them. They both shook their heads. 'No, me neither.' She turned her attention back to Jay. 'You've got balls, boy, I'll give you that. But this was the wrong direction to swing them in.'

'I don't work for you,' Jay shot back. 'I work for Chenna, and he gives me a quota. I've got to meet that quota, which means I have to sell my gear.'

'That ain't my problem,' Lily stated. 'That's *your* problem. And one you can solve wherever you like, *outside* the borders of my protection.'

'It's a pub, for fuck's sake,' he cried. 'Lil— *Argh*!' He cried out as George twisted his arm back hard. 'Ms Drew! Ms Drew, it's a pub. Gear is bought and sold in every pub in London.'

'Not in that pub,' Lily replied with a shake of her head.

'What does it matter to you anyway? You don't even peddle gear! I ain't stepping on anyone's toes.'

'But you are, Jay,' Lily responded. 'Because that pub pays us to keep trouble away and to keep it clean. The landlord's daughter died of an overdose five years ago, so he can't stand even the thought of it. Did you know that? No, of course you didn't,' she replied for him. 'Because a little prick like you don't stop to think about other people. Now, I told you before, you can sell it anywhere else but there. And you didn't listen.'

'I didn't know that,' he said, trying to recover as he saw the look she gave her men. 'Look, I'm sorry – I didn't know the story behind it all.'

'That doesn't matter. Whether you knew or not, I gave you a warning and you ignored it. And now it's time to pay the price. Hold him,' Lily instructed calmly.

'No, no!' Jay struggled to get up and pull away, but Andy and George held him tight. 'Get off me,' he yelled.

Lily stepped forward and stared at him for a moment. Reaching down, she undid two of his shirt buttons, revealing a bare pale chest. He struggled and fought to pull away but to no avail.

'What the fuck are you doing?' he cried. 'What, you want me or something?' The bravado in his tone was at odds with the fear on his face.

Lily barked out a laugh. 'A skinny little street rat like you?' she asked in a mocking tone. 'Not my type, darlin'. No.' Her smile grew cold and dropped. 'I want to leave a reminder. So that you won't forget this conversation the way you did the last.'

Flicking the ash from the end of her lit cigarette, she pressed the burning cherry into the centre of his chest. For the briefest moment there was silence as the shock set into his expression – and then he let out a high-pitched, blood-curdling scream.

Ignoring the screams and the smell of burning flesh, Lily held on, pushing harder as she made her mark. 'Scream all you like,' she said in a harsh tone. 'The machines make so much noise you'll never be heard over them.'

'Stop,' he screamed. 'Jesus, stop!'

She pulled the cigarette away then pressed it back into his skin an inch lower, and his screams rose once again. Tears fell down his pained face, and spittle broke free from his mouth as he lost control under the agonising burn.

Eventually she pulled the cigarette away, dropped it to the floor and used her high-heeled shoe to grind it out. She surveyed her work, looking critically at the two angry red weals now etched into his chest.

Leaning in, Lily grasped his chin with one hand, digging her nails into his jaw. 'You *ever* set foot inside that pub again, for any reason whatsoever, you'll be back here,' she promised. 'And next time it will be your balls. You understand me?'

He nodded, still sobbing.

'Good,' she snarled, straightening up. 'Get him out of my sight,' she ordered, turning back towards the factory.

*

Walking up to her office she sighed, irritated. As if she didn't have enough on her plate already without having to deal with a petty dealer causing aggro with a client. She rolled her neck as she walked around her desk and sat down.

As she pulled her chair in, her gaze rested on a photo she kept across the room of her three children when they were young. The boys smiled up at the camera. Ruby glared solemnly up from between them, not impressed with her game being disturbed. It had always been like that, from the start.

'Where are you, Ruby Drew?' she asked the silent, unmoving picture.

She'd tried all of Ruby's previously known haunts the day before and as many of her old acquaintances as possible – which was not a long list as Ruby had a tendency to drop people faster than hot bricks – but when she'd finally reached home last night, she'd still been no nearer to finding anything out. Or to knowing who the men searching for her were. No one seemed to know anything. Or if they did, they were too scared to let on.

The one thing she was fairly certain of was that Ruby was holed up somewhere in hiding. These men wouldn't still be staking out her flat if they had any clue as to where she was. So that was a good sign. She just needed to figure it out quickly and hope that she got to them before they got to Ruby.

Movement in the hallway outside the office caught Lily's eye through the internal window and she looked up. Scarlet was passing, heading towards her own office – the one that used to be her father's.

'Scarlet?' she piped up, catching her niece's attention.

Scarlet stopped and leaned into the office through the partly open door. 'Yeah?'

'Come in a sec.'

'What's up?' Scarlet came in and sat down at the desk opposite her aunt, crossing her legs and leaning forward with interest.

'We've got an event coming up,' she said, lighting a new cigarette.

'An event?' Scarlet frowned, her dark brows furrowing together. 'What kind of event?'

'You know how sometimes we have overflow cash mount up or we have a big job which gives us a spike?' She didn't wait for Scarlet to answer. 'Occasionally, we run it through another laundry. It's not something we can do often as it only has a certain capacity. But when we do go for it, we can shift a lot.'

'How much is a lot?' Scarlet asked.

'A *lot*,' Lily said. 'Anywhere from five to twenty times what we push through all our other avenues together.'

Scarlet's eyebrows shot up and she whistled. 'That really is a lot,' she replied in amazement. 'How do we manage that?'

'Through a charity,' Lily replied. 'I have a contact in a well-established children's charity – Sheila. Do you remember her? She used to come to some of our parties, back in the day. Had a bit of a thing for your dad.'

'Was she the tall one with the big nose?' Scarlet asked, screwing her face up as the dim memory shuffled forth.

'That's the one.'

'Oh, Mum hated her, didn't she?' Scarlet recalled with a laugh. 'I remember she used to huff and puff like anything when that woman came to things.'

'She did,' Lily replied with a grin. 'Well, she's in charge of overseeing all the income and expenditure for this charity. We came to an agreement years ago that now and then we'd put a large chunk through their books. They get to keep twenty per cent and they launder the rest back to us through a chain of fake invoices for services rendered.'

'Twenty per cent is twice what we usually let a laundry keep,' Scarlet noted.

'Yes.' Lily settled back in her chair. 'I have a lot of respect for their cause and wanted to give something back.' She thought back to her childhood, to when she and Ronan had struggled and barely survived through the cold lonely days after their parents had died. There hadn't been much help around then. But people like Sheila were trying to change that, and that was something she admired.

'OK.' Scarlet shrugged. 'Sounds good. So what's the event?'

'Shelia throws an annual dinner ball. It's a ticketed event to raise some extra funds and there's a live auction of various different things. It's good for us to show our faces…' she trailed off and watched the penny drop in Scarlet's eyes.

'And you manipulate the auction,' she said.

'Exactly,' Lily confirmed with a smile. Scarlet was whip-smart when it came to angles like these. The girl missed nothing. 'There are a couple of dud items we'll be bidding on. I'll let you know which ones. You can do one; I'll do the other. And if needs be we'll bid against each other to ramp up the price.'

'Of course.' Scarlet nodded, impressed. 'Seems like a lucrative outlet.'

'It is. Just a shame we can't use it more often,' Lily replied regretfully.

'When is it?' Scarlet asked.

'Day after tomorrow. It's black tie. Have you got something to wear?'

'I'll go shopping later after I've finished at the hairdresser's.'

'What time you picking up the keys?' Lily asked.

'Soon actually,' Scarlet replied, glancing at her watch. 'I just wanted to go through my emails first.'

'Then I won't keep you,' she said as Scarlet stood up to leave. 'Have fun.'

'Thanks.'

The door closed and Lily's gaze dropped to her phone. Chewing her lip thoughtfully, she reached for it and scrolled through her contacts until she found Ray's number.

She hadn't seen him in person for a while, which wasn't uncommon. Her relationship with Ray was unusual. They were both very independent people, each with their own firm to run and fires to put out. Over the many years they had known and loved each other, Ray had often pushed to take things to another level, but she'd always resisted. In truth, she believed that this was the main reason their relationship had survived so long. They were both alphas, neither willing to take a back seat. But that's exactly what changing things would require. One of them would have to move into the other's area; one of them would have to slow down in order to support the other, day to day. Lily wasn't willing to do that, and neither was Ray. So this worked, despite his occasional protests.

But it did mean that when one or both of them were under extreme pressure, they would go a while without meeting up. Ray was clearly very busy at the moment, but with everything going on, she really wanted to speak to him. Her worries about Ruby were growing and she wanted to talk them through.

The call rang through to voicemail and her hope dropped. She chucked her phone across the desk and put her cigarette to her mouth, breathing in deeply before she blew out the smoke and closed her eyes. What was she missing? Ruby couldn't have disappeared into thin air. She didn't exactly have many options to begin with, and when her options ran out, home was usually her next port of call. But that hadn't happened. And the men searching her flat were still looking for her, so they didn't have her.

A chill settled in Lily's stomach as another possibility crossed her mind. Whilst running from these men, had Ruby ended up being taken by someone else? Or worse still, was she already dead?

CHAPTER ELEVEN

Ray stared at the phone in his hand as it lit up and felt the familiar mix of longing and guilt swirl through him. He slipped it back into his pocket and cleared his throat.

'That my mum again, was it?' came a taunting voice from across the room.

Ruby sat on a sofa at the other end of Ray's large comfortable lounge, next to a burly man reading a newspaper. This man glanced up at his boss at Ruby's words, then quickly back down at the paper when he saw his face.

Ray picked up his cup of coffee and took a sip, before placing it back down on the side table with careful precision. He sniffed and turned his attention to Ruby, ignoring her question.

'How was your latest session with the doctor?' he asked. He was referring to the addiction counsellor he'd hired to see her once a week. Dr Townsend had been struck off a few years before for an inappropriate relationship with a patient and now took on private work throughout the underworld. He took the money, did his job and kept his mouth shut.

Ruby sighed. 'It went fine.'

Ray nodded and stared out of the window. Dr Townsend had explained what Ruby was going through – that the poison she had been pumping into her veins was technically out of her system and, physically speaking, she was better. She hadn't been at first, not for a while. Ray could still recall her pitiful cries and screams of pain as the evil drug had drained from her body.

He'd read somewhere that the body begins to rely on heroin to force it to create dopamine, the hormone that blocks pain. When a user stopped using, the body wouldn't create it on its own for a while, causing every movement, every breath to feel excruciating. It sounded terrible, and he'd felt genuine sympathy for the girl as he'd listened to her screams and as she'd begged for her life to be ended. But she'd worried him even more when she'd turned quiet. Her breath had become laboured, her body slick with sweat and shaking with fever. He'd had a nurse in with her around the clock then, though she'd been too out of it to realise. Eventually, though, she'd come out the other side and he'd been working on getting her back up to full health ever since. And it appeared that he'd done that. But now came the harder battle.

Mentally, the doctor had explained things weren't so simple. The mind could not be forced the way the body could. Right now, all she would remember was how good heroin felt when it flooded through her veins. It didn't matter how healthy her body was – whilst that memory remained, it would be hard to keep her away from it. But that wasn't going to stop Ray from achieving what he'd set out to do. Over his long and dark career in the underworld, he'd learned that there were many ways of getting someone to do something they didn't want to do.

'I guess the question is, what are we going to do with you now?' he asked, his cold gaze boring into hers.

Ruby shivered slightly, but then stuck her chin out defiantly. 'Well, you ain't going to kill me – I know that much,' she stated.

'Oh?' Ray raised one eyebrow. 'And why's that?'

Ruby studied him for a moment. 'You haven't gone to all this trouble and expense to make sure the body's clean before it gets stuffed under the tarmac.'

Ray hid a smile. She had her mother's fearless wit, though she had a sharper edge than Lily. 'That's true,' he said. 'Or maybe I haven't decided yet. Perhaps I'm just covering all my options until

I do.' He watched her face as she studied him, trying to work out how much of what he was saying was a bluff.

Eventually she shook her head. 'No,' she said resolutely. 'You love my mum far too much to do that. I mean, she's already going to be pretty pissed at you. I wouldn't want to be in your shoes when she finds out what you've done.'

Ray's jaw locked tightly and he looked away – she'd hit a nerve. The girl was right – there was no point arguing it. Lily was going to be furious when she found out he'd kidnapped her daughter and forced her to go cold turkey in a locked room. Whether or not it was for the greater good wouldn't matter. He'd crossed the line as far as Lily would be concerned. No one was allowed to meddle in her family, let alone keep one of them captive.

'I doubt she even realises you're missing, Ruby,' he said with a hard, level stare. It wasn't true – Lily was starting to realise something was wrong. She'd texted to tell him as much, but Ruby didn't know that. 'You've run off down the needle-lit path to hell and not surfaced again for months so many times that this won't be out of the ordinary. She'll just assume you're festering in some doss pit, wasting away your days.'

Her attitude remained nonchalant but the movement in her jaw as she clenched it gave her away. This truth stung, even if only slightly.

'And if I did decide you were too much trouble, if I did decide to just get rid of the cause of so much of Lily's pain' – he paused to let his words sink in – 'she'd never for a second suspect it was me. Why would she?' He sat forward and let his dark gaze turn colder.

Ruby swallowed. He saw a brief flicker of unease pass over her face. *Good*, he thought. He sat back in his chair and picked up his coffee once more, drinking as he watched her, never once looking away. She was quieter now, her attention more acutely trained on him than before.

'What's the matter, Ruby?' he asked after a few silent minutes. 'Cat got your tongue?'

Ruby swallowed once more. 'I still think you have other ideas,' she said. Her words were brave but they held much less attitude. 'So why don't you tell me what you intend to do?'

'That very much depends on you.' Ray sat forward and put his mug down on the coffee table, then laced his fingers together in front of him. 'I'm going to let you walk out of here for now. Tomorrow, in fact. No one will be watching you anymore; no doors will be locked. But by no means does that mean you're free to do as you please.' Ruby's brow furrowed slightly in confusion. 'You can go home or you can go on to something new; I don't particularly care where you choose to live. But you will *never* touch heroin – or any other drug – again.'

Ruby's eyebrows shot up and she snorted. 'You really think you can tell me not to do it and I'll just listen like some sort of sheep?' she asked.

'Oh I do, yes.' Ray nodded. 'And here's why. The moment I hear the slightest rumour that you're back on the gear, that you so much as toke on a spliff at a party, I will be back for you. I will take you just as easily as I did last time, somewhere you'll never see me coming,' he said with feeling in his deep rumbling voice. 'And at that point I'll have two choices. I can either throw you back in that room…' He saw the fear immediately light up behind her eyes. That room was her worst nightmare – being alone, writhing in the dark in the worst pain imaginable for weeks on end. 'Or if that proves to be too much trouble, I can just stage an accident somewhere. Make it look like you crashed a car or stepped out in front of a train while you were off your head on smack. You wouldn't be the first – or the last.'

'And what would that achieve, eh?' Ruby responded hotly, starting to look more than a little worried. 'That would hurt my mum more than me being on the brown does.'

'Would it?' Ray asked. 'Sure, it would hurt at first, but eventually she'd feel peace, knowing you were in a better place where you couldn't destroy yourself anymore. She wouldn't lie awake at night worrying about you, wondering where you are, what hole you've crawled into.'

'You wouldn't get away with it,' she shot back. 'The moment I get home, I'm telling her everything, *including* this conversation. So if something happens to me, she'll know it's you.'

'Now that's where you're wrong,' Ray replied. 'Because I'll admit to taking you and getting you clean. But I'll deny this conversation and suggest you made it up to keep her angry with me. Who's she gonna believe? Me, the person who's always had her back, who cared enough about you to get you clean? Or *you*, the skag head who's lied to her more times than she cares to remember?' He lifted an eyebrow. 'Nah, she'll think you're just playing your games again. You see, unlike you, Ruby, I'm actually good at lying. And I only lie to your mum when it's for her own good. When it's for her protection. And I'll protect her from anything – even her own family,' he added coldly.

Ruby drew back and darted her panicked gaze around the room as she processed what he was saying. It soon returned to his face, and he held her gaze as she searched for any signs of a bluff. She didn't find one though – eventually she gave in to horrified acceptance.

'I'm a dangerous man, Ruby, and I don't make false promises,' he said, forming his words with careful precision. 'You know that. You've grown up in a world where *everyone* knows that. So I know that I'll have no need to remind you of our conversation today.' He stood up. 'You can tell your mum I took you and got you clean. I'll accept her wrath. But the rest you'd be wise to keep quiet on and take heed of.'

'She will fucking despise you for this, Ray Renshaw,' Ruby spat. 'She'll never forgive you. Not ever.'

'Oh, she will. Forgive me, I mean. Eventually. She'll hate me too,' he added with a regretful look. 'And that's gonna sting. But I'll take it, because do you know what, Ruby? I love that woman.' His voice flooded with feeling. 'I love her with every inch of my being and that means I'd do *anything* for her. Even if it hurts me in the process.' He stared at her for one last long moment. 'Don't you ever forget that. *One* slip, Ruby. There ain't no more chances left for you in this world. Not anymore.'

He looked over at his man and clicked his fingers to gain his attention. 'Put her back in her room. Then tomorrow lunchtime drop her off at her mother's. They'll all be there. The family always get together for lunch on a Sunday.'

He left the room and crossed the hallway to his study, closing the door behind him with relief, before exhaling loudly and rubbing his forehead in agitation. The shit was going to hit the fan when Ruby got home tomorrow. And his relationship with Lily was going to take the hardest blow in nearly thirty years. But he'd had to do it. For her. Ruby's lifestyle had been slowly killing her. He just prayed that his actions didn't take her out of his life for good.

CHAPTER TWELVE

Scarlet stood outside the front of her new salon, the keys clutched tightly in her hand and a beaming smile on her face. It was hers. It was really hers. Well, technically it belonged to all of them, the whole family, as it was part of the firm. But this had been *her* idea and Lily had told her it was her baby. Her chance to make her own mark.

Natalie arrived and stood next to her, looking up at the faded old sign. 'Well,' she said cheerfully. 'That's the first thing that needs to go. We have to get our own name up there.' She glanced sideways at her friend. 'What's that going to be, by the way?'

'Salon Red,' she replied.

Nat pulled an expression of approval. 'Short and sweet – I like it.'

'Me too,' Scarlet replied with feeling.

She unlocked the front door then led the way in, leaving Natalie to look around the main space while she stepped behind the reception desk to have a closer look at what was there. The till was outdated and low tech, but she wasn't sure that was necessarily a bad thing. The simpler their system was, the easier it would be to hide money.

Natalie wandered over, looking thoughtful. 'There's a lot here already which is great. I mean, it needs a lick of paint and a restock, but if you're happy with how it's set up, I can't see any reason to change it.'

'Yes, it's fine.' She glanced around and made a mental note to shop for paint and accessories to cheer the place up. 'Can you go round and make a list of everything we need to buy?' she asked. 'Back room stock, towels, stationery, hairdryers and all that.'

'Sure, no problem. Have you hired any other hairdressers yet?'

'Not exactly,' Scarlet replied.

Natalie glanced at her. 'What's "not exactly" mean?'

There was a light tap at the door and they both turned as a blonde head popped in. 'Hi, Scarlet,' Sandra said with a smile.

'Hey, come in,' Scarlet said warmly. 'Nat, this is Sandra. She'll be working here as assistant manager, under you.'

'Oh, OK.' Natalie seemed surprised but she greeted her politely. 'Nice to meet you.'

'And you,' Sandra responded with a wide grin.

'As of right now, it's just the three of us,' Scarlet continued. 'But we'll hire more stylists ASAP. Sandra is going to help you hold the fort. You can't do everything, especially as you'll be taking on all the clients yourself at first,' she explained. 'Sandra can answer phones, take bookings, sort payments, make drinks, mix colour, sweep hair,' she reeled off all the tasks she could think of. 'Anything you need.'

Natalie nodded and sized Sandra up subtly. 'Have you worked in a salon before?' she asked her.

'Um, no.' Sandra shot a look at Scarlet, unsure how much to say. 'I managed a café once, for a few months.'

Scarlet decided to tackle this straight on and get everything out in the open. 'Sandra used to work for us elsewhere, but it didn't work out so I offered her this,' she said frankly. Whichever details Sandra wanted to share with Natalie were her business. 'She has no experience, but she's willing to do whatever is needed. Right, Sandra?'

'Absolutely,' Sandra said eagerly. 'I really am actually.' She smiled a wide genuine smile. 'It'll be nice to work with clients that end their visit by putting a tip in your hand rather than their cock in your mouth, to be honest.'

Natalie blinked, lost for words for once. After a few moments she nodded. 'OK, then,' she managed. 'Tips for the win.' She gave her an awkward thumbs up.

Scarlet moved the conversation swiftly on. 'OK, so that's Sandra. And Sandra, this is Natalie, the salon manager. The business is one of our fronts. It's set up mainly to be a laundry, and Nat will be running it behind closed doors. You two will be the only ones who know about that side though, OK?' Her gaze moved between the two of them and they both nodded. 'The less people who know, the better.'

She turned in a circle, surveying all that still needed to be done and ran her hands through her long dark hair.

'When do you want to be ready to open?' Natalie asked.

Scarlet twisted her lips to one side and turned back to face them. 'Within a week.' She placed her hands on her hips.

'A week?' Natalie exclaimed, her jaw dropping. 'But there's so much to be done!'

'Every second this is closed is costing money.' Scarlet's deep red lips formed a hard line. 'We start cleaning this up today,' she said resolutely.

'But it's Saturday – I had plans…' Then Nat saw the look in Scarlet's eye. 'Which I can cancel,' she continued grudgingly.

'I'm all yours,' Sandra said with a shrug. 'Just tell me where you want me to start.'

'It will be worth it,' Scarlet promised, giving Nat a smile. 'And I'll take you both out for dinner tonight when we're done.'

'As long as it's somewhere good,' Nat grumbled.

'It will be. Now, come on!' She clapped her hands together as a fresh wave of motivation washed through her. 'Let's make a list of supplies and I'll go get them. We'll chuck everything that's not staying, give it a big wash down and by the end of the day, it will be ready for us to start making our own mark.'

She marched off to locate a notebook and pen. Salon Red was going to be epic, it was going to be sensational and she was completely certain that nothing – absolutely nothing – could possibly go wrong.

CHAPTER THIRTEEN

Cath paused and pushed a stray strand of dark hair out of her face, checking in the mirror that nothing else had escaped the neat bun she'd adopted for the occasion. Happy that everything was as it should be, she stepped out of the car and let Scarlet hand her the large foil-covered dish she'd been holding on the drive over to Lily's house.

'Thanks, love.' She watched as her daughter tried to stifle a yawn. 'You're working yourself too hard, Scarlet Drew,' she admonished.

'I'm fine, Mum, honestly,' Scarlet replied with a dismissive wave.

Cath pursed her lips. There was no point trying to insist the girl rest – she was built the same way as her father had been. She'd never stop for something as unimportant as a rest.

Scarlet walked ahead and opened the door, holding it for her mother. Inside, the buzz of family gathered together made its way to her ears and she felt an instant warmth flush through her. The twins were bickering with the TV on in the lounge and Lily was shouting for peace over the music she played as she cooked, pots and pans clanging together as she moved around the kitchen. They'd been meeting every Sunday for a big family lunch ever since she could remember.

It was only a lunch, food on a table shared between people, but it had always meant so much more to them all, and these days more than ever. Now their Sundays were a little quieter, a little less crowded. Since Ronan had died, a few months before, his absence had left a gaping hole in all their lives, and it was never more obvious than when they gathered together on a Sunday. But despite this, Cath felt like these gatherings were what pulled her through the darker times. The five of them coming together no matter what was what made everything else bearable.

Coming around the corner into the kitchen, she gave Lily a broad smile and placed her dish on the white marble island with a flourish. 'Alright, Lil? Need a hand?' She pulled back the foil and balled it up. 'Here, I've made my famous bread-and-butter pear pudding for afters.'

'Lovely,' Lily said as she put the meat back in the oven. 'That's Connor's favourite.' She glanced over at Scarlet. 'How'd yesterday go?'

'Yeah, we made a good start.' Scarlet leaned onto the counter with her forearms and picked up an olive, popping it in her mouth. 'Cleared out all the crap the previous owners left behind and gave it a good scrub.'

'You talking about your new hairdresser's, Scar?' Cath asked, surprised. She'd known Scarlet was picking up the keys at some point but she'd come home late so they hadn't had a chance to catch up.

'Yeah, figured I'd just dive straight in, you know? I hate the thought of it just sitting there empty. It's a waste.'

'You should have said. I'd have come and given you a hand,' Cath said in dismay.

'Nah, that's OK, Mum. You don't want to be on your hands and knees scrubbing floors,' Scarlet said with a small laugh. 'It wasn't much fun.'

'Yeah, but…' Cath shifted her weight onto the other foot. 'It's not about fun; it's about helping you out.'

In truth, it would have been nice to have something to do, to be of use to someone for a change. She'd spent most of her life looking after Ronan and Scarlet and the house, but now Ronan was gone and Scarlet had grown so independent. With just the two of them, there was less washing, less cooking, less mess to clean up. Cath found herself twiddling her thumbs and questioning her purpose more often than she'd like these days.

'I'm OK, honestly, Mum,' Scarlet replied, not picking up on the underlying wistfulness in her mother's tone. 'Thanks though.'

Cath tried to swallow the ball of disappointment that appeared in her chest and cast her eyes away as Scarlet wandered off towards the lounge. As she looked back up, she saw Lily's shrewd gaze settle on her, lips pursed. She quickly plastered a smile across her face and moved to where she knew the aprons were kept.

'You alright, Cath?' Lily asked.

'Me? I'm fine,' Cath replied brightly. 'Come on – I'll give you a hand with the veg. What needs doing?' She surveyed the array of vegetables on the side as she tied the apron behind her back.

'Peppers and onions, Mediterranean style – but really, you OK?' Lily was not so easily distracted.

''Course I am,' Cath exclaimed, hearing her own voice go an octave higher than usual as she lied, then quickly bringing it back down again. 'I'm dandy, Lil. Bit tired,' she added. 'Can't stop worrying about those bloody pigs. They're still hounding her. They've pinned her for it, Lil,' she said, lowering her voice. 'They're certain she's involved and keep trying to trip her up. I know they ain't got proof, but they're like a dog with a bone.' Her lips formed a grim line.

'They've been back to the factory too with the same questions,' Lily said heavily. 'But there's no proof of anything. So long as she just sticks to the story, they've got nothing.'

'I hope you're right. I know you are,' Cath added. 'But with it hanging over her head like some noose waiting to fall, it's just…' She sighed and shook her head. 'I need a drink. Where's the wine?'

Lily gave her a sharp glance but answered her levelly. 'Fridge door. Help yourself.'

Cath poured them both a glass. After taking a deep gulp, she picked up a knife and a pepper. Lil stood beside her and reached for an onion, and for a few moments they chopped in silence. 'You sure there's nothing else?' Lil asked again.

'Honestly, Lil. I—'

Cath was cut off by the front door opening. She and Lil turned to each other and frowned. The twins were here, she and Scarlet were here, so who the hell was that? They each rounded the island on either side and entered the hall together.

'Ruby!' Lily cried, her hands shooting to her cheeks.

*

Lily rushed towards her daughter. 'Thank God you're OK,' she breathed, pulling herself up short as she reached her. Ruby was not one for physical affection most of the time, so Lily had learned to give her space. Today, though, Ruby reached forward herself and wrapped her arms around her mother tightly, surprising them all.

'Mum,' she said, her voice wobbling.

Lily blinked and pulled her in, holding her close with a worried frown. Scarlet, Connor and Cillian came into the hallway, having heard the exchange.

'Christ, Rubes,' Connor said. 'You alright?'

Ruby pulled back with a sniff and looked around at them all, a haunted look on her face. 'Not really,' she admitted.

Lily checked her over with a critical eye. She seemed to be OK. More than OK actually. After all this time on the run from those men, she would have expected her to be in a pretty bad state, but Ruby was clean and well dressed – she even looked as though she'd put a little weight on, which she had desperately needed.

'I went to your old flat,' Lily said. 'I know about the men looking for you.'

Ruby's brow furrowed in confusion. 'What you on about?' she asked, seeming not quite with it.

It was Lily's turn to frown in confusion. 'What do you mean, "what am I on about"? I'm sure you can't have so easily forgotten the men you've been on the bloody run from, Ruby.'

'On the run? Jesus,' Cath exclaimed, her eyes widening.

'Oh, them.' Ruby shook her head slowly as she remembered, then rubbed her eyes. 'I haven't been on the run,' she said tiredly.

Lily's concern began to grow. What was going on? Who was this calm, defeated creature in front of her? The fact Ruby was not angry and fired up about her situation was worrying her greatly. Angry and fired up was her natural state, even in times of peace. This wasn't the daughter she knew. Ruby Drew was a fireball. Ruby Drew was a force that had never been tamed, not even by her.

'If you haven't been on the run then where have you been?' Lily asked.

'Huh.' Ruby gave a short, bitter laugh. She looked up into Lily's eyes and finally Lily saw the spark of the rage she was so familiar with. 'I *was* running from them initially. But I didn't get very far before I was kidnapped off the street and locked up in a pitch-black room with boarded-up windows and nothing but a mattress on the floor and a bucket to shit in.'

Cath gasped, and Lily swallowed hard. The others were silent as they awaited Lily's lead. She studied Ruby's face. The girl had cried wolf so many times in the past that her initial instinct was to be wary, but something in the defeated stoop of her shoulders and the lack of emotion in her words told her that this was no embellishment.

'What happened?' she asked, touching her arm tenderly.

Ruby reached up and laid her hand over her mother's, another action that alarmed Lily. Ruby never wanted comfort. She actively fought against her family, fought the constant invisible battle in her head that kept her on the wrong side of self-destruction. But it was like all that fight was gone. Like her family was no longer the enemy. But Ruby always had an enemy – she had no idea how to live without one. Which begged the question, who could possibly have done something so terrible to her that they had taken her family's place?

CHAPTER FOURTEEN

'Who the fuck does he think he is?' Connor slammed his fist down on the side table next to his chair in Lily's study, where they had holed up to discuss the startling revelations Ruby had shared.

Scarlet sat in the chair next to him, leaning forward, her hands clasped on her knees; Cillian stood with his back against the wall nearby; and Lily paced, unable to stand still as she processed it all. After relaying everything that Ray had put her through, Ruby had been tired and asked if she could lie down. Cath had taken her upstairs to make up the bed and settle her in.

'We all know who he thinks he is,' Lily responded. 'We all know who he *is*.' She rubbed her temples, stressed.

'In all this time, he hasn't let on *once*? Even when you told him you were worried about her?' Scarlet asked again.

'Not once,' Lily answered curtly.

'This is fucking ridiculous. It's insane,' Connor continued. 'What right does he have to take her like that? It's an open invitation for us to go right for him. What's he after, a fucking war?'

'There will be no war,' Lily shot back. 'At least not one with you in it.'

'What do you mean? Of *course* there will be and damn right with us in it – she's our sister!' Connor declared hotly. 'She might be a fucking nightmare, but she's blood. No one gets away with that. Eh, Cillian?' He looked over to his brother. 'You're very quiet – you got nothing to add here?'

Cillian scratched his neck and exhaled a long breath. 'You're right,' he said slowly. 'It's an insult against us as a firm to take her the way he did. However, much as he shouldn't have done that, Ray has succeeded in fixing a problem we completely failed to.'

'What?' Connor spat, surprised at his brother's response.

'Oh, come on. Ruby was full-on running towards an early grave, shoving that shit in her arm whenever she could.' He held his hand up as Connor opened his mouth to protest. 'I'm not saying it's right; I'm not saying we should pat him on the back for it. I'm just saying that it's not black and white. He ain't done it to start up issues; he's done it to save Mum the heartache of burying her.' He reached into his pocket and pulled out a toothpick, putting it between his teeth. 'Much as I'm as outraged as you at the liberties he's taken, I'm glad he's cleaned her up. I've thought about locking her in a room myself from time to time.'

'And if you had that would have been our business to deal with. But this wasn't Ray's business,' Lily interjected. Both her boys looked across at her.

She continued her pacing, her eyes flicking from one to the other and then back again. She ground her teeth and rubbed her temples, feeling stressed. All kinds of feelings were raging inside her right now and she wasn't sure which to hold on to. She felt pure indignant fury at what he'd done. Yet gratitude too that he'd saved Ruby in a way she hadn't been able to. But that hadn't been his call to make, and the hell he'd put her through to do it – a hell which she'd not undergone willingly – sounded horrific. How could he do that? How *dare* he do that? But even as she thought this, she knew with resounding clarity that if someone were to give her the option to go back in time and stop him, she wouldn't take it. She felt torn, and that fuelled her anger even further.

'What do you want to do?' Scarlet asked.

'What we'll *do* is visit that cunt and put him back in his place,' Connor piped up, hatred dripping from every word.

'No,' Lily replied sharply. She shook her head. 'No, you won't. And that's a direct order. I'll deal with this. It has to be me.'

Her heart began to thud faster in her chest at the thought of her boys going to Ray in rage. They had every right to, and they were hard men who could hold their own, but Ray was dangerous. Far more dangerous than the boys understood. He would only allow them to step so far. *She* on the other hand was the one person in this world who could say or do what she liked and no matter how far she went, though he might push her back a little, he would never harm her. So it had to be her.

'Mum—' Connor began to protest, but she cut him off.

'No. I'll deal with this myself and that's final,' she said firmly.

She walked over to the drinks trolley she kept in the office, pulled out a bottle of whisky and poured a large measure into a glass. Lifting the glass to her mouth, she downed it in one and closed her eyes. The burn of the whisky calmed her as it rolled down her throat and into the fiery centre of her emotions. She took a deep breath and turned back around to face them.

'Right now, we're going to go back out there and have a family lunch, just like we always do. Then tonight, I'll visit Ray.' Her gaze darkened. 'And I'll leave him under no illusion of what our thoughts are on the matter.'

CHAPTER FIFTEEN

Ray watched from the upstairs window as the gates opened and Lily's sleek black Mercedes rolled through under the light of the lamps dotted either side of the long driveway. She parked up then got out and slammed the door hard, leaving him in no doubt of her current state of mind. He sighed and downed the brandy in his hand before turning to walk downstairs. It was time to face the music.

He made his way down the stairs and opened the door. Lily stood on the other side, her back ramrod straight, thunder in her dark brown eyes. There was no hint of a smile tonight, no welcoming twinkle.

'How did you know I'd be home?' he asked, breaking the ice. He stepped aside and gestured for her to come in.

She entered and stood a few feet away from him in the large open hallway. 'I knew you'd be expecting my visit,' she said in a controlled tone. 'And I imagined you'd rather take my wrath in private than in public.' She broke her gaze for a moment to look around the empty space. 'None of your men around tonight, I see,' she observed.

'Well, like you say' – Ray closed the door and turned to face her – 'I was expecting you.'

Lily nodded. 'No one to step in if I decide to claw your face off with my bare hands then,' she stated in a low, deadly voice.

'I don't need anyone else to stop you doing that, Lil. I can overpower you all by myself. It's one of the things you love about me, remember?' He stared at her and felt the strange mix of hatred and passion that was radiating off her, weighing down the air between them.

After a few long, tense moments, the corner of Lily's mouth lifted and her eyes narrowed as she let out a bitter, humourless laugh. 'And I don't need to get physical to hurt you, Ray. I can do that without moving a muscle. Remember?' Her words were laced with venom, and Ray almost stepped back as his heart missed a beat.

Lily turned in a circle, running her hands back through her wild curls as if the action might make them stay for once. They bounced back as she let go and pivoted to face him once more.

'How could you do it, Ray?' she demanded, all calmness gone. 'How could you *fucking* do that to me?' she yelled. 'Who the *hell* do you think you are? Huh?' She walked towards him, fire blazing in her eyes as everything she'd kept so neatly boxed finally began to erupt. 'Come on, who do you think you are?' she repeated hotly. 'Are you a member of my family? *No.* Are you a member of my firm? *No.* Did I give you my permission?'

As she took one menacing step nearer with each question, Ray couldn't help but admire how glorious she was in her fury, even though he knew he was in for it big time.

'Did I ask you to *kidnap my daughter*? Did I ask you to watch me worry and lie awake at night wondering if she was dead while you held her in a *fucking prison*? While she was locked up in *pain, terrified*? No?' Her voice had reached a crescendo and her steps had led her right up to his face so that she was only inches away, but still he did not move or respond. She stepped back and wiped a hand over her mouth, her rage still visible in every line of her body.

Ray sighed heavily. 'Look, I understand why you're upset.'

'Upset?' Lily rounded on him. 'No, Ray. Upset is how I feel when I've spent three hours cooking and accidentally burned the meat. Upset is how I feel when I spill red wine on a light-coloured dress. *Upset,*' she yelled, 'doesn't even come close. I am *fucking livid.*'

Ray put his hands up in the air in surrender as she lost it harder than he'd ever seen her lose it. 'Alright, Lil, I get it,' he shouted back, his deep voice booming around the hall. 'I get it, OK?'

'No,' she yelled back with feeling. 'No, you don't, because you never had kids, Ray. You never had someone who was part of you.' She balled her fist and thumped her chest. 'Whose heart beats because of you, who you'd do anything for – *kill* for, if you had to.'

'I'd kill for *you*, Lily,' he shot back. 'I'd do anything for you and you know it. And I'd do anything for your family too, *for you*,' he stressed. 'I love you. You might not have liked the way I went about it, but I got her clean. For *you*, for *her*—'

'Don't pretend this was for Ruby – you ain't her dad,' Lily snapped, shaking her head. 'You had your chance to be part of my family, to be a father and play happy families, many years ago. But you *blew it*,' she said, shaking under the weight of the emotions their conversation was stirring up.

Ray pulled back, stung. Stung because it was true. He'd had his chance when they'd first fallen in love as little more than kids. Lily had needed stability back then. She'd been raising her little brother all alone and needed to be with someone stable, someone who valued family. And he'd walked away, more interested in being free and playing the field. He hadn't realised then what a mistake that was, what a fool he'd been to throw something so precious to the wind. Lily had moved on, and once he'd had his fill of meaningless, empty fun, he'd had no choice but to sit on the sideline and watch as she settled down with someone else.

'And that was the biggest mistake of my life,' he said, his quiet voice full of raw emotion. Lily blinked and stared at him, silent now that he'd finally said the words out loud. In thirty years, he had never actually admitted that to her, but considering he may never get another chance, he figured it was time.

He held his hands out to the side helplessly and then let them drop. 'I fucked up. I was a kid; I didn't know what I was doing. And I've lived with the consequences ever since. But I'll tell you something.' He took a step towards her, his beseeching eyes looking into hers. 'The moment I got you back after that good-for-nothing Alfie took off, I made myself a promise. And that was to never let you down again. I made a promise that I'd always be there for you and I'd do everything I could to protect you.'

'I don't need protecting, Ray,' Lily snapped. 'I've never needed *that*.'

He held his hands up again. 'Not usually, no, but with Ruby you have a blind side. She's your weakness. She was running herself, and you in the process, to an early grave. And you wouldn't do anything about it.'

'I *couldn't*,' Lily corrected.

'You couldn't because locking her up and forcing her to get clean yourself would mean she'd never forgive you. Which is *why* I took that out of your hands. It don't matter than she won't forgive me,' he stressed. 'Don't you see? You've got her *back*. And you've got her *onside*. The only person she won't forgive for this is me. And I can live with that.'

Lily stared at him long and hard, and for the first time since she'd arrived, he couldn't work out what emotion was behind her beautiful brown eyes. He wanted so much to reach forward, to grab her in his arms and carry her upstairs to make love to her and make everything right between them again, but he knew that he couldn't. There was just a few inches between them, but it may as well have been a mile.

Eventually, Lily shook her head. 'No, Ruby won't forgive you for that, you're right,' she said. 'And quite frankly I don't know if I ever can either.'

Ray's heart constricted and his breath caught in his chest. He tried to find the right words to say, to convince her to stay, to make her understand, but he couldn't. They just weren't there.

With one last look, Lily turned away from him and walked back out the front door into the darkness.

CHAPTER SIXTEEN

Scarlet checked herself over one last time in the long mirror on her bedroom wall, turning each way slowly. The black dress she'd bought for the occasion hugged her figure down to the calf, with wide straps that sat off the shoulder and a sweetheart neckline. It was elegant and flattering on her tall, slender figure and just right for the charity event they were attending tonight. Or so she hoped anyway.

Hearing the car pull up, she fluffed back her long dark hair, set with voluminous waves, and quickly applied her lipstick. She rubbed her lips together and cast a critical eye over her face. The blood-red colour accented her pale skin and dark hair, just as she'd hoped. The horn sounded and she grabbed her stole and clutch, throwing the lipstick inside in case she needed it later, then walked out into the hallway.

Coming down the stairs, she smiled at her mother as she hovered in the hallway.

'Oh, Scar, you look gorgeous!' Cath exclaimed with a mixture of pride and love.

'Thanks,' Scarlet replied with a grin.

Cath gave her a quick hug and then stepped out of the way. 'Go on then, hurry up, or Lil will get the right arse,' she said. She pushed Scarlet gently out of the door and waved her off as she made for the car.

The back door opened and Lil leaned out, waved briefly to Cath then scooched over to the other side. 'Come on, get in. We'll be late.'

Scarlet got in and shut the door, then looked to see who was driving. It was George, one of Lily's right-hand men, and she nodded a greeting to him through the rear-view mirror.

'George is driving so we can both have a few drinks and let our hair down,' Lily explained.

'And because she hates taxis,' he added with a laugh.

'And because I fucking hate taxis,' she agreed with a grin back at him. 'You look nice,' she said in an approving tone. 'I recognise that stole,' she added.

'Yeah, I borrowed it from Mum,' Scarlet replied. It was one of her mother's prized possessions, a fur stole Ronan had gifted her before they'd married. 'You look lovely too, Lil,' she said.

Lily wore a dark burgundy satin dress that shimmered subtly in the dying evening light. With nails and lips to match, she was dressed to kill, as always. It was almost as if the events of the day before hadn't even happened. Scarlet shifted her body to face her aunt.

'Everything OK?' she asked.

'Yep,' Lil answered.

Scarlet bit the inside of her cheek. 'I mean, how did it go with Ray?'

Lily shot her a sharp look and Scarlet took the hint, turning to look out of the window at the passing scenery. Clearly, Lily was not up for discussing whatever had gone down between them.

They spent the rest of the journey mostly in silence, other than discussing a potential new customer for the factory. By the time they eventually arrived at their destination – a manor house somewhere just outside of London, in Kent – Scarlet was ready to enjoy herself.

'Now remember,' Lily said as they walked into the building, 'we're just collectors of antiques and unusual items. Just say we have a shop in Wanstead, if anyone asks.'

'Got it,' Scarlet replied.

They entered the main hall, gave their names and were directed towards their table. The schedule for the evening was drinks, dinner, then the auction over dessert. Someone handed Scarlet a glass and she couldn't help the smile that crept over her face. She'd needed some fun after all the long days she'd been pulling lately, and it seemed she was about to get it. She found her place name at the table and sat down, noticing her aunt had sat a few spaces away from her.

'Well, hello!' came a cheery voice from behind her.

She turned to see a man in his early thirties take the seat beside her. She smiled politely back at his beaming face and held out her hand to shake his. 'Hi, I'm Scarlet,' she said.

He took her hand and kissed it in a half-chivalrous, half-humorous motion. 'And I, my dear, am Henry,' he said in a distinctly upper-class accent. 'But most people call me Harry.' She opened her mouth to speak but he cut her off. 'You can call me Henry.' She blinked and he threw his head back with an embarrassingly loud guffaw. 'I'm just joking! You must, of course, call me Harry.'

'Er, OK then,' Scarlet replied. 'Harry it is.'

'Lovely to meet you, Scarlet,' he said in a merry tone. 'And may I say, you look positively stunning this evening.'

'Thank you,' Scarlet replied with a fixed smile.

'Andrew, Duffy, I must introduce you to Scarlet,' Harry continued loudly, as two more guests arrived at their table. 'And this gorgeous lady whom I haven't yet met,' he said, looking at Lily. 'You *must* tell me your name.'

As the attention shifted to her aunt, Scarlet pulled back and looked around at everything that was going on. The glittering people, the colourful stage, the opulence. This certainly was a different world, a world she hadn't encountered before. She felt out of her depth. But she was a Drew, she reminded herself, lifting her chin. And she could hold her own, whatever she was faced with.

CHAPTER SEVENTEEN

Scarlet put her hand to her aching stomach as she laughed for the hundredth time that evening. 'Oh God, stop, my muscles can't take it,' she said through tears of mirth.

Harry topped up her wine. 'Can I interest you in a shot of Patrón XO?'

'What's that?' she asked.

'It's a coffee tequila liqueur; it's really rather wonderful,' he enthused.

'Or rather terrible,' Duffy interjected. 'It depends how much you've already had to drink.'

'Two very contrasting reviews,' Scarlet replied. She glanced over at Lily, who was smiling at the conversation. They'd both had a great night. They'd sunk some ginormous bids on the fake items they'd set up, and after they'd got used to the crowd on the table, they'd found they were quite fun company. Even Lily had thrown her head back and laughed a few times.

'Waiter?' Harry caught the attention of a passing server. 'Hello, can we have six shots of your finest coffee patrón please?'

'I'm sorry, sir, we haven't got that in stock,' he replied apologetically.

'Oh blast! What do you have?'

'To shot? Um, I think we have some vodka left, or whisky, or Baileys.'

'Christ, we can't enjoy any of those,' Harry complained. 'Oh well, we'll just have to take the after-party back to mine sooner than I'd thought. Will you come?' He lifted an eyebrow to Scarlet and then Lily.

'Um—' Scarlet turned to her aunt, looking for the right words to decline gently, when Duffy interrupted.

'You really should come. Harry's house is incredible.'

'House?' Andrew scoffed. 'It's a bloody castle.'

'Castle?' Scarlet asked, surprised.

'No, it's a Grade II listed Jacobean manor house,' Harry corrected with a roll of his eyes. 'Which is why I am always the host of every after-party. Everyone always wants to play at mine.'

She paused, her interest piqued, and as she deliberated Lily made the decision for them.

'We can join you for a short while.' She met Scarlet's gaze. 'It's early and we have George to take us home later.'

Scarlet's eyes narrowed slightly. Surely she didn't really want to go on to an after-party with a group of drunken strangers? Fun as it sounded to her, she knew her aunt would usually see something like this as a waste of time that could be better spent elsewhere. Lily smiled sweetly at Harry across the table and suddenly it clicked.

Everything Lily ever did was for a reason, however big or small. And the most likely reason she had accepted this invite was that she was getting Harry onside for some sort of future hustle. It made sense. The guy was obviously rich, and it was clear from everything he'd said that he spent far too much time getting drunk with friends. Which likely meant that he was bored. Bored rich people were easily manipulated and potentially very influential, which was just the sort of asset Lily liked to acquire. As everything clicked into place, Scarlet gave Lily a look, which her aunt promptly returned. They were on the same page.

'Well then, I guess that's settled,' she said with a smile. 'Shall we?'

'Indeed we shall. Follow me, everyone,' Harry said, standing up. 'Let the after-party commence!'

*

As they made the long drive to Harry's home, following the line of taxis ahead carrying Harry and his friends, Scarlet's eyebrows shot up almost into her hairline. He hadn't been exaggerating – the place looked like something out of a Jane Austen novel. The sprawling house was set in what seemed like endless grounds, and lit up in the darkness, the yellow stone walls looked regal and impressive. With large window bays and tall columns leading up to the rooftop, she could see why Andrew had referred to it as a castle.

'Christ,' she exclaimed. 'Who are these people?'

'That's what I'm hoping to find out,' Lily said quietly.

'What are you thinking?' Scarlet asked, wondering if her aunt already had an angle in mind.

'I'm not sure yet,' Lily reflected as she stared at the imposing building. 'There's definitely an opportunity here. We just need to work out exactly what it is.'

George pulled up at the front of the house behind the taxi that was disgorging Harry and the others from their table.

'Let's find somewhere to leave the car…' Lily started, but George cut her off.

'Nah, it's OK, Lil; I'm gonna wait out here. You go on in. I've got some calls to make and a newspaper I haven't yet got round to,' he said in his deep crackling voice.

'You sure you don't want to join us?' Lily asked.

'What, stand around listening to a bunch of toffs go on about what they do with Daddy's money? Nah, I'm alright.' He gave them a lopsided grin.

Scarlet grinned back. She totally understood George's feelings on the matter. They came from a different world. When you worked as hard as they did for everything you had, it was difficult to respect people who'd had it all handed to them on a silver plate.

'We'll see you later then,' Lily replied.

They got out and joined the group of people assembling at the front door. Everyone seemed to know each other, and there was a lot of excited chatter as Harry fumbled around with keys.

'He doesn't usually need to open the door himself,' Duffy said with a chuckle. 'Don't know how to use the bloody key, do you, Harry?' There was a small wave of laughter and Harry cursed under his breath.

'What do you mean?' Scarlet asked with a frown.

'Usually his housekeeper and a few other household staff are here, so there's no need for it to be locked,' Duffy replied, swaying slightly as all the alcohol began to take its toll.

'Where are they all now?' she asked.

'He gives them all the night off when he's due to have a party like this.' Duffy and Andrew exchanged a loaded look.

Scarlet caught this and was about to probe further when there was a small cheer from the people around Harry.

'We're in!' he cried. 'Come on – to the bar!'

Scarlet fell into step beside Lily as they entered through the grand hallway. The interior was just as impressive as the outside, with intricate wooden panelling and large paintings hanging from the picture rails. They reached what appeared to be a library, one wall stacked with old books from floor to ceiling and with plentiful seating. Sure enough, in the corner of the room, a bar was set up, fully stocked, and Duffy headed straight over to it.

'OK, chaps and chapettes,' he said merrily, 'I'll take the first shift as bartender. Who's having what?'

Everyone flocked around him and soon the bar was no longer visible as everyone began shouting their orders.

Scarlet and Lily hung back, and a woman Lily had introduced Scarlet to earlier as Sheila's assistant Amanda came over to join them.

'How are you, Lil?' she asked pleasantly. 'Did you win any bids tonight?'

'Oh yes, we did very well, thank you,' Lily replied.

'I'm glad,' Amanda replied. 'You do so much for the charity. You're one of our biggest benefactors, you know.'

Scarlet averted her gaze. Amanda was not in the know about who they were or what they did. She made her excuses and walked over to a painting which had caught her eye.

Art was an interest of hers. She'd studied fine art at A level and had even got an A*. She hadn't had time to go to a gallery for a while, but seeing impressive artworks still gave her great pleasure whenever she got the chance.

Harry came over and handed her a glass of wine. 'Here,' he said. 'I bagged you one before the rabble completely took over.' He swayed, slightly worse for wear, and a little of the wine sloshed out of the glass.

'Thank you.' She accepted it with a smile of thanks and took a sip, looking back up to the painting.

'German artist, that one,' Harry said. 'Not usually one for contemporary work, but this caught my eye and apparently he's one to watch, so' – he shrugged – 'maybe it will go up in value. We'll see.'

'It's lovely,' Scarlet remarked. 'I really like his use of light here.' She pointed to one side of the painting. 'It's unusual.'

'You're into art?' Harry asked, his tone surprised.

'Yes,' she replied. 'I'm more of a classics fan though.'

'Me too.' Harry looked her up and down not very subtly. 'You know, I have some more interesting pieces in the next room if you'd like to see?'

'Er…' Scarlet glanced back to check on her aunt, but Lily was engrossed in her conversation with Amanda. 'Sure. Go on then,' she replied.

They entered an adjoining room and Harry tried to push the door closed behind them. Scarlet stopped it with her foot and left it half-open. She smiled as he looked to her questioningly.

'I need to keep an eye out for my aunt,' she said. 'In case she looks for me.'

'Oh, right, right. Yes,' Harry bumbled, almost tripping over the foot of a side table.

He was incredibly drunk, Scarlet realised. She wondered whether she should try and draw Lily into their conversation now.

'Anyway, here, look at these bad boys.' Harry swept his arm in a wide arc, in front of a wall of paintings. Scarlet looked up and her breath caught in her throat. She immediately recognised several artists' work and blew out a long, slow breath. This was the most impressive collection she'd ever seen outside of an art gallery. But then again, she realised, she'd never been in an art collector's home before, let alone one with this much wealth.

She walked across the room slowly, drinking in each painting with her eyes. Harry followed close behind, explaining each painting in turn, slurring his words and hovering just a little too closely. She could feel his body heat now and then as he swayed too close, and each time she stepped quickly forward.

As they came to the end of the room, she took one more wistful look at the wall, then turned towards the half-open door. 'That really was a sight to see. Thank you so much.' She glanced over his shoulder towards her aunt, who she could just about see through the gap. 'I'd better get back to Lil. She—'

'Wait,' Harry said quickly, cutting her off. 'There's something else you need to see.' He glanced over his shoulder at the door, then back to her. 'Please – it will only take a moment. An art lover like yourself can't leave here without seeing this.'

'Hmm. I really should get back.'

'Have you ever seen a Rembrandt?' Harry said suddenly, with a hiccup.

'What?' she replied, her head snapping back towards him. Her attention was immediately sharpened by his question, all thoughts of Lily gone.

'I said' – he smiled – 'have you ever seen a Rembrandt?'

Scarlet's eyes narrowed and her quick mind assessed the situation. He couldn't own a Rembrandt. He seemed well off, but Rembrandts were worth millions – hundreds of millions, some of them – and most were in museums. There was no way he could be in possession of one. Plus, there was next to no security around the house. Even his staff were away for the night. Who would be so lax with their security if they owned a piece of artwork worth millions?

'I can show you it, but you have to promise not to tell anyone,' he slurred.

Scarlet's frown deepened. He seemed genuine, but he couldn't be. She couldn't work out whether he was so drunk he was making things up, or whether he was so drunk he was confusing one artist for another. Either way, her curiosity was piqued and she wanted to find out what was behind the crazy claim.

'You know, Rembrandt is actually my favourite artist,' she said slowly, watching his face for any sign of deceit. 'I know his work quite well.'

'Then you'll love this,' he replied with a chuckle and a swagger.

Scarlet studied him with interest. He seemed very confident for someone she was sure could not possibly back up his claim. 'OK then,' she replied. Her eyes narrowed. 'Show me.'

CHAPTER EIGHTEEN

They walked over to the other side of the house. Harry swayed a few times, babbling about how this had to be their little secret because no one was supposed to know. She tuned him out, looking instead at the artwork and sculptures they passed with interest. Eventually they reached a study, and he closed the door firmly behind them. Scarlet turned in a circle, scanning the walls.

She frowned. 'I knew it was too good to be true,' she declared. 'There's no Rembrandt here.' Her intrigue turned to annoyance. Why had he dragged her all the way over here?

He held his hands up in protest. 'You didn't really think it would be out in plain view, did you?'

Scarlet pursed her lips. Harry stumbled around the desk and tugged out a drawer, reaching underneath it awkwardly. He pulled a pained expression and stuck his tongue out of the corner of his mouth as he reached and rummaged. Eventually there was a quiet clicking sound and one of the wooden panels in the wall behind him popped open. Scarlet's eyes widened in surprise.

She watched with open curiosity as he pulled the panel open to reveal a keypad. He keyed in the code and tried to cover what he was doing with his hand, but in his drunken state he didn't do a very good job and, after moving slightly, Scarlet was able to see what he keyed in. She noted the number and quickly committed it to memory. Once the keypad light had turned green, Harry pulled on a small handle and a larger section of panels pushed inwards and slid to one side.

Her hands flew to her mouth as she tried to process what she was looking at. It couldn't be real. The painting she was faced with hadn't been seen in decades. She knew, because she'd written a piece on it for her A level coursework.

'It can't be,' she breathed, stepping forward to take a closer look. She stopped just in front of it and put her fingers up towards it, not quite touching, but hovering above it reverently.

'I can assure you it is,' Harry boasted, walking up behind her.

Scarlet shook her head slowly. Her eyes flew over all the little details, looking for any sign it could be a copy. She was no expert on artistic fakery, but it certainly did seem like it was the real deal. 'How do you have this?' she asked.

'That's a secret, I'm afraid.' Harry swayed and blinked, apparently unsure. 'I shouldn't have shown you really. I've had a bit too much to drink, I think.' He reached forward over her and pulled the sliding panel back into place, covering the Rembrandt back up.

Scarlet wandered over to the desk, her mind whirling. What she'd just seen was both shocking and incredible. She wasn't sure yet what to do with this information; she needed to discuss it with her aunt. She turned and then pulled back in surprise as she realised Harry was suddenly right behind her.

'Oh, er, thank you. For showing me that,' she said quickly, trying to skirt around him. Each time she moved though, he moved with her, blocking her exit. She exhaled uncomfortably, realising he'd backed her against the desk.

'That's OK,' he slurred with a slow smile. 'It got you alone. Finally,' he added, with a roll of the eyes. 'I didn't think it would take so much, but at least we're here now, eh?'

He leaned towards her and with startling clarity Scarlet realised his intentions.

'Oh!' she exclaimed, placing her hands flat on his chest to bar his way. 'No. No, sorry, Harry. This isn't what I was…' She laughed awkwardly, trying to dispel the tension. 'I just wanted to see the painting.'

Harry made a groaning sound of annoyance. 'Painting, yeah, sure. Well, you saw it, sweetie, and now we move on to the good stuff.' He leered forward again, moving her hands off his chest with his own and kissed her on the lips, sticking his tongue into her mouth.

Scarlet gagged as it probed down her throat and pulled back as far as she could, leaning at a precarious angle over the desk he now had her pinned against. 'Jesus, Harry, I said no,' she said emphatically.

Harry paused and stared at her through bleary, drunken eyes and for a moment she thought he was going to back off. But then a dark look flashed behind his pupils and she realised that wasn't going to happen. She pushed forward in an attempt to break free, but with surprising strength and precision for someone so drunk, he shoved her back onto the desk.

'I don't think so,' he snarled.

She tried to get up, but in the position he'd put her in, she couldn't quite get a hold on anything to propel herself and he stood staunchly above her, weighing her down.

'Harry, get off me,' she shouted, getting angry. She kicked out, but his legs just pushed forward between her own, and in one swift movement he bent and hooked his arm under one of her knees, bringing her leg up high. She heard her dress rip as her legs were forced apart, and she felt the blood rush to her cheeks as embarrassment and fear began to take hold. 'What are you doing?' she demanded, beginning to panic.

'Oh, come off it,' he moaned. 'You're up for this. You've been chatting me up all night.' He gave her a leery grin. 'I know you want a piece of me.'

'I don't want a piece of anything,' Scarlet cried. 'Let me go right *now*!'

'Oh shut up,' he snapped. 'No one's going to hear you, you know. Not out here. Even if you scream the place down, no one will hear a sound,' he taunted. 'Just enjoy it, will you? Stop pretending you're anything but the East End whore we both know you are.'

'What?' Scarlet asked, aghast.

Harry pushed her legs apart painfully, and her dress rode right up to her waist. She cried out and tried to pull it back down but to no avail. He was horrifyingly strong, and her attempts came to nothing. He looked down between her legs and chuckled.

'Oh, Scarlet,' he moaned, a dark excitement in his tone. 'You call that underwear?' He was referring to the slim thong she'd worn to avoid a visible underwear line beneath her dress. 'That's nothing but dental floss, you saucy thing.'

Scarlet let out a sound that was somewhere between a snarl and a shout of frustration at his words. How dare he uncover her this way! How dare he do any of this to her! Her heart rate increased as she realised he had no intention of stopping here. Already she could feel his mounting excitement as he pressed against the inside of her thigh.

He reached forward and gently pushed the flimsy thong aside.

'Get off me,' Scarlet screamed at him, bucking and writhing as she tried to get into a better position, a position where she had the power to be able to push him away. But no matter how she tried, she couldn't seem to move.

'Oh, you sexy bitch,' he groaned. He moved his hand down to his own privates, massaging them through his trousers.

'Get the fuck off me, Harry,' Scarlet yelled. 'Get off me now.'

'Oh, would you *shut up*,' he yelled back. 'Stop pretending you don't want it. *You*, the working-class little nobody from the East End. The little tart who's been parading around in that low-cut little black number. Who came back to my home after knowing me just a few hours. Don't pretend you aren't up for it,' he said, pushing forward and gyrating against her. 'Why on *earth* would I invite common muck like you and that brassy old whore you came with into my home if it wasn't for this, hmm?' he sneered. 'Do you know who I *am*? Do you really think I associate with people like you?' He laughed. 'You're not here for your company, sweetheart. So just do what girls like you do best and take my dick like it's the last dick you'll ever ride, eh? You love this. Stop pretending you don't.'

Scarlet's panic reached a crescendo and she felt tears prick at her eyes as he pulled back her thong once more. He was going to rape her. She struggled against his vice-like grip, and her legs flailed in the air as they desperately searched for something to push against. Harry's hand fumbled with his flies, and she whimpered as she heard the zip open. Looking down in horror, she saw him pull himself out. His penis was already large and swollen, ready to carry out what he had planned.

'That's it, have a good look,' he said, following her gaze. 'This is what you like, isn't it? You must see a lot of these, a girl like you. Those blokes in the East End are lucky fellows, having you in the local buffet. Now come on…' He shifted and hoisted her leg up higher, lining himself up. 'Oh, yeah!'

He closed his eyes as he went to press forward, but as he moved into position, Scarlet saw her chance. Her leg was now high enough that she was certain she could push her foot into his chest if she just moved it a little higher. Without waiting to deliberate, she pulled her leg back and let out a ferocious roar, pushing him back with her foot and every ounce of her strength.

Harry stumbled, momentarily shocked, and Scarlet quickly rocked up off the desk into a standing position. He blinked and rushed forward to try and push her back down, but she was too quick for him and dodged to the side. The drink made him misjudge the distance and he bounced against the edge of the desk, falling over on to his side.

'Jesus Christ,' he yelled angrily. 'What the bloody hell do you think you're doing?'

He reached out to grab her leg, but she kicked his hand. He cried out in pain and cradled it with the other one as he sat on the floor, his trousers around his knees.

Angrier than she could ever remember being in her life, Scarlet stepped forward and stamped with all her strength on the area between his legs. Harry let out a blood-curdling scream and curled into a ball, letting her know she'd hit her mark.

She pulled back, breathing heavily as adrenaline and fear mixed with triumph and anger. She pulled her dress down as best she could and pushed her hands back through her hair as she processed all that had just happened.

'You cunt,' she said, her voice trembling under the weight of her emotions. 'You foul, disgusting, *evil* cunt.' She backed away from him to the door, horrified, on top of everything else, that she'd been so stupid.

She ran down the hallway and through the house back to the party, slowing as she reached the library doors and calming her breath. She didn't want to cause a scene; she just wanted to get Lily and get out of this place before he could follow after her.

'Ah, there you are. I was just saying to…' Lily frowned. 'Scarlet?' she asked, grabbing her arm.

'I need to leave,' Scarlet said quietly, glancing up into her eyes just once. 'Now.'

Lily's hold on her arm immediately tightened. 'Amanda, I'm so sorry, we'll continue this another time.'

Without waiting for a response or further detail, Lily turned Scarlet around and the pair walked swiftly out of the room. Scarlet let out a silent sigh of relief as they passed through the front door and out into the fresh night air. She knew Lily wouldn't need any further explanation.

They marched towards the car where George sat with the light on, reading his paper, and only once they were inside did Lily turn to Scarlet and search her face properly.

'What happened?' she asked sharply.

Scarlet opened her mouth to reply but found the words stuck in her throat and instead a sob made its way out. She immediately shut her mouth, embarrassed at showing such weakness in front of her aunt. She swallowed and tried to talk again but this time tears fell from her eyes. Unable to communicate, she just shook her head.

Lily's forehead crumpled in concern and her quick eyes latched onto the rip in Scarlet's dress. 'Did he...' She looked up into her eyes for the answer.

George turned round and a flash of anger rippled across his face as he caught on to Lily's meaning. Lily put a hand up to stop him as he opened his mouth, so he closed it again and waited to see what she wanted him to do.

Scarlet shook her head. 'No,' she managed, through the tears. 'No, I stopped him.'

Lily and George exchanged a dark look. 'Shall I take care of him?' George growled.

'No,' Scarlet said quickly. 'Please, I just want to go home.'

After a long pause as she deliberated, Lily shook her head and indicated that he should drive them away. With a disgruntled sound, George did as he was bade and made off down the long driveway.

The further they moved from the house, the safer Scarlet felt, and as the darkness of the night enveloped them, she leaned into her aunt's embrace and allowed her silent sobs to flow.

Lily held her tightly and stroked her hair. 'George,' she said quietly, 'Scarlet will stay with me tonight – don't worry about dropping her off.'

Scarlet squeezed her eyes closed with relief. She could tell Lily what had happened and they could deal with it themselves. But

Cath could never know. It would upset her too much. It would also upset her to know that Scarlet planned to get even with the man who'd tried to rape her tonight. He'd messed with her because he thought she was some common little nobody and that he could get away with it. But that was not the case. She wasn't a nobody.

She was a Drew. And Harry was about to find out exactly what that meant.

CHAPTER NINETEEN

Cath wandered round the large, empty house clutching her half-full cup of coffee feeling strangely adrift given it was the home she'd lived in for twenty years. Scarlet hadn't come back, but that wasn't worrying her, as she'd sent a text to say she'd stay at Lily's. But it did mean that the house was horribly silent this morning, and that there was even less for her to do than usual.

She headed for the kitchen with a sigh. She didn't even want this coffee – it had just been something to do. She dumped the cup in the sink then leaned back against the side and looked around the pristine space. It was a beautiful kitchen – white marble tiles and worktops, all the best appliances and with big windows looking out into the garden. Ronan had spared no expense, knowing how much she loved to cook. As her thoughts rested back on her late husband, the sadness threatened to overwhelm her once more and on instinct she moved towards the fridge.

She opened the large door and her gaze lingered on the open bottle of white wine within. She could almost taste the cool, crisp liquid in her mouth. No one was here. No one would even know she'd had a drink first thing in the morning. It wasn't as though she had anywhere to be or would need to drive later. If she just reached forward and grasped the neck, took a few sips, it would take the edge off. It would calm the anxious, lost feeling she always struggled with now.

But she'd been so good these last few weeks. She'd stopped drinking alone and losing herself in a haze the way she had after

Ronan had died. For Scarlet. Scarlet needed stability. She needed her mother to do her job.

She tried to close the door but found she couldn't. A little voice began to whisper in the back of her mind. *Scarlet isn't here*, it said. Whether she drank or not wouldn't affect Scarlet at all. Barely realising she was doing it, Cath reached in and pulled the bottle out. She put it to her lips, tipped it up and took two deep gulps.

Almost immediately she pulled the bottle away, aghast. Had she really just done that? Her hand flew to her lips, still cool from the liquid. The feeling of it hitting her stomach was comforting, and even as she hated herself for her weakness, she relished the familiar relief that came with drinking.

She closed her eyes as guilt and shame washed over her, then placed the bottle back in the fridge and closed the door. What had become of her? Once she'd had such purpose. But now she was no use to anyone. She was no longer a wife with a child to raise. And she had no profession. Ronan had insisted she had no need to work. He'd kept her busy and happy and she'd never given anything else a second thought. But now what? She was still so young, decades of life ahead of her.

As her thoughts moved towards Scarlet, she remembered something her daughter had said just a few days before. She'd complained that she needed to sort through her clothes and organise her drawers but that she never had the time. That was something Cath could do. She could sort them out for her.

Her head snapped up as her mind clung to this thought. Yes, that was exactly what she'd do.

Turning on her heel, she marched out of the kitchen and up the stairs to Scarlet's bedroom. It wouldn't fill her whole day, but it would distract her enough for now.

Kneeling down at her daughter's chest of drawers, she pulled them out one by one and carefully emptied the contents. As she reached the back of the third drawer, her fingers touched something hard and cold that rustled. With a frown, she reached further in and pulled it out. It was something wrapped in a plastic bag. She unwound the carefully wrapped plastic and peered in, her face paling as she saw what was within.

It was a knife, but it wasn't just any knife – it was one she recognised with horrifying clarity. It was the knife Jasper had wielded the night Scarlet had killed him. He'd been chasing her with it, trying to kill her. Cath shook her head. It didn't make sense. Why on earth was it here?

As her mind made the connections, she groaned and closed her eyes. 'Jesus Christ, Scarlet,' she muttered. She remembered now – as the boys had taken his body away, the knife had been a few metres away on the ground. Scarlet had picked it up. Lily had told her to get rid of it. But Scarlet was so fresh to this life, barely eighteen, and she would have no clue how to safely dispose of something like that. She'd likely hidden it here assuming it was the safest place. But it wasn't.

Cath exhaled slowly through puckered lips as she thought it through. It had to go immediately. That much was a certainty. If the police found even a smidgeon of evidence that linked their family to Jasper they'd be here with a search warrant in moments.

She rewrapped the bag and stood up. It wasn't the first time she'd had to get rid of evidence. There had been many occasions in the past when Ronan had asked her to take care of things like that. He'd told her what to do and where to do it and she'd carried out his wishes without question.

Biting her lip, she thought over her options. She could bury it, but without Ronan's direction, she wasn't exactly sure where the best place for that would be. Fire wouldn't do much for the blade, even if it did take the handle. So it would have to be the river. She nodded to herself and hurried off to get dressed.

The Thames had swallowed many tainted weapons into its murky depths over the years. And today it would take one more.

CHAPTER TWENTY

Scarlet leaned over the breakfast bar in Lily's kitchen and stirred her tea, the spoon moving in small, slow circles as she stared off into the distance. She was so lost in her thoughts that she didn't notice anyone come into the room until Ruby stood right in her light of sight.

''Ello? Earth to Scarlet?' Ruby waved her hand in front of her face. 'I said, where's the coffee pot?' She gestured towards Scarlet's mug.

'Oh.' Scarlet shook her head to clear it. 'This is tea.'

Ruby rolled her eyes and sighed loudly, then trudged over to where the coffee was kept. 'How come you're here anyway?' she asked with an edge of annoyance. It was no great secret that she wasn't a fan of Scarlet. Scarlet wasn't much a fan of hers either. 'You both got in very late. Where'd you go?' She glanced back at her cousin with a sly curious gaze.

'Charity auction,' Scarlet replied in a short tone, ignoring her first question. 'Then on to an after-party.'

'Oh right, partying for the greater good, were you?' Ruby retorted, her tone laced with sarcasm.

'For the firm, yes.' Scarlet looked out of the window, bored of the conversation already.

'Oh, for the *family*,' Ruby sneered. 'The firm is all for the family, right? That's what you lot always say. Funny, my invite must have got lost in the post.' She shot over a humourless smirk as Scarlet looked back round to her.

'Trust me, you wouldn't have enjoyed this one.'

Ruby opened her mouth to respond but paused as Lily marched in. She was dressed for the day in her signature black knee-length leather skirt and polo-neck top with sleek heels and deep red lipstick. She was busy fastening the clasp of her bracelet, but her gaze flickered between the two young women.

'Good morning,' she said, caution in her tone. 'And how are you both today?'

Neither of them answered immediately. Scarlet wasn't sure how she felt this morning, and it was obvious from Ruby's expression that she didn't feel much better than she had when she'd first turned up.

'Fine,' Scarlet lied, needing to say something to break the silence. Lily glanced up at her and pursed her lips before looking back at her bracelet and walking over to the fridge. Evidently, she could see the lie for what it was. 'When will the boys be here, did they say?'

When they'd arrived home in the early hours, Scarlet had told her aunt everything. Even before she'd stopped talking, Lily had had an idea. They'd discussed it in detail and between the two of them – with Scarlet's knowledge of art and the strategically twisted underworld way in which Lily's brain worked – they'd come up with the plan of the century. Lily had messaged the twins to join them as soon as they were up, so they could fill them in before they took it any further.

'They've just pulled up,' Lily replied. She took the coffee pot from Ruby's hands and set about making drinks. Ruby sat down at the other end of the breakfast bar from Scarlet and waited.

A minute later, the front door opened and the twins entered, both impeccably groomed as always, in smart matching suits. They greeted their mother with a dutiful kiss on the cheek.

'Alright, gang?' Cillian asked cheerfully.

'So, what's on the cards?' Connor asked, taking a seat on the bar stool next to Ruby. 'Why've you called a meeting here? The laundry packages are at the office, ain't they?'

'This isn't about the laundry drops,' Lily replied, pouring the hot coffee into several mugs. 'And this is best discussed where no other ears may be listening.' She slid two mugs across the bar to Connor and Ruby and then handed another to Cillian. 'Scarlet, why don't you start?'

All eyes swivelled over to Scarlet and she sat up straight, turning slightly to address them. 'We've come up with an idea, a job. Something we've not done before. It started last night at this charity ball.' She paused, biting her lip as Ruby watched her with open curiosity. 'Shall we sit in the study?' she suggested, standing up.

'Oh, I see,' Ruby said bitterly. 'Can't talk in front of Ruby, right? She ain't part of this family or anything.'

'Ruby...' Lily started.

'Nah, forget it,' Ruby spat, cutting her off and standing up abruptly. 'I'll go sit in my room, shall I? That's best, ain't it? Ruby Drew, the cuckoo in the nest. Ignore her or get her out the way, right?'

'Ah, come on, Rubes,' Cillian said, holding his arms out in a placating manner.

'Nah, fuck ya,' she cried as she walked off, throwing daggers with her eyes over her shoulder.

Scarlet watched her leave and sighed. She had little time for Ruby's dramatics. But as much as there was little love lost between them, she didn't want to cause her aunt more trouble. Lily had a lot on her plate too – the last thing she needed was Ruby kicking off. She cleared her throat and looked up at Lily.

'Sorry,' she said. 'I didn't mean to cause issues. Do you want me to go smooth things over?'

'No, don't worry,' Lily said. 'I need to talk to her anyway after this. I'll sort it out.'

'Come on then,' Connor said. 'What's going on, Scar?'

'Let's go through.'

Scarlet led the way across the hall to the study. The twins followed and sat down on one of the comfortable sofas around the edge of the room. Lily closed the door behind them and claimed her favourite armchair, crossing her slim legs and reaching for her cigarettes. She lit one, then nodded for Scarlet to continue.

'After the charity auction last night, we went on to an after-party.'

'Really?' Cillian asked, looking at his mother doubtfully.

'A guy called Harry Chambers. He was a drunk, bored toff,' Lily replied. 'Money to burn. We got invited; I figured he might be worth getting friendly with.'

'Except he tried to get a little too friendly with me,' Scarlet followed.

'How friendly?' Connor asked sharply.

Scarlet swallowed and looked past him out of the window. 'Far too friendly. Actually,' she said, pulling a face, 'it wasn't very friendly at all.' She forced herself to look back at him. 'Apparently, the reason he'd invited *low-class trash* like us to the party was because he believed I'd be up for some fun. When I wasn't, he tried to have it anyway.'

'What?' Connor cried, his tone as thunderous as his face.

'He didn't succeed,' Scarlet swiftly assured him. 'I managed to get away, before…' She trailed off and swallowed again as her throat constricted. 'Then I stamped really hard between his legs.' She shrugged.

'Good,' Cillian said angrily. He pulled a toothpick out of his pocket and put it between his teeth with a dark frown. 'We'll go finish the job,' he said resolutely.

'No,' Scarlet replied, shaking her head.

'It wasn't a question,' he replied curtly. He stood up and looked down at her with a serious expression. 'There are certain things that have to be dealt with, without mercy and without question. This is one of them. No one touches a member of this family that way.' The look he gave her made it clear that his decision was final. 'Come on, Connor. Mum, send us the details.'

'No, stop,' Scarlet said a little louder. 'I'm not saying no to retribution – we just have a better idea. Hear me out.' Cillian and Connor both paused, and she exhaled heavily, looking over at Lily then back to them. 'Please, just sit back down.'

Cillian glanced at Lily, who nodded in agreement, then reluctantly sat back in the seat he'd just vacated. 'Go on.'

Scarlet sat forward, her eyes gleaming with a keen steeliness. 'Before he did that, I was looking at his collection of paintings. They have money – a *lot* of money.'

'They?' Cillian questioned.

'He and his wife. The house is hers, left to her when her parents died,' Scarlet replied.

'He's married?' Connor asked, lifting an eyebrow. 'It just gets better,' he murmured.

'Indeed,' Scarlet said heavily.

She'd only found out he was married after they'd started to research him when they got home. Lily had suggested that with the sort of wealth Harry possessed, there was likely to be information online – magazine articles and notices perhaps – and she hadn't been wrong. Details of his wife and their marriage came up, and suddenly the reason he'd dismissed all his staff for the party became blindingly clear. His wife was away and he wanted to play, but he didn't want to be caught out.

'Anyway, we were looking at this painting and the conversation turned to art.'

'Oh yeah, you're into all that stuff, aren't you?' Cillian remembered.

'I am,' she replied. 'So he was trying to get me alone and it wasn't working, then in his drunken desperation he blurted out that he had a Rembrandt.' She waited and looked at both the twins in turn, expecting them to understand. But she was met with blank looks. 'Rembrandts don't just sit in people's houses – most of them are in galleries or in known collections,' she explained. 'I didn't believe him, but he seemed dead certain. So I went to have a look.'

'You should have asked Mum or George to go with you,' Connor pointed out.

'Yes, well, hindsight's a charm,' Scarlet replied drily. 'Anyway, we went to this study and he uncovered this keypad, typed in a code, and the wall opened up revealing a secret hideaway.'

'And was it a Rembrandt? A genuine one?' Cillian asked, his interest sharpening.

'It was,' Scarlet said, her tone tinged with her own disbelief as she confirmed it. She shook her head in wonderment. 'It was insane. Incredible. But more than that – the painting behind the wall was *The Storm on the Sea of Galilee*. Which is a painting – a very, very famous painting – that hasn't been seen or its location known to anyone in over thirty years.'

'Really?' Cillian asked. The twins exchanged a look.

Scarlet's own eyes gleamed with fevered excitement. 'I mean, there's a chance it's a fake. But why go to all that trouble and expense to hide a fake?' she asked. 'And as collectors, *true* art collectors like them, I just don't think that it would be.'

'When you say it hasn't been seen in over thirty years...' Connor said, his brow furrowing.

'It was in a museum in Boston, but in 1990 two men dressed up as police officers broke in and stole twelve paintings, including this one. It was the biggest art theft in American history and they never caught them or recovered the paintings.'

There was a long silence, then Cillian suddenly grinned and slapped Connor on the chest with the back of his hand. 'Eh, that's like what we did with all that weed,' he said.

Connor grinned back at the reminder. 'Oh yeah,' he said with a chuckle. 'We should have gone bigger.'

'I told you two never to discuss that day again,' Lily snapped, her eyes flashing dangerously.

Scarlet watched as her cousins quickly righted their expressions and looked away. She shook her head. They were referring to a heist they'd pulled off a few months before, off the cuff. They'd stolen a bulk load of weed from a rival's safe house after it had been raided, posing as a police clean-up crew. It had been a stroke of genius but also complete madness, and Lily had had to work very hard to cover their tracks and ensure none of them ended up being hacked to death with machetes by the men they'd stolen it from. Her cousins were smart men, hard, feared and respected with good reason – but they could be reckless beyond belief at times.

'What are you thinking?' Cillian asked, moving the conversation on and holding his mother's daggered gaze with caution. 'You want to blackmail him with it?'

'No,' Lily replied, pulling out a cigarette and lighting it. 'We're going to do better than that.' She adopted a look of dark anticipation. 'We're going to steal it.'

CHAPTER TWENTY-ONE

Lily lifted her hand and knocked lightly on Ruby's bedroom door. There was no answer, so after a moment's deliberation she walked straight in. Ruby was curled up in the chair by the window, staring out into the street beyond.

She turned at the sound of her mother entering with a frown of annoyance. 'You know, when someone doesn't answer that usually means they don't want to be disturbed.'

Lily nodded and sat down on the bed. 'I know.' She took a deep breath. 'You said when you came back that you wanted to rest and needed space, and I've given you that.'

'For two days,' Ruby cut her off flatly. 'Is that my quota?'

'I've given you time to settle in, but, Ruby, we need to talk,' Lily replied in a stronger tone. 'Other than telling me that Ray forced you clean, you haven't talked about anything.'

'What is there to say?' Ruby asked sulkily. 'It ain't like there's a lot to tell you. We didn't travel the world or go off adventuring – he locked me in an empty room, Mum. What exactly do you think there is to share here?'

Lily looked out of the window, stifling a sigh. Her heart bled for Ruby. Her heart was always bleeding for Ruby. For some reason, her daughter was completely lost in this world. None of them were perfect; they all had their faults, but the rest of the family were at least functional. But Ruby was like a lost soul, floating towards all the dangers in life as she blindly turned her back on those who could help her.

'The men at your old flat, who were they?' she asked, turning back to her and searching her face.

Ruby shrugged. 'I don't know. I owed money to a few dealers. I think they work for a guy called Ash.' She shook her head. 'That's all I know about him. I had to be put in contact with him and he didn't talk much.'

'Who is he? He can't be a bottom-level dealer to have that sort of manpower,' Lily pushed.

Ruby frowned. 'I told you, I don't know,' she snapped. 'I was off my head most of the times I saw him. I was told not to ask questions, so I didn't.'

Lily bit the inside of her cheek. She needed to try and find out who he was, then pay him off to ensure there was no longer a target on Ruby's back.

'What do you want to do now?' Lily asked quietly, changing the subject.

'What do you mean?' Ruby glanced back at her before returning her gaze to a point outside the window.

'I'm hoping you might stay on here for a while,' Lily said carefully. Ruby was volatile at the best of times and this had always been a touchy subject. Instead of a sharp retort though, Ruby just sniffed and continued staring out of the window. 'You know you're welcome here as long as you like. This is your home.'

'Is it?' Ruby replied scathingly.

'Yes, it is. And it always will be, whatever you do,' Lily replied.

She cast her eyes over her daughter with a sad smile. She'd put on a little weight under Ray's care – if care was what you could call it – but she was still very slim, her pale skin almost translucent under the light from the window. Her bright red curls, tightly wild and untamed, much like her own golden locks, hung down below her shoulders, longer than they'd been for many years.

'The real question though is what are you going to do with your time?' she continued. 'You need to find something to

focus on, something to keep your mind busy and away from…
You know.'

'Heroin,' Ruby stated. 'The word ain't gonna bite ya.'

Lily looked up at her. 'OK. Heroin. We need to find you
something to keep you busy and focused away from heroin.'

Ruby snorted and folded her arms across her chest defensively.
'Oh, Mum,' she said tiredly, the fight leaving her voice in the
same worrying way it had the day she'd come home. 'There's not
a thing in the world that could pull my mind away from heroin.
My body no longer needs it – Ray made sure of that. But once
you've known that feeling…' She closed her eyes. 'It's not like
anything a person can feel without it. It's another level completely.'

'That's because it ain't real, Ruby,' Lily said in a matter-of-fact
tone. 'It ain't like anything you can feel normally, because it isn't
a real feeling. It's an illusion.'

Ruby shook her head. 'It's not *natural*, I'll give you that. But
it *is* real. You can't understand that though. No one can.' She
sniffed. 'No one that hasn't been there.'

Lily closed her mouth, feeling helpless. Ruby was right, she
couldn't understand it. Lord knew she'd tried. But Lily's feet had
always been firmly planted in the real world. She couldn't imagine
craving one that wasn't even really there.

'Listen. I can't stop you wanting what you want. But if you
will open yourself up to at least trying to focus on building up
the other areas of your life, I'll help you.'

'How?' Ruby asked.

Lily blinked, surprised. She'd been expecting a swift rebuttal,
perhaps an explosive argument or two before Ruby even allowed
her to continue. She shifted in her seat as her mind began to work
through the options. 'Well, I can help you find a job. I can help
with interviews and preparation and…'

'No.' Ruby shook her head and frowned. 'I can't work for
someone else. We've tried that before and it never works out – you

know it doesn't. You know that I'm not, you know, great with people,' she added awkwardly.

Lily pursed her lips. It was true. Ruby's temper usually ended up ruining her relationships with friends and employers alike. But what options did that leave?

'If you want me to work,' Ruby sighed as though the idea pained her to voice it, 'then it has to be within the firm. I mean, you say I'm part of this family, so let me into the firm.'

Lily felt the icy fingers of dread creep into her stomach and make a fist. 'I don't know, Ruby, that's…' She tried to find the right words. 'It's a big responsibility. And as much as you seem to think it's a free ride, I can assure you it's not. The boys and Scarlet all work twice the number of hours anyone in a normal job would do. There is no clocking-off time, there are no breaks; when you're in, you're in. It becomes your daily life, and it's a heavy burden to hold up. One that can't be dropped. One that's dangerous to ignore.'

'I know all that,' Ruby snapped. 'I grew up here, remember?' She turned to face her mother. 'I know all our dirty secrets, despite how hard you try to keep me out of them.' She tutted and rolled her eyes. 'I mean, Christ, you might push me out of meetings, but I've seen you wash blood off your hands. I've seen you destroy evidence. I know who we are and what we do.'

'That may be true, Ruby, but I don't know if you'd really be up to doing all we do,' Lily replied frankly. 'The reason we stay ahead is because all of us have our full focus on the ball at all times. You've already admitted all you think about is heroin. And you don't really want to be here. I don't think you would be able to focus on things the way I'd need you to.'

Ruby stared at her. 'If you want to keep me on the straight and narrow and you want me to work, what other choice do you have?'

Lily tried to think of anything else she could suggest, but nothing came to mind and she floundered. She sighed and shook her head. 'How do I know that the moment you're settled into a job and I start to rely on you that you won't run off and get back on the gear again?'

'If I was going to do that, I'd already be out there scoring, not sitting in here talking to you,' Ruby replied, turning back towards the window.

Lily frowned. 'Why aren't you?'

'What?' Ruby's brow crinkled as she turned back to her mother.

'Well, why *are* you still here? Don't get me wrong, I'm glad you are,' she added, 'but usually you *would* already be gone. What's different?'

'I guess I just feel a bit more motivated to stay off it this time,' she finally answered.

Lily's gaze narrowed. 'What did Ray say to you?' She had an inkling already. There was no way Ray would let her go without some sort of warning to stay off the gear. 'Did he threaten to take you again, if you went back on? Put you back through cold turkey?'

A ghost of a humourless smile crossed Ruby's lips. 'Something like that.'

Lily nodded. It must have been hell to go through it once. She imagined Ruby was in no hurry to be forced through it again. As this small reassurance washed through her, her thoughts returned to Ray and the feeling swiftly returned to anger. With difficulty, she pushed these thoughts and feelings away. She didn't want to think about him right now.

She took a deep breath and exhaled slowly. Ruby was right – there really was no other option for her right now. And at the end of the day, she was family. The firm, everything she and Ronan had built up over the years, was all for the family. To provide for them, to protect them. And that was exactly what Ruby needed right now. Lily nodded.

'OK,' she said quietly. 'I'll give you a chance. But this isn't going to be an easy ride, Ruby,' she warned. 'You have to work hard, and you don't get to choose what you do and don't do. If you're in, that's it.' She eyed her hard. 'You work for me. You show me respect in front of other people and you don't question my judgements. If I ask you to do something, you do it. Whether it's midday or midnight. Do you understand?'

Ruby nodded back solemnly. 'I do.'

'You may also have to work under Scarlet or one of the boys,' she added.

Ruby retorted, 'I ain't working under my kid cousin.'

'You'll work under whoever I *say* you work for, if you come onto my payroll,' Lily responded, her voice hard. There was no point sugar-coating it. 'And that includes Scarlet. It's up to you, Ruby, but I am deadly serious about that.'

Ruby made a sound of disgust and looked away. After a short silence she replied in a flat tone, 'You're the boss.'

Lily stood and brushed down her skirt. 'That's settled then. You can start tomorrow.' She paused at the door. 'I'm popping to the shops this afternoon – maybe you could come with me and we can pick you up a few new outfits. You know, nice bits for work.' She smiled hopefully at Ruby.

'I'm actually pretty tired so I'm going to rest today. If you see anything you want me to wear, just get it and I'll wear it,' Ruby said.

'Oh, OK. Sure.' Lily swallowed her disappointment. Baby steps, she reminded herself. Ruby was home and she was clean. That this continued was all that really mattered right now. 'I'll leave you to it.'

As she descended the stairs, she exhaled heavily. The rest of the family were not going to be pleased with her decision today. Ruby was a liability, and liabilities could be deadly in their game. To have her thrown in the mix just as they were about to make some big moves was not ideal. In fact, it was outright reckless, something Lily had never been. But Ruby was blood. So she was their responsibility whether they liked it or not. And the others were just going to have to deal with it.

CHAPTER TWENTY-TWO

Lily marched through the factory and up the stairs towards her office. Riley, one of the more senior machine workers, hurried over and she paused halfway up. 'What is it?' she snapped.

He blinked and pulled back, surprised by the aggression in her tone. 'Um, you've had a delivery,' he said slowly.

Lily smiled tightly at him. 'Thanks,' she said, her tone less sharp. 'Everything else OK? Did that new part work out? No more issues?'

'Oh, yeah, all fine now. Running better than it did before,' he answered.

'Great stuff. I'll catch you later.' She dismissed him and continued stalking up the stairs.

Her mind still preoccupied with the question of what to do with Ruby, she opened the door to her office then stopped dead in her tracks.

'What the fuck?' she breathed. Her jaw slowly dropped as she stared around the room.

Her usually neat, minimalist office was covered in boxes and boxes of bright red roses. They covered the desk, the sideboard and even littered the floor in a gigantic over-the-top display. Three balloons were tied together on the biggest bunch, swaying slowly, the words *Sorry, I love you* and *forever* emblazoned in bold across their shiny surfaces.

Rage bubbled up from the pit of her stomach, and she began to breathe deeply and loudly through her nose. Turning on her heel, she marched back out, down the hallway past Scarlet's office, and opened the cleaning cupboard. Rummaging through the shelves, she found the roll of bin bags and stalked back into her office. She grabbed her largest pair of scissors, then immediately began hacking away angrily at the nearest bunch.

As the heads fell to the floor, there was a knock on her open door. She looked up to see Cath walking in.

'Hi, Lil, I just need to... Aww, look at all this!' Cath exclaimed, a big smile crossing her face as she swooned at the sight that angered Lily so. 'Ah, Lil, he's such a... What the *hell* are you doing?' Her smile turned to a frown.

'How *dare* he send all this here?'

'Um...' Cath tilted her head to the side and squinted as she tried to follow.

'I mean, did he *really* think this would work? Did he really think that after all he's done, I'd just fall to my knees and simper over a few fucking flowers? Really?'

'They *are* very nice flowers,' Cath said placatingly, in an attempt to instil some reason.

'They could be the nicest flowers in the world for all I care, Cath,' Lily shot back, moving onto the next box, not stopping as she cut mercilessly through the bunch. 'They could be made of solid fucking gold, and it would make no difference. He can't *buy* me,' she said indignantly. 'It's nothing but an insult that he thinks *this* is the way to making things right.'

Cath crinkled up her nose. 'I don't think he's trying to buy you, Lil,' she said. 'I think Ray, more than anyone, knows you can't be bought. I think he's just trying to show you how sorry he is.'

'It's the same thing, Cath,' Lily replied. All the boxes on the table and the floor demolished, she pulled the balloons down and angrily stabbed them with the scissors one by one. 'And *that* is what I think of *that*,' she said, a pinch of triumph sounding through her fury. She moved on to the boxes on the sideboard and carried on her ruthless beheading.

Cath cringed. 'Fine, but do you *have* to destroy them all? I know you're angry, but they're so pretty. And it's not their fault.'

'They're *guilt* flowers, Cathleen,' Lily stressed, throwing the box she'd just decimated to the floor with the others. 'Guilt flowers that are going to decorate the area just outside his front gate very soon.'

She finished the next box and was about to move onto the last when Cath swooped it out of her grasp. She wrapped her arms around it protectively and pulled back.

'Nope,' she said, moving further out of reach. 'Not this one. You've murdered enough innocent flowers for one day. I'm saving these ones from your wrath,' she continued firmly. 'They can brighten my kitchen for the next week or so, if you don't want them.'

Lily stared Cath out for a few long moments, poised with the scissors still in her hand. Cath held her gaze defiantly until eventually Lily conceded.

'Fine,' she said grudgingly. 'But the rest of them are littering his drive, so he knows exactly what I think of this little display.'

'Oh, I think he'll know,' Cath replied wryly, setting the box of saved roses down by the door. She surveyed the damage and then looked up at her sister-in-law. 'Feel better?' she asked.

'No. Not particularly,' she replied.

Cath nodded and picked up the roll of bin bags. 'Come on then – I'll help you clear this up.'

Lily took one of the bags from Cath then knelt down to start clearing the mess. As they cleared in silence, she looked over at Cath with a small frown of curiosity. 'What were you here for anyway?'

'Oh.' Cath paused for a moment and then carried on carefully gathering handfuls of petals and thorns. 'Yes. The knife…' She glanced over her shoulder and lowered her voice. 'Jasper's knife.'

Lily's attention immediately sharpened, her irritation with Ray momentarily forgotten. 'What about it?'

'I found it hidden at home.'

'Jesus! Scarlet said it was dealt with.' She closed her eyes. The girl was so capable she sometimes forgot there were certain things she just didn't know or had no experience in yet.

'It's OK, I got rid of it,' Cath replied.

Lily nodded. Cath may not have been part of the firm, but they had always been able to count on her to protect them and help cover things up. There had been several occasions she'd helped them dispose of evidence. 'Where is it?'

'The river,' Cath replied.

'OK, good. I'll speak to her about it,' Lily said.

Cath nodded then reached for another bag, the one in her hand already full. 'Are you going to deliver these yourself?' she asked.

'No,' Lily growled, thoughts of Ray darkening her mood once more. 'I'll send someone else. I'm not giving him the chance to talk to me.'

'I'll take it,' Cath offered suddenly. She looked up at Lily. 'It's not like I have anything else to do. It will keep me busy for a while.'

Lily was about to refuse, but then she saw the wistful loneliness flash across her sister-in-law's face and hesitated. 'You really want to litter his drive with all this? You can't just leave it neatly to the side – this has to be a clear message,' she said firmly. 'He needs to understand.'

'Poor Ray,' Cath said with a small grin. 'But yes, I'll do it however you want. Honest.' She looked up in hope.

'OK then. You can take it. But no more *poor Ray*,' said Lily sharply. 'What he did was unforgivable. Ruby went through hell. And whilst it's great that she's clean, she should never have been put through it like *that*.'

Cath bit her lip. 'I agree with you, of course I do.' She stood up. 'But just remember, Lil, for all his mistakes, he had good intentions. That man's loved you for thirty years. He's stood by you through thick and thin.' Her serious gaze held Lily's. 'He fucked up. But life is too short to hold grudges. Because you never really know how long you've got with the people you love. And you know that.'

With one last meaningful look, she turned away and started filling the next bag. Lily cast her eyes away. She did know that. She missed Ronan every day. She still felt as though she'd lost a limb. But could she ever forgive Ray for what he'd done? Her heart still loved him fiercely, but the feelings of anger and betrayal were all-consuming. And right now, she just couldn't see a way back.

*

Ray looked down from the upstairs window as Cath scattered the bags of petals and thorns all over the front of his drive and sighed heavily in frustration. As she emptied the last bag, she looked up and saw him. She shot him a sad, apologetic smile, held her arms out and shrugged. He nodded back and she got back in her car, then drove away. His gaze dropped to the mess of red petals. From this distance, they looked like the kind of bloodstain left behind from someone who'd been stabbed through the heart. Then with depressing clarity he realised that that was exactly what it was.

CHAPTER TWENTY-THREE

A knock on the salon door caught Scarlet's attention and she pulled herself up from where she'd been sitting on the floor behind the reception area. She was ready to tell whoever it was to come back when they were open, but then she paused and smiled.

'Hello, Mum,' she said as Cath walked in with a beaming smile. 'What are you doing here?'

'Oh, Scar, it looks amazing!' she cried, looking around in excitement.

'Yeah, it will be when we're done,' Scarlet replied with a grin.

'I brought you girls some lunch,' Cath said, holding out a hamper laden with foil-wrapped food. 'I figured you must be starving, doing all this yourselves.'

'Ahh, thanks, Mrs D,' Natalie said, popping her head out from the back room. 'We were just saying about getting something actually. Good timing.'

'Yeah, perfect timing. Thanks, Mum.' Scarlet beckoned Sandra over. 'Mum, this is Sandra – she's going to be the assistant manager working alongside Nat. Sandra, this is my mum, Cath.'

'Hi, Cath.' Sandra came over and held her hand out with a smile. 'It's nice to meet you.'

'You too,' Cath replied, shaking her hand.

'I was so sorry to hear about your husband,' she added. 'He was a lovely man.'

'Oh, er...' Cath blinked and swallowed, her smile fading at the reminder. 'Yes. Thank you. You knew my husband?' she asked.

'Yes, he was always very nice to me,' Sandra said.

'Sandra used to work in one of our other laundry sites,' Scarlet quickly butted in. 'In a, er, like a front-of-house role.' She shot Sandra a meaningful look. 'We pinched her from there.' She smiled at her mother, hoping this would be a sufficient explanation and that Sandra would catch on quickly.

Her mum had no idea they ran an escort service. It was something Ronan and Lily had always kept from her, knowing she would disapprove. She should have warned Sandra of this before now, but she hadn't realised that it would come up so soon.

'Oh, lovely,' Cath answered politely. 'And will you like it here better, do you think?'

'Yes,' Sandra replied with a fixed smile. 'Definitely.' She stepped back. 'I'd best get on. Scarlet wants us up and open in just a few days.'

'Crikey,' Cath exclaimed, turning back to her daughter. 'Do you really think you'll be ready? Do you have clients?' She looked around with a small frown. 'Do you even have *stylists*?'

'The clients will come,' Scarlet said with a dismissive wave. 'And as for stylists, yes. Nat will be taking her own clients on, and someone she used to work for wants to join us too, so that's two.'

Cath looked around pointedly. 'But you have' – she quickly counted under her breath – 'eight, ten, *twelve* chairs!'

'I have adverts out and CVs are already coming in – I'll have them filled in no time. Plus,' she added, 'I'm only using half of them.'

'Half? Oh, I see,' Cath said, catching her drift. She walked around, looking at the walls they were halfway through painting.

Scarlet took the hamper over to the reception desk and put it down, then turned back to her mother.

'That side's going to be a nice fresh white,' she said. 'Then this side is this midnight blue.' She pointed at what she'd done so far. 'Then I'm going to add a lot of greenery around – ferns and the like.'

'That sounds lovely, Scarlet,' Cath enthused. 'That's really in at the moment too, isn't it? Midnight blue.'

'Yeah.' Scarlet rested her hands on her hips as Cath continued exploring. 'Are you staying for lunch with us?' she asked.

'Oh, no, I've already eaten,' Cath replied.

'OK. Well, we really appreciate you bringing that over.' Scarlet looked at her watch. 'We'll break in a bit, but I just want to get this paint that I've already poured out on the walls.' She pulled an apologetic smile. 'Sorry, don't mean to rush you out; I just don't want it to dry up.'

'No, that's OK,' Cath said brightly. She bit her lip and her gaze flicked towards her handbag. 'I could always stay and help you out?' she asked hopefully.

'We're fine; don't worry about all this,' Scarlet replied. 'I don't think I've got another brush anyway,' she added.

'That's alright,' Cath replied quickly, reaching into her handbag. 'I brought my own.' She held it up in front of her, her features almost pleading.

'Nice one. We could definitely use an extra hand,' she said with heart. 'I think there's one of the old colouring aprons in the back, if you want to put it on over your clothes.'

'Great, I'll go find it,' she said happily, putting her handbag to one side. 'Let's get cracking then, shall we? You know what they say, Scarlet,' she continued over her shoulder as she went out to the back.

Scarlet mouthed the words as her mother said them, knowing exactly what was coming. 'Many hands make light work.'

The front door opened again and Scarlet swivelled round to see who had entered. She hadn't realised she hadn't locked it again. But it was only her aunt Lily. She smiled in greeting and walked over.

'Christ, it's like King's Cross in here today,' she joked.

'Oh, I'm not your first visitor?' Lily asked.

'No, Mum's here. She wants to help with the painting.'

'Oh, right. You should let her,' Lily said, seeming distracted.

'Yeah, I am. You alright?' Scarlet asked.

'Yes, I need to talk to you about something.'

'Sure, what is it?'

Lily levelled her gaze to Scarlet's. 'Ruby's joining the firm.'

Scarlet's brows shot up in horrified surprise. Lily had never wanted Ruby in the firm before – in fact, she'd actively argued against the possibility in the past. So why now? She frowned as the implications of what it could mean began running through her mind.

'Really?' She wasn't sure how to respond. She didn't like the idea in the slightest, but she couldn't argue. This was Lily's decision to make as head of the firm, and whether they liked it or not, Ruby was family.

Lily nodded. 'Yes, really. And I've been thinking about what to do with her. Where I can put her where she can do the least damage and get in the least trouble.'

As Lily's gaze bored into hers, Scarlet felt her heart slowly sink and turn to ice. She couldn't be saying what she thought she was saying. She shot through all the options in her head and one kept standing out with bright, horrific clarity.

She began to shake her head. 'No, uh-uh…' she muttered.

'It's the best place to put her, Scarlet,' Lily implored. 'I know you can see it too – you came straight to the same conclusion.'

'Come on,' Scarlet pleaded. 'You can't be serious.'

Lily's expression turned stonily resolute. 'Ruby will be coming to work in the salon.'

CHAPTER TWENTY-FOUR

Scarlet hurried up the last few steps towards the office. It was late, the rest of the factory in darkness as the machines rested and the people who worked them dreamed in their beds. The light from Lily's internal window lit her path as she reached the top and entered.

Everyone they trusted was already there. Lily sat behind her desk, lit cigarette in hand, one leg crossed over the other. Cillian sat to one side of her and Connor the other, along with George and Andy, the two men who had worked alongside Lily and Ronan for as long as she could remember.

The last person in the room, who studied Scarlet with open curiosity, was Bill Hanlon. Bill wasn't part of their firm. In fact, he was actually part of a bigger firm – the Tylers'. But they all had history going back many years and Bill was a slight anomaly among the underworld in that although he aligned his loyalties with the Tylers, he had a unique skillset that could be hired out to other friends. As soon as they'd begun forming this plan, Lily had suggested they ask him to come in for this discussion. It wasn't a certainty that he'd take on the job, but even if he didn't, he might offer some valuable suggestions.

'Here she is,' Lily said.

Scarlet closed the door behind her and quickly greeted everyone, then took the last seat in a strategically arranged circle.

Lily sat forward and rested her forearms on the desk. 'Now we're all here, let's get into it. Everyone here is aware of what you've uncovered, Scarlet, and knows we've put together a rough plan to steal the painting. Let's begin by explaining about the painting in more detail.' She gestured for Scarlet to take the floor.

Scarlet took a deep breath. 'Right now, the painting they have hidden in their home is worth somewhere in the region of a hundred million pounds.' She watched as eyebrows shot up and an air of surprise came over their faces. She nodded. 'Yeah. And it's a wanted painting. There's a reward with the FBI for information leading to its return, even now, after more than thirty years. They wouldn't be able to report it as stolen, as that would land *them* in trouble for having it in the first place.' She smiled. 'Which means the possible consequences are already limited.'

'That doesn't mean there won't be any though,' Bill warned gravely. 'When that sort of money goes missing you can definitely expect a comeback. And it won't be friendly.'

'I think we can get around them finding out it was us,' Lily said.

Bill's expression remained unconvinced.

'Lil and I have been doing some digging,' Scarlet continued. 'The man of the hour, Harry Chambers, throws parties like the one we went to a lot. Whenever his wife is not in town, which is often, he switches off all the security measures and sends the household staff away for the night. He only locks the place up once his party is over and everyone's gone. This allows him to bring women back and do whatever he likes with no witnesses other than his own friends, who turn a blind eye.' She swallowed and glanced away, flashes of her own experience running through her mind.

'Which leaves him vulnerable,' Lily said, flicking the ash from the end of her lit cigarette into the ashtray.

'What does he do for a living?' Bill asked her.

'Nothing much. He's on the board for a couple of local charities and owns a racehorse over in Newmarket. But he mainly relies on the trust fund his parents left him,' she answered.

'And his wife?' he asked.

'Grace Dupont,' Lily continued, sitting forward as everyone watched and listened. 'She kept her name when they married. The house is hers and she inherited an import-export company that runs between the US and Europe.'

Bill exhaled loudly and crossed his arms, his attitude still sombre.

'What don't you like, Bill?' Lily asked.

Bill shook his head slowly and mashed his lips together before answering. 'I'm just trying to work out where the painting has come from? I mean, what pies have these two got their fingers in to have something like that in the first place?'

Scarlet edged forward. 'I have a theory on that,' she offered. Everyone turned to hear it. 'I don't think it's them who acquired it. The study, the wall, none of it looked new. It was tired; looked like it had been there for quite a while. The house belonged to Grace's parents, who died five years ago.' She glanced between their faces. 'The painting was stolen back in 1990. Maybe they were the ones who bought it from whoever stole it, or possibly even stole it themselves.'

Bill nodded. 'Possible. But we can't be sure. There won't be a paper trail to follow and find out.'

'Well, no. But does it matter?' Scarlet asked.

'It makes a big difference, knowing whether they're tied up in this sort of business or whether they're just lucky idiots.' He exhaled, clearly unhappy about this.

Scarlet glanced at Lily, but Lily was watching Bill intently. She silently prayed that he'd accept the job and work with them. The risks were high, yes, of course they were. But there was no reward without risk.

Bill raised his gaze to Lily's. 'How do you want to do it?'

'The next party is this Saturday night. The wife is away, he and his mates are set to go to an event for another charity that he's on the board for, then they'll head back to party. This is what I'm thinking.' She stubbed out her cigarette and clasped her hands together in front of her. 'We can get a ticket to the event for Sandra, one of our former escorts who now works for us elsewhere. She was a top biller – she'll catch his attention and make sure she prises an invite out of him for the after-party.'

'You've talked to her about it?' Connor asked.

'I have and she's game,' Scarlet replied. 'Once she's in, the idea is for her to seduce him, with a small camera running somewhere nearby so it catches it all.'

'*That* I can help you with,' Bill said.

'To blackmail him later?' George asked.

'Possibly,' Scarlet said slowly. 'It's more of a fallback plan in case he finds out who we are. He won't want to rock things with his wife.'

Lily continued. 'The other reason we need Sandra in there is for later on. We assume he probably gets his girls to leave with the rest of the party before he locks up. And once it's locked up and the security system is turned back on, that makes things a lot harder. So once they're done, Sandra will slip off, pretend to leave, then hide somewhere in the house. After he sets the cameras and alarms back on, she'll wait until he goes to bed and then turn them back off.' She glanced at Bill. 'I was hoping you'd be able to help us with that too.'

Bill nodded. 'I'll have to scope it out first, but it shouldn't be a problem.'

Scarlet smiled. This was sounding promising.

'At that point, the rest of us can move in,' Lily continued. 'We'll need a van. George, if we go ahead, I'll need you to be the driver and stay outside on lookout.'

'OK,' he said.

'Cillian, Connor, you'll go with Scarlet to the study,' Lily ordered. 'And once she's opened the panel, you'll bring the painting out in a protective box which Scarlet is going to source. Andy, you'll go with them and clean down everything they've touched as they leave. We'll all be covered up, but just in case.'

'Clean down, gotcha,' Andy replied.

'What happens if Harry wakes up?' Cillian asked. 'I imagine he isn't going to just roll over and accept it.'

'Scarlet had an interesting suggestion which I think has merit,' Lily said, looking over towards her.

'At first I was going to suggest we talk to Ray about him lending us a couple of his men.' The icy look on her aunt's face reminded her that Ray was still in her blackest of bad books. 'But then I thought, what about bringing Chain onto the job – him and Damo?'

'Chain?' Connor and Cillian both exclaimed loudly.

'You have to be kidding,' Cillian said, exchanging a horrified look with his brother.

'I'm deadly serious,' Scarlet replied. 'He's a dangerous man, but one with a code. We trust him with a lot of our business.'

'Not *this* sort of business,' Connor interrupted strongly.

'I wasn't suggesting we tell him what we're taking,' Scarlet argued. 'We'll keep it vague and pay him well for his silence. He honours the code among thieves – you know that as well as I do.' She held Connor's glare. 'We'll have them keep guard outside Harry's room and deal with him if there are any complications.'

He looked away, shaking his head. 'I think that's ludicrous.'

'I think it's a good idea,' Lily stated. 'They can keep that side of things running smoothly, and I'll keep communications going between the two teams. He's ideal. Like Scarlet said, he has a code and we have a good relationship. Plus, if Harry does end up waking and sees anyone, better it be them than us. It will throw them off completely, down the line.'

'It's a good red herring,' Bill agreed.

'What if they end up finding Chain?' George asked.

'Chain has no connections to them, not even loose ones,' Scarlet replied. 'They won't find him. Plus, he'll be masked up too – him and Damo. Harry might get a general overview if it comes to it, but he'll never see their faces.'

'Have you already spoken to Chain?' Connor asked, his strong feelings on the situation still clear in his face.

'Not yet. He's the last puzzle piece. No point bringing it up unless we're all in and ready to go,' she said with a shrug.

'So that's the plan,' Lily finished. 'We get it in the van and disappear. Then we hide it, get a good fence and sell it on through the black market.'

'How are we going to make those sorts of connections?' Cillian asked, rubbing his chin thoughtfully.

'I can make the connection,' Lily said with quiet resolution.

'You gonna talk to Wiley?' Bill asked her. She nodded.

'Who's Wiley?' Scarlet asked.

'Sam Wiles,' Lily answered. 'Bill and I have both known him for years, though I haven't seen him in a decade or two. He moved into these circles a while ago. He fences jewellery mainly, and some antiques, but he's in with some of the bigger fish and can make introductions.'

There was a long silence. 'These are waters you ain't swum in before, Lil,' Bill said.

Lily lit another cigarette and blew the smoke out in a long thin plume. 'True,' she conceded. 'But seas weren't conquered by people who stuck to the land.'

Bill nodded and pulled a grim expression. 'I'll help you with the set-up. The cameras and the security system override. But that's as far as I can go.'

'Then that's all we ask,' Lily replied.

Bill stood up and grasped her hand across the table briefly before heading over to the door. 'Send me the address; I'll do a recce on their security and come back to you in a couple of days.'

As he left and the door closed, Scarlet looked around at the rest of them. It was a big job. Bigger than any of them had ever attempted – or even *dreamed* of attempting – before.

Cillian and Connor were sharing a look and Lily was studying them from her desk. George and Andy turned to each other, doubt clear in their eyes.

'Look.' Lily suddenly drew everyone's attention back towards her. 'I know this isn't our usual game. But we're *good* at what we do. And when opportunity knocks, only fools ignore the door.' She stared round at each of them in turn. 'This painting is worth a *hundred million*,' she said with emphasis. 'That's more money than we could hope to make doing what we do in a lifetime. Now, I don't know if we'll get that on the black market,' she admitted. 'I don't know exactly how that works yet. But even if we sold it for half, imagine what we could do with that. And everyone in this room here today will get a cut.'

Scarlet saw everyone's attitudes change and marvelled once more at the quiet power her aunt held over people.

'We do this and we move up into the big league,' Lily insisted. 'We do this' – she paused – 'and we're set for life.'

CHAPTER TWENTY-FIVE

Scarlet determinedly crossed the small square between the tall high-rises, her dark hair fanning out behind her and her long black jacket flapping in the wind. Her eyes were trained on the run-down pub, but she didn't see the metal cages over the windows or the rust in the old sign swinging above the door. All she saw was a means to an end.

She reached the one-storey building and pushed open the door, holding her head up high as the customers all fell silent at her entrance. Dark, menacing looks faced her all around, but she didn't flinch. Instead, she cut slowly and deliberately through the middle of the room, down to the end where the man she was looking for sat chuckling and shaking his head.

'You're brave, girl, I'll give you that,' he said. 'Very brave. Either that or stupid, one of the two.'

'Oh, I think we both know I'm far from stupid, Chain,' Scarlet replied. 'I knew you were here.'

'And while I'm in this castle I am its king,' he replied with a grin. 'Which means you're welcome.'

'I know.' She sat down on a vacant stool opposite him, and slowly the low chatter resumed behind her.

'I wouldn't come here if I'm not though,' he added quietly. 'You nah'm sayin'?'

'I do,' she replied. She glanced at one of the two men beside him. Someone she didn't know.

Picking up on her meaning, Chain clicked his fingers and both of them stood up and melted away, leaving them to talk alone. He picked up the half-empty pint glass in front of him and took a deep drink, staring at her over the rim. Putting it back down, he narrowed his gaze for a moment.

'What was so important it couldn't wait for the shop then, Scarlet Drew?' he asked, his tongue rolling playfully over the syllables of her name.

'I have a proposition for you. A one-off job,' she replied.

He tilted his head to one side and studied her thoughtfully. 'One-offs tend to be more trouble than they're worth.'

'Not this one. I need you and Damo. Five grand for a couple of hours' work,' she said.

'Five Gs for just a couple of hours?' His gaze narrowed once more.

'For that and your silence,' she added severely. She stared at him across the table, her gaze unmoving as he returned her scrutiny.

'What does it involve?' he asked, taking another sip of his beer.

Scarlet watched him. Five grand was a lot of money for such little work, but she could tell he wasn't convinced. She glanced around warily before continuing. 'A few nights ago a man called Harry Chambers tried to rape me,' she said, cutting to the point. Conversation with Chain seemed to go a lot smoother when she left out the crap. 'Apparently, no one taught him that no means no.' Chain's brow furrowed and the wariness disappeared. She finally had his attention. 'I'd like to teach him a lesson.'

'Surely your cousins would be first in line for that job,' he stated.

'They were. But I don't plan on leaving him with just a kicking. I plan on taking the most valuable thing he owns. Along with his marriage,' she replied, then paused. 'Anything I say from now, can you assure me it's between us?'

'All conversations I have stay between me and the person I'm having them with,' he said. 'It wouldn't do my reputation much good if they didn't.'

Scarlet nodded. She'd known as much, but it didn't hurt to confirm it. She was still slightly nervous about bringing Chain into this at all. It had been her idea, and even though she had her aunt's approval, if it backfired, it would be all her fault. She prayed that her instincts weren't wrong.

'We're planning a heist Saturday night. He lives in this big mansion outside London, filled with artwork. *Expensive* artwork. There's a piece in there that's not officially on his books.' She'd decided to stick to the truth as much as possible, without revealing the true extent of what they were doing. 'It's pretty valuable. I'm going to steal it.' She leaned forward onto the table. 'We have everything covered, except for him. He'll be asleep in his room, but ideally I'd like you and Damo stood outside. If he sleeps through it all, then it's the easiest money you'll ever make.' She pulled a face. 'But if he wakes, then I need you to tie him up, threaten him and keep him out of the way, nowhere near a phone or anything else he could use to alert anyone. What do you think?' She pulled back and waited.

Chain looked up and past her, out of the window for a few moments, obviously considering the job. 'That's a lot of money for a little security work,' he mused. 'You sure there ain't more to it than that?' He turned his deep brown eyes back towards her, his gaze boring into hers.

Scarlet held her head higher and locked her jaw. 'What he tried to do to me defies the most sacred of my personal laws. You know, I respect someone who wants to *kill* me more than I respect someone who wants to use my body against my will.' Her eyes blazed. 'I'm offering that much because I'm hoping that means you can't bring yourself to refuse me.'

Chain pulled himself up from his relaxed slouch and leaned over the table on his forearms. 'We'll do it,' he said in a low voice. 'I have no time for men who do that. You've got your muscle.' He nodded. 'This is a one-off though,' he added in a warning tone. 'Don't think I'm joining your firm or anything. I don't work for no one but myself.'

Scarlet stood up. 'That's fine. You weren't invited.' She gave him a grin, which he returned. 'I'll be in touch before Saturday with the details, but just be ready, and bring masks and gloves.'

He nodded just once, and she turned towards the exit, leaving as swiftly as she had arrived.

As she burst out into the chilly air outside, she breathed in deeply with relief. It had worked. Chain was on board and everything was ready to be set into motion. Now all she had to do was get back to normal life and pretend as though none of this was happening.

CHAPTER TWENTY-SIX

Cath awkwardly pushed the salon door open with her hip, her hands full with the tray packed with precariously balanced plates of food. Sandra rushed forward to help her, taking the tray out of her hands.

'Oh, wow, look at all this,' she exclaimed. 'You expecting the army, Mrs D?'

'You can't have an opening without providing decent nibbles, Sandra,' she replied, brushing down the front of her dress now that she had her hands back.

Lily looked at Scarlet with a flat, accusatory expression from the other side of the room, then walked over to Cath.

'That looks lovely, Cath,' Scarlet heard her aunt say. 'A really nice spread.'

'I was a bit surprised when I heard last night it was all going ahead today,' Cath replied with a flustered smile. 'But I managed to make almost everything I had in mind.'

'Yeah, I think we all were,' Natalie said with a laugh, as she began unwrapping the clingfilm from the seemingly endless plates of food. 'The bloody sign only arrived an hour ago.'

Scarlet exhaled slowly and looked down to the reception area she was setting up. She was beginning to understand why Lily smoked. The tension in the room was palpable, and she wished she had something to take the edge off.

Lily had advised her to wait, to give it another week before she opened. They were up to their necks sorting everything for the heist and this was another thing they didn't need to be juggling, she'd said. But Scarlet hadn't seen it that way. By throwing them in at the deep end, she'd ensured all the people who needed distracting were taken care of. And she was also painfully aware that every hour that passed, the salon was costing money, rather than making it. But now they were here she was beginning to see the wisdom in her aunt's words. Perhaps she should have waited.

Ruby entered with a carrier bag from the local shop. 'Here are the balloons,' she said sullenly to Scarlet. 'They had red but no navy so I picked up a few silver instead.'

'Great. Silver will do,' she replied.

Ruby stood awkwardly, holding the bag. 'So, what now?' she asked, the dislike for her cousin as clear as could be.

'You could blow them up?' Scarlet suggested tersely.

She was losing patience with Ruby already and they were barely a few hours into her first day. She silently cursed her aunt once more for landing her with the abominable nightmare that was Ruby Drew. Unable to stand and watch her moody face and slow, grudging movements, Scarlet marched across the room to her aunt. She stood beside her and took a deep breath, exhaling with a long hiss as she watched the activity around them.

'I can't believe you're opening this place. It's not ready, Scarlet,' Lily said to her disapprovingly.

'It's ready enough,' she replied with confidence she didn't really feel. 'I always planned to open quickly. Time is money after all.'

'You're holding an opening that you haven't told any of the locals is happening,' Lily replied. She turned to Scarlet grimly. 'I know this is a laundry, but you need to make it look as legitimate as possible to everyone else. And you need to make friends of the local business owners, act like that matters to you, so none of them catch on to what we're doing. Believe me, the last thing you want to do is rile the locals. Rule number one in this game: keep those around you onside.'

Lily's phone rang and she looked down at the screen. Scarlet glanced at it too and saw Ray's name flash up. Lily declined the call with a sound of annoyance, then turned back to the room with a sigh.

'I'd have sent out fliers and put ads in the local rags,' she continued. 'Maybe offered the neighbours a fifty per cent discount for their first visit. No one even knows this is going ahead. It looks odd, Scarlet, for a business like this to open and not be fussed about making a noise. And your poor mum – look at all that food,' Lily admonished. 'I bet she stayed up half the bloody night making that.'

'She did,' Scarlet admitted guiltily. 'I did tell her not to.'

'You know as well as I do that telling Cath not to cook for an event is like telling ice not to bleedin' melt,' Lily shot back scathingly.

'Well… I guess at least we all know what we're eating for the next few days,' Scarlet replied.

Lily couldn't stop her face breaking out in a grin of amusement and they both began to laugh, the tension dissipating as quickly as it had risen.

*

Across the room, Ruby scowled resentfully. She hated the way Scarlet always sidled up to her mother. She had a mother of her own, for Christ's sake – why could she not buzz off back to her? But even as she thought this, she answered her own question. Because Cath wasn't as powerful as Lily, *that* was why. Cath didn't open doors or pave her way with gold, the way Lily did. It was cupboard love, pure and simple, that Scarlet was displaying. And she was sick of it.

The only reason she was prancing around like queen of the castle in this poxy little hairdresser's was because Lily had stumped up the money to set it up. And yet Scarlet had the audacity to look down her nose at *her*, Lily's *actual* daughter, bossing her around like she was nothing but a skivvy. She tied the balloon aggressively and threw it to the side with the others.

Her mother had told her she had to work here now, help with the running of the place, help Scarlet make a go of it. But she'd soon realised she was just being kept out of the way when she saw Nat and Sandra were already there doing just that. That realisation had left her even more depressed than she already was.

It wasn't that she'd been looking forward to working here. Work was boring and unrewarding, whatever form it came in. Nothing compared to the feeling of pure happiness and energy that came from shooting up heroin. Nothing even came close. And now she'd tasted it – no, now she'd spent a good portion of her adult life *gorging* on it – she couldn't think of anything else. Her heart felt empty. Her very soul felt grey and tired, as though sunlight would never warm it again. And that was something no one could fix.

She envied them, at times, the rest of the family. They found pleasure and reward in such simple things. Work, family, a drink, a good night's sleep. These things did nothing for her. But the one thing that did, she could never go back to. Because she believed Ray when he said he'd kill her. His words came back to her now, the look of cold promise in his eyes as he threatened to take her life. She shivered.

His love for her mother was absolute and as unforgiving as it was passionate. He would walk through fire or on broken glass for Lily. And he'd have no qualms sending his soul straight to hell if it meant protecting her from harm. And he saw Ruby as harm. So despite her longing, Ruby knew she could never return to the poisonous love of her life, if she wanted to continue breathing.

The door opened and her brothers walked in. As Cillian turned and grinned at her, the heaviness in her heart lifted ever so slightly. She and her brothers were at odds a lot of the time, but love was still there underneath. She tilted her head upwards in greeting and he sidled over to her.

'Alright, Rubes?' he asked, taking the balloon she'd just blown up out of her hands and bouncing it lightly off the top of her head. 'How's it going?'

She scowled and pushed the balloon away towards the others. 'Don't do that – you'll make me barnet frizzier than it already is.'

'I like your frizzy barnet,' Cillian said fondly, playing with the toothpick he seemed to constantly have in his mouth these days.

'You never were known for having good taste,' Ruby replied with a half-grin.

'How's it going here then, eh?' he asked, searching her face with a look of genuine interest. 'Think you'll like it?'

'What, playing court to Queen Scarlet?' she replied, glaring at her cousin.

Cillian turned his back to the room and leaned close. 'You've got an opportunity to change the game here, you know,' he said quietly.

Ruby rolled her eyes. 'Yes,' she snapped. 'So I keep hearing. Don't worry, I'm changing my evil ways and—'

'No,' Cillian cut her off. 'That ain't what I mean. What I'm saying is, you have a chance here to show Mum what you can *really* do.' There was a challenge in his expression. 'You don't like playing second fiddle to Scarlet? Then change it. Don't just plod – make your mark. Scar won't be here all the time, but *you* will. Show everyone how well *you* run things. You might have everyone else fooled, but not me. I know you've got it in you.' He straightened up. 'Show *them* that, surprise them, and you'll be out of here and running your own shit in no time.'

Ruby frowned, surprised by his words. Did he really believe in her so much? It had been a long time since anyone had believed in her for anything.

'Look, I'm sure this ain't your idea of a dream life, but what are your choices, eh?' Cillian brushed down the front of his suit jacket. 'You can sulk under Scarlet's watch, or you can carve your own path. But either way you're stuck here, from what I understand.' He glanced at her with a small smile. 'I'd love to see their faces if you *do* decide to show them what you've got.'

For the first time in as long as she could remember, something warm pierced her heavy heart. Cillian really believed in her. He really thought she had something to show the world. She blinked and shifted her weight onto her other foot as she tried to find an appropriate reply.

'Cillian?' Scarlet's voice pierced her thoughts and shattered the fragile moment. 'What are you doing Saturday morning?'

Cillian nudged her arm. 'I'll catch you later.' He drifted away from her and over to Scarlet.

Ruby swallowed, feeling upset and irritated by the interruption. Even when Scarlet didn't *know* she was doing it, she trampled all over everything Ruby had like an elephant in a greenhouse.

Perhaps Cillian had a point, she thought as she blew sharply into the next balloon. She was stuck here whether she liked it or not. Maybe she should play the game and get out from underneath Scarlet at least. She didn't get much out of working. But rising up to where Scarlet sat was at least something to focus on. And if she got that far, she could just keep climbing.

As the next thought occurred to her, she smiled her first genuine smile in weeks. If she got that far, she could climb further and further up through the family firm until their precious Scarlet was so far beneath her she could crush her younger cousin and get her out of the way for good.

CHAPTER TWENTY-SEVEN

Lily lifted the still heavily laden tray of food from the car and walked into the house behind Cath and Scarlet, who were carrying similar loads.

'I just can't understand why you wouldn't tell anyone about your big opening, Scarlet,' Cath said as she reached her kitchen. 'I made all this food and no one barely touched it.'

Lily shot Scarlet a pointed look, and the younger woman had the good grace to look away guiltily.

'Sorry, Mum. It was all very nice though. Sandra mentioned how much she liked your sausage rolls.'

'*Sandra* was taking the Michael out of my food actually,' Cath said with a disapproving sniff.

'What you on about?' Scarlet asked. 'Sandra had nothing but praise for your food when she spoke to me.'

'She referred to my mini gherkins as mini *stiffies*,' she replied indignantly.

Scarlet almost choked on a laugh and Lily hid a smile.

'Well,' Scarlet replied, 'you know what they say. If the pants fit.'

This time Lily couldn't quite contain her laughter and it slipped out, despite the look on Cath's face. Cath glaring at her just added to her amusement, and she and Scarlet fell into raucous laughter.

'Well… probably a good thing I didn't put the mini pickled onions on the same plate then,' Cath said, deciding to join in on the joke.

Scarlet howled, and Lily shook her head with a wide grin. 'Oh holy mother of God,' she said. 'What are we, fifteen? Come on, let's get this in the fridge.'

She walked over to the big American fridge and opened the door, looking for a space on the shelves to offload the first tray. As she slipped it into the middle shelf and moved a couple of things aside to make room for the next, the doorbell sounded.

Cath hurried off while Lily continued putting away the food – until she heard who was at the door.

'Is Scarlet here?' she heard him say.

'Oh, for Christ's sake, I've told you lot—' Cath started.

'I have a warrant for her arrest,' he cut her off.

'What?' Cath gasped.

Lily whipped around to face Scarlet, the food forgotten. Scarlet stared back at her with wide, horrified eyes.

'Why?' she whispered across the kitchen. 'What for?'

'I don't know,' Lily mouthed. Her mind raced through the possibilities.

'Well, she ain't here,' Cath asserted.

'This would be a lot easier if she just came with us now,' the officer continued, obviously not believing her.

Lily stepped forward to meet her niece and grasped her hands as a look of fear flitted across the girl's face. She cursed internally, knowing what she needed to tell her next wasn't going to go down well. They had been here before a few times over the years. And they had learned that the more they delayed the inevitable, the guiltier they looked of whatever they were being pulled in for. Which meant, much as she hated to admit it, that the officer was right – it would be a lot easier if Scarlet just went with them now.

'Listen to me,' she said, her voice low and urgent. 'You need to go with them, find out what they want but answer *nothing*. Do you hear me?' she asked, the iron strength in her tone mirrored in her expression. '*Nothing*,' she stressed.

'No…' Scarlet breathed in horror, squeezing her aunt's fingers tighter in horror.

'I told you, she ain't here,' Cath repeated with a growl.

'Shit,' Scarlet said, closing her eyes as she tried to get her head around what Lily was telling her. 'OK. What do I do?' she whispered.

Lily's heart lurched with a mixture of fear and the urge to protect her niece, but she ignored it. She needed to keep a straight head. This was serious, and Scarlet had to play this just right if they were going to get her back unscathed. Especially considering they had no idea why the police had come for her.

'Just go with them, be pleasant, act confident but give nothing away,' she instructed. 'I'll send our lawyer. Do *whatever* he says but don't say a *word* until he arrives, do you understand?' She braced Scarlet's forearms and gave her a small shake. 'Do you understand?'

Scarlet nodded. 'Yeah,' she breathed.

'Her car's on the drive,' the officer commented.

Lily searched her face, a feeling of dread settling into the pit of her stomach. They'd all been arrested in the past and questioned over things they'd done – sometimes even things they hadn't. She, Ronan, the boys, even Cath, were seasoned at dealing with these situations. But Scarlet wasn't. And without knowing what they were pulling her in for, there was no specific advice she could give.

'I guess she went out without it,' Cath replied in a tone of contempt, holding them off as she always had, until Lily or Scarlet decided how to handle this.

With a sigh, Lily squeezed her arms in encouragement, then nodded, gently pushing her towards the hallway. 'Stay strong,' she whispered. 'And remember you're a Drew.' A heavy feeling of dread plummeted to the bottom of her stomach as she let go. What the hell was happening? What did they have on her?

Scarlet paused, then straightened her back and went out into the hallway. Lily leaned against the door frame just out of sight of the officers at the door.

'What's going on?' Scarlet asked in a calmer tone than Lily had expected. *Good girl*, she thought. *Don't let the fuckers see you're scared.*

'Scarlet Drew, I am arresting you on suspicion of murder. You do not have to say anything, but it may harm your defence if you do not mention, when questioned, something which you later rely on in court. Anything you do say may be given in evidence,' the officer stated.

'What?' Scarlet demanded. 'What the hell are you on about?'

'This way, Miss Drew,' another voice said.

'You can't take her,' Cath cried. 'She ain't done nothing!'

'Mum, don't worry about it. I'll be home later. I've done nothing,' Scarlet said. 'Don't worry,' she repeated, her voice receding as the officers escorted her out of the house.

Lily waited until she heard the car doors open and shut, then the car drive away before she walked out into the hallway. Cath's hand was to her mouth, her face pale and stricken. Lily felt the same fear in the pit of her own stomach, but she knew she had to keep it together for Scarlet's sake. And Cath's.

'There was no evidence,' Cath whispered in a shaky voice. 'They had nothing. How could they have something now?'

A claw of ice grasped her insides as something suddenly clicked in Lily's mind. Her eyes widened. 'Where did you put that knife, Cath?'

Cath's jaw dropped in horror. 'Oh shit,' she whispered.

'*Where*, Cath?' Lily pushed.

'In – in the Thames,' Cath stuttered, her eyes darting around as she thought back over what she'd done.

'Whereabouts?'

'I chucked it in from the bank at Lyle Park,' she said. 'I weighted the bag and threw it as far as I could…' She trailed off as Lily closed her eyes and put her hands together in front of her mouth in a prayer-like manner.

'It's shallow there,' she said flatly. 'There's a shore when the tide goes out.'

'Oh God,' Cath breathed again. 'I didn't realise.'

Lily cursed and turned around, placing her hands on her hips. Her head pounded and her blood raced as she tried to figure a way out of this for Scarlet. For all of them. The knife would have Scarlet's prints on it and Jasper had nicked his hand when he'd used it to saw himself out of his binds – that much she'd noticed when they got rid of his body. She shook her head as the options began to drop like flies. She needed to get the lawyer in there fast. If it was the knife that they'd found then this was bad. Very bad indeed.

CHAPTER TWENTY-EIGHT

Connor paced the room as Cillian leaned over the breakfast bar, his head in his hands. Lily stood by the door on the phone, still trying to get hold of their lawyer, and Cath hovered, not quite able to stand still. Ruby sat by the window, watching them all with detached curiosity as the situation unfolded.

The call connected and Lily almost danced for joy. 'Dana! It's Lily Drew. Sorry to call on this number but it's an emergency. How soon can Robert get down the station?'

Robert had been their family lawyer for many years and Dana was his faithful secretary. They'd tried Robert first, but despite several attempts, they just kept getting his voicemail.

'Oh, Lily, hello,' Dana replied with a note of surprise. 'Um, who's been arrested? You?'

'No, Scarlet,' Lily replied grimly. 'I need him there urgently,' she said with feeling. 'It's her first pull and it's serious. Serious enough that they'll be trying to press her before Robert gets there to protect her. They know she's green; they'll be playing on it.' She heard the worry that she wasn't quite able to mask. There was a hesitant pause on the other end of the phone and her brows knitted together in a frown. 'Dana?'

'Yes, I'm here. But there's a small problem.'

The dread that had taken seed in Lily's diaphragm began to grow. 'What kind of problem?' Cath grasped her arm and she gently eased her off, needing space to think.

'Robert's been away for the last two weeks visiting relatives.'

'And?' Lily demanded.

'In Australia,' Dana continued, the cringe in her tone detectable.

Lily felt the dread in her stomach turn colder and her heartbeat quickened. 'When is he back?'

'He's in the air right now and he's due to land in the early hours of tomorrow morning. I can get him there first thing. He'll go straight there,' Dana replied.

Of course he'd go straight there, Lily thought. He'd leave his own funeral to attend one of the Drews, with the amount of money *they* paid him. He was on retainer, paid a lot of money cash-in-hand to make sure he was there whenever, wherever and however they needed him. He was as bent as they came, so they could tell him straight when they *had* done something, then he figured out the best play to defend them or cover up the ugly truth.

But today, the day they needed him more than any other occasion, he was hundreds of miles up in the air, unreachable. Lily ran her hand down over her mouth as she tried to work out what they were going to do. They couldn't leave Scarlet without a lawyer for that long. This left the police way too much time alone with her.

'I could see if another associate could come,' Dana continued.

'No,' Lily cut her off sharply. 'It has to be Robert.' They couldn't risk this falling into the hands of a straight lawyer if Robert was going to be able to do his job properly when he landed. 'Just tell him the moment he lands he needs to call me. I'll have someone meet him.'

'Of course,' Dana replied.

Lily ended the call and turned towards them all with a grim expression.

'What's going on?' Cath asked urgently.

'Robert's currently on a long-haul flight and doesn't touch down until tomorrow. Which means Scarlet's on her own until then,' she said tartly. She walked over to the kitchen table and sat down in one of the chairs.

'You're not serious?' Cillian said, looking over at his mother, aghast. 'What's she going to do? She can't sit in there overnight! Shit, she…' He began shaking his head slowly as he thought it through. 'They're going to question her until she cracks.'

'They're going to try,' Lily replied in a foreboding tone. 'We've just got to pray she doesn't say a word.'

'You think she's going to be tripped up?' Cath asked with a wobble of fear.

Lily turned and met her gaze solemnly. 'They're going to try, Cath. And they're going to try hard. Right now, Scarlet is alone in there, facing God only knows what, with no counsel and none of us to pull her out of it. She's a smart girl, but that ain't a good position to be in for anyone, let alone someone who's never faced the police in this capacity before.'

She turned to look at Cillian, seeing her fears mirrored in his eyes. 'She's on her own now. And all we can do is hope she's strong enough to hold out until Robert gets there. Because if she isn't…'

She stood, went to the fridge and pulled out a bottle of wine. She needed a drink. Really, she needed something stronger, but she knew Cath didn't keep whisky in the house.

'If she isn't, what, Lil?' Cath asked, her eyes darting between Lily and the twins.

Lily turned to her with a slow, heavy exhale and stared at her for a moment. 'If she isn't and they somehow trip her up, it's not just her alibi that crumbles for the night of Jasper's murder.' Lily looked up at her sons gravely. 'We are all each other's alibi. If she falls, Cath, the whole family falls.'

CHAPTER TWENTY-NINE

Scarlet sat on the hard ledge with her back to the cold concrete wall, staring at the door of her cell. Various names were scratched into the paint, but though she was staring right at them, Scarlet barely registered they were there.

She wrapped her arms around herself defensively and shivered. They'd taken the jacket she'd grabbed on her way out away, along with her shoes and loose personal belongings, and the temperature in her cell left much to be desired.

Her aunt had said she was sending a lawyer, but as yet no one had arrived. She had no idea how long it had been since she'd been put in here, but it had to have been at least a couple of hours. Her stomach rumbled and she pulled her arms in tighter, wishing she was still back home with her mother and aunt eating the mountain of food from the opening and laughing over stupid jokes.

She imagined the police had left her for so long in the hope the solitary cell would begin to frighten her and pull down her defences. In truth, the former was working. She was terrified, and these feelings were only growing with each passing minute. She wasn't stupid – she knew the score. The Drews were on the police radar, and from time to time, one of them got pulled in and questioned about something or other. But it was a rare occurrence and she'd not expected to cross this bridge herself for a long time yet. She'd only been part of the firm for a few months. And what's more, she couldn't understand what they could possibly have on her to pull her in in the first place. They'd questioned her over and over again about Jasper once they'd realised their connection, but she'd been careful. She'd solidly stuck to the story each time. So despite the fact they desperately wanted to pin it on her, they'd never had even the slightest bit of evidence to tie her to the scene. What had changed?

Dull, heavy footsteps beyond the door sounded and slowed as they reached her cell. There was a teeth-clenching screech of metal on metal as the grille in the door was pulled back and a pair of eyes peered through at her. She stared back, trying to look a lot cooler and more confident than she really felt. The eyes disappeared and the door was pulled open, groaning at the movement.

'Come on then,' the young officer behind the door said. 'They're ready to question you.'

Scarlet stood up, her heart rate quickening. Had the lawyer arrived? Surely he wanted to speak to her alone before they went into the room, didn't he? She had never been in this position before, but that would have made more sense to her, so they could make sure they were both on the same page.

She followed the officer down the hallway and up to another level where a series of rooms led off to one side. He paused outside one of them and knocked, before opening the door and gesturing for her to go in.

Inside the small bare room was a table with an empty plastic chair on one side and the two officers who'd arrested her sat waiting on the other. She swallowed hard, trying to quell her rising fear. She desperately needed to calm down. Right now she could barely think straight.

'Take a seat,' one of the officers ordered curtly.

Scarlet did as she'd been told, glancing at him as she sat. She knew this one. He was DC Jennings. He was the officer who'd questioned her time and again about Jasper. He was rude and domineering and she didn't like him in the slightest. The other was a woman with short, cropped dark hair and a face that reminded her of a pixie. DC Crawley, her name was. She'd joined Jennings on the last visit he'd made to the house.

Scarlet sat down and stared at Jennings with what she hoped was a look of defiance. He smirked and looked down at the closed file in front of him, strumming his fingers across the front cover. After a few seconds, he reached across to the tape recorder and pressed record, then declared the date and time and names of the people in the room, before turning back to look at her.

Scarlet took a deep breath in and steeled herself, trying not to let her gaze slip down to the file she knew had to contain something bad. Her fingers began to feel damp, and she clenched her fists together under the table.

'Miss Drew, you have been detained on suspicion of your involvement in the death of Jasper Snow. We have reason to believe you were with him on the day he died and that you lied to us about your whereabouts. We're going to ask you some questions,' Jennings said.

'Jasper killed himself,' Scarlet said, her inexperience and natural instinct leading her to defend herself – causing her to forget her aunt's warning to stay silent until the lawyer had arrived.

'Did he?' Jennings asked, his eyes boring into her.

'You know he did,' Scarlet replied flatly. 'You told me that yourself, remember?' She shifted in her seat. 'You told us about his suicide note.'

'Yes, the note that was so conveniently placed in a sandwich bag to keep it dry. Bit odd that someone so consumed with guilt that they wanted to take their own life would stop to think about such a minor detail, don't you think?'

'You're the policeman,' Scarlet replied in a slow, sarcastic tone. 'Why don't you tell me?'

There was a short silence and Jennings nodded, lowering his gaze to the file. He touched it, holding his fingers to the edge for a few moments as if savouring the moment of revelation. Scarlet's heart rate increased once more as the tension became almost too heavy to bear. What did they have on her?

'You mentioned to me on several occasions that the night Jasper died, you and your family were at your aunt's house having dinner – is that correct?' he asked.

Scarlet swallowed as something prickled at the back of her neck. Somehow she felt as though she was being lured into a trap, but this wasn't something she hadn't already told him numerous times. So how could it be a trap?

'That's right,' she replied cautiously.

He opened the file and looked down the first page. She couldn't read it clearly but from here it looked like a simple summary of the facts they'd gathered so far. Perhaps they didn't have anything after all, she suddenly thought. Perhaps this had all been a mind game, the police applying excessive pressure in the hope that she might crack. That had to be the case. What else *could* it be? She sat up slightly taller and her shoulders relaxed.

'And that was yourself, your cousins Connor and Cillian Drew, and of course your aunt Lily, yes?' he asked, looking up at her for confirmation.

'Yes,' she replied irritably. 'I've already told you all this.'

'Jasper's whereabouts were accounted for right up until seven thirty that evening – then he wasn't seen again until his body was found,' Jennings continued. 'And you were at your aunt's from about seven, right?'

Scarlet sighed heavily. 'For the last time, *yes*,' she said.

'And you hadn't seen Jasper for a few days before that, according to your statement,' he continued.

'Are you going to get to a point or did you seriously drag me here to go over the same old questions you've already asked me a million times?' Scarlet demanded. 'Because I've got better things to do than sit around here with you lot, you know.' She shook her head and rolled her eyes. 'I've just opened a new hair salon. *Today*, in fact.'

'Another laundry?' Jennings asked, not missing a beat.

Scarlet felt her insides constrict, but she was careful not to show it in her face. They weren't going to trip her up that easily. Clenching her jaw, she forced herself to answer levelly. 'You deaf?' She gave him a look of scorn. 'I said hairdresser's. We wash hair, not clothes,' she said, purposely mistaking his meaning.

'Clothes. Cute,' he replied drily. He turned the next page and pulled out a series of prints, pushing them across the table and twisting them around to face her. 'Tell me, have you ever seen this knife before?'

Scarlet looked down at the prints with a frown, but as her eyes came to rest on the familiar blade, her heart almost stopped. Her insides turned to ice, and a strange cold tingle of fear rippled over her skin. Her breath caught in her throat and she had to remind herself to breathe. How had they got hold of that knife? It was stashed safely at home in her drawer – she'd not moved it since the day she'd killed Jasper.

'Should I take it from your silence that you *do* recognise the knife?' Jennings asked.

Scarlet shook her head, dread seeping into every pore. She looked around the cold, stark room with its white walls and camera in the corner monitoring her every move and suddenly felt as though she couldn't breathe. How did this happen? She closed her eyes and willed herself to snap out of the panic that was slowly taking over. She had to stay calm.

'No, I don't recognise it. I've never seen it before in my life.' She swallowed and sat up straighter, trying to clear her head. 'Why are you showing me this?' she asked. 'What has that knife got to do with anything?'

'It's interesting that you don't recall it, as this knife has your prints all over it. Yours as well as Jasper Snow's,' Jennings continued.

'So?' Scarlet asked, sounding much more defiant than she felt. In reality, she felt cornered. She felt as though she was backed right up and the walls were closing in. 'Maybe we used it for some reason when we met up, I don't know.' She was floundering. 'I don't exactly remember everything we talked about or did or touched when we met. So what if it has both our prints? That doesn't mean anything.'

Except it did mean something. It meant that it was the knife he'd tried to kill her with after he'd escaped from his binds, right before she'd put a bullet in his brain. It was the knife that had clattered to the floor in the factory basement and skidded to a halt a few feet away from his body as he'd gone down. It was the knife that her cousins had left behind, that she'd picked up and taken away to hide. But they didn't know that. Not for certain, at least. They couldn't, could they?

'I think you do remember the knife, Scarlet,' Jennings pushed. 'And I think you were there when he died. Jasper had a cut on his left hand, you see. A cut that the forensic pathologist who undertook the autopsy discovered was made only a very short time before his death. And the DNA on the knife shows that it was the knife that made that incision. So' – he shifted in his seat and studied her gravely – 'we have a knife that cut the victim's hand right before he died that also has your prints on. I suggest we start over and you tell me exactly what happened from the very beginning.'

CHAPTER THIRTY

The small bell above the door of the old antiques shop tinkled as Lily entered. She let it close behind her and looked around the dark, cluttered room with little interest. She had always enjoyed antique shops, but she had too much on her mind to appreciate this one right now. She'd barely slept, lying awake in the dark wondering whether Scarlet was OK. She'd stayed with Cath and had heard her pacing the floor through the early hours. None of them would be able to relax until they found out exactly what was going on, but they were still no nearer to finding anything out. Robert's flight had been held up and he wasn't going to land for another couple of hours yet.

What would happen when he did land? He was their best shot, but he wasn't a get-out-of-jail-free card. He was only a lawyer. Sirens sounded elsewhere down the street and she tensed. Would they be coming for her soon? Would they be coming for all of them? Trying to focus on the task at hand, Lily made her way slowly through the shop to the back, where she knew the person she was here to see would be sat, hidden away behind the counter, watching her on his many CCTV screens.

'Lily Drew, the lioness of the East End,' came a calm, crisp voice. 'Much time has passed since you last graced these humble halls with your presence.'

A small smile curled up the corners of Lily's mouth as she rounded a large mirror and reached the counter. She stared down at the small, thin man stooped over the desk, soldering a broken trinket back together again.

'Humble?' Lily lifted one slender brow. 'It's not the first word I'd use when describing this place, Sam.'

'Ah,' he replied, still staring intently at the jewellery in his hand. 'But that is because you are an intelligent woman. Most people look in here and see tired old junk.'

'Whereas I see your treasure trove,' she finished.

'Precisely.' Sam Wiles put the soldering iron down, his work complete, and finally looked up. 'How's tricks?'

'They could be better,' she said carefully, running her hand across the polished wood of a nearby piano lid. Whether or not Scarlet's arrest was common knowledge yet she wasn't sure, but she wasn't about to share the news herself. She wasn't here about that. She was here to continue setting things up for the heist. Things might be dire, but business needed to continue as normal until something happened which stopped her ensuring that it did.

'I was sorry to hear about Ronan,' Sam said.

Her hand paused for moment. One of these days she would get used to hearing that, to getting the reminders of her loss and the wave of grief it elicited every time. One day. But not yet.

'Thank you,' she said, lifting her hand off the end of the musical instrument. She turned to face him. 'And how are things here? Trade good?' She couldn't have cared less about the things she was asking, thoughts of Scarlet – alone and out of her depth – circling round her mind. But small talk was expected.

'Not bad. But then this ain't where I make my real money, as we both know. And I'm guessing the other side of things is what you're likely here about,' Sam replied, sitting back in his chair and studying her a little more closely.

'You guessed correctly,' she confirmed.

'What you got for me then?' He leaned forward, eager and curious.

'Actually, I need an introduction,' Lily replied. 'I've got something big. So big I'm not even sure with all your connections I can get high enough to deal with it. But I'm hoping you can at least connect me to someone who can pass me on further.'

Sam frowned. 'It would have to be pretty big to be out of *my* league. I've not come across anything I haven't been able to fence or sort out yet, not in fifty years.'

Lily wandered back to the counter and leaned over it. 'I think I might just be the one to throw your record off, Wiley.'

The intrigue on his face intensified. 'Really?' he asked slowly. 'Hm. What sort of fence you after? What level we talking here?'

'I need someone who deals in fine art, at the very top. I'm talking *top* top. I've got something that hasn't floated through the black market for thirty years. And I highly doubt anything this big has come around since it was last there either.'

Sam's curious expression sharpened and Lily wondered if he realised what she was talking about. 'Price range?' he asked.

'Above-board value is somewhere around a hundred mill,' she said quietly, double-checking that no one else had entered the shop. 'Street value I'm not sure.' Sam's eyes flew wider and his jaw dropped. 'I'm out of my depth,' she admitted.

Sam nodded, his eyes darting around as he processed what she was saying. 'Well, fuck me,' he exclaimed eventually in disbelief. 'I think you're right. I think you have just broken my record.' He shook his head with a crooked smile. 'I know someone who *will* be able to put you in touch with the right person. I can arrange a meet,' he offered.

'That would be great. When can I meet your guy? The sooner the better,' she added.

Sam stood up and dusted off the front of his trousers. 'Danny, his name is. We can go now. He has a shop not far from here.'

He moved to go through a door behind and then hesitated, turning back to her. 'You know, these guys at the top, they ain't like us. They play by different rules. And they don't stick to the shadows – they hide in plain sight.' A flicker of concern flew through his frown. 'I'm not saying that's a bad thing, it's just… different. I hope you know what you're doing.'

Lily lifted her sober gaze to meet his. 'So do I, Sam. So do I.'

An hour later, Lily and Sam parted ways, their business complete. After vetting her through Sam, Danny had agreed to arrange the meeting. The guy he knew dealt purely in fine art. He was the best of the best apparently. She'd asked to see him today, very aware that the heist was now almost upon them if things did somehow go to plan, but he wasn't in the country. According to Danny, he lived, most of the time, on a yacht in Monaco.

She checked her watch. The meeting had taken longer than she'd anticipated and now she would need to move fast if she was going to catch Robert on his way to the station. Scarlet had been on her own now for about eighteen hours. It was a long time to be locked up surrounded by police with no lawyer. What did they have on her? How hard had they pressured her? Had she kept silent as Lily had told her to, or had she given them the opportunity to trip her up?

As she pulled her sleeve back down, she noticed a movement out of the corner of her eye. She turned her head and slid her gaze sideways. There was a man in a dark hoodie walking down the quiet road behind her, watching her. She frowned and her senses sharpened.

As she passed the next few shopfronts, she watched him in the reflection and quickly realised he wasn't alone. Behind her to the other side was another man in a dark hoodie, keeping pace. She sped up as much as she could without it looking suspicious and they sped up with her.

Her heart began to race and she quickly assessed her surroundings. The road was practically deserted. Ahead of her, the main road where her car was parked was getting closer, but when she checked again, she realised they were too. She calculated the distance and realised they were going to try and get to her before she could make it out of the road. She swore under her breath and pulled her handbag to the front. Here, out of their line of sight, she reached in, pushed aside her lipstick and phone and wrapped her fingers around the Swiss army knife she kept in there.

She passed another shopfront and checked to see where they were. They were close now. In a few moments she would have to try and make a run for it. She could see them gearing up to grab her. The one across the road stepped off the pavement and headed towards her. Swearing under her breath, she felt the adrenaline kick in. But how far was she really going to get in heels and a restrictive knee-length skirt?

As she geared herself up to run, a group of men suddenly turned the corner into the street ahead, laughing and chatting jovially.

'Hey!' she yelled loudly, waving to get their attention. 'Hey, excuse me!'

The men looked over and she hurried towards them in a trot.

'Hi, everything OK?' one of them said, looking over her shoulder with a frown.

'Yeah, sure,' she replied. 'Sorry, I was just wondering if you could help me find this shop…' She pulled out her phone and began scrolling to buy time. Out of the corner of her eye, she watched as the two men passed by and quickly scooted off out of sight.

Her heart began to slow and she breathed out a sigh of relief. Who on earth were they? And what the hell did they want with her?

CHAPTER THIRTY-ONE

Robert Cheyney rubbed his eyes as he approached the exit that led to the airport arrivals hall. He was exhausted beyond belief, having had a long stopover and an additional unscheduled delay on his way back from Australia. He'd been in transit for over twenty-four hours now, but it would still be a while before he could get home and crawl into bed like he so wanted to do.

He'd managed to access his messages during the last stopover and had quickly caught up with what was going on. He'd cursed, wishing he'd picked any other time to visit family in Australia. His usual clients were not an issue; if they had a problem, they could be temporarily dealt with by someone else, but he was supposed to be at the Drews' beck and call. That was what they paid him so handsomely for. He'd figured he'd be OK to slip away for just a couple of weeks without anything happening, but clearly he'd been wrong.

The double doors opened in front of him and a sea of faces stared eagerly in, searching for their loved ones. As he stepped through, he looked around for a face he knew and eventually spotted one. He made a beeline for George, who took his bag and gestured for him to follow.

'Where are your other bags?' George asked.

Robert shook his head. 'They got lost in transit when we got rerouted.'

'Have you got all you need to work?' he asked with a frown as they made their swift exit from the building.

'Yes, everything important is there,' Robert replied, pointing towards the hand luggage.

'Good,' George replied. 'We're headed straight there. Scarlet's been in there on her own a long time, Robert.' His serious expression betrayed his worry.

'I'm aware,' Robert replied, feeling a flutter of unease in his stomach. 'It will be fine. I'm sure we can sort this out quickly.'

He glanced at George, who didn't answer, and prayed that he was right. Because if he couldn't sort this out – if Scarlet had already condemned herself by talking without caution because he hadn't been around to protect her – then he wasn't sure even God himself would be able to protect him from Lily Drew's wrath.

An hour later, Robert was seen through to a small room and told to wait for Scarlet. He tugged at his tie, feeling hot. Ignoring the chairs, he paced instead, too stressed about the situation at hand to sit.

A few minutes later the door opened, and a pale and drawn-looking Scarlet walked through, the door shutting behind her. He quickly guided her to one of the seats at the desk and sat beside her.

'Quickly, tell me what's happened so far. We only have a couple of minutes before they come in,' he said urgently.

'Has Lily told you anything about Jasper Snow?' she asked.

'Yes,' he said quietly. 'I know what really happened and I know the story for everyone else. What have they got?'

Scarlet licked her lips. 'There was a knife,' she whispered. 'Jasper had it on him that night. I hid it at home; it was safe. I don't know how they got it.'

Robert nodded. Lily had told him she suspected as much and explained that it might have been found following Cath's relocation of it. 'OK. Have you said anything to them?' He watched her intently, willing her to tell him that she'd stayed silent. But her guilty look told him she hadn't. He sat back and rubbed his forehead. 'What did you say?'

'Nothing really, just that I hadn't seen it before and that if it had my prints on then maybe I touched it another time. We met a couple of times before,' she said quickly. 'But then they started talking about my dad and kept trying to trip me up.' She frowned. 'So I said I wasn't talking anymore until you got here.'

'Good!' He grasped this like a lifeboat, glad that she'd had the sense to stop before she incriminated herself too deeply. 'Good. OK.' Footsteps sounded down the hallway towards them. 'Don't say *anything* more, alright? Just let me handle things from here on out.'

'OK,' she whispered gratefully as the door opened.

Jennings and Crawley came in and sat down opposite them. Jennings tried and failed to hide his annoyance at the fact Robert was now in attendance. He waited as they restarted the tape and noted the appropriate facts before launching straight in.

'My client informs me that she was questioned intensively alone despite expressing clearly that she wanted to wait for me to arrive. Can I ask why that was?' He lifted his brows enquiringly, directing his gaze at Jennings.

'Your *client*,' Jennings said in an irate tone, 'didn't state in the meeting until towards the end that she wished to have you present. That is clearly recorded on the tape.'

'No, she told you before the tape started rolling, didn't she, Officer?' Robert countered, knowing exactly how things would have gone.

Her initial request for a lawyer would have been when she'd arrived at the station. They'd taken their chances that she wouldn't repeat that on tape until later, meaning their bending of the rules could not be proved. He'd hit a nerve though, Robert noted, spotting a pale flush creeping up the detective's neck.

'What are you charging my client with?' he continued sharply.

Jennings narrowed his eyes slightly. 'As yet, nothing. We would like to ask a few more questions—'

'You've already asked my client questions,' he cut in.

'And yet we've still not reached the bottom of the situation,' Jennings replied. He opened the file and pushed the pictures of the knife towards Robert. 'A knife was handed in to the station yesterday with your client's prints along with the prints of Jasper Snow, a man whose death is under investigation.'

'A man who I understand from my client committed suicide, is that not correct?'

'A man whose death is being treated as suspicious due to certain discrepancies.'

'And why do you think that has anything to do with my client?' Robert pushed.

Jennings sighed, exasperated. 'The knife – with her prints on it – was also used to cut Jasper Snow's hand shortly before he died. It then ended up in the river about a mile downstream from where his body was found.'

'You've got nothing,' Robert said bullishly. He shook his head with a cold smile. 'My client and Jasper Snow were connected and had met previously, which you're aware of. My client could have touched that knife at any point – it does not tie her to the time or place of his demise. And as for its location, I imagine if he'd had it with him when he fell into the river, it could easily have travelled downstream to where you claim it was found. The Thames is a mysterious and powerful force, Officer. As you well know.'

'Scarlet.' Jennings turned to her in desperation as he watched his thin connection crumble before his eyes. 'We *will* find more proof, and when we do this won't go well for you.'

'I think we're done here,' Robert said.

'If you tell us what happened now, we may be able to look at a reduced sentence,' he continued. 'This man murdered your father. And whilst that doesn't make what you did legal, it does go a long way to—'

'My client will not be discussing this any further.' Robert cut his plea off in a loud, firm voice. 'Now, you've held Miss Drew here for nearly twenty-two hours, so your twenty-four-hour hold is coming to a close. You also have absolutely no evidence of any crime, meaning you have no grounds on which to hold her any longer either. This link through the knife is tenuous at best, and to be honest, your constant badgering of my client over the last couple of months has not gone unnoticed. The girl lost her father to the man you keep questioning her about. The emotional distress that this is putting her through has become a very real issue.' He eyeballed Jennings hard, daring him to come back at him. Jennings's face contorted as he struggled to contain his frustration. 'You are to release my client immediately, or I will file harassment charges against you personally.'

The tension in the room rose at the rate of Jennings's fury. He could argue that they needed more time, but they both knew he didn't have solid enough grounds. The time he spent arguing whilst she sat in a cell would go against him, if and when Robert did file for harassment.

Jennings pulled a face of pure frustration and ended the recording. He narrowed his eyes across the table at Robert. 'I'll arrange the release papers. But be advised that there may be need for further questioning down the line. We *will* get to the bottom of the circumstances surrounding Jasper Snow's death.'

With that, he abruptly stood up and left, Crawley following close behind him. The door closed and Scarlet let out an audible sound of relief. She turned to him with a grateful smile.

'Thank God,' she exclaimed. 'Thank *you.*'

'Don't count your chickens yet,' he warned, glowering at the door. 'You'll be going home now, but we need to make sure nothing else concerning Jasper can be linked to you again.' He turned his serious gaze back to her. 'You should know, you've made an enemy for life today. One that is most likely going to haunt you for years to come. Men like that may grudgingly concede a battle, but they don't give up their wars. Not ever.'

CHAPTER THIRTY-TWO

The auctioneer stood up above the crowd on an old fruit crate and called out the lots, one by one. There was a breeze in the air, whistling through the open space and dancing playfully through everyone's hair. About thirty people stood in the cold, huddling in small groups and talking in hushed whispers as they guessed what could be behind each rolled metal door.

'Why are we here again?' Connor asked with a frown, glancing up at the CCTV cameras. They looked fairly new, compared to the rest of the old storage site.

'We're buying a storage unit,' Scarlet replied, her eyes trained on the auctioneer. It was the day after her release and although the experience had shaken her, she had jumped straight back to business.

'But *why* are we buying a storage unit? And here of all places?' Connor questioned. 'This is not a good idea,' he said gravely. 'These have to be registered properly. Our names will be all over the paperwork.'

'I know that,' Scarlet said levelly.

'And they're tiny,' Connor continued. 'Look at them. They're no bigger than a standard garage. If you only need something that small, we can buy one of the garages closer to home.'

'I want one of these,' Scarlet said simply.

Connor rolled his eyes. He really didn't know why she'd insisted on coming here, *or* why he'd had to join her. Or how Cillian had managed to get out of it. In just a few hours they were setting off on the biggest heist they'd ever attempted. A heist that was out of their comfort zone and that they'd had very little time to prepare for. A heist that they were pulling off despite the fact that Scarlet was still under the police spotlight. They had to be careful now, more cautious than ever. It was absurd, in his opinion, that they were not back at the factory going over every inch of the plan again, making sure they were as prepared as they could possibly be.

Connor ran one hand back through his thick black hair and then down across his chiselled jaw. He checked his watch and sighed.

Scarlet glanced sideways at him. 'I need this unit. We'll be done soon – I promise,' she said placatingly.

Connor glanced up at the CCTV once more and shook his head. She was leaving their family prints all over this little venture of hers, whatever the hell it was for.

'Lot number eighty-two,' the auctioneer cried.

Scarlet's grip tightened on the paper in her hand, outlining the lot numbers and their details. Connor watched her and wondered what it was about this particular lot she favoured. They seemed all the same to him.

'… previous owners passed away and no living relatives have been located. The unit contents are to be sold as one lot and bids will be blind…'

'What does he mean, *blind bids*?' Connor asked.

'He means the unit won't be opened for people to see the contents,' she replied. 'There are too many of them to do that; the contents will just be sold as bulk lots, pot luck.'

'… bidding will start at three hundred pounds…'

'So you want the contents?' Connor asked.

'I'll be taking on the contract for the storage unit, plus buying the contents, yes,' she replied.

Connor felt totally confused but decided not to bother questioning her further. If she wanted to buy a load of random old stuff then that was her prerogative.

'… four hundred…'

The bidding continued, with Scarlet occasionally raising her hand. The bidders were whittled down further and further until it was just Scarlet and one man left. He scowled at her across the open space.

'Five hundred and seventy-five?' the auctioneer continued.

Connor glanced down at his cousin. Scarlet was as cool and collected as ever, her grey-blue eyes never wavering from the auctioneer.

'Six hundred?'

Scarlet raised her arm again. As the bidding continued, Connor pursed his lips and waited. He already knew what the outcome would be. When Scarlet had decided she wanted something to happen, it happened. She was much like his mother in this way. She was strategic and always a step or two ahead of where everyone else assumed she would be.

When she had initially joined the firm, her presence had concerned him. She was just a young girl of eighteen, someone who'd never had to bloody her hands the way they'd had to, to keep the firm on top. He had worried that she would be a target for those searching for their weakness, someone he would have to go out of his way to protect. But she had proved those worries to be baseless. She'd worked hard to carve out her own place in the firm, had put in just as much graft as the rest of them, had stood her ground unfalteringly, even under police interrogation, and when it had come to it, she'd blooded herself in without a second thought. She'd impressed him in the few short months since she'd stepped up. She'd impressed all of them.

'Going once, twice… Sold – to the lady in the red dress for six hundred and fifty pounds.'

'Well done,' Connor said quietly.

'Thank you.' She shot him a quick smile and then beckoned him to follow her to a man sitting at a small trestle table set up at the side. 'I just need to register my details and pay and then we can get off.'

'Which one is it?' Connor asked, squinting as he tried to make out the numbers down the long line of storage units.

'Oh, I don't know. I think it's down that way somewhere,' she answered, waving dismissively. 'I'll figure it out when I'm next over here.'

Connor blinked. 'Surely you want to see what you've spent all this time and money on getting?'

'Yeah, some other time. We really should get back and go over things a few more times before tonight. And time's getting on.' She grinned and turned to give her details to the man at the table.

Connor wandered away as Scarlet filled out all her details. His mind turned to the heist. Not for the first time, he felt a sliver of doubt about their ability to pull it all off. Had they really had enough time to organise it? Was this really a sensible plan? He and Cillian had pulled some stunts in their time, but this job had him spooked.

He turned back and watched his cousin laugh with the man at the table. Was Scarlet truly up to this? Or would this be the job that sent them all down and ended the Drew firm for good?

CHAPTER THIRTY-THREE

Cillian paced up and down in the small waiting area. He couldn't sit – he was too wired. He rolled his neck once more, closing his eyes and flexing his upper arms.

'That won't do you no good, you know,' came a voice from behind him.

He opened his eyes and turned to find himself looking into a pair of clear blue eyes. They broke contact and roamed over his upper body critically.

'You're just tightening it up even more.'

He tilted his head as he stared at her. 'I don't think even you can loosen me up today.'

Once more he wasn't sure why he'd come here. It wasn't so much that he didn't believe in her abilities this time, but today was the day of the heist. He should have been preparing himself, going over all the possibilities of what could go wrong and working out solutions ahead of time. But the appointment had already been booked before they'd known the heist was going ahead, and something had stopped him from cancelling it. Perhaps this was what he needed – something to ease him up before it was showtime. Or it could just be a totally unnecessary distraction.

Billie's eyes narrowed as they searched his face. It was clear she could see his internal struggle, even if she didn't understand exactly what it was. She circled him slowly.

'Whether or not I can loosen you up depends more on whether or not you want it. If you're fighting against me as I work, then no, I probably won't be able to,' she said in her calm, practical voice.

'And what then?' Cillian found himself asking, watching her carefully. 'What if I do fight you as you work?' He caught the flicker of interest in her eyes and it stirred something within him. Something that usually lay dormant, unanswered by the women he encountered day to day.

'Then I'll just have to push you harder, won't I?' she replied in a low, challenging tone. She raised one eyebrow defiantly. 'Come on then. You're on the clock and I have clients back-to-back all day.'

He followed her back into her room, watching her hips sway. Was she moving them a little more purposely than before? He bit the inside of his cheek. He really should be concentrating on work, not on exploring the boundaries of his new masseuse. But something about her intrigued him and he couldn't help but want to explore that intrigue further.

He closed the door behind him and watched as she began getting her oils ready.

'Strip off then,' she ordered. 'And lie face down on the bed.'

'You not gonna leave this time?' he asked, a note of amusement in his tone.

'Do you want me to?' she asked, looking round and meeting his stare. After a moment, she looked away with a smile. 'I won't look, don't worry.'

'Feel free,' he replied, pulling his shirt off. 'It's nothing you ain't going to see once I'm on the table anyway.'

'True,' she replied, turning back to face him.

He paused and they stared at each other for a few long moments, a strange battle of wills silently raging between them. Billie slowly bit her bottom lip and Cillian narrowed his gaze.

'What do you propose to do for a man who's so tense he has no chance of being able to relax?' he asked.

'What's making you so tense?' she asked, walking forward to stand directly in front of him.

'A highly stressful job,' he replied, not missing a beat.

'Manager on your case?' she quipped, subtle sarcasm in her tone.

'I don't do the kind of work that would apply to,' he replied, his dark gaze boring into hers.

'I know,' she replied, not fazed in the slightest. 'I know exactly what you do.'

'Oh, I don't think you do,' he replied.

'I do,' she responded firmly. 'And if your body is intent on fighting me…' she said, leaning forward and placing her hands on his shoulders. He closed his eyes momentarily as he felt her breath on his chest. 'Then I'm just going to have to fight it back.' She pushed a pressure point and Cillian let out a roar of surprise and pain.

On instinct, he grabbed her by the upper arms and marched them both forward a couple of paces, looking intensely into her face. As quick as lightning, Billie twisted out of his grip and pushed another pressure point in his neck, causing him to spin to the side and stand awkwardly in pain as she held it. Her smile grew and her eyes sparkled as he held her gaze, intense interest and pain burning in his own.

'That's what I would do, Mr Drew,' she whispered. 'But I think you already knew that. And I think you wanted me to do it.'

'I think you wanted to do it too,' he replied breathlessly as he struggled with her hold.

She released the pressure point and he straightened up, looking down at her in wonder. She couldn't be much more than five feet tall, her large blue eyes and sunshine-blonde hair making her look almost angelic to the normal eye. But not to him. He could see the viper that lay beneath the pretty façade, and that viper excited him. He knew he wasn't normal in his tastes, and finding women who held the same interests as him was difficult at the best of times. But here Billie was, right in front of him. She was exactly the sort of woman who could hold his attention.

'Exactly how much do you enjoy these sadistic moves of yours, Billie?' he asked in a low, dangerous voice.

'How much do you want to find out?' she asked, the challenge and her own excitement very clear.

Cillian reached forward and grabbed her once more, pulling her towards him. This time she didn't twist free and overpower him the way he knew she could. This time she moved with him, and when his mouth met hers, her lips were as hungry as his own. Bending down, he grabbed her thighs and pulled her up, wrapping them around his waist. Her fingers reached up and wound into his hair, pulling it hard, and he groaned, grabbing her buttocks in return with all his strength.

He was going to find some release from all the tension he felt today after all. But it was going to be in a very, very different way than he'd initially planned.

CHAPTER THIRTY-FOUR

Suddenly, as if it had crept up on her like a thief, Saturday night came around. Scarlet and Lily were in Lily's bedroom, changing into the black catsuits and accessories that would protect their identities in the hours ahead.

Scarlet took a deep breath and tried to find some calm. It had seemed achievable when they'd talked about it – planning all the ins and outs of the heist – but now it was here, she had to wonder, could they really pull it off? They weren't the kind of firm that took on jobs like these. They didn't conduct business from yachts in Monaco; they made deals from the shadowy alleys of the East End. They stole transported goods from the backs of trucks which the police forgot about once the trail ran dry. But the eyes of the world were searching for this painting. Eyes that hadn't given up in over thirty years. The pressure of this realisation bore down upon her and she closed her eyes as she exhaled a long, slow breath.

'Are you OK?' Lily's voice broke through her thoughts.

'Yeah, 'course,' Scarlet replied, trying to sound convincing.

Lily paused and studied her face critically. 'You need to be,' she said. 'This is it, Scarlet. You need to be fully focused tonight.'

'I am,' Scarlet confirmed with more conviction. She met her aunt's gaze. 'I'm focused.'

'Good.' Lily turned away to pull on her black leather gloves. 'Because this is the one, Scarlet. This is the job that's going to elevate us to a whole new level. Once we pull this off, doors will open in

ways we hadn't even thought possible before.' She glanced at her niece
with a smile. 'And you should feel proud about that. Because none
of this would have been possible if you hadn't seen that painting.'

'Yeah.' Scarlet swallowed the lump of unease that had gathered
in her throat. It was true – none of this would be happening if
she hadn't seen it that night. Which also meant it would be her
fault if it all went wrong. As the weight of responsibility settled on
her shoulders, she felt more out of her depth than ever. Sending
up a silent prayer, she looked to the heavens and hoped that she
hadn't made a terrible mistake.

*

The start of the evening went exactly as planned. Sandra attended the
dinner, paraded around and flirted in the way she was so skilled at
doing, and soon gained her invite back to the infamous after-party.
Standing there among the rich and the interesting, she threw her
head back and laughed heartily at the terrible joke that had just been
told. Out of the corner of her eye, she watched as Harry's gaze slid
down to her bronzed cleavage. Her white gauzy floor-length dress
clung to her perfect curves and didn't leave much to the imagination.
With her golden hair pinned up at the nape of her neck, she made
sure to draw his eyes to her bare skin as much as possible.

It hadn't taken long to gain his attention. He was as straight-
forward a target as Scarlet had promised. Getting here had been
easy. Seducing him would be too. Her years as a high-class escort
made this part of the job no more challenging than buttering
bread. It was later on in the evening that she felt tense about.

'Can I get you another drink?' Harry asked, wobbling slightly
as he sauntered over.

'Thank you,' she said enthusiastically. 'I'll have another spritzer.'

'A spritzer? What about something a little stronger, eh?' he
pushed. 'You're barely even tipsy. Come on, you have to try and
catch us up.'

Sandra smiled and leaned close to his ear. 'The thing is, Harry, too much alcohol makes me sleepy. And I really wouldn't want to be sleepy when you finally get around to showing me the master bedroom.' She let her fingers rest lightly on his chest for a few moments and felt his heart rate quicken in excitement. Then she turned and walked back to the group she'd been chatting to.

Another thirty minutes or so passed as she regaled the group with stories, maintaining the centre of attention and ensuring Harry couldn't yet pull her away. She had been avoiding getting to the point too early, as she didn't relish the thought of having to hide out for too long. After getting the video footage of Harry, there was nothing much she could do until the party was over. Eventually, though, she decided it was late enough and allowed someone else to hold court.

Stepping back, she sidled up to him and pretended to sip at her drink. In truth she was stone-cold sober and had been ditching the wine all night whenever he hadn't been looking.

'So, do you fancy that tour now?' Harry asked, leering down at her in his drunken state.

'Lead the way,' she whispered back conspiratorially.

They slipped off from the party, which she noted was luckily beginning to dwindle, and she followed him up the stairs towards the back. They passed several doors, then finally turned into a large bedroom.

'This is the master suite,' he said in what she assumed he meant to be a seductive tone.

'Oh, it's so grand,' she enthused, giggling.

'All the more so for having your gorgeous self in it,' he replied, coming to a stop in front of her and catching her gaze with his.

She noted the dilation in his pupils and the fever that took over his expression and prepared herself. He lunged forward and kissed her, sloppily and with groans of excitement.

'Oh, Harry,' she moaned as he moved his lips down her neck and pawed at her breasts. 'Oh, you're everything I'd anticipated.'

Spurred on by what he assumed was a compliment, his efforts increased and he pulled one of the straps of her dress down, frantically trying to free her breasts. She stepped back with a smile, gently prising his hands away with her own.

'Do something for me?' she asked.

'What?' he replied breathlessly.

'Go and have a shower, freshen yourself up.' She saw the doubt and annoyance cross his features and quickly pressed herself against him. 'I promise I'll make it worth your while,' she purred.

He instantly relaxed and grudgingly agreed to her request. 'Well, OK. But don't you go anywhere.'

'Of course not,' she replied. 'I'm going to get myself ready for you right here.' She sat down on the bed and stroked the covers.

Harry took one last lingering look at her and departed the room. 'I'll be five minutes,' he promised.

Sandra waited until the door closed and then jumped off the bed. She opened her handbag and pulled out the tiny camera Bill had given her – among other things – earlier that day.

Pressing the little switch on the back, she waited until the small red dot of light came on then looked around for somewhere to hide it. The camera was a top-of-the-range nanny cam. It was wireless, and once it was on, it could transmit live to a device up to half a mile away. They'd already paired it to a laptop Scarlet had in the van down the road. It would now record everything and they would have their video of Harry cheating on his wife.

There was a stack of books on the windowsill not too far from the bed and she positioned it against them discreetly.

Stepping back she looked into the camera with a nervous grin. 'OK,' she whispered. 'It's showtime.'

She turned back to the bed, took a deep breath in and pulled her dress up over her head, revealing the sexy white underwear she wore beneath. She felt immediately self-conscious but reminded herself that Scarlet and Lily were the only ones watching. Whilst the others were all in the van, Scarlet had assured her they would keep the screen out of everyone else's view.

After a few minutes, she heard Harry hurry down the hallway and he burst into the room with gusto, wearing nothing but a towel beneath his slightly podgy belly.

'Here I am,' he announced loudly.

'Here you are,' she agreed with a wry smile.

'Oh dear God, you really are stunning,' he said, running his eyes over her body in awe. 'I guess I really do still have it after all,' he then muttered, more to himself than her.

'You certainly do,' she replied with a smile.

He swaggered over and pulled away the towel. 'You mentioned you were going to make this shower worth my while. What exactly were you thinking?'

Sandra smiled and looked down at his – rather unimpressively sized – erect penis. He pushed his hips forward, displaying it proudly.

'Well.' She slipped off the bed and pulled him over to it, kissing him as she turned him round to the best position for the camera. She pushed him down into a seated position on the bed. 'Lay back on your elbows,' she instructed.

'OK,' he agreed in a husky voice. He did as he was bidden and waited.

Sandra leaned over him and kissed him deeply, then slipped her hand down though the sparse hair on his torso, over his pelvis and wrapped her fingers around his penis. As he whimpered with pleasure, she began rhythmically pulling his shaft back and forth, building his excitement up slowly. After a couple of minutes, she kissed his neck and trailed her tongue down his chest, licking and nipping at his belly and then finally, after a moment or two of teasing, she took him fully into her mouth.

He groaned loudly as she sucked hard, caressing his balls with one hand and holding the base of his shaft with the other. She moved backward and forward, until he was almost crying with excitement. After a couple of minutes, she pulled back. That should be more than enough to incriminate him on the tape, she decided.

'No, no, don't stop,' he pleaded. 'Please don't stop.'

'You want more?' she asked.

'Yes,' he begged, 'please.'

'I want to fuck you,' she said enticingly. 'Do you want to fuck me?' She bit her lip and ran her hand over her own body as he watched.

'Yes, yes, I do,' he replied urgently.

'Tell me though, Harry. How much do you *really* want me? Am I the only woman in the world to you right now?' she asked.

'Literally no other woman has ever or will ever exist to me,' he replied in a heartfelt strangled voice.

'Thank you,' she said. If what she had already done wasn't quite enough, hearing those words should seal the deal for his wife. 'I needed to hear that.' She pushed him back. 'Lie on your back up at the top of the bed,' she ordered. 'I want to show you a very special move.'

'What kind of move?' The interest in his eyes grew.

'A move I can promise no other woman has ever shown you before,' she teased in a low tone. 'Lie back with your hands behind your head and spread your legs as wide as you can.'

'Ooh, you are *saucy*,' he said in a low growl, licking his lips. He shuffled quickly up the bed, raised his arms and spread his legs wide, his manhood standing strong as his anticipation reached new heights.

Sandra smiled and retreated to the back of the room. 'This is my signature move. I call it the flying fuck.' She giggled and bit her lip. 'I'm a bit of a gymnast, you see. What I'm about to do is going to make you feel things you've never felt before.'

'Oh my God,' he breathed, quivering with suspense as his eyes widened. 'Do it.'

'OK.' Sandra pushed off her back foot and ran towards him, leaping up as she reached the bottom of the bed and thrusting herself forward towards his waiting body.

As she flew through the air, she pulled her knee up tight and fast, making sure it scored a perfect goal in between his splayed legs.

As the sickening sound of her knee connecting with the lower bones of his pelvis sounded, there was a momentary silence, then an almighty strangled scream escaped Harry's lips.

Sandra rolled to the side as he curled into the foetal position and screamed loudly again in pain. Hiding the smile of glee that threatened to take over, she plastered on a fake look of horror and bent over him, feigning concern.

'Oh, Harry, I'm so sorry! That has never happened before,' she said.

'Gah – my – argh!' He tried to speak but was in so much pain all he could manage were incoherent sounds of agony.

'What can I do? I'm so sorry. It must have been the drink – it threw me off,' she claimed.

'Gah!' he wailed, pushing her away. 'You fucking bitch!' he screamed through the tears of pain.

'What?' Sandra pretended to be surprised and offended. 'Why would you say that, Harry? It was an accident. I thought I was the only woman who existed for you?' She had to turn away for a moment to hide the smile that wouldn't be quashed at these words.

'Get – argh!' he cried pitifully as he cradled his privates. 'Just get out,' he finally managed.

Sandra stepped away, slipping back into her dress as swiftly as she could. Sniffing dramatically, she made a wide circle in order to snatch the camera off the side, then ran out of the door, as if she was too upset to say anything further.

She hurried down the hallway and checked over her shoulder to make sure she was alone, before lifting the camera to face her. 'And *that*,' she said quietly, 'is the flying fuck. The one I'll never really give.' She winked and slipped the camera into her handbag.

*

In the dark van just outside of the estate walls, Scarlet's face broke into a wide grin and she gently closed the laptop.

'That looked like it hit the spot,' Lily said.

'It certainly did,' Scarlet replied. She felt a calm wash over her that she hadn't felt since before Harry had tried to rape her. It didn't undo what he'd done, but knowing that she now had the ability to crush his marriage and get her revenge made her feel a lot better – like she had regained some of the power he had taken from her that night.

'Whatever she just did, and it sounded fucking awful,' Connor said, 'it was no less than he deserved. Scumbag. Now let's just hope she's as good at hiding. Because if she ain't, this all goes down the pan.'

'She will be,' Scarlet piped up with confidence. 'I know Sandra – she can do this.' But as the van fell silent once more she felt her confidence waiver.

Was Sandra up to this? She fervently hoped so. Because she couldn't come this far and return home empty-handed. She just couldn't. Her jaw locked hard at the thought. No. One way or another, they were stealing that painting tonight. Whatever she had to do to get it.

CHAPTER THIRTY-FIVE

Sandra peered through the slit between the door and its frame to the hallway beyond. She had pretended to leave earlier, had run to Harry's friend Duffy and feigned concern after their unfortunate incident in the bedroom. It had distracted those who were left enough for her to slip away without them noticing she'd never actually left. As Duffy had run upstairs and the rest of them began talking worriedly between themselves, she'd slipped into the morning room the other side of the hall.

The party had eventually moved back to the library and she'd crept out to slip the small device Bill had given her behind the security box on the wall near the front door. She followed his instructions to the letter, pulling out the yellow wire from the back and clipping it on, then tucking it out of sight. Later, after everyone had gone and Harry had set the code, all she had to do was pull it back out and press a button and it would take the system back offline without needing the code. All the cameras and alarms would be off, leaving the place open for Scarlet and everyone else to make their way in.

Harry eventually shuffled painfully down the stairs, aided by Duffy, swearing and complaining about the clumsy bitch who'd maimed him. She grinned widely in the darkness as he came into view. His face was puffy and red from crying, and he winced as he took each slow step.

'Good,' she muttered under her breath. 'I hope it bloody well falls off.' She wasn't a hateful person particularly. But when it came to men like him, she could barely stand to breathe the same air. Hopefully she'd inflicted some long-lasting damage, though even if she hadn't, he'd be suffering soon when Scarlet shared the video to his poor unsuspecting wife.

After he'd garnered all the sympathy he could from his adoring crowd of late-night drinking companions, Harry finally called an end to the evening and said his tired goodbyes to the last of them at the door. She was glad, already regretting her choice of hiding place. Wedged as she was between the back of the door and a tall wooden armoire, she was beginning to feel stiffly uncomfortable. Careful not to make a sound, she stepped out of her heels and allowed her feet to rest on the cold wooden floor.

She watched as Harry locked the door and set the alarms and cameras back up as they should be – and wondered if his wife ever noticed he regularly took them down. He lowered the flap to the security box, and she breathed a silent sigh of relief. Not long now until she could slip out there and undo his work.

He shuffled off, and she waited a couple of minutes before slipping back out. She crept around the door and straightened up, rolling her neck from side to side to alleviate the tension, then moved through the large hallway towards the security box.

As she rounded the bottom of the stairs, she glanced down the hall towards the back of the house and jumped nearly out of her skin. Harry stood barely a few feet away, staring down at something on his phone. She twisted around and ran back to her hiding place with a grimace. But as she rounded the door and ducked behind it, she knocked it, and it let out a loud, groaning creak as the old hinges were disturbed. She froze and her eyes widened.

'Hello?' Harry called out.

She pulled back as far as she could behind the door and leaned her head against the wall, silently pleading to the heavens for him to just go. Her prayers went unanswered though, and he began to awkwardly shuffle towards the room she hid in.

'Is anyone there?' Harry called again, doubt and worry in his tone.

He was nearer now, only just outside. After a second's pause, he continued, and Sandra held her breath. There was a small click and light flooded the dark room. Sandra's heart dropped to the bottom of her stomach. If he saw her here, he would eject her from the house instantly. Everyone had gone home and she was hardly in his good graces anymore. But she couldn't get thrown out – she just *couldn't*! She'd be letting everyone down. The whole operation would have failed, because of her. Without her on the inside, all was lost.

Her panic began to rise as he walked further into the room. If he turned around, if he moved even slightly to the left, he would see her. There was nowhere for her to go.

She squeezed her eyes shut. Was she going to be the reason the job failed? Why hadn't she picked a better hiding place? Why had she not gone upstairs and just watched them all leave from a window?

Harry took another step. He was listening hard, and Sandra kept a controlled hold on her shallow breathing. 'Grace?' he finally whispered tentatively, naked fear clear in his tone.

She figured that Grace must be his wife. He certainly should be afraid, if he suspected she might be home, after his antics earlier in the evening. But luckily for them both, Grace was not in the building tonight. It was just her.

'Haunted bloody pile of old stones,' he grumbled to himself, turning back around.

Sandra's hopes lifted. Was he leaving?

'I really do hate this place.'

The light turned off and she heard him walk back to the stairs and then mount them with a few sounds of unease as he went. She put her hands to her face and allowed the relief to spread throughout her body. She was still here. He hadn't found her.

She let a few minutes of complete silence pass this time before she ventured out, and when she did, she was careful to peer round each corner with caution. This time Harry was nowhere to be seen and she was able to get to the box without issue. Gently she prised the little device out from where she'd tucked it earlier and pressed the small button on the front, just as Bill had told her. She held her breath and stared at the small glowing green screen on the front of the box. After a few seconds, the message changed to show the system was offline and she silently rejoiced.

*

Scarlet and the others reached the top step and the front door opened. Sandra appeared, beckoning them inside. They filed in silently, trepidation settling into Scarlet's stomach as their plan began to roll into motion.

'Sandra, is Harry asleep?' she whispered as they all waited for her instruction.

'He's gone to bed,' she confirmed. 'He should pass out pretty fast – he's drunk a lot.'

Lily stepped forward. 'Show Chain and Damo to his room so they can stand guard. I'll come too so I know where to go,' she ordered, her tone brooking no argument. 'After that, go to the van and sit with George.'

Sandra nodded and led the way up the stairs – Lily, Chain and Damo following closely behind. As they departed, Scarlet turned to Cillian, Connor and Andy. She swallowed, trying to quell the turbulence she felt inside. Coming up with this idea and actually going through with it were two very different things. Now they were actually here, it all seemed so much crazier than it had before. Could they really pull this off? She tried to shake the question off. Of course they could. It was a simple in-and-out job. They just needed to be quick and quiet and they'd be out before any of them knew it.

'Come on then – let's go. Do you need a hand?'

'Nah, we've got it,' Cillian whispered back.

They were carrying a long, thin wooden box that Scarlet knew was heavier than it looked. It was padded and lined, a case to keep the painting in, until they sold it on. Andy stood behind them, carrying a small box of cleaning supplies by the handle, ready to rub down anything they touched. They were dressed from head to toe in black, ski masks over their heads and faces, and gloves on their hands. But Scarlet didn't want to take any chances. When they realised their painting was gone, they would spare no expense looking for the slightest trace of DNA, she was sure.

She led the way through the darkness towards the study. At first, the moonlight coming through the windows around the front door lit the way, but the deeper they entered the house, the darker it became. She had to pause and turn on a small torch to see where she was going. Eventually they arrived.

'Here,' she whispered, opening the door gently. They filed in and Scarlet went around to the other side of the desk. Pulling out the drawer that contained the switch, she searched with her fingers until she found it. As she flicked it and heard the panel move behind her, she grinned at the men who stood waiting.

Cillian nodded in admiration. 'That's a pucker set-up,' he said. 'Ain't it?' he asked, glancing at Connor.

'It's impressive,' his brother agreed.

Scarlet ran her gloved fingers over the simple keypad. She'd memorised the numbers easily. It was only a four-digit code, and Harry had been so drunk he'd been unable to hide it from her eyes.

'Seven, three, two, two…' she mumbled as she pressed the buttons. 'And bingo!'

She widened her smile in excited anticipation, but instead of the green light and the panel wall moving, she was met with a red light and stark stillness. She blinked and frowned. Perhaps she'd hit another button by mistake. She tried it again, slower this time. But as she hit the last digit, the red light blinked once more.

Could she have got it wrong? But no, she'd watched so carefully. She was sure that was the exact code he'd entered. Which meant only one thing.

'What's happening?' Connor asked.

Scarlet turned to him, horror slowly creeping over her expression. 'They've changed the code,' she whispered. 'We can't get in.'

CHAPTER THIRTY-SIX

Lily's hands were pressed flat together and against her mouth in her familiar prayer-like manner as she paced the study back and forth. Cillian, Connor and Andy stood silently around the edges of the room, tensely watching her. Scarlet sat in the chair behind the desk, bent forward over her legs, her hands held to her head in despair as she tried to wrap her mind around this catastrophe.

Lily exhaled a long, slow breath as she cycled through their limited options one last time. It really only boiled down to two choices. Either they walked away and gave up on the plan entirely, or they woke Harry and forced the code out of him. This would take things to a whole new level, a level they hadn't planned to reach; one that made everything much less predictable and a lot more dangerous. But Lily was not one to walk away from a plan. Not when they had this much to gain.

'Here's what I propose,' she said. 'We get Chain and Damo to wake him and shake him down for the code. They might have to beat him around a little, but hopefully that, coupled with the fact they got all the way into his house and to his bed whilst he slept, will be enough to scare him into handing it over.'

'It should be us,' Cillian interjected. 'Our skills are more precise.'

'Your skills *are* more precise, yes,' Lily agreed, cutting him off. 'But don't forget the reason we brought Chain and Damo along in the first place.' Her gaze met his. 'They're our decoys.

They don't look or sound anything like you, so when he gives a description tomorrow, no one will think to look at you down the line when we're in possession of the hottest painting this side of the millennium.'

'I still think we're more likely—' Connor started.

'Lil's right,' Scarlet said, cutting him off. 'You know she is.' She shrugged and sidled up to her aunt. 'If we can avoid him seeing any of us, even masked up, we need to. Come on – let's get on with it. We don't know how long he's going to take to break. He might only be a soft toffee but that's a hundred-million-pound painting.' She breathed in and exhaled heavily. 'Even the weakest of men would fight to guard that one. We might be in for a long night.'

*

Nearly two hours later, Scarlet paced the hallway outside Harry's bedroom. Lily sat on a chair by the door, Andy sat on the top stair further down the hall, out of the way, and the twins loitered against the walls. They all stayed silent, listening to the sounds coming from within.

Low threats and raised voices alternated around the dull thuds of the thumps and kicks that were being doled out to Harry as he cried pitifully and begged them to leave. He offered them money, other pieces of art, anything else he could think of – anything except the one thing they were after. This, as Scarlet had predicted, he was protecting with every ounce of strength he had. And they had to give it to him – he had held his ground for a lot longer than they'd thought he would. Chain and Damo were terrifying people, and they were giving it their all, but it seemed this still wasn't enough. He would still rather take the beating of his life than hand over that painting.

Cillian sighed and pushed away from the wall, walking over to his mother. 'This isn't working,' he said, his voice quiet but his tone firm. 'You need to let me in there.' He held her stare with a hard look, silently battling her will with his own. After a few moments, she looked away and twisted her lips to the side. He pushed, seeing her resolve waver. 'If he hasn't broken under them by now, he ain't going to. They're hard but they're blunt and they've got one speed. You *know* I can get it out of him.'

Lily exhaled slowly and Cillian waited, knowing there wasn't another solution. Eventually she gave him a short, sharp nod. 'But you go alone,' she added in a warning tone. 'Just you.'

Connor let out a small growl of annoyance and folded his arms across his chest, but he didn't voice his irritation. They all knew it would be pointless. Lily's word was final on things like this. Cillian nodded and silently opened the door to the bedroom, slipping in and closing it behind him.

Inside the room, Chain and Damo circled the man who lay in a battered heap on the floor. They paused in their attack as Cillian entered.

'I'll take over,' Cillian said simply, stepping to the side to allow them a pathway to the door.

Chain kissed his teeth and gave Harry's thigh one more vicious kick before walking out, Damo following close behind.

Harry's breath was laboured as he dealt with the pain the other men's kicking had inflicted. Cillian put his hands in his pockets and made a slow semi-circle around Harry, studying the man. He was curled up at the foot of the bed, his wrists bound around the bedpost with a cable tie. Blood from his swollen nose poured down his face, and bright purple bruises were already coming up around his puffy eyes. Cillian couldn't see what damage had been done to the rest of his body, but he suspected it looked much like his face. Harry stared up at him, frightened.

'They certainly did a number on you, didn't they?' he asked calmly.

'P-Please,' Harry snivelled, 'I can't give you that code. I don't know it. Only my wife knows and she's not here.'

'That's a lie, Harry,' Cillian countered darkly. 'You *do* know and you *will* be telling me what it is, a lot sooner than you think.'

CHAPTER THIRTY-SEVEN

Harry shook his head, fresh tears falling from his eyes as he squeezed them shut in despair. 'You don't understand,' he whimpered. 'That painting isn't mine to give. I can give you anything else but that. You want money? Take it,' he pleaded. 'However much you want, name your price and I'll give it to you.'

'I highly doubt you'd have the sort of money that painting is worth, Harry,' Cillian replied, looking around the room. He walked over to the dressing table and began searching through its small drawers. 'People like you tend to be asset rich and cash poor. Though,' he added, 'your version of cash poor is probably still pretty rich. But not a hundred-mill rich.'

'But you'd have to sell it on through the black market,' Harry argued. 'Think of the risk, the stress, the, the…' He floundered as he tried to bulk out his argument. 'You wouldn't even get close to full value. I might not be able to offer that sort of cash but what I could give you would be hassle free. A-A-And you could take any of my other paintings,' he added, trying with all his might to direct Cillian onto another path. 'I have several that are worth a lot but would sell in a much smoother fashion. I-I could even sign them over into your possession. They'd be legal. Think about it – please,' he begged.

Cillian paused in his search and picked up a small thin metal nail file. He closed the drawer and turned back to Harry.

'I ain't interested in any other paintings. Or a smooth ride,' he added. 'You see, I like a bit of adventure. I like diving into the unknown. Gives me a bit of a thrill, you know? Some people like skydiving, some like race cars; I'm into this.' He shrugged. 'It's that diversity that makes the world go round, I guess. Life would be boring if we were all the same.'

Harry bowed his head and began to sob anew. Cillian slipped past him and sat down on the edge of the four-poster bed near his bound hands.

'So let's get to what I'm here for, Harry. 'Cause I'm sure you don't want to continue down this path any longer than you have to. What's the code?'

'I can't give it to you,' he sobbed.

'Yes, you can,' Cillian replied. 'I know you have it. And I'm not leaving here until I have it. So how hard you make that on yourself is down to you.' He twiddled the nail file in between his gloved fingers.

Harry groaned between his sobs. 'I can't give it to you,' he said tiredly. 'You can kick and punch me all you like, but I still can't give you that code.'

Cillian nodded in the dim light of the room. 'I guess we're going for the hard way.' He grabbed one of Harry's bound hands and pulled his fingers out straight.

Harry immediately let out a cry of fear and surprise. 'What are you doing?' he screamed. 'Wait, what are you doing?'

'I'm getting that code,' Cillian answered calmly. 'The sooner you tell me, the sooner this stops.' Holding the nail file steady, he forced the sharp end in slowly underneath the first of Harry's nails.

As the metal broke through the skin and deep into the nail bed, Harry let out a blood-curdling scream. He bucked and writhed as true agony set in, trying and failing to pull his hands back through the tightly bound cable ties. His screams intensified and reached fever pitch as Cillian pushed right to the end and prised it off completely. Dropping the bloody nail to the floor, he pulled the file away and waited as Harry's screams began to slow, and deep heavy sobs took their place.

It was all very well taking a beating, bracing your body as hard punches and sharp kicks inflicted dull wounds, but it was another thing entirely to stay strong through this sort of precise torture. It was the sort of pain that the mind could not detach itself from. Which was why it was so effective.

'I don't need to punch and kick you, Harry. What would be the point in tiring myself out that way? Clearly, you've got the ability to handle it. I have to say, you surprised me with that,' he admitted. 'I didn't have you down as quite so strong a character.'

'I can't give you the code,' Harry cried pitifully, a long spool of dribble falling from his open mouth, mixing with the blood and tears that had smeared all down his face. 'You don't understand. She'll kill me.'

'No, *I'll* kill you, Harry,' Cillian replied. 'Your wife? She'll be furious, I'm sure. She'll probably divorce you too, especially after watching the tape your little lady friend made for us earlier.' He watched as Harry's face visibly paled even under all the swelling and bruises. 'But as for who'll kill you, it's me you need to be afraid of.' He twiddled the nail file. 'You see, I don't stop until I get what I want. So I will take each nail off one by one.' Harry whimpered. 'Then if we haven't got anywhere, I'll make a start on your teeth with the pliers. Then your ears, then your fingers and toes, and if we *still* ain't getting anywhere, I'll have no further use for you.' Cillian glared at him hard through the eye slits in his ski mask. 'So you'll be nothing more to me than evidence to destroy.'

'Wh-Wh—' Harry tried to speak but collapsed into another bout of tears, making a high-pitched keening sound as he rocked back and forth, shaking. 'I can't,' he managed eventually.

Cillian grabbed his hand once more and isolated the next finger.

'No! No!' he screamed with terror and pulled back and forth hard, trying desperately to get free, despite knowing that he couldn't. The heavy, solid-wood bed frame barely even moved as he struggled against it like a half-crazed wildcat.

'Last chance,' Cillian said, pressing the nail file into the skin. When Harry didn't reply, he pushed forward mercilessly, piercing through the skin under the nail bed once more.

Harry's screams curdled in the air and as Cillian reached halfway, his choking voice broke through. 'I'll tell you – stop, stop!'

Cillian paused and waited for the screams to dull into pants.

'Take it out please,' Harry begged. 'I'll tell you.'

'Tell me first, then I'll take out the file.' Cillian put some pressure on and Harry screamed once more.

'OK, OK, it's twelve eighty-seven,' he cried, the agony clear in his words.

Cillian pulled the file back out, and Harry's body slumped in pained defeat as he sobbed even heavier than before.

'There it is,' Cillian said, wiping the bloody file on the bedsheet next to him. 'You did well, you know. Don't beat yourself up about it.' He glanced over at the wreck of a man on the floor.

'It doesn't matter,' Harry mumbled through his sobs. 'None of it matters now. She's going to kill me.'

'Probably,' Cillian replied.

He stared down at Harry. He so dearly wanted to tell him the reason why he'd suffered so much tonight. To make it clear that touching Scarlet the way he had came with retribution and that this was it. But to do that would shed light on who they were. So he was just going to have to take this punishment without ever knowing exactly why it had happened.

'I'm sure once you show her your injuries, she'll feel sorry for you. After all, she can't blame you for being robbed, eh?' He stood up and placed the still slightly bloody nail file neatly on the dressing table.

'No, she won't,' Harry wailed. 'You don't understand.'

'Probably not,' Cillian agreed, bored of the other man's woes already. He walked over to the door, opened it and gave his mother the code. He closed it again and returned to Harry. 'That better be the right code,' he warned. 'Because they're off to try it now, and if you're mucking me about, it ain't going to go well for you.'

'I'm not mucking anyone about. It's the right code,' Harry spat resentfully. 'How did you know the painting was there anyway?' he asked, curiosity starting to bring colour back to his voice. 'Nobody knows it's there – no one who would steal it anyway.'

'No one who'd steal it? I think you'd be surprised at how many people would turn to theft at the thought a hundred million pounds that you can't even report to the police as missing,' Cillian replied.

Harry shook his head resolutely. 'You clearly don't know my wife.'

'Or perhaps I just don't care about being snubbed out of polite society by her, eh?' Cillian countered. No, none of their friends would dare to steal the painting. It would ruin their precious reputations. All these rich people cared about was staying in the right cliques. Keeping their wealth within the right circles and keeping the societal hierarchy in place. God forbid they ever did something so scandalous that they were denied an invite to the next boring fundraiser one of them threw to look charitable to the masses.

Harry just closed his eyes. 'Can you undo these ties please?' he asked.

'No,' Cillian answered, looking down on him in contempt. 'I need confirmation that we're in first. And then I think we'll leave you there for your wife to rescue when she gets home tomorrow. We don't want you calling anyone when we're travelling with that painting now, do we?' The door opened and Connor appeared. Cillian turned towards him. 'Well?' he asked.

'We're in.' He glanced at Harry and then retreated again without a word.

'All's well that ends well, eh, Harry?' He swept his gaze over the room once more to check he hadn't left anything behind that he shouldn't have, then he made his way towards the door to follow his brother and help with the painting. 'Good luck with the wife,' he called over his shoulder as he let the door swing shut behind him.

*

Harry stared at the closed door through the one eye that hadn't yet swollen shut. Every part of his body, every bone, every muscle screamed in agony after the hours of brutality he'd endured, but none of it came close to the overwhelming fear he felt coursing through his veins now that he'd given over the code.

Grace was going to kill him. That painting was everything she had saved for their future. And now it was gone. Whilst he had been here with the security off and no one around to help safeguard it. It wouldn't matter that he'd put up a fight – not to her. This was his fault. And she was going to make him pay. He shivered, despite the warmth in the room. He was royally screwed.

But at least he would be able to give her something, one small offering of information that might save him from the highest levels of her wrath. The men who'd been in here before, they were just lackeys, that was clear. It was the second man, the quieter one who'd taken his nail who was the real business. And the man who'd come in just now, he had the same eyes. *Exactly* the same eyes. It had only taken a second, but he'd seen it. It was like looking at the first one's double. They were brothers – he was sure of it. He'd even go so far as to guess they might be twins.

Same build, same arch between the same dark brown eyes, the same strong top of the nose. They even had the same deep voice, the same East End accent. It was little enough, but it was something. Which meant Grace would have something to go on.

And when Grace had something to grab on to, she didn't let go until she had exactly what she wanted.

He closed his eyes and prayed for a miracle. He really was screwed now, whatever way he looked at it. And these people had no idea what they had just let themselves in for.

CHAPTER THIRTY-EIGHT

Lily carried a tray of Buck's Fizz through to the study from the kitchen, where Scarlet, Cillian and Connor all sat waiting. It was early still, only just turned eight thirty in the morning, but none of them had yet been to bed. After extracting the code from Harry in the early hours, they'd dropped everyone else off home, then hidden the painting securely in one of their off-the-record storage barns. Finally, they'd reached home just as the sun rose, and after a shower and a quick incineration of their heist outfits, they were now all winding down from the night's escapades.

'OK, grab a glass,' Lily said with a smile. 'I think we've all bloody earned it. Come on.' She handed one to Connor, who was rubbing his eyes tiredly. 'Let's make a toast.' She raised her glass. 'Last night held a few challenges we hadn't expected, but we got through it. Not through luck, but because we're a bunch of determined bastards with good heads on our shoulders and balls of steel.' She grinned at them all as they laughed. 'I'm proud of you all, you know.'

'How many of them you had?' Connor asked.

'None, you cheeky sod,' she replied. 'I know I don't say it often.' She pursed her lips for a moment. Letting her feelings out was not a natural action for Lily, but they'd earned some praise so she was going to give it. 'But last night we upped our game. And we pulled it off.' She turned her gaze on each of them in turn, resting on Scarlet last. The girl had done well. 'Your dad would have been proud of you, Scar,' she said.

'Thanks, Lil,' Scarlet replied.

'And, boys, I'm bloody proud of you too,' she continued.

'Oh, come off it,' Cillian said, swiping the air as if to push the compliment away. 'You'll give Connor a big head if you keep going.'

'Oi!' Connor punched him on the arm playfully. 'You're the one with the big head.'

'Well, I am. You're fine young men with impressive skills. I guess most mothers would probably see those skills as a bad thing,' she added with a grudging tilt of the head. 'But not me. You're good boys at heart. I know, because I raised you that way.' Lily felt her heart swell as she thought back over the years to all the times her boys had shown who they were. 'But Lord help the fuckers that ever try to mess us about, because you know *exactly* how to handle yourselves and protect your own.'

She held her head higher with pride and raised her glass. 'Here's to you. To all of you. May your families grow with love and your enemies fall behind you like broken blades of grass as you walk through the field of life. To our family. To the Drews.'

'To the family,' they repeated. They all raised their glasses and drank.

'And,' Lily added after a few moments, 'to the smooth sale of this painting. Much as last night was impressive, we still have a way to go.'

Her reminder dulled the light-heartedness of the moment somewhat as they each nodded in agreement.

'What's happening with that side of things?' Connor asked with a frown. 'Have you met that contact yet?'

'Tuesday,' Lily replied. 'Scarlet and I will be meeting him then to hopefully start arranging the sale – or at least to set things in motion.'

'Do you think it's safe to leave it out there for so long?' Cillian asked. He'd been unsure about leaving it where they had.

'It's as secure and as hidden away as we can possibly make it,' Lily replied.

Cillian had wanted to take it to the factory, to hide it in the basement, but she'd decided against it. As successful and as careful as they'd been, there was still a chance of reprisals. Harry couldn't call the police, no, but what about a private investigator? He and his wife certainly had money, and they weren't just going to shrug this off. And if their PI found any evidence that they'd missed, they could be discovered. If that happened, Lily didn't want the painting sitting somewhere obvious.

The barn might be remote, but it was sturdy, and they had strong locks on it. They had hidden the painting in a concealed basement with old bales of hay on top of it. The chances of anyone stumbling across the barn were minimal, let alone getting in and then finding that. And best of all, should anyone come sniffing around the family, there was absolutely no paper trail between them and the barn at all.

'It's two days,' she continued. 'And then we'll at least know where we stand with it, what we're planning to do with it. Just hang tight. As long as we stay vigilant, this will all be over before we know it.'

'And then what?' Scarlet piped up.

Lily sat down in the seat beside her. 'What do you mean?' she asked.

'When this is over, we're going to have more money than we've ever handled before. Illegal money. How the devil are we going to launder it all? We had problems before, but no amount of new salons are going to solve this one.'

Lily rubbed her forehead. Scarlet was right, and it was something she'd been thinking about since they'd first put the plan into action. 'We're going to need to look into opening some offshore accounts for this sort of money,' she said slowly.

'But we don't know anything about offshore accounts,' Scarlet replied, picking up on the issue, sharp as ever.

'No, we don't,' Lily agreed. 'Which is why I'll be asking this contact on Tuesday if he can also connect us to a higher-level accountant who deals with this sort of thing. He'll have one for sure, someone who already deals with his side of the transactions. We'll have to see if we can start something with him ourselves and learn what we need to know about handling this kind of cash.'

'More risk,' Cillian said, niggling the toothpick in between his teeth with his tongue. 'This is a lot of people we have no experience of.' He locked his jaw tightly. 'What's to say we aren't going to be done over.'

'I'm to say we aren't,' Lily replied in a hard tone. 'This is new ground, yes. But we weren't born yesterday. We know how people work; we know what to watch out for. We'll be fine. We'll make our way in this new world the same way Ronan and I made our way into this one. We just need to stay vigilant.'

They all paused as Ruby descended the stairs and into the room, tucking her blouse into her green cigarette trousers. Her sharp gaze flicked between them all and she pursed her lips.

'Out late again then,' she said in an accusing tone.

'Actually only just got back,' Cillian replied jovially.

'How nice for you all,' she responded sarcastically.

'Morning, Ruby. You look nice,' Lily said, taking in her outfit.

'You're up early for a Sunday,' Scarlet remarked. 'You going somewhere?'

Ruby paused and shook her head in disbelief, narrowing her eyes at her cousin. 'Salon Red opens Sundays, *remember*?' she said scathingly. 'And seeing as this is the first weekend and neither you nor that tart you hired as an assistant manager is around, I'm the only one in there other than Nat. So yes, I am going somewhere. I'm off to keep the *family salon* running.'

Scarlet's gaze tightened. 'I'm well aware of when *my salon* is open, thanks. And that's great that you're putting some of your hours in today. I'll mark it on your payroll sheet,' she said coolly.

Ruby's cheeks flared red. Lily watched the pair of them with a grim expression as their subtle battle tinged the air with tension.

'Thank you, Ruby,' she said, trying to break some of that tension. 'Though do you have to go? Are there actually any bookings today? It's just that it's Sunday, so the family get-together will be in a few hours, and—'

'And what?' Ruby asked sharply, cutting her off. 'That's nothing to do with me. I haven't been to one of your get-togethers for years – why would I start now?' She raised an eyebrow at her mother, then grabbed her bag off the side and walked out through the front door, slamming it behind her.

Lily swallowed the lump of disappointment that rose in her throat. It didn't matter how many years it had been, Ruby's rebuttals still hurt every time. What would it take for Ruby to truly come back into the family fold? Would she ever fit in to her own family? Or was that just a pie-in-the-sky wish that could never come true?

She took a deep breath and turned back to the room. 'So – the painting. We still have a long way to go, and as Cillian pointed out, we've got some new people to feel out before we can actually do business with them. So stay alert. Listen to your hunches.' She eyed them all hard. 'And bring your best game, every step of the way. Because this deal is either going to make us or break us. And if it breaks us, we won't just be scraping our knees and getting back up again.' She exhaled heavily. 'If this goes south, we're going to be staying at Her Majesty's Pleasure for a very long time.'

CHAPTER THIRTY-NINE

Ruby paced up and down outside the closed shutters of Salon Red and huffed for the hundredth time. Natalie was late once again. Not ideal for Ruby, who was half an hour early after storming out of the house the way she had.

She'd been late the day before too, though she'd been grudgingly tolerant towards Ruby for a change, not having Sandy there to run all the errands she needed. Today though, Ruby imagined the other girl would go back to being her rude bolshy self, as Sandy was due to come back in and she was no longer really needed – despite what she'd said to Scarlet.

But that was OK. Ruby wasn't bothered by being treated that way. She was used to getting other people's backs up. It was par for the course in her life. What *did* bother her though was having to wait on the pavement when she could be inside. Being out in the open like this made her feel uneasy. She still owed a lot of people a lot of money. The chances of those people being around here were slim, but the longer she lingered on the street, the greater the chance someone would spot her.

Eventually, Natalie bumbled down the street, her arms full of bags. She grappled around in her handbag trying to find the keys.

'Finally,' Ruby complained as she reached the front of the salon. She rolled her eyes.

'Oh, do one, Ruby,' Natalie said, scowling. 'I had to run some errands on me way over.'

'Then why don't you call one of us to open up if you know you're going to be late?' Ruby asked irritably. 'Saves us standing here on the street like gormless idiots at least.'

'I only see one gormless idiot,' Natalie retorted as she turned the key in the lock. 'And anyway, you don't have a key.'

'Then give me one,' Ruby replied.

'Not bloody likely,' Natalie scoffed, rolling up the shutter. 'You've still got to prove you can be trusted, from what I hear.' She opened the door and stepped inside, holding her nose up in the air.

Ruby glared at her, biting back a retort. Who did she think she was? Couldn't be trusted with a key indeed! She shook her head. At least *she* was actually here on time. She walked in and hung her bag and jacket on the coat stand beside the reception area with a sigh.

She had to admit, although the idea of working for a living still didn't thrill her, she did like having somewhere to escape to. Hanging around her mother's house was driving her insane. Even though she'd lived there before and had her own room, it wasn't her space. Nothing felt like hers, she couldn't properly relax and whenever she tried to find some peace, Lily would pop up and want to talk or suggest some activity, and it was wearing hard on her sanity. At least here she could escape and the work kept her fairly distracted from the overwhelming sense of despair and grief she felt at losing her access to heroin.

That was something. And after her conversation with Cillian, she'd decided that whilst she was stuck in this hell-like existence, she might as well focus on trying to outshine her cousin. It wouldn't be hard. Scarlet might have been working for the family for longer, but she was juggling too many balls. She couldn't keep her eye on this one long enough to make a difference. So Ruby would be the one to do that. Slowly, she would prove herself invaluable here and take it from under Scarlet's nose. Then she would do it again and again right across the business, winning battle by battle until without Scarlet even realising what she was doing, she'd won the war.

It was these thoughts that kept her going. That helped her drag her empty soul out of bed every day and forced her to keep coming back.

Pulling the booking diary towards her, she ran her finger down today's date and noted the appointments. Despite the fact they hadn't advertised, they were already getting calls and walk-in bookings. They weren't exactly busy yet, but they were as busy as they could be with only one stylist working. Two more girls were set to start later next week too, and she'd already begun filling their slots.

The door opened and Sandy walked in with a bright smile and a coffee in her hand. 'Hi, girls,' she said cheerily. Ruby frowned and looked back down at the book.

'Hey, Sandy, did you get my text that I'd be late?' Natalie called from the back.

'Yeah, thanks for the heads-up,' Sandy replied, taking off her jacket and fluffing out her hair.

Ruby swallowed down the shot of resentment that jumped up into her throat. So Natalie had texted Sandy to make sure she wouldn't be standing on the pavement, yet hadn't bothered to text her too. She felt her cheeks burn with anger, but continued studying the page as if nothing was untoward. She didn't want to give Natalie the satisfaction of seeing her react. Natalie had been a cow to her from the off, but this was shitty even for her.

She flipped the page back to the day before and her gaze paused on one of the bookings. It had been crossed out and the word *Cancelled* was written next to it. But it hadn't been cancelled. Ruby had been the one to book it in. She'd greeted the client when she'd arrived and had even made her a hot sweet tea to drink whilst she was waiting for her colour to develop. She frowned.

'Nat?' she called out.

'What?' came the short response.

'Why is Mrs Wilks's appointment struck through and marked as cancelled? She didn't cancel – she had a full colour, cut and blow-dry.'

There was a short silence and Natalie returned to the main salon space, tying her dying apron around her waist. 'Mind your own business,' she tutted.

'I *am* minding my own business,' Ruby responded sharply. She looked up at Natalie with a hard glare. 'This is *my* family business and I'm here to work, just like you. So I'll ask you again: why does it say cancelled?'

'Christ, don't get your knickers in such a twist,' Natalie responded, holding her hands up in surrender. 'It's nothing you need to worry about,' she added. 'It's all just to do with how I'm fiddling the books, alright? Just leave that to me. That's my job.' She flapped her hand dismissively. 'Anyway, can you please get the antibacterial wipes and go over the chairs with them before my first lady? That one last night was coughing and sneezing all over the show.'

'Sure,' Ruby said quietly as Natalie disappeared again. Her eyes narrowed. That cancellation was nothing to do with the laundry. To launder money through the books they needed to add clients, not take them away. So what on earth was Natalie really up to? And why was she lying?

CHAPTER FORTY

'… And I'll go for a nice thick cut of that salt beef too, Mrs Franks,' Lily said, peering through the Perspex counter at the fresh produce beneath.

'How much do you want, Ms Drew?' Mrs Franks asked, pulling up the large slab of meat and placing it on the chopping board. She measured up to a certain point with her knife and paused. 'Will this do?'

'That's perfect, thank you,' Lily replied with a smile.

'I'll throw some of my kosher pickles in with them too,' Mrs Franks said as she wrapped the salt beef in paper. 'I know how much your boys like them.'

'Oh, they'll love that, thank you.' Lily waited patiently as her goods were packed, then paid her bill and walked out with the full paper bag under one arm.

She'd been going to the Franks' deli for years, a small family-run shop that made the best salt beef in London. She hadn't had time to run over for a few weeks, but she'd decided to take a break Monday lunchtime and treat herself and the rest of the family. She'd make up salt beef sandwiches later and drop them off round each of their houses. Perhaps she'd stay at Scarlet and Cath's for a while for a glass of wine and a natter. It was becoming more and more clear these days how lonely Cath was. And Cath didn't deal with loneliness well.

Loneliness was never something that had bothered Lily. She'd always been so fiercely independent and kept herself so busy that what little time she ended up having to herself was always a welcome respite from the constant stresses of life. But she understood that most people were not built like her.

She crossed the street and glanced over her shoulder down the road, which was buzzing with lunchtime activity. As someone in the distance caught her eye, she paused, squinting to get a better look. The person she'd clocked melted back into the shadows – just out of sight – and she pursed her lips. She knew she hadn't been imagining it. She was being followed. And she'd bet her last penny that it was the same guys as before.

Taking a deep breath, she repositioned the groceries more tightly under her arm and pulled her handbag to where she could easily reach in. She debated pulling her knife out but decided against it. Whoever they were, they were following at a distance, and in the bright daylight, with people all around, she doubted they'd get much closer. Her Mercedes was only a few cars down on the main street, so she'd be in it and away before they had a chance to get too close.

She continued towards her car, speeding up as fast as her heels would allow. When she drew near, she searched her bag for the keys, but as she did, someone grabbed her from behind, pinning both her arms and propelling her forward. Before she could even turn her head to see who it was or open her mouth to utter a word, a car door opened right beside her and she was manoeuvred into the back.

As the door slammed and she righted herself, her hand shot straight into her handbag without a moment's pause. Quick as lightning, she pulled out her blade, twisting to jam it up against the neck of whoever was next to her in the car as it pulled off down the road.

Ray pulled back and held his hands up in surrender, his gaze holding hers with caution as the blade bit into the skin of his neck.

'Jesus Christ, Ray,' Lily cried in equal amounts of anger and relief. She lowered the knife. 'What the hell do you think you're doing? You nearly gave me a heart attack. I nearly cut your bleedin' throat, for fuck's sake.'

'I think you actually did a bit,' he replied in surprise as he touched the small nick that she'd inflicted.

Lily looked over to assess the damage. 'Good,' she said, after ascertaining that it wasn't anything serious. 'You deserve it.' She slipped the blade back into her bag.

Ray chuckled and pulled a handkerchief out of his pocket, holding it to his neck to soak up the small droplets of blood before they soiled his white shirt. 'That's probably true.'

Lily crossed her arms. 'This isn't OK, Ray,' she said, looking out of the window. 'You can't just take me off the street like this.'

'What else am I supposed to do, Lil?' he asked, a note of helplessness in his deep craggy voice. 'You ain't answering my calls or texts; you murder my roses and dump them on my drive – or rather, you get poor Cath to do that,' he added. 'You're avoiding places I go…'

'And there's a *reason* for that.' She turned and gave him a hard stare, trying desperately to ignore the turmoil being near him made her feel.

She loved him dearly. She loved him in a way she had never loved and never would love another man. But he'd crossed a line. He'd messed with her family in a way that was inexcusable. And her family was the one thing she loved in this world more than him.

'Come on, Lil,' Ray begged. 'Don't shut me out like this. I know you're angry and I get it – I overstepped. Would I do it again? Yeah, I would,' he said honestly. 'I'm not gonna lie to you, Lil. I'd do it ten times over if it meant cleaning her up for you and getting her home where she belongs. She don't have to like me for it, so long as she don't hate you. I did it so I could take that rap. And you can scream at me for how I went about it, Lily Drew. You can shout and scream and hold as many knives to my neck as you want. But *please* don't shut me out like this. Not me, Lil.' His deep blue eyes bored into hers, beseeching her.

Lily felt the overwhelming pull that she always did when she was in close proximity to Ray as he opened his soul to her – and looked away stubbornly. She heard him sigh and bit the inside of her cheek to stop herself from replying. What could she even say? She'd said everything she wanted to already. And although every part of her body ached to just turn to him and forget it all, she couldn't. It wasn't that simple. He couldn't just snatch her up and force her to talk to him before she was ready. If she ever would be ready. Many people might just let it go, but this kind of intrusion burned too deeply for her.

With a hint of hope in his tone at her silence, Ray moved on to another subject. 'I hear you made a visit to Wiley last week. What you running that you need his services for?' he asked.

'Frank?' Lily leaned across to address the driver. 'Can you please pull over?'

Frank's gaze darted from hers to Ray's in the rear-view mirror, his question clear. She turned to Ray and raised her eyebrows defiantly.

'Are you kidnapping me too, or am I free to go?' she asked bluntly.

Ray sighed and nodded his agreement to Frank, who pulled the car over to the side of the road. As it came to a stop, Lily opened the door and stepped out onto the pavement. She paused and looked back in towards Ray.

'It don't concern you, what I'm running with Sam,' she said. 'That's *family business*.' She took one last look into his pained expression and slammed the door.

CHAPTER FORTY-ONE

'You're telling me that this happened Saturday?' The cultured tone sounded calm enough to any normal ear, but the three men standing in the room before the tall, elegant woman winced at her words. 'And you then waited until *today*, two days *after* the event, to inform me?'

'Technically it was the middle of the night, s-so only really yesterday morning, sweetheart,' Harry stuttered in a placating tone. 'Not exactly *two days*, and I knew you were getting back today. I didn't want to worry you when you were so far away and couldn't be here to do anything.'

'I may have been out of the country,' she shouted sharply, cutting him off, 'but I could have put the wheels in motion to get the painting *back*.' She glared at Harry through icy pale blue eyes as he cowered before her. She rolled her neck and looked up to the heavens before turning to pace the large magnolia lounge at the back of the house. 'If you'd rung me immediately, I could have had them followed,' she continued in a dangerously low voice. 'If I'd managed to get them followed, we could have already had it back safely by now.'

'I was tied up,' Harry said helplessly. 'I couldn't even get to a phone until nearly lunchtime yesterday when Mrs Parker finally found me. They cable-tied me to the bed frame, Grace,' he stressed. 'There was nothing I could have done.'

Grace frowned and her eyes narrowed. 'And where was Mrs Parker when all of this was happening? Surely it woke up the whole house?'

Harry glanced at Duffy, who stood to the other side of Grace, looking down at the carpet. 'No one was here at that time but myself.'

'What do you mean?' Grace glanced over to Duffy and then back to Harry. 'Where were the staff? There are three other people who live here, Harry. Are you seriously telling me they were all off somewhere else?'

'There, um, we had some friends back here; it was going to be late and loud, so I suggested they might be better off going away for the night,' Harry mumbled, his cheeks turning red underneath the angry bruises that covered his skin.

Grace felt her anger rise in a tidal wave of rage as it all finally clicked into place. Harry had got rid of the staff so that he could drink and whore the evening away without being watched. She'd suspected he'd been doing this for a while, but her suspicions had never been confirmed until now.

'And let me guess,' she said in a low growl, through gritted teeth, 'the security system was offline too, yes?'

'Y-Yes it was. I think there was some sort of glitch—' Harry started.

'Do you take me for a fool?' Grace roared, finally setting her temper free. She sneered down at him as he tried to pull back. 'You've pulled these games for far too long. I should have taken you in hand before now,' she spat, 'but no. I turned a blind eye to your drinking and your parties, feeling guilty for leaving you alone so often. Ha!' She laughed bitterly, then turned in a circle and ran her hands down her face with a groan. 'But I hadn't realised you were sending the staff away and taking down the cameras. And that would be for only one reason, wouldn't it?' She looked at him and saw the guilt flood his features. 'To hide your women,' she finished simply.

'N-No, I wouldn't do that to you, my love,' he pandered, holding his hands out to her. 'Grace, sweetheart, you're the only one—'

'Shut up, you snivelling shit,' she snarled.

He recoiled and she stared at him as if truly seeing him for the first time. His guilt was as clear as day, and he was afraid. And now that she'd found out for sure that he'd been unfaithful, it was as though the final cord of responsibility had been severed. Harry had been a weight around her neck for a long time. Dead weight that needed to be cut. But as he was her husband and had so loyally stood by her through her climb to power, she'd allowed him to tag along on the tails of her success.

He had never brought much to the table, throughout their marriage. Harry had a modest trust fund, but he was useless with money, so she had realised very early on that it was down to her to fund their lifestyle and find the money to keep the dilapidated family home from falling apart.

Her parents had left her the house but next to nothing in terms of money when they died. Luckily, she was smart. She'd worked hard, using her degree and her family connections to climb the ladder to success. But even her generous salary couldn't keep them in the manner they were accustomed to, so she had turned to the dark shadows of the upper classes to make more. Moving in the murky circles of the rich and illegal, she'd brokered many deals and bought and sold many stolen gems in her lifetime. People thought that criminals were only found among the poor and the desperate, but she'd realised as she'd grown that the most criminally minded of all could be found among the rich.

Over the years, she had grown into a very powerful person. And the more she'd grown, the greater the gap had widened between her and her gormless husband. She looked him up and down, no longer feeling anything but disgust for him. At university he'd been handsome, interesting and entertaining. He'd dreamed of going places with his career. Now, fifteen years on, he was nothing but a balding beer can who wasted his days away and cheated on her in her own home whilst she was out hustling to pay for their future. And to top it all off, he had somehow managed to lose the single most important and expensive possession she had.

Only a few years before, she had finally managed to persuade an old dying crook she had done a lot of work for to sell it to her at an absolute bargain of a price. On the black market, it would have gone for double what she'd paid, and she was counting on exactly that, when the time came for her to retire. It had taken all her unlaundered savings from her entire career and more. But she'd done it. She had paid her dues and the painting was hers, outright.

Except now it wasn't. Now it was in the hands of a bunch of common thieves who'd taken advantage of the fact that her husband was a bumbling idiot.

'You're a fool, Harry Chambers. I should have cut you loose a long time ago.' She watched him pale. 'And if I had, perhaps this could have gone another way. For both of us.' The question of what to do with him had been swimming through her mind, but her decision slowly cemented. 'Nobody knew about that painting. Which means you talked.'

'I didn't, Grace, I swear!' he cried in panic.

'It wasn't a question,' she cut him off in a clipped tone. She shook her head and looked him up and down in contempt. 'I can't have you talking about anything else. There's too much at stake.' She clicked her fingers at the third man in the room, who'd been standing silently on the sidelines. 'Get him out of my sight,' she spat.

'Grace, please,' Harry cried as the other man grabbed his arm and pulled him away. 'Darling, please listen to me!'

'Put him somewhere he can't disturb anyone.' Her cold glare landed on her husband dispassionately. 'I'll deal with him later.'

'I-I have details – of the men who took it. It could help catch them, Grace. We can find them together. We can sort this all out,' he pleaded with her.

She turned to the man gripping his arm. 'Ivan, get all these details and I'll see if they are of any use.'

Her gaze rested on her husband as he was dragged away and she wondered if she should feel some sort of sorrow. But she no longer owed him anything. Not now. She'd met his loyalty with her own, but that had been destroyed, along with her financial future. She could put up with many things, but not infidelity and definitely not the level of incompetence it took to lose a hidden painting worth a hundred million pounds. He'd sealed his own fate.

As Henry's muffled complaints faded away down the hallway, she turned her gaze towards Duffy, who was now watching her warily. She narrowed her eyes as they met his. 'You're lucky I still need *you* on my payroll,' she growled.

'Y-Yes,' he managed to stutter. 'Thank you, Grace.'

'Get my men together. And call Archie,' she ordered. She walked over to the tall windows and stared out across the sunny manicured grounds with a hard look. 'Because I will *not* give up until that painting is back in my possession where it damn well belongs.' Her fingers curled up into tight fists as her rage burned hotter than ever before. 'And whoever took it is going to rue the day they ever set eyes on that painting.'

CHAPTER FORTY-TWO

Lily and Scarlet stood side by side in the lift as it travelled up to the floor where they were meeting Lily's contact Danny and the man he was about to introduce them to. Scarlet smoothed her fitted burgundy dress down. She had dressed to impress for this meeting, too stressed to give it anything but her best effort all round.

Next to her, Lily stood as collected and confident as always. She glanced at her aunt. 'How are you so calm and relaxed?' she asked quietly.

'There's no reason not to be calm,' Lily replied. 'A calm head fixes many problems. As for being relaxed' – the corner of her mouth lifted slightly in amusement – 'I'm far from it. But we don't want our new friends seeing that, do we?' She looked back at her niece. 'And you need to hide the fact you're not too.' She turned to face the lift doors as it slowed to a stop. 'Fake it till you make it, darlin'.'

The doors opened and they stepped into an elegantly stylish bar with panoramic views across the city. Scarlet looked around with interest – this was the nicest bar she'd ever seen.

'Welcome to Galvin at Windows. Do you have a reservation?' a young man asked.

'We're meeting someone,' Lily replied. 'Danny Myers. Is he here yet?'

'Ah, certainly. Mr Myers and his other guest are already seated. Please follow me.'

They wove their way through the tables to the farthest corner where two men sat by the extensive wall of windows with a bucket of champagne on ice.

'Here you are,' the man said. 'Now, can I get you ladies anything to drink?'

'Just two more glasses please,' one of the seated men said with confidence. 'I'm sure these ladies will be game to enjoy this bottle of Bolly with me.' He stood up and pulled one of the seats back for Scarlet, whilst the waiter pulled back the other for Lily.

Scarlet sat down, taking him in with curiosity. Was this Danny, Lily's London contact, or the art fence from Monaco? He was dressed in an expensive-looking blue suit with a red patterned handkerchief sticking out of his breast pocket. His cream shirt was dotted with pearlised buttons, and the watch on his wrist was a Rolex. So he was rich, that much was obvious. He was very attractive too, she noted, with deep olive skin, thick black hair and warm brown eyes that reminded her of melted chocolate.

She turned her gaze towards the other man. He was dressed well too and with an air of sophistication about him, but his tastes gave off more of a London vibe than the first man. She placed her bets on this being Danny.

Lily gestured towards the second man. 'Scarlet, this is Danny Myers. Danny, this is my niece Scarlet.'

Her guess had been correct. She smiled at him across the table and nodded in greeting. 'Lovely to meet you, Mr Myers.'

'And you, Miss Drew,' he replied, his smile not quite meeting his eyes. 'And this is Arj.' He stopped there and picked up his drink.

The message was clear. There would be no last name or further details about Arj. They didn't trust her or Lily any more than they trusted them. That was fair enough. Trust would take time.

The waiter returned with two glasses and poured the champagne.

'Thank you,' Lily said as he finished and walked away.

Danny cleared his throat. 'I have relayed our previous conversation to Arj already, so, assuming everything went as you expected, he's pretty much up to date with things. *Did* everything go as planned?' he asked.

'It did,' Lily confirmed. 'We have the painting somewhere secure until we have a buyer ready to make the transaction.'

Arj's gaze narrowed as he leaned on the arm of his chair and studied her. 'Who exactly, other than yourselves, has seen the painting?'

'No one yet,' Lily replied.

'How do you know it's the real deal?' he asked, watching her closely.

'It's real,' Scarlet said confidently. 'I'm not an expert, but I'd stake my life on the fact that it's the original.'

Arj turned his gaze back to her, an unreadable look in his eyes. 'I'd be careful with your words, young lady. In this business, the art is often much more valuable than a person's life.'

Scarlet stifled a shiver as she watched his warm eyes turn cold.

'Well then, I'd stake a lot of money on it,' she said, holding his gaze.

He broke away first, taking a sip of his champagne. 'What makes you so sure?' he asked. 'What do you know of art?'

'I studied it.' She stopped there, not wishing to admit that it was only at A level. 'And I studied Rembrandt in particular. I'm as sure as I can be without officially testing it.'

'I'll need to have it properly verified,' he replied. 'But assuming you are correct, I already have two buyers in mind who I know will be very interested indeed.'

'Who are they?' Lily asked.

'People who value their privacy,' he responded bluntly. After a moment, his tone relaxed slightly. 'They're clients who particularly covet paintings like this one. One lives in Dubai and the other currently in the US. They're two of my most wealthy and determined clients.' His expression rose and fell as he considered his thoughts. 'In fact, I think with these two players in the mix together, we could get a much higher price than I'd usually expect. They'll most likely end up in a bidding war.'

Scarlet exchanged a look with her aunt. 'What sort of price would you usually expect to see?' she asked.

Arj shrugged. 'It varies through the market. Younger items – contemporary paintings – usually fetch between seven and ten per cent of their value on the black market. But older more classic pieces painted by the greats' – he tilted his head to the side with a smile – 'twenty, sometimes twenty-five per cent.'

'And you say you expect this to go for more. How much more?' Scarlet probed.

'My guess is that this could go for up to maybe fifty per cent. I know these clients would probably go up to that sort of price before they capped out,' he estimated.

Scarlet picked up her glass and took a long sip of the icy bubbly liquid within as she processed what he was saying. Fifty per cent would be fifty million pounds. It was more money than she'd ever imagined earning in a lifetime, let alone on one job.

'And what would your fees be, Arj?' Lily asked calmly. 'For brokering this deal.'

'Fifteen per cent of whatever it sells for,' he replied. 'And for that I take care of everything, beginning to end.'

'That's a lot of money for making a few connections,' she replied.

'It's a lot of risk too,' he responded, unfazed by her remark. 'And at the end of the day, it's *you* who needs *me*, Ms Drew, not the other way around.' He shrugged and topped up his glass. 'If you'd like to try touting the painting yourself to someone with that sort of money who's into stolen artwork – after getting it professionally appraised, of course – then by all means be my guest. It's your painting – you can do whatever you want with it.' He smiled, the action as casual and light as his words. 'But if you require my services, then that's my fee.'

Lily nodded and Scarlet followed suit, trusting her aunt's judgement. It was a lot of money to hand over, but as he'd pointed out, they didn't really have much choice.

'Then we have a deal,' Lily said with a tight smile.

'We have a deal once the painting has been verified,' Arj warned. He regarded them solemnly. 'I'll feel out the buyers and get the ball rolling, but we'll need to arrange a meeting soon to verify its authenticity.'

'Who will be doing that?' Scarlet asked with a small frown. The more people who knew about the painting, the higher the risk that word would get out and that could cause all sorts of issues.

'I have a guy – a professional forger. The best in the world, I personally think. He can spot another forgery a mile off. He's my go-to man for anything of this nature,' Arj replied.

'No problem. Just let us know when you want to meet and we can arrange something,' Lily replied. 'Here are our details,' she continued, opening her purse and taking out one of her factory business cards. She handed it over, and he handed her one back. She took one last sip of her champagne and then stood up. 'Thank you, Danny, for the introduction. And it was great to meet you, Arj. We look forward to doing business.'

Scarlet got to her feet also. Evidently, the meeting was over.

'Oh, must you go so soon?' Arj asked, surprised. 'We were hoping you might stay and have a few more drinks with us. Eh, Danny?'

'Arj doesn't get to London very often these days,' Danny said with a laugh. 'He likes to get as much partying in as he can before he heads out again. It will likely be a fun night, if you want to come along.'

'No thank you,' Scarlet said quickly. After the last party she'd attended with people they weren't familiar with, she'd decided to stay firmly in her own lane for a while. 'We really must get on.'

'Next time,' Arj said graciously.

'Sure. Enjoy your evening.' Scarlet nodded to Danny and then she and Lily turned to leave.

'By the way,' Arj added, 'if the painting fails to prove genuine, obviously the deal will be off and you will be required to cover the costs of getting it checked over.' His steely gaze flickered between the two of them.

Lily turned back. 'It won't,' she said.

CHAPTER FORTY-THREE

As they stepped out into the bright autumn sunshine, Scarlet heaved a great sigh of relief. 'Christ,' she said, looking back over her shoulder. 'What do you make of him?'

'Smooth and dangerous,' Lily immediately replied. 'He seems professional enough, and from what information I've been able to get, he's well established.'

'Yeah?' Scarlet glanced at her aunt as they quickly made their way down the street.

'I didn't have much to go on, but that was the gist of what I was able to find out,' she replied. 'There ain't exactly tales being told about him through our usual circles, so it's hard to get a rounded view.' She paused while they crossed the busy road. 'But you were there. He's friendly enough, but I wouldn't want to get on his bad side.'

'No,' Scarlet agreed.

She thought back over their meeting. The man could go from jovial chatter and warmth in his stare to thinly veiled threats and cold, hard steel within a matter of seconds. And Scarlet had no doubt that his words were not exaggerated in the slightest. He was the real deal and much higher up the underworld tree than the likes of them. The law and the lives of anyone who might get in the way were very much beneath him.

'I need a drink,' she said, feeling the weight of what they were doing press down on her slim shoulders.

''Course.' Lily looked around at the selection of posh-looking bars surrounding them.

'Let's find a proper pub. One we can actually relax in.'

'Best idea you've had all day,' Lily agreed. 'There – look.' She pointed down the road at a small pub with a black front and a gold-painted sign that read The Rose and Crown.

As they walked in, Scarlet looked around at the tables. They were almost all full already, but there were a few stools at the bar that were still vacant. Lily went over and took a seat.

Scarlet pulled herself up onto the stool next to Lily's and leaned on the bar, finally letting her muscles relax for the first time all day. The barman came over and they gave him their order.

'What do you think we should do when it comes to this guy verifying it?' Scarlet asked, turning to face her aunt.

Lily twisted to face her too and leaned her arm on the bar. 'What do you mean?' she asked, pushing her tight curls off her face and reaching into her handbag for her small compact mirror.

'We don't want them knowing about the barn,' Scarlet said.

'Obviously,' Lily replied, pulling out her red lipstick and popping off the lid.

'Where do you want to meet? Or do we let them decide?'

'Absolutely not,' Lily said with a hard glance, carefully applying the lipstick. She rubbed her lips together then closed the compact. 'We need to maintain the advantage, so we'll pick the location and let them know only a short time before they need to be there. That will leave no opportunity for foul play.'

'You think they'd try something then?' Scarlet asked.

'It's always better to take the chance out of the equation.' She met Scarlet's gaze. 'I'll figure it out. Don't worry about it.'

'OK.'

The barman slid their drinks across the bar and Scarlet took her large vodka and Coke with a grateful smile. She put the glass to her lips and drank deeply, relishing the refreshing feel as it slipped down her throat.

'I've got some stuff I need to go over with you later, when you get into the factory. I'm assuming you'll pop to the salon first?' Lily asked, sipping her gin and tonic.

'Yes, I need to,' Scarlet insisted. Her feelings about the salon were so conflicted.

She'd been so eager to open it and excited by the venture, but since her aunt had persuaded her to take Ruby on there, she felt as though it now sat under a dark cloud. Every time she walked in, Ruby was there with some snide remark and a dirty look; every time she got personally involved with the day-to-day running of things, Ruby went out of her way to try and make her feel unwelcome. And that bothered her. The salon was *her* baby. And she was proud of that. She hated the fact that her troublesome cousin was trying so hard to take that away from her.

She didn't even understand why. It wasn't like Ruby had any real interest in the family business or even in running a salon. She'd made it clear from the start that the only reason she was involved at all was because she physically had no other choice.

Lily's phone went off in her bag and she pulled it out to have a look. 'We'll need to go over exactly what we need to—' She slowed to a stop as she focused on reading the text. 'Bollocks,' she muttered. 'Listen, I need to run. I'm sorry. Stay and finish your drink and I'll catch you back at the factory later, yeah?' Lily said distractedly, slipping off the stool and making sure she had everything.

'Sure. Everything OK?' Scarlet asked, concerned.

'Everything's fine. I left my car down that little side street by the butcher's – you know the one?'

'Oh yeah, I know.' Scarlet often parked there herself. It was one of the few places they could park without restrictions if the factory car park was full.

'Apparently my alarm keeps going off. And I've got the keys.' She rolled her eyes. 'Should have left them in the office. Never mind. I'll see you later.'

'No worries. See you later.' Scarlet watched as her aunt left, waving over her head as she swept out the door, then she turned back to the bar.

Picking up her drink, she took another long sip and leaned back into the wooden embrace of the bar stool, looking around with interest. It was a nice pub. Traditional with warm colours and an inviting feel. There was a friendly buzz, chatter between groups of friends and some upbeat background music playing from somewhere. It wasn't often she got the chance to just sit and enjoy a quiet drink by herself. Like her aunt, she'd always enjoyed her own company, so this was a welcome respite.

As she sipped her drink, a man sidled up to the bar next to her. She pulled slightly out of the way, allowing him room to get the barman's attention.

'Hey, what's up?' came a gruff voice.

She turned, realising he was speaking to her. Smiling with polite coldness, she ignored the question and turned back to her drink.

'Hello?' he said rudely, nudging his head closer towards her, revealing a crooked grin.

'Hi,' she replied curtly, giving him a look that should have left him in no doubt of her lack of interest.

'Ooh, icy,' he mocked in a leery manner. She could smell stale beer on his breath and had to make an effort not to wrinkle her nose. 'What's the matter with you then, moody?'

Staring forward, Scarlet frowned and clamped her jaw. She had no intention of entertaining this lout and had no qualms about making it known, but she decided to hold her tongue a little longer in the hope that he'd just give up and she wouldn't have to bother with the argument.

'Christ, right snooty one you are, eh?' he remarked when she didn't respond. He leaned in so close his torso was almost pressed against her arm. 'Am I not good enough for you love, no?'

Scarlet's patience snapped and she turned, ready to tell him where to go, when another voice piped up behind her.

'There you are. Sorry I'm late.' A tall man in his early twenties stepped forward to stand between them, subtly forcing the other man back. 'Everything OK?' He raised his eyebrows at Scarlet with a friendly smile, then pointedly turned to the other man with a steely look behind the smile. 'Who's your friend? I don't think we've met.'

Taking the not-so-subtle hint, the other guy sulked off and ambled back to his group of friends. The man who'd just approached and defused the situation watched him go, then turned back to her.

'You alright?' he asked. 'Sorry for the pretence – you just looked like you could do with a hand.' He grinned.

Scarlet turned to face him. 'I was about to tell him where to go,' she said, wanting him to understand that she could have dealt with the situation herself. 'I was just waiting to see if he'd fuck off without a scene first.'

He laughed. 'It sounds like I probably did *him* a favour then.'

Scarlet couldn't help but grin. 'Probably,' she agreed.

She looked at him with curiosity. He had a friendly face and an air about him that made her feel strangely comfortable. He was tall with dark brown hair and thick heavy eyebrows above a pair of bright green eyes. His wide mouth was naturally upturned, and his cheekbones and jaw strongly defined his long and slightly narrow face. He wasn't what she'd call classically handsome, but somehow the way he was put together was very attractive.

She squeezed her gaze for a moment as she deliberated whether or not to pursue the conversation.

'I'm Scarlet,' she said eventually with a smile.

'John,' he replied, offering his hand.

She shook it and gestured to the seat Lily had recently vacated. 'Feel free.'

'Thanks,' he said, taking her up on the offer. 'I'm not in anyone's way?' He looked around expectantly.

'No, my aunt just left. It's only me.'

'Ah, OK.' He caught the barman's attention and ordered a beer, then asked if Scarlet wanted a refill.

'No. Thanks, but I have to get on,' she replied, shaking her head at the barman.

John sat down and shrugged off his jacket. 'So, Scarlet. What brings you here on this fine day?'

'I had a meeting around the corner,' she replied.

'Yeah? What is it you do?' he asked.

'Oh, it's…' She trailed off reluctantly.

John pulled a face. 'This is such a clichéd conversation, isn't it?' he asked. 'Why do people do that? Why do we always jump straight to the life list? It's like bingo, checking off the boxes. Job, check. Family, check. Local residence, check.' He shook his head. He paid for his beer and drank some of it, then placed the pint glass down neatly on the bar mat in front of him. 'OK, better question,' he said. 'What's something that makes you feel happy?'

'Happy?' she repeated, surprised by the question.

'Yeah, you know, like…' He paused, puffing out his cheeks. 'I don't know, something that, when you experience it, makes you smile?'

Scarlet laughed and searched her brain. Personal happiness wasn't something that was usually high on her list of priorities. 'Art,' she said suddenly. 'I like looking at art. When I get the chance. The good stuff makes me smile.'

'Wow, that's actually a really sophisticated answer. I was just going to go with this beer in front of me – but now I can see I'm going to have to up my game.'

Scarlet laughed once more, thoroughly amused. 'Beer isn't a bad answer,' she offered.

'Don't give me that pity save,' he replied with a groan. 'It was a terrible answer. I'll think of something else – just give me a minute.'

'While you're thinking of a better answer, let's go back to bingo.' Scarlet was enjoying their conversation. It felt refreshing to chat to someone with such a light-hearted sense of humour. 'What do *you* do for a living?'

'Eugh.' He recoiled in mock disgust. 'Let's not. My job is boring and I'm here to escape it after a very, *very* long shift. So think of something else. I'll answer any question you can come up with that's completely random and unexpected.'

'OK, um…' She took a sip of her drink and teased a frayed corner on her beer mat as she thought. 'What's your favourite Scottish city?'

'Well, I've never actually been to Scotland but definitely not Glasgow,' he replied with certainty.

'Why not Glasgow?' she asked, pushing a stray lock of her dark hair back behind her ear.

'I've heard terrible things about Glasgow from a mate who lived there once. I'll have to do some research and let you know next time we meet up.' He looked over at her with a small smile and a captivating sparkle in his bright green eyes.

'Oh, so we're meeting up again, are we?' Scarlet asked with a laugh. He had a lot of confidence for someone who'd just met her. But she found to her surprise she wasn't bothered by that.

'Oh yes,' he replied, holding her gaze as the first spark flew between them. 'We most definitely are.'

CHAPTER FORTY-FOUR

Lily sighed in annoyance as she marched down the street and heard her car screaming away. She turned the corner into the narrow dead-end street and pulled out her keys, pointing them towards her car and clicking the button to make it stop.

'There, you little fucker,' she muttered to the car, as if it could understand what she was saying. 'Going off like that in the middle of the bloody day!'

She turned to walk back up to the main street and realised just a moment too late that she'd been followed in and was now cornered by two thickset thugs merely a few feet behind her. They glared down at her as she began backing away from them towards her car. She moved to open her handbag, but the nearest one closed the gap between them with a jog and grabbed her arm.

'I don't think so,' he growled.

'Get the *fuck* off my arm,' Lily shouted at him indignantly. 'Who the hell do you think you are?' she asked, her words curling into a snarl. She glared up at him as she tried and failed to pull away. 'Do you know who I am?' she asked, her anger rising. 'Because if you don't, I can promise you this is a *very* big mistake. And if you do,' she added, 'you really are the most stupid cunt walking if you think you can get away with this.'

The other man reached them and leaned over her menacingly. 'Know who you are?' he asked, in disbelief. 'I don't give a flying monkey's who you think you are, love,' he spat, his lip curling.

'But you sure as hell should know who *I* am. I'm the man your junkie slag of a daughter owes a small fortune to.'

Lily's fury burned brighter at the man's disrespectful words about Ruby. It didn't matter what her kids had done, *no one* was allowed to speak of them that way in front of her. But at the same time as her fury raged, realisation dawned. She looked the man who had spoken to her up and down in contempt.

'Ash, I take it?' she said through gritted teeth.

'So you *do* know who I am,' he replied, ignoring the vitriol coming off her in waves.

'*Get* off me,' Lily said once more, this time managing to rip her arm out of her captor's grip. 'If you wanted to get the money she owed from me, you could have approached me civilly, instead of following me around and setting off my fucking car alarm,' she declared angrily. 'I'd have happily settled this with you a long time ago.'

Ash stepped forward menacingly. 'I don't take kindly to being told what to do,' he replied.

'Those are your issues, not mine,' Lily replied in a severe tone.

The smack across the face was unexpected. Her head snapped to the side and she twisted around, then fell to the ground from the force of the backhander. As she hit the pavement, she blinked, momentarily stunned. The pain set in a moment later, as her confusion cleared.

Ash had just hit her. Hard. She barked out a hard laugh of disbelief and amusement at the absurdity of the situation. The man had just made the biggest mistake of his life.

'Something funny, old woman?' he sneered, incensed by her reaction.

She looked up at him, a dangerous glint in her eyes. *Old?* Her rage boiled even hotter. Lifting her hand to her mouth, she pulled it away and looked at her fingers in surprise. They were red with blood. He'd split her lip.

'Oh dear,' she said in a low deadly tone. 'Now that wasn't very nice. Or very clever,' she said, pushing herself up off the ground, her movements awkward as several aches began to complain at once through her body.

She stood tall, lifting her chin defiantly, her features ablaze with something that most men would have recoiled from. Ash, however, was too full of his own importance to notice.

'Oh it ain't clever? Feel clever down there on the floor, did ya?' he mocked nastily, flexing his muscles. 'You're lucky that's all I gave you. You can pass that little message on to Ruby for me. And as for the money she owes, I want that *now*. And I want it from you.'

Lily wiped the blood from her chin with the back of her hand, not taking her eyes away from his for a second. 'How much does she owe you?' she asked, her tone low and controlled.

'Twelve hundred,' he spat. 'Though for the inconvenience of having to chase it this long, that's now gone up to *fifteen* hundred,' he leered.

Lily almost laughed again. All this for twelve hundred quid? Instead she nodded, keeping her feelings on the matter hidden for now. 'Right. I don't have that in my purse,' she said flatly. 'I'll have to get the money out and give it to you later tonight.'

'Damn right you will,' he hissed. 'I want it by nine o'clock, without fail. Do you understand me?'

'I do,' she replied.

'And if you try and mess me about, you'll regret it,' he warned. 'You call the police and I'll make sure a nasty end comes to your little girl. And if you try to put me off or short me in any way, it will be *you* that suffers.'

'Nine o'clock tonight,' she said, ignoring his threats. 'You know the factory around the corner, I presume?'

'Your workplace, yes, I do,' he said smugly, as if he held all the knowledge in the world, though it was clear he had absolutely no idea who she even was, or what he was setting himself up for.

'Yes,' she said drily, 'my workplace. I'll be there tonight at nine. Come by then – I'll have someone see you to my office where we can settle what you're owed. Is that suitable for you?' she asked.

'How very civil,' he said sarcastically. 'Yeah. That'll do. I'll be there. And remember what I said.' He pointed his finger at her and then turned and walked away, the other man falling into step beside him. 'You'd better pay up, or you'll regret it.'

'Oh, you'll get what you're owed,' Lily said under her breath as she watched him retreat through cold, narrowed eyes. 'You'll get everything that's coming to you.'

CHAPTER FORTY-FIVE

Lily waited in the dimly lit factory basement. She was sitting in a large wooden throne-like chair, one of Ronan's random purchases that had sat down there for years. She'd thought about throwing it away, but it came in handy from time to time, being particularly heavy and sturdy. Especially when they needed to restrain someone who didn't want to be confined. She raised her arm and took a sip of the whisky in her hand, ignoring the sting as it touched the bruised, broken skin of her lips. The ice clinked against the glass, the only sound in the otherwise silent room.

A brooding Connor stood against a wall, his arms crossed tightly over his chest as he waited. Cillian paced, twiddling the ever-present toothpick with a thunderous face, unable to contain his anger quite as well as his brother. Andy sat on a stool the other side of the door, looking grimly down at the floor.

Lily's own anger bubbled quietly beneath the surface of her cold, hard mask. It had been a long time since she'd encountered anyone on the wrong side of the law who didn't know who she was, let alone one who'd dared to disrespect her. But Ash had gone way over the mark on that front. And he was about to learn exactly how big a mistake it had been.

The sound of footsteps descending the stairs came through the door and Connor pushed away from the wall, moving to stand at his mother's shoulder. Cillian went to stand next to Andy, out of sight in the shadows.

The door opened and Ash and his heavyset friend from earlier that day bowled in with misplaced confidence. George followed behind them and gestured towards Lily.

'Well, here we are. Where's the cash?' he cut bluntly to the point.

His gaze flickered up to Connor and back down to Lily, who was now staring at him with a confident and dark expression. A fleeting look of uncertainty passed across his face, and as George shut the door behind him, he swivelled around, realising too late that this was a set-up.

Cillian and Andy emerged from the shadows, cutting off the only exit in the room. Ash's eyes darted between them. His panicked gaze darted around, then paused on Cillian. He looked at Connor and then back again, and realisation suddenly dawned.

'You're the Drew twins,' he whispered with heart-sinking horror.

'There's a clever boy,' Cillian replied quietly.

'Shit!' He turned back to Lily aghast, his eyes drawn down to the swollen side of her mouth. 'Oh God, I didn't know. I didn't know who you were…'

'I did ask, if you remember,' Lily said in a clipped, deadly tone. 'I asked very clearly if you knew who I was.'

'Y-Yeah, but—' he stammered.

'But you were not concerned with finding out,' she continued. 'You were too full of your own importance. Which was stupid,' she added. 'Very stupid.'

'Right, OK, yeah,' he replied awkwardly as he tried to come up with the right words to free himself from the corner he was now wedged into.

Lily watched him squirm. There were no correct words, of course. There was no way out now. But somehow watching him try made this moment even sweeter.

He stared at Connor beseechingly. 'Look, if I'd known, I would never have—'

'Look at me when you're speaking,' Lily thundered, cutting him off. 'It may be my sons you recognise' – her voice lowered to a dangerous hiss – 'but it is *me* who heads this firm and who decides what will happen to you now.'

He looked back to her, real fear now showing behind his eyes. 'I-I'm sorry,' he stuttered. 'Alright? I never would have touched you if I had any clue who you were. And – and your daughter's debt.' He swallowed and closed his eyes momentarily, kicking himself for not finding out who she was when he had a chance. 'That's nothing. It's gone. No longer exists. As an apology from me to you for this – this misunderstanding,' he said, his eyes pleading with her.

Lily frowned and tilted her head as she stared at him from her seat. 'This wasn't a misunderstanding. We all very clearly understand what happened. *You* are a stupid, vicious little bully who likes to get his kicks beating on anyone he thinks is weaker than him. You say you would never have touched me if you'd known who I was.' She shrugged. 'That much I believe. Not out of respect, of course.' She rose and slowly approached him. 'But because if you'd known how fucking powerful I am, you'd have been too afraid. That's what bullies do. They steer clear of anyone who could put them in their place and take pleasure in hurting the weak.' She looked him up and down in contempt. 'And I fucking hate bullies.'

'I'm sorry,' he pleaded. 'Like I said, I would never have even come near you if I'd known. I would have just written it off, I swear.'

'You're not getting it, are you?' Lily asked, shaking her head. 'Ruby's debt was never the issue. As I said to you before, I would have happily paid you what she owed, had you approached me in a normal manner.' She stared at him coldly. 'Business is business.

She took your products – she owed you payment for them. Fair's fair.' She circled the two men slowly. 'No, the issue is that you followed me, lured me into a trap, threatened me and smacked me to the ground for absolutely no good reason.' Her eyes flashed darkly as they met his.

Connor reached behind the large wooden chair and picked up a bat, testing the weight in his hands and stepping forward.

'Alright, easy now,' Ash cried, raising his hands in the air and stepping backward. 'I've said I'm sorry. And I've told you I'll wipe the debt as an apology. There ain't nothing more I can do about it, OK?'

He jolted forward as Cillian poked him with another bat from behind. Cillian rounded on him as Andy and George grabbed the other guy and forced his arms behind his back. This one cried out and tried to pull free, but Andy and George were stronger than he was.

'OK, wait!' Ash cried, holding his hands out in front of him as a barrier. 'I'll work for you,' he said in an almost pained tone.

'Excuse me?' Lily asked, blinking in surprise.

'I said, I'll work for you. For free. Until you feel my debt to you has been settled. I have connections and I ain't afraid to get my hands dirty. I'm an asset – this is a good deal for both of us.'

There was a short silence as Lily stared at him and then she threw her head back and laughed. 'Jesus Christ,' she exclaimed, looking at her sons. 'The balls on this one!' She shook her head, amused. But as her gaze moved back to his, her smile cooled and the hardness she'd adopted moments before returned with fury. 'Do you really think I would allow a piece of shit like you to work for me? To come into the business my brother and I built up from the ground over decades?' Her lip curled up in contempt. 'I wouldn't hire a thick, self-important nobody like you if you were the last man left on the planet. And you offer yourself to me like you'd be doing us some sort of favour?' she asked in disbelief. She shook her head. 'The men in this firm are smart. They're fair; they live by a code. They're good people. Oh, don't get me wrong,' she said when she saw Ash was about to open his mouth, 'they do bad things. People can do bad things and still be good people. Like my boys here.' She turned and looked at them both in turn with an expression of pride. 'They're good people. They'll do bad things when needed. I mean, we run a criminal firm' – she shrugged – 'which technically falls under *bad things* in the eyes of the law. And they'll even get a little bit nasty with people, when the protection of our business or family requires it. But' – she pointed a finger at Ash with a steely look – 'they do it for the right reasons. They dole out retribution to the deserving. They don't prey on the weak to make themselves feel big. And *that* is the very big difference between you.'

Picking up her whisky from the wide flat arm of the chair where she'd left it, she walked past the two men towards the door.

Ash watched her go, blinking in surprise. 'Was that all? Can I go?'

'Go?' Lily asked, turning back to him with a smile of amusement. 'No, Ash. You cannot.'

He swallowed and exhaled heavily. 'What you gonna do to me then? Eh?' he asked, trying to put some bravado behind his words.

'Me? Nothing.' She stared at him for a few moments. 'My sons, on the other hand, have a couple of bones to pick with you. Yours, I should imagine.'

Feeling satisfaction hit home at the look of fear that flooded into his eyes, Lily turned and left, the sound of splintering bones and screams of agony following her down the hall as her boys set to work.

CHAPTER FORTY-SIX

Lily stood outside Ruby's room and paused, laying her hand on the door for a few moments before lifting it and knocking. There was no sound from within, no reply, but she knew her daughter was in there. She lifted her hand and rapped again, a little louder.

There was a sigh and the sound of the bedsprings creaking. 'What is it?' came the irritable response.

Lily pushed the door open and leaned in. 'Were you sleeping?' she asked.

Ruby was sitting on top of the bed covers, still fully dressed with a notebook and pencil next to her. 'No,' she replied moodily. 'I was just writing some stuff down for work.'

Lily couldn't help but smile at these words. 'That's brilliant, Rubes,' she said.

'Oh, don't patronise me,' Ruby said with a scowl. 'I'm not some kid who you need to praise for doing her fucking homework.' She closed the notebook and shoved it on the side in annoyance.

Lily bit the inside of her cheek and cast her eyes towards the window. 'I wasn't trying to patronise you,' she said levelly. 'I'm just pleased that you seem so invested. It's good for you. It's good for all of us, to have another Drew looking out for the family business.'

This seemed to appease Ruby slightly, as she gave a slight nod. 'I'm tired and I'm sure you have loads to do. Another party to go to perhaps,' she added scathingly. 'Or whatever else you and your best mate Scarlet like to do.'

Lily sighed. This issue between Ruby and Scarlet was becoming a more serious problem than she'd anticipated. It was something that needed to be resolved. This was a tense time already – the last thing any of them needed was distraction or for unnecessary attention to be drawn their way. But not yet. It was a delicate subject and she hadn't yet figured out the best way to approach it.

If she went about it the wrong way, it could force a wedge between her and Ruby, and she'd only just got her back. As her mind rested on this, it naturally turned towards thoughts of Ray. Ruby wouldn't be here if it hadn't been for him. Irritably, she pushed this from her mind.

'I'll let you get some rest,' she said, pulling back. 'Oh, and you don't need to worry about Ash anymore. Your brothers and I took care of him. He won't bother you again.'

'What?' Ruby's head snapped around in surprise. 'You found him? How? What happened?'

'It doesn't matter,' she replied.

Ruby finally looked at her mother's face properly and her gaze lingered on her swollen lip. A frown of concern lined her forehead, and she looked back up into her mother's eyes.

'It doesn't matter,' Lily repeated firmly. 'It's done.' She smiled. 'No more looking over your shoulder. Are there any more people you owe who will come looking?'

'No.' Ruby shook her head. 'A few small debts but they'll just have blacklisted me. Nothing worth them chasing.'

'Good. OK, I'll see you in the morning.' Lily made to leave.

'Mum,' Ruby called out.

Lily looked back at her in question and found a softer, more open face looking back.

'Thank you,' she said quietly, her tone genuine and grateful.

Lily's heart warmed and lifted with more hope for their relationship than she'd felt in many years. 'You're welcome, my love,' she replied. 'Always.'

CHAPTER FORTY-SEVEN

Cillian paced up and down outside the small house in Wandsworth, debating whether or not to wake its occupant. It was barely five in the morning, but he was wired and he needed a release – and the only way he could seem to find a release these days was with her. He'd barely known her for five minutes, but since he'd met her, she seemed to consume his mind. She was all he could think about, and the darker his day, the more he craved her.

He'd never met anyone like Billie before, not really. He knew he had kinks, and he knew he could satisfy them in many places throughout Soho, but he'd never met a girl – a *real* girl, one that wasn't paid to play out his pleasures – that understood him on the level she did. Even before they'd got down to it, before they'd even discussed it in the open, he'd sensed it in her. Because it wasn't just sexual – it slipped into everyday life, the desires they shared. In his line of work it wasn't hard to mask. His was a violent profession where a show of dominance was mandatory anyway. But with Billie it had been a lot more obvious. She enjoyed the power. She enjoyed the euphoric mix of pleasure and pain, of controlled dominance. And just like him, she liked it both ways.

'Fuck it,' he muttered to himself, marching towards her door.

He paused and knocked, waiting a few moments before knocking again. Eventually he heard a stirring within and waited for her to come downstairs. The gauze curtain behind the glass in the door moved aside and Billie's frowning face appeared. Her bright blonde hair was ruffled from sleep, and she was still rubbing one tired eye, but she lowered her hand with a look of surprise when she saw who it was.

She unlocked the door and pulled it open wide, stepping back to let him in. 'Jesus,' she said. 'What are you doing here? What time is it?' She winced at the weak early morning light then closed the door.

'It's nearly five.'

'*Five in the morning?*' she exclaimed.

'Well, it ain't in the afternoon,' he replied with a crooked smile of amusement. 'And as for what I'm doing here…' He moved forward and grabbed her waist with both hands, pulling her towards him roughly. 'I needed you,' he whispered in a hoarse tone.

Billie's expression contorted between annoyed defiance and lustfulness, and she narrowed her gaze at him. 'I have a busy morning, you know,' she said. 'I need to be up and at it in a couple of hours. I have two people to interview for the room before I head to work.'

'Sack 'em off,' he pushed, his lips trailing across her cheek and down to her neck.

Her breath became heavier, and she melted into his arms as he teased her skin in just the right place. 'I can't,' she breathed. 'I need to get someone into that room.' She found some strength as she said these words and pushed back against him, but he held fast.

'No, you don't. Because I want to rent it,' he replied, running his hands up her spine from the bottom of her back.

'What do you mean?' she asked.

He bit the curve between her neck and her shoulder, then pulled her nightie up and over her head. 'I mean, I'll pay that rent from now on.'

'Cillian…' She pushed him with an element of force this time and he stepped back. 'We barely know each other.' She pushed her hand up and back through her hair and laughed. 'You can't just start paying my rent.'

'I'm not,' he argued, pulling her hand down and grasping both her wrists. Her breath caught in her throat, and a spark flew between them. He tightened his grip and watched her own excitement grow with his own. 'I'd be renting the room for myself. I have a storage issue. This would solve that issue, if you aren't against the idea.'

Billie had been renting a two-bed house with a friend, but recently that friend had moved away and she'd been looking for someone to take her place. She couldn't afford it on her own, Cillian knew. He also knew that she was fiercely independent and had too much pride to take any handouts, but she couldn't argue with him paying to use the space legitimately. He didn't really need it, but that was beside the point. He enjoyed being able to visit her like this without the worry of a housemate getting in the way. If she *wanted* a housemate, of course, that was a different matter. It was her home – she could do what she liked. But now at least she had the option.

'I'll think about it,' she replied, pulling her wrists away from him in a quick, sharp movement.

The move was unexpected, so he hadn't been ready to stop her. He grinned. He loved it when she played with him like this. As Billie said, it hadn't been long since he'd met her, only days since they'd started seeing each other really, but already they couldn't get enough of each other and were sneaking off at every possible opportunity. It was the start of something interesting – he could feel it. And this was new for Cillian. He'd dated before, many women, one after the other. But all of them had been for convenience. They'd been pretty faces, willing girls that had proved to be amusing distractions. But Billie was different. They were two of a kind, and there was already an underlying bond forming that he couldn't quite explain.

She reached up and grabbed his lapels, pulling him towards her hard. He didn't resist, and she kissed him hungrily, biting down on his lip before undoing the top buttons of his shirt. He shrugged off his jacket and let her continue down, but she paused as she reached halfway.

'There's blood here,' she said.

He looked down and saw the dark splatter of crimson across the crisp white of his shirt. He'd missed that. He'd have changed before he came over if he'd realised.

'Yours?' she asked.

'No,' he replied, holding her gaze. She claimed to know who he was, so what would she make of that? he wondered.

Her clear blue eyes showed no strong reaction. 'Good. I'd hate to have to be careful with you.'

Cillian's mouth curled up into a slow grin and he ripped the rest of the buttons apart, pulling the shirt away from his tight, muscular torso. 'I'll burn it later. Don't you want to ask me whose blood it is?' he challenged.

'Not particularly,' Billie answered. She ran her nails down his chest and bit her own lip in anticipation of what was to come as she raked her eyes down his body. 'I'd rather not know, then if I'm ever asked I can just forget I saw it. The less lies, the less there is to remember.'

'Good girl,' Cillian said huskily. She knew how to play the game clearly. That impressed him. A lot of girls would be put off or even frightened to learn he was covered in someone else's blood. But apparently not Billie.

'Now take those clothes off and get upstairs,' she ordered, her voice authoritative.

'Not today,' he replied, grabbing her wrists again and pushing her back against the wall – hard. He leaned into her ear. 'Today I'm in charge.'

CHAPTER FORTY-EIGHT

The black Range Rover behind made the same turn as they did and Lily frowned in the rear-view mirror. It had been following them for some time now. She and Scarlet were on their way out of the city to check on the Rembrandt, but she couldn't go there with a tail.

They reached the next roundabout and Lily turned right.

'Where are you going? The barn's that way, isn't it?' Scarlet asked, looking back over her shoulder with a frown.

Lily watched in the mirror as the Range Rover followed them once again. Her lips formed a grim line. 'I think we've got company,' she warned.

Scarlet glanced back through the wing mirror. 'Who are they?' she asked.

They were on the outskirts of London now and the road they'd taken had led away from the network of streets towards fields. As Lily watched in the mirror, the Range Rover sped up and overtook them, revealing a second identical car behind it that quickly moved closer to their rear.

'I'm not sure,' Lily mused. 'But I think we're about to find out.'

The car behind pulled out beside them and the car in front slowed, then turned down a narrow dirt track. The adjacent car edged in closer, giving Lily no choice but to turn in after the first one.

'Shit,' she cursed. Who was in those cars? Several options swirled in her mind, but none quite made enough sense.

'Scarlet,' she said urgently as the car in front pulled to a stop, 'reach into the glovebox carefully – don't let them see. There's a knife. Slip it up your sleeve. *Quickly*.'

'What about you?' Scarlet asked worriedly as she did. 'Is there anything else in here?'

'No,' Lily admitted. 'But I've got my wits. They're sharp enough.' She subtly pressed some buttons on the centre console, dialling Cillian's number, then muted him. Hopefully he would catch on and listen in.

'Lil—'

'Come on,' she said, cutting her off as people started getting out of the two cars. 'There's no point putting it off.'

They exited the car and exchanged a tense look over the roof. There were six of them in total. Five men and a woman. The men had created a wide circle, but as Lily assessed them critically, she noted they appeared to be unarmed and made no attempt to move closer.

Lily's gaze narrowed as she studied the woman. She was tall, slim and elegantly dressed. Her movements were graceful, her naturally golden hair pinned up in a soft style that prettily framed her face. But her pale blue eyes were as hard as stone, and her steely expression took away any illusion that she was as gentle as her outward appearance indicated. Lily's grip tightened around the keys in her hand.

'What do you think you're doing, running us off the road like that?' she asked in a low, menacing growl.

The woman's eyes glinted with a note of amused interest. She looked her up and down pointedly. 'What do *you* think you're doing breaking into my home and stealing my property?' she asked, her accent clear-cut and distinctly upper class.

Lily swallowed, surprised. It had occurred to her that this could be related to the painting, but it had seemed a less likely option than some of the others. They had been so careful to hide their tracks.

'What the hell are you talking about?' she bluffed.

'You know exactly what I'm talking about,' the woman replied in an icy tone. 'My painting. You took it and I intend to get it back. One way or another.'

As Lily let her gaze wander towards the two men behind her, she suddenly recognised one of them. It was Duffy, one of Harry's friends from the party. She cursed inwardly. How could he have known it was them? What had they missed?

'What painting is that then?' Lily asked, stepping forward with fake confidence. 'We don't deal in paintings. We deal in a lot of things: stolen clothes, bags, shoes. We supply protection and escorts. And we deal in heavy handling too,' she added, the threat underlying her tone. 'The breaking of bones, the silencing of men.' She let the words linger for a moment, holding the woman's stare. 'But paintings are not our forte. So you have the wrong people.'

The woman smiled coldly. 'Oh, I don't think so. You see, very few people actually know about that painting. And of those, none would ever talk of it outside a very small circle.' She gave a cold, tight smile. 'How rude of me, I haven't yet introduced myself. I'm Grace Dupont. It was my house you came back to for that party, not so long ago. Where Harry tried to seduce *you*.' She pointed at Scarlet. 'If I'm not mistaken.'

Scarlet let out a sharp, humourless laugh. 'If that's what you call it. Your shitbag of a husband wasn't really in the mood to seduce – he just tried to force what he wanted instead. Whether I wanted it or not.' Her eyes blazed with anger.

Grace lifted her chin and looked down at her through narrowed eyes. 'Yes, I've recently been told of this penchant for other women. I even hear you have a video of him with one of your friends. Taken to be used for blackmailing purposes, I presume. But that doesn't really matter anymore. He's no longer an issue I have to deal with.'

Lily noted the menacing tone and wondered at it. Why was Harry no longer an issue?

'Anyway, that aside, I've been told at this party, in his drunken state, he decided to show you my prize possession,' she said in a bitter tone. 'God only knows why. That useless shit of a man really outdid himself on that one.' She turned and glared at Duffy, who quickly looked down.

Lily watched the exchange with interest. What had happened *there*?

'That much I know,' Grace continued. 'Then, a heartbeat later, my painting is stolen from my house by a team of people with East End accents like yourselves.' Her cold smile returned. 'Two of whom were distinctly alike. A likeness apparently not very well hidden by their disguises. You have twin sons, I hear?' She lifted one slender brow. 'We don't know many East Enders. In fact, I believe you were the first my husband had met in a while. Except for our plumber. But he had no idea about the painting and has been in hospital following a car crash the last few weeks. So I doubt very much it was him.' She tutted. 'It didn't take long with my connections to follow the breadcrumbs.'

Lily locked her jaw. There was little point in arguing it – there was no doubt left in Grace's mind. But she wasn't about to admit it. She looked around at the men surrounding her. None of them looked particularly hard. And if Duffy was anything to go by, they were probably there for show more than anything else.

'These your men?' she asked with a note of amusement. 'Where'd you pick them up then, the local book club? What they gonna do, stare us to death?' she scoffed and lifted her chin.

'They're not going to do anything to you,' Grace replied. 'Violence is not the purpose here. Of *this* meeting anyway.' She let the words settle. 'I merely wanted to meet you and ask you *politely* to return the painting.'

Lily exhaled and shook her head with a wry grin. 'If I *had* gone to the trouble of getting a team together, breaking into your house and stealing your painting,' she replied, 'then I doubt I'd be persuaded to bring it back, just because you asked politely.'

'Oh, I'm sure,' Grace said, stepping forward to stand directly in front of Lily. 'But when you realise, first, that no one at your level is equipped to deal with a sale of this size and that you can't safely sell it on without being discovered and arrested,' she said, pausing to let the words sink in, 'and second, that if you don't hand it back, I will systematically burn to the ground everything you've ever built, I'm sure you'll see things in a different light.'

She glared down at Lily, her gaze boring into hers. 'You don't have a clue what you're dealing with. This isn't some second-rate lorry you can pilfer and sell off for a few pennies. This is a piece of history. A piece people would kill for. A piece *I* would kill for.' She held her stare seriously. 'This isn't a game. This is millions of pounds, and you fucked with the wrong person.'

There was a short, tense silence before Lily responded. 'Are you quite done with asking politely?' she asked, dry sarcasm dripping from her words. 'Only, if that's all this meeting was, I can't see why we're all still here. And I have things to do.'

Grace gave a short, silent, humourless laugh. 'You're very *brave*, aren't you, Lily? I wonder how much you'll regret this show when you're in prison or watching your life burn to ashes.' She studied her in a strangely detached way for a few moments then pulled a business card out of her pocket. Reaching forward, she slipped it into the pocket of Lily's suit jacket. 'You have a week to return my painting. If it's not back in my possession by then, you can't say you didn't have fair warning.'

'I hope you find who took it soon,' Lily replied, turning back to the car and glancing at Scarlet to let her know to do the same. 'I'd say it was a pleasure meeting you, but…' She tilted her head dismissively before slipping into the driver's seat and closing the door.

She started the engine and turned the car around. No one stopped her. The men moved out of her way as she passed, watching in eerie silence as they left.

'Fucking hell,' Scarlet breathed, looking back over her shoulder and running her hands through her hair in stress.

Lily unmuted the call to Cillian. 'You catch that?' she asked.

'Some of it. What the hell was that?' he asked.

'That was trouble,' Lily replied grimly. 'But just how much I'm not yet sure.'

*

'What do you want to do now?' Duffy asked her as the black Mercedes drove away.

Grace narrowed her gaze. 'When I spoke about not being able to sell the painting on, it didn't faze her. Not one flicker of doubt, and somehow the younger one seemed more confident.' She twisted her lips to the side as the car turned out onto the main road and out of view. 'I suspect they're further along than we gave them credit for.'

'You think they have a buyer?' he asked, surprised.

'I think they may have made some connections,' she said carefully. 'It's not sold. Selling that would take time. Even if they caught on to the right track, they'd be new to the market. Certain assurances would need to be made before anyone would even show an interest. And I haven't heard anything through the usual channels. No,' she mused, 'they still have it. But I think I know how we can head them off and get the painting back.' Her features darkened. 'And I think I also know how we can bring them down at the same time.'

CHAPTER FORTY-NINE

'You did *what*?' Cath shrieked, dropping the towel she'd just picked up back onto the kitchen counter. 'You're pulling my leg?' She glanced from Scarlet to Lily, looking for confirmation that this was a joke but found none. 'You can't be serious,' she continued. 'Jesus R. Christ, Scarlet,' she admonished, planting her hands on her hips. 'You lot were supposed to stick to nicking knickers of the back of lorries, not famous bloody paintings! Clothes and bags is risky enough but *this*…' She put her hand to her head. 'They won't write this off like they do the other stuff – they'll hound you till your dying day for stealing that!'

'The police won't be looking for it,' Lily said quietly from her seat on the bar stool next to Scarlet. 'It's been missing for decades – they have no idea it's even in the country, much less with us.'

Cath frowned, confused. 'That makes no sense,' she said. 'How…' She paused and shook her head firmly. 'No. I don't want to know. I wish I didn't know *this* much.'

'You asked,' Scarlet said. 'You know we won't tell you anything unless you ask, Mum.'

'Well, I wish I hadn't,' Cath replied, annoyed. 'For God's sake, I'll be up all night worrying about you all now.'

In all the years she'd been married to Ronan she hadn't once got involved in the family business. He'd respected her wishes to stay out of it and had kept it separate, only letting her know the basics. But Ronan was gone. Now she had too much time on her hands and found herself rattling around a mainly empty house with too much and yet too little on her mind. For the first time since she could remember, she found herself wanting to be more involved, despite her fears and reservations.

'OK, fine, what do you mean it's been missing for decades? And what's worrying you if not the police?' she asked, pulling one of the bar stools around to her side of the kitchen island and sitting down to face them.

Lily and Scarlet exchanged a surprised look. 'You really want to know?' Lily asked.

'No. And yes. So just tell me,' Cath replied, reaching for her now rapidly cooling cup of coffee.

'The painting was stolen from a museum back in 1990,' Lily replied. 'The thieves were never found, and it was never recovered. Obviously,' she added. 'Turns out Henry, who we met at a recent charity ball, and who then—'

'Who then got very drunk and accidentally revealed it to me,' Scarlet said quickly, cutting Lily off with a meaningful look.

Cath frowned, glancing from one to the other.

'Yes. Well, he had it,' Lily finished. 'Or rather, his wife did. Hidden behind a secret panel in their study.'

'Oh, wow,' Cath declared, her eyebrows lifting in intrigue.

'So we stole it. They can't report it stolen, as it was already illegally in their possession, and it was a clean sweep. Or at least we thought it was,' she added.

'It wasn't?' Cath asked slowly, trying to keep up.

'Apparently not,' Lily replied shortly.

'Grace, his wife, cornered us earlier today,' Scarlet explained. 'She's demanding it back.'

Cath sipped her coffee, taking it all in. 'What are you going to do?'

'Nothing,' Lily replied. 'She's made some threats, but we're well equipped to handle her. Now she's shown her hand, we know to prepare our defences.'

'You make it sound like some sort of battle,' Cath commented worriedly.

'It is, in a way,' Lily replied. 'And we need to be prepared.'

'For what exactly?' Cath asked, frowning.

She glanced at Scarlet. Her daughter, her only child. She was all grown up now and making waves in the family business. Cath was so proud of her, with her strength and her work ethic and her clever ideas. But Scarlet was still her baby. Scarlet would always be that little girl she'd sheltered from this world all her life. And her heart still constricted every time she was reminded of the danger within it.

She sighed and braced herself. 'Well, go on then, tell me,' she demanded.

'For anything,' Scarlet answered. 'She threatened us, the business, but it was vague. So we don't know exactly what to expect. We all need to keep our wits about us.'

'Which includes you,' Lily added. 'So it's probably a good thing you do know.'

Cath sighed and stared past them both out of the kitchen windows into the well-tended garden beyond. 'You're already on the police radar at the moment, Scar. I know they ain't got the proof, but they want you for Jasper's murder – you know they do.' She turned to look at her daughter, deep worry in her eyes. 'This was a big move to be making when you're at the top of their shit list.'

'They want her, but they're not tailing her,' Lily answered. 'I would have cancelled it if they were.'

'And how can you be sure?' Cath asked.

'I've been keeping close watch. There's no one keeping tabs on her movements right now.'

'Still…' Cath trailed off with a worried twist of her mouth as she exchanged glances with a now sombre Scarlet. 'How are you going to shift the painting?' she asked. 'It don't exactly sound like it's something you can flog on the market.'

'No, we've had to make new connections,' Scarlet said. 'It wasn't too hard – there are only so many people at that level on the black market who deal in art.'

Cath bit her upper lip as she turned this over in her mind. 'If there are only so many people in that area of the market, the circles will be very small,' she pointed out. 'And if this Grace woman is well connected and deals in art herself, then she's likely in those circles already. Which makes you the outsiders.'

There was a short silence. 'This had crossed my mind,' Lily admitted, looking at Scarlet grimly. 'It's good business sense for him to work with us quietly as arranged, but it's true. We don't know if he already knows her.'

'Oh, come on, there's more than one art dealer on the black market,' Scarlet argued. 'And even if he does know her, like you say, business is business. He's hardly likely to screw himself out of the sort of money he's set to make with us.'

'Maybe,' Lily conceded.

Cath regarded them both for a few moments, a feeling of dread settling over her like a cloak. She stood and took her mug over to the sink, pouring away the cold residual liquid. 'I just hope you know what you're doing,' she said darkly. 'Because if you don't, God help us all.'

CHAPTER FIFTY

Dropping the lemon-and-mint teabag into the cup of hot water, Ruby put the glass lid on the jar and placed it back on the shelf. Her gaze swept over the neat row of matching jars and she felt a small tug of approval. It had been in total disarray before she'd decided to tidy up.

Natalie had said it didn't matter, because it was behind closed doors away from the eyes of the clients. She'd claimed it was a waste of time and profit and that Scarlet wouldn't approve that Ruby had bought the jars with some of the petty cash. But whether or not Scarlet approved she didn't much care. Ruby needed things to be very clean and very tidy, more and more these days. Mess and dirt had begun to make her feel anxious. When she saw it, it reminded her of the way she used to live, when she'd been on the gear. All that had mattered back then was getting her next fix, so everything else had fallen to the wayside.

Now when she saw unnecessary chaos, it sent her mind straight back there, and the familiar feeling of empty longing returned. But she could never go back. Not now Ray had decided her fate if she did. So instead she focused on doing all she could to keep that longing at bay. It was all she *could* do.

'Sandra,' she heard Natalie call out. 'Get Ruby to do that.'

She walked through and saw Sandra was sweeping the hair from the last client up off the floor. They locked gazes for a moment and Ruby made her way over, resigned.

'I'm fine, Nat,' Sandra replied. 'Ruby did the last two.'

'Well, as she should,' Natalie replied in a bolshy tone, shooting her usual disapproving look through the mirror.

'As we all should, I guess,' Sandra replied. 'We've all got to earn our bread, haven't we?'

Ruby blinked at the unexpected person in her corner, surprised. Sandra winked at her with a quick smile and then carried on with the brush. Looking down at the appointment book, Ruby felt a small prickle of warmth in her chest. She hadn't really paid much attention to Sandra; had mainly ignored her before now. She'd assumed, being so close with Scarlet, that Sandra would have the same natural aversion towards her as Natalie. But perhaps that wasn't the case. Perhaps she'd judged too soon.

Feeling slightly less defensive now, Ruby turned her focus back to the book. She scanned the page of appointments then flipped back a page. Sure enough, there was another appointment scribbled out with the word *Cancelled* next to it. Her eyes flicked up to check that Natalie was still busy, then she reached into her handbag and pulled out her own notebook. She opened it up and ran her finger down the list of names and times she'd written down until she found the one that corresponded with the appointment book, then marked a small star next to it.

'Right, now you just relax and enjoy your tea, Mrs Bevel,' Natalie said, walking away from her client and towards the reception desk.

Ruby swiftly closed the notebook and shoved it back down into the bottom of her handbag.

'I'll be back in twenty minutes to see how that colour's developing.' Natalie glared at Ruby as she rounded the desk. 'Out the way,' she said irritably, almost barging Ruby aside.

Ruby scowled and glared but bit her tongue. It didn't come naturally, holding back the things she wanted to say. But she was learning to do so more often with Natalie.

'Why you just hanging around anyway, eh?' Natalie demanded. 'Go and get the Windolene – give the mirrors a good clean. Go on,' she repeated in a rude tone.

Ruby retreated with a seething hiss. Natalie enjoyed bossing her around and talking down to her, but it wouldn't be for long. Because Ruby had uncovered what she was *really* doing with the books.

She'd patiently waited, gathering the evidence, and very soon she'd be ready to expose what was really going on. And when she did, the rest of the family were going to be truly shocked. She couldn't wait to see the look on her mother's face when she finally revealed her findings and took the step that would reveal Scarlet for the fool she really was.

CHAPTER FIFTY-ONE

'Arj, darling,' Grace said in a low, seductive voice. 'You know it makes sense.'

They were seated at a table on the busy rooftop bar above Selfridges. Beautifully draped foliage hung above and around them, and the busy chatter of happy parties of friends and couples surrounded them.

Arj sat back in his chair, twiddling the thin stem of his wine glass between his fingers, watching her with a fixed smile. 'I've done you a favour already, Grace,' he warned. 'You asked and I divulged information I really shouldn't have. What you do with that is your business, but I cannot be involved.'

'Why not?' she asked.

'I have a reputation to uphold,' he said. 'I can't be seen to screw over my own clients. Who on earth would come to a black-market dealer who did that?' He arched one eyebrow in question.

'They aren't clients,' she said with a dismissive tut. 'They're idiots who got lucky. *I*, on the other hand, *am* one of your clients.' Her smile dropped to an icy stare and the two other men at the table tensed. 'How much money have I put your way over the years, hmm?' she asked.

Arj's eyes glinted coldly back above his fixed smile. 'You've been a *wonderful* client on a number of occasions, but I do not work exclusively for you. I work for many clients, whether that's as a one-off or on a regular basis. But the only person I *serve* is myself.' He shrugged and took a sip of his crisp white wine. 'Even if I were willing to get involved with your personal dramas, which I'm not,' he added, 'I would be a fool to do myself out of the commission that sale is going to reward me with.'

Grace exhaled slowly. 'What if you didn't need to give up the commission at all?' she asked.

Arj's foot tapped the leg of the table. It hadn't been an immediate no, which gave Grace hope.

'And what exactly am I going to say when the Drews come knocking on my door, hmm?' he asked. 'I don't want to have to deal with that sort of drama, nor do I wish to be in their line of fire. You know, for all your dismissive talk about them,' he said, studying her closely, 'I don't think you really know that much about them.'

'Oh?' Grace declared. 'And you do I suppose?' she asked drily.

'I research all potential clients.' He shifted in his seat and looked out across the city in the swiftly falling dusk. 'They're a lot more organised than you think. And they're known for dealing with people who cross them brutally and efficiently.' He blew out a long breath and shook his head. 'I wouldn't want to be their next target.'

'You wouldn't be. I plan to deal with them too,' she replied. 'They won't be able to get to you or anyone else all after I'm done with them.'

'How?' Arj's interest grew and his gaze narrowed.

Grace sat back and watched him with a cold smile. '*Those* are details I'll divulge once I have confirmation that you're on board.' Her gaze bore into his. 'So are you with me or not?'

*

Lily swept into Scarlet's office with her mobile to her ear, gesturing frantically with her other hand for her niece to end the call she was on herself. Scarlet did so quickly, making swift excuses. Lily sat down opposite her at the desk and placed the mobile between them, putting the call on speaker.

'That's great to hear,' Lily said.

What's happening? Scarlet mouthed.

The forger's in town, Lily mouthed back.

'He has a very packed schedule though,' Arj's smooth voice sounded through the speaker. 'It's going to have to be first thing Saturday morning. As in crack of dawn, 7 a.m.'

Lily frowned at Scarlet over the desk. 'That *is* early,' she mused. 'That's really the only time he can do?'

'Like I said, he's packed out this trip. It's either then or we can set a better time on his next visit, but that's not going to be for a couple of months.' Arj sounded resigned. 'It's up to you. I'm happy to wait until then and we can make it to suit your diary.'

'No, no,' Lily said with a small shake of the head. 'That's fine. It makes no difference really, but I'd rather get things moving now. As for where—'

'It will have to be at the airfield where he's due to catch his next flight,' Arj said, cutting her off. 'Sorry. Again, if we wait until next time we can find a more convenient location, but he's due to fly out to Edinburgh straight after. It's only a tiny airfield just outside of London, barely even used most of the time; his next client has a little two-seater thing he wants to meet my guy there with.'

There was a short pause as Lily bit her lip and exchanged a look with Scarlet. They had wanted to control the meeting. As clients in possession of a painting like theirs, it should have been *their* choice of location and time.

'Hello?' Arj's voice came down the line into the room.

'Yes, we're here,' Lily responded. She took a deep breath and exhaled slowly.

'Is that OK?' he asked. 'Like I say, if you'd prefer we can arrange something more convenient on his next trip. I can find out in maybe a few weeks when he's planning to come back this way again. It's no issue.' His casual tone was polite and a tad bored.

Lily bit the inside of her cheek as she and Scarlet exchanged another glance. Scarlet pulled a face and looked away, leaning back in her chair, leaving Lily to decide how to proceed. 'Let's do it,' she said eventually. 'Send me the details of the airfield and we'll be there.'

'Good stuff,' he replied. 'Sending it over now. It's very discreet. Pretty old and basic, not much in the way of security. We'll have plenty of privacy, you can rest assured.'

'We'll check it out,' Lily replied. 'See you Saturday.'

Lily put the phone down and ran her hand over the bottom half of her face.

Scarlet regarded her with a serious expression from the other side of the desk. 'It's settled then?' she asked.

'It is,' Lily said, meeting her gaze. 'This wasn't what we wanted, but he's taken the choice out of our hands.' She frowned, then looked down as the text with the location address came through. 'We just have to trust that our instincts are right on this. And I really do think they're right,' she added with a nod. 'I can just feel it.'

Scarlet nodded. 'Your instincts haven't led us astray yet,' she said. 'So I guess we're doing this.' She looked over at her aunt with a sudden excited grin. 'Just a few more days and we'll be coming out the other side. We'll have actually pulled this off.'

'Absolutely,' Lily agreed with confidence. 'Just a few more days and that painting will be gone.' She smiled. 'And then all there will be left to do is decide what we're going to do with the money.'

CHAPTER FIFTY-TWO

Scarlet entered the crowded coffee shop on the corner and looked around. As her eyes swept the busy tables, she caught sight of John waving at her from the front of the queue.

'I'm sorry, I didn't anticipate it would be this busy,' he said with a grimace as she reached him.

Scarlet laughed. 'What, in a coffee shop right near Green Park at lunchtime on a Friday?' she asked wryly. 'No, I can't think why anyone would think *that* would be busy.'

John chuckled. 'Alright, smart ass,' he replied. 'I'm new to London – I'm still learning these big city ways.'

'Oh, really?' Scarlet asked as he passed her a coffee and picked up his own.

'Yeah, though I'm only from Essex. So, to be honest, I still don't really have much of an excuse.'

She laughed again and looked around. There were no free tables. 'Shall we walk through the park?' she suggested.

'Yes, come on.'

John led the way back through the crowd and out of the door. Once outside, they crossed the street and walked through the nearest entrance into the large park, taking a quieter path between the rows of trees away from the crowds.

Scarlet wrapped her fingers around her coffee cup, glad of its warmth. It was only autumn and the skies were still blue, but the days were definitely getting colder.

'Thanks for the coffee,' she said, taking a sip.

'You're welcome. Sorry I didn't reserve a table,' he joked, his bright green eyes twinkling in the sun.

She smiled and breathed in the cool air of the park. 'It's good to be out,' she said. 'I feel like all I've been doing lately is running from the car, to the office, to the car, to another office, to the car…'

'Oh no, are we back to life bingo again?' John groaned.

Scarlet laughed. 'Sorry. I do have some questions though that probably do count as life bingo.'

'Eugh.' He rolled his eyes and laughed back. 'Go on then. Get them out of the way.'

'OK.' She appraised him thoughtfully. 'How old are you?'

'Twenty-four,' he answered.

'Last name?' she continued.

'Richards. John Richards,' he said in a suave James Bond manner.

'Psychopath?' she asked, almost cringing as she realised she wasn't even joking. With her dating history it was wise to check.

John spluttered his coffee slightly, his dark brows shooting upwards in surprise. 'Not that I'm aware,' he replied with a grin.

'OK.' Scarlet nodded. 'That's all I wanted to ask.'

'I did my research by the way – on Scotland,' John said.

'And?' Scarlet asked.

'Inverness,' he said with a decisive nod. 'I'd like to check out the Highlands, and I can't pretend I'm not just a little bit curious about the Loch Ness Monster either.'

Scarlet grinned once more. 'That's pretty solid reasoning,' she agreed.

'What about you? What's your favourite place in Scotland?' he asked, sipping his coffee. He pushed his free hand down into his smart Barbour jacket as the wind pulled playfully at his golden-brown hair.

As they strolled through the park together, Scarlet noticed once more how attractive he looked. He seemed like a nice, genuine guy too. It felt good to be talking to someone who wasn't involved in their murky way of life, and who didn't have an urgent, life-threatening situation to deal with. Someone who just wanted to spend time with her for her company.

'I haven't actually been either, but it would have to be Fife.'

'Fife,' John said with a nod. 'The ancestral home of the old Scottish monarchs.'

Scarlet turned to him with a look of surprise.

'Like I said, I did my research. That was on the list of possible winners for a while, but the monster won out. So why Fife?'

Scarlet looked away without answering for a moment. 'I was ready to move there, just a few months ago,' she said. 'I got into St Andrews university and was ready to take my place.' She swallowed and their pace slowed to a more casual stroll. 'I was so excited, but then my dad died and my family needed me. My aunt and cousins were maintaining the family business, but they couldn't do it alone.' She glanced at him. 'And so I never went. Joined the firm, took over my dad's office.' Her gaze drifted away as the memory of her father intensified. It was always close, but sometimes it grew stronger, especially when she spoke of him. 'I still feel him there,' she admitted quietly, more to herself than to John. 'It's still his really.'

It took her a moment to realise they'd both stopped walking and that John was staring at her intently, understanding and sympathy in his eyes.

'I'm sorry,' she said, feeling her cheeks colour. 'That's not where I meant to take this conversation.'

'Don't apologise for being real,' he replied straight away. 'Don't ever apologise for that.'

At the same time, they both realised that, on instinct, John had put his hand on her back. He glanced at it and gently pulled it away. 'There's a bench if you want to sit?' He gestured towards it.

'Sure,' she replied as she did so, feeling foolish for spilling her emotions like that to someone she barely knew.

John turned his body to face her, but as he lay his arm along the back of the bench, he looked away, staring into the distance as if considering his next words. 'I get it. That feeling,' he said simply. 'I lost my mum three years ago. And that pain was just' – he shook his head – 'unimaginable. Unbearable, for a time. And it doesn't get better – ever. It just becomes, I guess, manageable – eventually.'

Scarlet nodded, understanding what he meant entirely. The pain never lessened, the love never weakened. But she'd learned the art of distraction and had developed the ability to control when her grief could come out of the carefully constructed box she kept it in. Most of the time anyway.

'I still can't walk into my kitchen at home, when I go back to visit, without expecting her to turn around with a tray of something she's just baked,' he continued with a small smile. 'I don't think I ever will.'

'I'm sorry,' Scarlet said softly, resting her hand on his arm.

His gaze locked with hers, and for a moment they connected through their mutual pain on a level that she'd never been able to share with anyone else. John understood her. He'd felt that same pain, the same loss.

'Well,' John said, clearing his throat and bringing them both back to the present. 'We got to the deep sharing part a lot faster than expected. I usually don't put out until at *least* the third date.'

He pulled a face to lighten the mood and Scarlet laughed, the sombre note to their conversation shattering. 'I guess that makes you an emotional hussy then,' she joked.

'Er, I think you'll find that stands for the both of us. And you made the first move, so…' He left it hanging and they both laughed.

As their laughter quietened, he studied her. 'I would like to try out that third date anyway,' he said. 'Even if I did already give up the goods.'

'Would you now?' Scarlet asked with a slow smile.

'I would.' He looked down at her hand, which still rested on his forearm, then gently lifted it and ran his thumb along her palm.

Scarlet felt a thrill rush through her body at the touch of his skin on hers and was both intrigued and embarrassed by it. What was she, some sort of schoolgirl? But as he met her gaze, she felt it intensify. What was it about him that captured her so? she wondered.

John's thumb paused, and her breath caught in her throat as they regarded each other across the bench. His gaze flicked around her face and rested on her lips, then his free hand gently touched her chin and guided her mouth to his, as he finally leaned in to kiss her.

She pressed into his arms as his warm lips brushed hers in a strong yet sensual motion, and she closed her eyes, giving in to the unexpected moment. She hadn't planned for this when she'd agreed to coffee. She hadn't thought much at all, actually, about what would happen when they got here. So many other pressing matters dominated her mind, like whether Saturday would go as planned, or whether the police would unexpectedly arrest her again. In fact, the last five minutes were not something she could have predicted if she'd had all the time in the world. But for some reason, kissing him, this almost complete stranger, on the bench in Green Park felt so natural, despite its randomness.

Eventually John pulled away, and he bit his bottom lip as he searched her face for her thoughts.

'Well,' she said, 'I guess that was a yes, to the third date.' She laughed, feeling self-conscious, and pushed her hair back behind her ear.

John reached forward and pushed a few strands she'd missed into place. 'Good,' he said finally. 'Because honestly those were my best moves – I had nothing if you still weren't sure.'

She laughed, then grimaced. 'Not sure we've actually reached the second though yet. Does the pub really count?' She shifted as she realised a discarded newspaper was wedged underneath her leg. She picked it up and glanced at the front page.

'I *was* counting it,' he replied. 'But I guess we could put that down as more of an introduction.'

'Shit!' she cried, pushing away from him and pulling the paper open fully.

'What?' he asked, frowning. 'What's wrong?'

'This, it's…' She shook her head as the picture stared up at her. 'Hang on, let me read this.' She scanned the words and her heart sank in horror.

John glanced at the paper. 'Did you know him or something?' he asked.

'Um, sort of. He…' Scarlet put her hand to her forehead. She needed to show her aunt straight away. 'I'm sorry, I need to go.' She stood up and refolded the paper. 'I'm so sorry.' She looked down at him, at the confusion on his face and felt terrible for breaking up the date. 'I've had a lovely time,' she said. 'And yes to the next date, definitely – second, third, whatever. I just really have to go right now.'

'I'll text you later,' he said with a look of understanding. 'I hope everything's alright.'

Scarlet reached for his hand and squeezed it. 'Me too,' she said. Then without further pause she turned and marched up to the main road to hail a cab.

CHAPTER FIFTY-THREE

Lily stared down at the newspaper in front of her as she leaned on the desk, her laced fingers pressed to her mouth. Scarlet paced the room and Connor leaned over her shoulder, reading the article. He exhaled loudly as he reached the end and stood up, his features set in a sour line.

'I can't say I feel bad for the bloke, after what he tried to do to Scar,' he said bluntly.

'Me neither,' Lily agreed. 'We're not concerned by the fact he's dead, but it has confirmed some suspicions.' She looked up and met Scarlet's gaze, a grave look in her deep brown eyes.

'What?' Connor asked, looking from one of them to the other. 'You think he was killed?'

'Grace practically admitted it when she ran us off the road,' Scarlet replied.

'When Scarlet told her what he'd done to her, she dismissed it, saying he was no longer an issue for her anymore,' Lily explained.

'Which could just mean divorce,' Connor reasoned.

Lily looked up over her shoulder at him with raised eyebrows and pointed back at the article.

He blew out a long breath. 'Fair enough.' He frowned and peered down at the page again. 'How's she done it?'

'I don't know,' Lily pondered. She began to read out loud. *'Found dead in a ditch by Anna Vickers, who was walking her dog… Terrible accident… Police believe Mr Chambers was making his way home after a night out with friends and was hit by a speeding car, forcing him head first into the ditch where it appears his neck was broken on impact. Police are looking for any witnesses.'* She pursed her lips. 'They're putting it down to a drunken hit and run.'

'If it were me,' Connor said, sitting down on the edge of his mother's desk, 'and I was trying to make it look like a hit and run, I'd have probably forced him to drink enough alcohol that he passed out drunk, staged him in the road, maybe got someone to hold him then jump out of the way at the last minute.'

'You'd have a car ram him for real then?' Scarlet asked.

'Yeah,' Connor replied with a nod. 'Definitely. The closer it is to the truth, the better. Less to fake for the police.'

'If it was hard enough to send him flying into a ditch at a force that his neck could break, there'd likely be a pretty big dent left over,' Lily mused.

'Yeah, but she wouldn't use one of their own cars,' Scarlet added, catching Lily's train of thought.

There was a long silence.

'It would have been Duffy's,' Lily said suddenly as she thought back to the odd exchange between them. She sat up straighter. 'It had to be someone she trusted. And you saw the look he gave when she spoke about Harry, didn't you?'

Realisation dawned on Scarlet's face as she thought back. 'You're right,' she said.

'What's that got to do with anything?' Connor asked.

'Maybe nothing,' Lily replied. 'But I wonder if we could find out where Duffy lives. If nothing else, we can bluff it as leverage if things get rough.'

'It's definitely worth keeping in our back pocket,' Scarlet agreed.

Connor bit his lip and nodded. 'And you still definitely want to go ahead with the plan?' he asked.

'Of course,' Lily replied emphatically.

'We don't even know if we can trust these people,' he argued.

Lily watched the stress reappear on his face. She knew he hated the idea, but everything was in motion. They were in deep, and she intended on seeing their plans through to the end.

'We can trust them,' she said firmly, hoping as she said the words that they were right. 'I know we've not done anything like this before.' She squeezed his arm. 'But sometimes you just have to play with the hand you've been dealt.' She took a deep breath. 'Just think of the millions,' she said with a grin. 'And how good it's going to feel when Grace realises what we've pulled off.'

CHAPTER FIFTY-FOUR

Cillian glanced up through the darkness at the camera facing the wide-open area below. 'It only covers this bit here by the entrance,' he said, turning to Scarlet. 'So as long as we go through the back, it won't pick us up. There's no other surveillance – I'm certain.'

'One hundred per cent?' she checked, looking up into her cousin's face.

He nodded. 'You want to do a run now or just wait till we set the area up tomorrow?'

'It can wait. Let's just check the fence round the back though – make sure we can definitely get through.'

They walked in silence around the old partially broken wire fence surrounding the area where it would all go down. It was eerily quiet and dark. Lily had asked them to come and scope out the area ahead of time, to make sure that there would be no unpleasant surprises when it came to transporting the valuable piece undetected.

Cillian had thought he was going to have to disconnect the one low-quality camera that faced the entrance, but discovering its inadequacy had already solved the problem. All in all, the trip appeared to be for very little. But it didn't hurt to be over-prepared. He glanced sideways at his cousin.

'How you doing anyway, little Scar?' he asked.

'Less of the *little*, thank you,' she immediately retorted.

He was glad the darkness hid the smile on his lips. She would always be little Scar to him, no matter how old she was. Even if she rose above him in the ranks.

'I'm good,' she said. 'I had a date today,' she continued casually.

His eyebrows shot up in surprise. Scarlet usually showed little more than disdain for the possible suitors that came her way. He'd watched her scathing rebuttals a few times and once or twice had even felt quite sorry for the poor guys. Not *too* sorry for them though. He liked to keep a silently protective watch over his strong, beautiful cousin.

'How'd it go?' he asked.

'Actually, really well,' she replied. He heard the smile curl into her tone, even though he couldn't quite see it.

'Nice. Seeing him again?' Cillian asked. 'Who is he? What's his name?'

'John. John Richards,' she said. 'Just some guy I met in a pub. He saved me, actually, from this total twat.'

Cillian frowned. 'You don't need saving,' he scoffed.

'I didn't say I *needed* it, just that he did,' she replied. 'Obviously, I let him know I was perfectly capable of handling it myself.'

That sounded more like the Scarlet he knew. 'John Richards,' he mused. He couldn't place the name. 'So he's not anyone I'd know?' he asked.

'He's not one of us,' Scarlet responded, correctly guessing the underlying question.

They continued tramping around the dark site in silence for a minute or two, Cillian swatting the low branches of a tree they passed out of the way.

'That's going to cause you all sorts of problems, you know,' he said. 'It's not quite as hard for me and Connor. If we date a girl who don't know who we are – which ain't often to be fair…' He ducked under another low branch. 'A guy going about his business, disappearing late at nights, not coming home. Most women can be persuaded to not ask questions, with the right assurances. But *you*. A woman heading out into the dark night to conduct some vague business, not coming home and all that. It's eventually going to raise some questions with your fella.'

'See, that just pisses me off,' Scarlet scorned. 'Why is that fair? Why is it one rule for one and one for the other?'

'No one said life was fair, Scar,' he replied. 'And I ain't saying I agree with it. But it's the truth.'

'It's downright fucking sexist,' she replied with an angry huff. 'But I know what you're saying,' she grudgingly admitted. She sighed. 'I don't want to think about that right now.'

'Fair enough. Enjoy what you've got going on, worry about the rest later.'

'What about you?' Scarlet asked. 'I haven't seen you with anyone for a while. Not since that Chastity.'

'That was Connor,' Cillian corrected.

'Oh, that's right. I only saw her once, sorry.'

'Easy mistake. I hear we look alike,' he replied with a grin. 'But yeah, I'm seeing someone, as it happens.'

They finally reached the part of the fence they'd eyed up from the other side. Cillian stepped back and surveyed it, looking for a weak spot. Scarlet found it first. 'There.' She pointed. 'It's already half broken. If we bolt cut to the ground, we'll slip through easy enough.'

'OK. We'll have to cut it tomorrow; I didn't bring cutters,' he said.

Scarlet turned to walk back. 'So what's she like? Does she know who you are?'

'Yes and no,' he answered. 'Yes, she does. But...'

'But not fully,' Scarlet finished.

'Yeah. Though I'll give her her due, I turned up covered in blood the other day and she didn't bat an eyelid. Just calmly got her story straight for if she ever got questioned by the filth like that.' He clicked his fingers on the last word, his tone impressed. 'She's actually a pretty interesting woman.'

'Wow. I don't think I've ever heard you describe a woman as interesting before,' Scarlet replied in mock shock. 'Are you finally growing up or something?'

'Don't be silly, Scarlet,' he replied. 'Why the hell would I want to do that?' He nudged her with his shoulder playfully and she laughed. 'Nah, but seriously, I actually really like her.' He reached into his pocket and pulled out a fresh toothpick, placing it between his teeth. 'I think Mum will too. Eventually.'

He heard his cousin snort. '*That* I can't wait to see. The day a woman is good enough for you or Connor.'

'Well, you will,' he replied with certainty. 'And sooner than you think.' He grinned in the darkness. ''Cause I'm bringing her to Sunday lunch.'

Scarlet stopped dead in her tracks.

'Are you mad? You can't bring her to Sunday lunch,' she said in horror. 'You *know* the rules.'

'I can and I will,' he replied. There was another short silence.

'I was wrong,' Scarlet said finally in a low serious voice. 'It ain't Grace we need to worry about at all. 'Cause that ain't nothing compared to the nuclear bomb that's going to blow when you rock up to the sacred family lunch with a girlfriend.'

CHAPTER FIFTY-FIVE

Ruby glanced at the clock as she mixed the colour up for one of the new stylists. Two of them had started now, both girls that had worked with Natalie in her previous salon. They seemed OK so far, though it had only been a few hours, so she was holding off forming any solid opinions of them.

Like clockwork, Natalie set down the last magazine she'd been straightening in the waiting area, put her hands on her hips and declared she was popping out for her break. Every day she took her lunch at twelve thirty, and every other day she'd leave via the back door that led out into the car park. Curious, Ruby had watched her once to see why and had found Scott, Natalie's boyfriend, hanging around there waiting.

Ruby moved into the back room, purposely taking her time with the colour. After a few seconds, Natalie swept past her, pushed open the heavy fire-escape door and walked out, letting it slowly close behind her. Quickly, before it could close and stubbornly jam again, Ruby shot her foot out to stop it. The door would swing easily without a noise, but it complained loudly when being pushed away from its tight frame. And she wanted to be able to follow Natalie out today without alerting her or Scott to her presence.

It had taken a while to figure out what Natalie was doing and, once she had, Ruby realised she'd need some sort of proof before she could try and trip the other woman up. Natalie was Scarlet's lifelong friend. Her *best* friend. She wasn't going to believe Ruby's story easily.

Over the last couple of weeks, Natalie had been religiously keeping the two sets of books that Scarlet had asked, but having watched these as carefully as she could, Ruby was now sure she'd figured out a third secret angle of Natalie's that would put her in the dog house and turn Ruby into a hero forever more, when she finally spilled the beans. And this was Ruby's greatest hope right now. To be able to stare Natalie in the eye as she sent the nasty bitch down and show Scarlet up for being naïve about her friend in the first place too. But if her hopeful suspicions were right, there was still one more element of it all that she hadn't quite figured out yet. Today she hoped to rectify this.

She waited a few seconds to allow Natalie time to cross the car park to Scott, then peeped out through the crack. Sure enough, Natalie had reached their usual corner and they were kissing each other passionately. She grabbed a nearby towel and replaced her foot with it, ensuring the door would remain open, then crept outside.

The good thing about the small car park behind the salon and the shops next door was that it was surrounded by an old crumbling wall with wide pillars sticking out here and there and patches of overgrown ivy. So Ruby could creep fairly close to the couple and remain concealed.

Natalie pulled away from Scott, and Ruby ducked behind a pillar, peeping through the greenery towards them. She pulled out her phone, switched it to video and pointed it towards the couple through the leaves.

They started a mundane conversation about their days. Ruby watched the seconds tick on through her screen. Scott told Natalie a long, boring, drawn-out story about a guy at his work and she began to wonder whether she'd been wrong about these meetings after all. Perhaps they really were just catching a few minutes together.

A sliver of doubt crept into her mind. Had she been wrong about the whole thing? She so desperately wanted to bring Natalie down, to see her fall from grace after the way she'd been treating her. In her desperation to do that, had she turned something simple into something sinister? She shook her head. No. She knew she was right. Natalie was a bad egg, through and through. And she was about to prove it. She just needed to be able to show Lily the whole picture, and these little meetings with Scott were part of it – she knew they were.

The back door to the salon opened and she ducked as Sandra's head popped out. She cursed. Had she been spotted?

'Nat?' Sandra called out. 'You seen Ruby?'

'Ruby? She's mixing colour for Rox, I thought?' Natalie called back across the car park.

'Don't matter; I'll do it.'

'Fuck's sake, where's she gone then?' Natalie moaned. Her voice lowered as she turned back to Scott. 'The miserable little beast.'

'Who's Ruby? The cousin?' she heard Scott ask.

Ruby noted with relief that Sandra had left the towel in place as she'd gone back in. She lifted her arm and aimed the camera towards the couple.

'Yeah, that's her,' Natalie grumbled. 'Still can't believe I'm stuck with her. She's only here so the family can keep her busy and out of the way. They don't want her around the real action, but they have to find *something* for her to do. So I have to play bloody babysitter.'

The words stung, despite the fact it was a truth Ruby already knew. She swallowed hard.

'At least it's an extra pair of hands,' Scott offered.

'That ain't much help – she's bloody useless,' Natalie argued.

Ruby bristled, feeling a stab of hot anger pierce through her abdomen. She was many things, she knew. But *useless* was not one of them.

'Anyway,' Natalie said in a bored tone. 'Here, take this.'

Ruby's attention sharpened and she watched as Natalie reached into her waistline and pulled out a small plastic bag. Her anger subsided and a smug feeling of glee took its place. She'd been right. This wasn't just a lovers' meeting – something else was afoot. She checked the screen to make sure the video caught what she was seeing.

'Nice one.' Scott took it from her outstretched hand and slipped it into his inner jacket pocket. 'I'll catch you tonight then, yeah?' he said.

'Yeah, I'll call you when I'm done. Here…' She pulled him towards her. 'Gimme another kiss.'

As they embraced once more, Ruby crept towards the salon and into the back room. She removed the towel from the door and let it close gently.

'Oh, there you are,' Sandra said, walking in with some dirty colour pots. 'Where'd you go?'

Ruby looked up at her, a wide smile on her face. 'I just had to catch a snake,' she replied mysteriously.

'A snake?' Sandra's eyes widened. 'Jesus Christ, in the *salon*?' she asked, horrified. 'Gordon Bennett.' She groaned and ran her hands up through her hair. 'I was just feeling comfortable with that damn toilet.'

Ruby blinked, confused. 'What are you on about?'

'Snakes, Ruby. *Snakes*,' Sandra said, looking at her in horror. 'Do you know how deadly snakes can be? I had this mate, right – Sally her name was – said that her friend Jamie was on the loo and a massive ten-foot-long snake came up through the pipes and bit her right in the arse. And it was poisonous and she ended up being hospitalised for weeks. Was never the same again according to Sally.'

Ruby stared at her. 'A ten-foot snake in the toilet?' she repeated.

'Swear down. It was in the news and everything, so it was definitely true,' Sandra insisted. 'Ever since then I've never sat down on a toilet without checking it first. Not once,' she said, nodding sagely. 'Not now I know that can happen. And I always try to go on a higher floor too. You know. To lessen the odds. They can't all be ten foot.'

Ruby narrowed her gaze at Sandra. 'You know that's not, like… here though. Right?' she said slowly. 'I mean, that's like Australia or the Congo or something.'

'So you'd think, Ruby,' Sandra said. 'But yet here *you* are finding snakes in the bloody salon.'

'I'm pretty sure this wasn't the toilet-lurking kind,' Ruby replied.

'You never know, Ruby,' Sandra warned. 'But I'll be double-checking before sitting on that loo again, I tell ya. And you should too.' She pursed her lips and walked back out onto the salon floor.

Ruby stared after her, amazed, and for a moment she completely forgot the reason she'd been out there. She was soon reminded when Natalie returned and gave her a withering scowl.

'Oh, turned up then, have you?' she asked, brushing past her.

Ruby narrowed her eyes hatefully at her retreating back. 'Your time is coming, Natalie,' she hissed under her breath. 'And a hell of a lot sooner than you think.'

CHAPTER FIFTY-SIX

Grace looked critically at a small building on the edge of the abandoned airfield. She squinted for a few moments and then looked away, satisfied that she couldn't spot an inch of her hidden car. It hadn't been easy wedging it between the back of the building and the tree, but it was the only place it wouldn't be spotted.

She smoothed her hands over the rough material of the clothes she'd borrowed from her good friend Archie – who'd taken them from the spares locker of the SWAT team – for the occasion. They came with a mask that covered her hair, so when they did jump out on the Drews, they'd have no idea they were not legitimate policemen. Four of her men were dressed in a similar fashion, and Archie was giving them a quick lesson on how to surround and approach.

She and Archie went way back to their school days – lifelong friends who had always had each other's back. He was the head of the art and antiques unit of the Metropolitan Police. This position had served them both well over the years, as Archie was as bent as they came. Whilst he ran the team who searched for the crooks of the art underworld, behind the scenes he was one himself, giving Grace tips and sliding her the occasional piece to sell on the black market.

Today was an entirely different operation to what they usually ran, but one that would prove financially worthwhile all the same. Archie had told his team that they were setting up a potential hand-off, but that they were not to arrive until 8 a.m., ready for the suspects to arrive at 9 a.m. In reality, the Drews were set to arrive at 7 a.m., to meet Arj and his contact. Arj would be there, the bait to lure them in, but once they got out of their vehicle, Archie and Grace and a handful of armed men in stolen SWAT gear would rush out and surround them, forcing them into the back of the nondescript van they'd been hidden behind and locking them away. Then, Grace and her men would take their car and the painting, Arj would disappear, and by the time the real SWAT team arrived at 8 a.m., the Drews would already be safely cuffed in the back of the van and the anticipated action would be over.

Archie would tell his team a tale full of bravery and luck, about how he'd managed to arrest them alone when they'd arrived unexpectedly early, and explain that some of their firm managed to escape with the painting. He would be labelled a hero, the Drews would go down for many years, and Grace would sell her painting, giving Arj and Archie a cut for their troubles. It was a win-win situation all round.

It had taken some persuading to get Arj in on the deal, especially when he'd heard Archie was involved. They were natural enemies under usual circumstances. But eventually the money had been too hard to resist, so he'd made the call to the Drews and had set them up for the biggest and last fall they would ever encounter.

'You ready for this?' Archie asked, walking over to her.

She smiled. 'More than ready. These ingrates have been the biggest ever thorn in my side.'

'We'll move hard and fast, get them locked down before they have time to think,' Archie replied.

'Huh.' Grace laughed. 'I wouldn't fear they'd do something as dangerous as that.'

'Don't underestimate them, Grace,' Archie warned. 'Rule number one of making a smooth arrest. Remember, they were smart enough to get the painting in the first place.'

Grace's jaw tightened at the reminder. 'Yes, well.' She turned to look out over the horizon. 'At least after today we can be sure they won't be able to attempt anything like that again.'

'Yes. Two of them anyway,' he agreed.

They had got Arj to call back and insist a condition of the meet be that only Lily and Scarlet attend. Overpowering the two women alone would be no issue. And even if the others were not too far away and decided to try and intervene, by the time they caught up, Grace and the painting would be gone.

She turned in a small circle and breathed in deeply. Since she'd arrived back from that fateful business trip, it had been one stressful problem after another. Every day had been full of dark tension and frustration. But not today. Today was going to be a good day. Today she would get her painting back and set all her plans back on the right track. She no longer had that useless, cheating husband hanging around her neck either, which meant her finances could stop taking the hits of his debauched weekends.

Sure, it hadn't been easy to stage his death in a way that would ensure nothing came back on her. But she'd managed it in the end. Quite neatly too, she thought with an element of pride. The police hadn't caught so much as a whiff of foul play.

She smiled, lifting her cool blue eyes to the weak morning sun. Yes, today was a good day. In just half an hour she'd have the painting back, the Drews would be on their way to prison for many years and there would be nothing but bright sunny days ahead.

CHAPTER FIFTY-SEVEN

'I still think we should be there with you,' Cillian's voice travelled though the speaker in the car. 'I don't like this. You shouldn't be walking into a situation like this without backup, with people you don't know.' He added, 'What if this all goes tits-up? Or what if it's some sort of set-up? They don't give a shit about *us*; all they care about is the painting.'

Lily shook her head as she looked down the road ahead, her hands tight on the steering wheel. 'It's too late for all this now, Cillian. Stop carrying on and remember who you're speaking to,' she replied sharply. 'I was building up this business and cutting shady deals before you were even cutting teeth.'

In the seat beside her, Scarlet couldn't help but grin. Her aunt had always had a way with words, and she knew her cousin wasn't going to like that response. The hiss of his exhaling breath down the line confirmed as much.

'This plan is the best one we've got, given the cards we've been dealt. Is it ballsy? Yes,' she admitted frankly. 'But that's exactly why it's going to pay off. Now, I have to go. We're nearly there.'

'Call me when you're out.' Cillian cut the call and silence fell over the car once more.

Scarlet felt the same tug of worry Cillian was feeling pull in her chest, and she lifted her hand to rub it. Lily glanced at her, clocking the action.

'You OK?' she asked quietly.

'Yeah, I just…' Scarlet looked out of the window, trying to quell her rising anxiety. 'There *are* a lot of wild cards at play. I get why he feels like that.'

'I do too,' Lily admitted. 'We just need to get this over with, keep our wits about us and stick to the script.'

'Stick to the script,' Scarlet repeated, nodding.

Lily took a deep breath and let it out slowly, the weight of the risk they were about to take showing in her face. 'You're a smart cookie, Scarlet Drew. As smart as they come. It's why I wanted you here in the family business where you belong. Where that brain of yours has room to thrive. And yes, this job may be slightly bigger than our usual ones, but that don't mean it will be any less effective. So have a little faith, yeah?' She waited until Scarlet nodded.

'Yeah,' she said with the level of confidence she wished she felt. 'It's going to be fine.'

Lily slowed to a stop in the road, the engine idling as they stared at the next corner. Just beyond it was the entrance. And once they turned in, there was no going back.

'You're ready for this?' Lily asked, glancing at Scarlet.

Scarlet took a deep breath and nodded. 'It's now or never, right?' She turned and met her aunt's gaze, ignoring the jangling nerves that danced in her stomach. 'So let's do it.'

CHAPTER FIFTY-EIGHT

Lily pulled the car in through the old front gate and slowly made her way over the crumbling tarmac towards the two men standing beside the black van in the middle of the wide-open space. They watched her approach patiently, not moving until Lily drew to a stop and opened the car door.

She stepped out, slammed the door and walked towards them, just a half step behind Scarlet. She started to gear herself up for the play ahead of them, but as their view of the area behind the van changed, she suddenly saw several other men she hadn't noticed before. As she caught sight of them, they clocked her too and they began to move together towards them.

Fear spearing through her like ice, Lily gripped Scarlet's arm and pulled her to a sharp stop. Scarlet froze, already on high alert for anything that could go wrong.

'It's alright, ma'am,' came a deep American voice from the man in front of them. 'They're with us – they're just here to help us verify the painting and take photos for our documentation.' He stepped forward towards them, his hand outstretched and a friendly grin on his face. 'I'm Agent Reynolds of the FBI, and it's a pleasure to meet you.'

*

'Where the hell are they?' Grace growled, pacing the small area behind the riot van where they waited. She checked her watch again. It was already twenty past seven. Only forty minutes before the *real* SWAT team was set to arrive. The Drews should have been here by now. They should already have them cuffed in the back of the van and *she* should be halfway back to London with the painting.

Arj pulled the phone down from his ear and shook his head, making a sound of frustration. 'They aren't picking up,' he said.

'You *said* they would be here on time,' she said through gritted teeth.

'I insisted that this was important,' he replied, holding his hands out. 'They said they would be here at seven on the dot.'

'This meeting is worth millions of pounds to them, or so they think,' Grace continued, stressed. 'Why would they not be on time for that?'

'I don't *know*, Grace,' Arj seethed. 'Maybe something happened. Maybe they – I don't know, had a car accident or something.' He raised his hands up and shook his head at her, widening his eyes to let her know he was plucking options out of thin air.

Grace made a loud sound of annoyance and turned sharply away from him. She folded her arms and exhaled through her nose, her cool eyes flashing dangerously as she thought the situation over. Could they have known they were being set up? Of course they couldn't have, she reasoned. They had been meticulous, and there was no one in the mix who would have tipped them off.

Archie walked over, looking at his watch. 'It's coming up for half past, Grace,' he said with a look of regret. 'We're going to have to pack this up.'

'No,' she breathed, grabbing his arm and pleading with her eyes. 'Archie, we're so close. They could be here at any moment. I can't just walk away.'

'You *have* to,' he said firmly, squeezing her hands as he removed them from his arm. 'My real team are on their way over, and if they find any of you here, there will be questions,' he pressed. 'This is over, Gracie. It didn't work. If they were going to come, they'd have been here by now. I'm sorry.' He turned and began collecting the batons and cuffs he'd given to each of her men.

Grace watched him walk away, stunned. This couldn't be happening. It had been the perfect plan – how could it have failed so spectacularly?

She closed her mouth, her jaw locking in anger, and she turned back to Arj. 'This isn't over,' she hissed. 'Come with me. We're getting that painting back, one way or another. If they think they've outsmarted me, they can think again. They haven't got a *fucking* clue who they're dealing with.'

CHAPTER FIFTY-NINE

'And that's when I saw it,' Scarlet continued. 'I couldn't believe it when I first looked.' She paused and shook her head with a small frown of disbelief to add depth to her story. The semi-circle of men in front of her watched intently, their gazes open and intrigued. 'I thought, well, it must be a fake. I mean, I *recognised* it of course. We studied Rembrandt at school. But I assumed that the real one must be hanging in a gallery somewhere. It was only when I looked it up online that I saw about the robbers who took it back in the nineties.' She pulled a face and blew air out through her cheeks. 'Then my aunt said maybe we should get it checked out to be sure.'

'And that's when you called us?' Agent Reynolds asked, making notes in a little pocketbook.

'Yeah. I mean, I googled who would be best to call. I nearly called one of the London museums.' She paused to laugh. 'But then my aunt saw online how you guys still had it under an open investigation and that you were offering a reward for information pertaining to its recovery.' She shrugged to admit she was only human. 'So I called you.'

Agent Reynolds nodded and rubbed his stubble. 'Well, that was a good call, young lady.'

'I'm just hoping it is the real thing now, and that I haven't wasted your time.' She gave him an anxious look. 'I would have hated to call you all the way out here for nothing.'

'Hopefully that's not the case,' he replied reassuringly. 'Let's take a look.' He flipped the cover of the notebook over and slipped it back into his breast pocket. 'Which one is it?' He looked up and down the row of units at the edge of the wide-open yard.

'It's this way,' Scarlet offered, stepping forward to lead the way. 'Number eighty-two.'

'And you only recently purchased this unit, you say?' he asked, falling into step beside her.

'Yes,' she answered enthusiastically. 'I needed some extra storage to keep bulk supplies in. Works out cheaper than buying the things I need for my salon as and when,' she explained.

'Oh, yeah, I get that,' he agreed.

'I heard they were auctioning off old units, contents and all, and figured it was a good idea. I thought I might find some interesting things inside, maybe some stuff to do a car boot sale with. Anyway' – she paused to find the key in her pocket as they reached her unit – 'I'm glad I did, because when I finally did manage to get in here the other day...'

'Which was the first time you'd entered the unit?' he checked.

'It was, yes. You can verify that with the manager if you like,' she said sincerely, holding his gaze with wide clear eyes. 'I didn't get a chance to open it up the day I bought it as I had to rush off. Anyway, that's when I noticed the box.' She put the key in the lock and turned it.

'The box?'

'Yes, it's in a box. Here,' she said, pulling up the shutter. The rumble of metal on metal resounded as it rolled up, then she stepped aside, allowing them room to enter. 'It's right there, at the back. I left it in the box. I didn't want to disturb it too much.'

'Thank you. Wow,' said Agent Reynolds as he moved further into the unit, past piles of old bits of furniture and general discarded junk. 'It's quite the, er...'

'Treasure trove,' Scarlet said with as much enthusiasm as she could. 'I know.'

'Yeah,' he agreed politely, eyeing up an old broken lamp. 'That's what I was going to say.' The FBI men and their team clustered around the box and began talking hurriedly about how best to check it. 'We're going to take it over to the truck,' he explained as two of them gently lifted the box.

'Of course,' Scarlet responded.

She hung back with Lily as the men climbed up into the van to check it over and Agent Reynolds walked off out of earshot to make a call.

'Nicely done,' Lily murmured.

'Thank you.'

They'd realised the connection between Arj and Grace when he'd made that call to set the time and place. They'd done their research beforehand and knew it was standard etiquette for the seller to decide the location for verification. This allowed for the painting to be moved around much less, reducing the risk of discovery or damage. So when Arj – a supposedly respected and experienced art broker – had insisted on the opposite so force-fully, they knew something was amiss. They'd then looked into the airfield and found it was barely a twenty-minute drive from Grace's estate, cementing their suspicions.

As soon as Arj had revealed his cards, they'd fallen back to plan B. Scarlet had been the one who'd come up with that idea. The FBI had offered a substantial reward for any information leading to the recovery of the painting ever since its disappearance. Five million pounds, to be exact. It wasn't the fifty million they'd been expecting it to reach at auction on the black market, but it was better than nothing. It was also a legitimate payment. Meaning the stress of having to try and find a way to launder it back into their pockets was taken away. It was all legal and above board and could be simply deposited into their bank account.

Both twins had been strongly opposed to the idea, pleading instead that they hold off and try to find another broker on the black market. But Scarlet had argued that they could never be sure Grace wouldn't infiltrate those connections too, and while she knew the painting was still in their possession, she would stop at nothing to get it back. In the end, Lily had made the final decision, decreeing Scarlet's plan to be the best way forward, all things considered.

Agent Reynolds finished his call and wandered back over, waiting beside them and watching the flurry of activity in the back of the open van with his hands shoved down deep in his trouser pockets. Eventually one of the men who'd tested it jumped down and gave him the thumbs up.

'Well.' Agent Reynolds' eyebrows shot up in surprise and he looked down at Scarlet. 'It turns out your suspicions were right,' he said. 'We'll have to run a few more tests back at the lab to make sure protocol is followed, but the ones they've just done are pretty accurate.' He shook his head and made a sound of amazement. 'I can't believe that's really it. After all these years. Stuck here in the back of an old storage unit.' He scratched his head. 'I'll need to take some details about the previous owner, if you have them?'

'Oh, he's dead,' Scarlet replied with a shrug. 'And no family left either. That's why it was all for sale. It was the end of the road. But' – she turned and pointed towards the small hut where the general manager of the site had a small office – 'they'll have his name and all those details for you to verify.'

'OK. Thanks. We'll need to get an official statement from you too, if you don't mind. And you'll need to fill out all the paperwork in order to get the reward money,' he added.

'Of course,' Scarlet agreed with a nod. 'I can come back with you now, if that's best?'

'Sure. Why don't you follow us back to the embassy and we can go from there?' he suggested.

'Sounds good.'

Scarlet and Lily secured the unit and returned to Lily's car. They strapped in and waited for the men to pull away in the van before following them out down the road.

'I can't believe we pulled this off,' Scarlet whispered.

'We're not out of the woods yet,' Lily warned. 'We need to get back and get our things in order. Because once we've done that, we still need to deal with Grace.'

CHAPTER SIXTY

Ruby entered her mother's office without bothering to knock. Lily looked up from the desk in surprise.

'Ruby!' she exclaimed. 'What are you doing here?'

'I need to show you something. Scarlet too. Is she in?' she asked cheerily.

Lily's face grew immediately wary. 'She is, but we're a bit busy right now.' She bit her lip as Ruby's face fell. 'What's happened?' She stood up, walking around the desk. 'Come on, if you're quick, we can talk. Scarlet's through here.'

Ruby let her mother lead the way and followed behind, clutching her bag tightly. Lily knocked briefly on the door to her uncle's old office and then walked in, leaving it open for Ruby to follow. Scarlet was searching through a filing cabinet for something.

'Hey, what's up?' she asked, before looking over. Surprise followed by swiftly masked annoyance crossed her face as her gaze landed on Ruby. She then looked enquiringly at Lily.

Lily shrugged. 'I'm not sure yet,' she replied. 'Ruby needs to speak to us both.' She closed the door and hovered.

Ruby took a deep breath, ignoring their obvious desire for her to leave. She put her bag down on the desk, then pulled out a notebook. She glanced at Scarlet severely.

'I noticed some discrepancies with the accounts,' she began.

'The accounts aren't your job,' Scarlet replied sharply. 'And there will be discrepancies. It's a laundry – that's the point.'

Ruby's hatred towards her cousin spiked, but she pushed it back down. Her issues with Scarlet could be dealt with later. This was more important right now.

'I'm aware of that,' she said witheringly. 'Let me finish.' She glanced at her mother, who was now watching her with interest. 'The discrepancies I noticed weren't the right sort.' She gripped the book tighter. 'To launder, Nat needs to be adding fake clients, not crossing out those who came in as cancelled.'

'What are you talking about?' Scarlet demanded with a frown.

'I noticed soon after we opened that she was crossing off clients and putting them down as cancelled or to be rearranged when they had actually been in. The till reflected those changes too, despite the fact they paid. So I started copying the appointments over into this.' She tapped the notebook. 'I kept track of who came in and who she marked off as a no-show. There's been one or two every day. Some of them spend quite a lot of money.'

Lily's expression rose into one of disbelief and anger, and she turned towards Scarlet. Scarlet held Lily's gaze for a moment before turning back to Ruby with a shake of the head. 'You must be mistaken. Have you asked her about it? Maybe it's not what you think.'

'It's *exactly* what I think,' Ruby said sharply. 'She's been skimming the money off the legitimate clients for herself. While still laundering the other like you asked.'

Scarlet stared at her for a long few moments, her features contorting until they settled into angry accusation. 'You're making this up,' she stated. 'You've not liked Nat since the moment you stepped foot in there.' She stood up and turned to Lily. '*This* is what I didn't want to happen. I *knew* there would be some issue, some *game*.'

'That's enough,' Lily said in a tone that brooked no nonsense.

Ruby laughed bitterly. 'Of *course* that's where your mind goes. It can't be true of your precious mate, can it?' she cried. 'Of me, your own cousin, sure. You'll believe anything. But not when it comes to your friends. You're as blind as a fucking bat when it comes to them.'

'I said, that's enough,' Lily snapped. She got to her feet and stood between them, glaring at them each in turn. 'Turning on one another is pointless,' she said sternly. 'That's the sort of shit that destroys families like ours, and we didn't raise *either* of you to do that.' She pushed her mess of tight curls back off her face and sighed. 'Let me see that.' She held her palm out for the notebook and began to flip through the pages when Ruby handed it over. 'Do you have anything else to back this up?' she asked.

'Yes,' Ruby replied, pulling out her phone.

She glared at Scarlet across the desk, then scrolled to find the video. She pressed play and ran the footage to just before the hand-off. Passing it over to her mother, she watched as Scarlet leaned in and they both witnessed the same thing she had.

'Every other day she meets him out back and hands it over,' she added as she heard it get to the right spot.

Scarlet's face paled and her hand shot to her mouth. Lily's expression hardened, her jaw locking grimly.

'She's even using the bags we use for the cashing up,' she continued.

'I can see that,' Scarlet snapped sharply, cutting her off. 'I can see that,' she repeated in a less aggressive tone, catching Lily's look of warning. 'Fuck!' she muttered, walking away and running her hands down her face before placing them on her hips.

Ruby couldn't help but feel smug at the way things had turned out. Natalie had looked down her nose at her since day one, and Scarlet had swanned around like queen bee whilst treating her like she was some sort of low-life peasant. Well, now the tables had turned.

Natalie had made a colossal mistake. She'd disgraced herself in the worst way possible. And Scarlet had made a mistake in hiring her. She'd made herself look naïve and blind and, worst of all, had put their business at risk by bringing a thief into the mix. This was not something her mother would stand for, and Scarlet's error of judgement would be remembered for years to come.

She, on the other hand, had come out of this situation smelling of roses for once. Already she'd surprised them all by actually turning up to that salon each day and doing her job. None of them had expected her to last even this long. But she had. And now she had been the one to uncover the sordid plan that was being carried out right underneath their noses.

'This needs to be dealt with,' Lily said. 'Now, before we deal with the other.' She gave her a meaningful look.

Scarlet nodded. 'I'll see to it,' she said severely, then swung her cold gaze away. 'They'll both be dealt with before the day is through.'

'They need to be,' Lily warned. 'You have three hours. Go get the boys and get it done.'

Ruby caught her breath as Lily turned back towards her. Because for once she'd seen something she'd longed to see aimed in her direction for many years. For the first time since she could remember, Lily actually shot her a look of approval and respect. And for the first time since she'd been off heroin, Ruby felt a flood of genuine, warm happiness wash through her heart.

CHAPTER SIXTY-ONE

Scarlet watched Natalie approach the front of the factory and went to open the door for her friend.

'Ta,' Natalie said brightly, stepping in and unwinding her scarf from her neck. 'Christ, brass monkeys are beginning to shiver out there now, I tell ya,' she exclaimed. 'Summer's definitely over, ain't it?'

Scarlet nodded with a tight smile that didn't reach her eyes. She couldn't bring herself to answer her best friend of so many years, not trusting what might come out of her mouth.

'You alright?' Natalie asked with a concerned look. 'What did you want to talk about anyway that couldn't wait until tonight?' she asked.

'Come with me,' Scarlet finally said, clearing her throat of the huskiness she heard there. She turned and moved through the factory towards the stairs to the basement. The last machine was still winding down for the day, but all the workers were gone. They had sent them all home early.

Not picking up on the unusual quiet, or the tension in the air, Natalie fell casually into step beside her. 'Is it about that witch of a cousin of yours?' she asked. 'Tell me she's done one,' she continued in a wishful tone. 'I 'ope she bloody has. Little cow only went and walked out today during our busiest period.' She tutted in annoyance. 'If she was anyone else I'd have sacked her on the bloody spot,' she claimed indignantly. 'She went off to mix a colour for Roxanne and never came back.'

As they passed the steps that led to the offices, Scarlet glanced up. Her aunt stood at the window of her office, watching them. One arm crossed over the other, a glass of what looked like whisky in one of her hands. Her expression was sombre but unreadable. After a moment, Lily turned away out of sight.

They reached the stairs to the basement and Scarlet gestured for Natalie to descend ahead of her. Still chattering away, Natalie happily complied, walking down and looking back at Scarlet over her shoulder as she went.

'The client was sat there for ages, just waiting like a lemon. As was Rox. Expecting Ruby to come back with the colour. We looked like right bloody prats. Sandra had to mix it in the end. But it didn't look good, Scar.'

They reached the bottom of the stairs and Natalie pushed through the closed double doors, stepping into the basement beyond.

As the sight that met her registered, she gasped loudly in shock. Scarlet closed the doors then leaned back on them, watching Natalie's reaction through cold eyes.

In the middle of the wide-open space, Scott was trussed up, his hands and legs tied by ropes as he knelt on a plastic sheet on the floor. One of his blackened eyes was swollen shut, and blood trickled from his nose and the corner of his gagged mouth. He appeared to be crying, and as they watched he swayed, dangerously close to passing out from the force of the beating he'd already received.

Connor paced behind him with a bat in his hand, his jacket discarded, his shirt sleeves rolled up and buttons undone to the waist, revealing a tightly fitted vest beneath. His hands were gloved, to protect them from the blowback of his punches, and his neck and forehead shone with perspiration.

Cillian appeared from the shadows nearby and stood beside her at the door. He was in a similar state but slightly more composed than his brother, indicating to Scarlet that Connor must have been the one having most of the fun. She hadn't seen Scott's retribution so far. She'd been too busy locked in her own personal hell upstairs, torturing herself over what to do with her friend.

Natalie swivelled round, the shock and fear clear on her face. 'Oh my God, Scarlet,' she exclaimed. 'What's going on? What's happening?'

Scarlet stared back at her coldly, her anger growing at the fact that Natalie had put herself in this position in the first place. 'I think you know exactly what's going on, Nat,' she replied steadily.

'N-No, I don't,' Natalie argued.

But Scarlet could tell from the look of guilt that flooded across her face that she did. She nodded and looked down sadly.

Scott tried to call out to her, but only muffled sounds came through the gag.

'Shut up,' Connor spat, stepping forward and backhanding him hard across the face. He fell to the ground, his sobs intensifying.

'Scott!' Natalie began to run forward on instinct, but Cillian grabbed her arm and yanked her back.

'I don't think so. We're going over here.' Ignoring her whimpers of protest, he pulled her roughly over to the large, wooden throne-like chair that faced the gruelling scene a few metres away and forced her down.

Scarlet followed slowly, her stiletto heels clipping out a sharp rhythm that echoed around the eerie basement. She stopped in front of Natalie and looked down on her with contempt. Natalie peered up, her eyes wide with fear.

'Scar,' she whimpered softly. 'What are you doing? You're scaring me.'

'Good,' Scarlet answered bluntly. 'You should be scared.' She nodded to confirm her words. 'You should have been scared before now,' she added. 'At least enough to not steal from me and my family.'

'What?' Natalie asked, her voice shaking. 'I haven't. I wouldn't!'

'You *have*,' Scarlet roared, bending down into her face and grabbing the arms of the chair in which Natalie sat with both hands. 'And clearly *would* have continued, had you not been caught out.'

Natalie pulled back in terror, away from her furious friend. Tears began to fall from her eyes, and she sobbed loudly as she tried to find the right words. 'I-I-I didn't mean…' She sobbed again, her eyes darting all over the place as she tried to find a way out. 'Please – I – Scar – I'm your best mate.'

'Exactly,' Scarlet spat with a furious glare, pushing back off the seat. She walked away, suddenly unable to be so near to her. 'You were my *best friend*.' She shook her head, unable to wrap her head around the betrayal. 'How could you do that to me? How could you be so fucking disloyal?' She ran her hands through her hair. 'I gave you an opportunity to leave a job you hated and take over a salon. I paid you more than you've ever been paid. And *this* is how you repay me? By *stealing* from me? What were you thinking?'

'I-I wasn't,' she stammered through the tears. 'I wasn't thinking, Scar. It was just a stupid mistake.'

'No,' Scarlet said firmly with a shake of her head. 'No, that's not a mistake. A *mistake* is accidentally putting the wrong kind of bleach in a customer's dye. A mistake is forgetting to charge them for an extra treatment they added at the last minute. *This* is purposeful dishonesty. This is stealing money from a friend. A friend who's part of a world that *should* be on your list of things never to fuck with. I mean, I thought you were *that* smart, at least.'

'I-I'm sorry, Scar,' she said pitifully through her tears.

'Sorry don't cut it,' she replied savagely. 'You stole from an organisation much bigger than me, Nat. And those who steal from us have to pay the price.'

She nodded at Cillian, who grabbed Natalie by the arms and yanked her into a standing position.

'No!' Natalie screamed in terror. 'No, please! It wasn't even my idea! Please don't hurt me!' Her screams echoed loudly around the large room.

Scarlet stood face to face with her, rage and disgust battling for top position in her eyes. 'Not your idea? Who's was it then? His?' she asked, pointing at Scott.

Natalie clamped her mouth shut, and her features filled with pain and fear as she looked over to her battered boyfriend on the floor. It was clear she didn't know what to say. Scarlet narrowed her gaze, then turned and began pacing from side to side.

'Well, if you ain't gonna talk…' she said after a few moments. She lifted her hand as if to give Cillian a signal but was cut off by Natalie's next words.

'No, wait, it was him,' she admitted, through her sobs. 'OK? It was his idea. He said you wouldn't miss it – that the legit money didn't matter to you so long as you covered your costs and could launder enough money through.' Her chest heaved as she drew another panicked breath in. 'I knew it was wrong, but I just went along with it.'

Scarlet lifted her eyebrows with a smirk of disbelief. 'Do you hear that, Scott?' she asked, turning to the bloodied man on the floor. 'Your beloved girlfriend just threw you under the bus to try and save her own skin.' She shook her head in disgust. 'I guess none of us mean that much to her after all.'

She nodded at Connor, who took a running start at Scott and kicked him hard in the stomach. He pulled his leg back and kicked him again and again, the dull sounds of the impact nothing compared to the man's cries of agony.

Natalie started forward once more, screaming for Connor to stop, but Scarlet grabbed hold of her, wrapping her arm around her chest and pinning Natalie's arm, then grabbing a handful of her hair in a fist. Natalie's free arm shot up to try and loosen Scarlet's, but in her rage, Scarlet was too strong. She forced the other woman forward, pushing her head towards the violent scene.

'Look at what you've done,' she roared. 'Go on, look! *That's* what happens to thieves around here, Natalie Baker. *That's* what happens when you cross a family like mine.'

'Stop, please,' Natalie begged. 'You're killing him!'

'Perhaps,' she replied, no emotion in her voice.

'Please, I'll give it back, every penny, I swear!' She sagged under Scarlet's vice-like grip as Connor kicked Scott again and again.

'It ain't about the money, Nat,' Scarlet replied. 'It's about the betrayal. It's about the disloyalty. And it's about the fifteen years of friendship you've just thrown down the drain,' she spat.

Her heart hurt as she held her sobbing friend. As she held the one person she'd thought she could trust over anyone else outside her family. The person she'd whispered her dreams and her fears to for as long as she could remember. The person she'd have taken a bullet for and who – up until this very day – she'd thought would do the same for her. She squeezed her fist tighter, making Natalie cry out.

'This ain't you, Scarlet,' Natalie wailed, changing tack. 'This ain't who you are.'

Scarlet twisted Natalie round and pressed her face to hers. 'This is *exactly* who I am,' she growled through gritted teeth. 'It's who I've always been, who I was *born* to be. Only you were too stupid to remember that.'

She locked gazes with the friend she loved and hated so dearly for a long, painful moment. Then, in one swift, hard movement, she threw her to the side. Natalie landed on the floor, putting her hand to her aching head as she curled up in pain and sobbed louder.

Scarlet took a deep breath in an attempt to compose herself, then signalled for Connor to stop. He did so, stepping back with a sniff, wiping the sweat from his brow with his shirtsleeve.

For a few moments the room fell silent, apart from Natalie's sobs and Scott's weak, laboured breathing. 'You can keep the money,' Scarlet concluded in a controlled voice. 'You'll need it, when you leave here, to help set yourself up somewhere new.' She sniffed and placed her hands on her hips, her emotions still in turmoil, despite her cold, calm exterior.

'What do you mean?' Natalie asked between sobs.

'I mean that for old times' sake, I'm letting you go,' she said, swallowing hard. 'Both of you. We'll drop Scott at the hospital. He'll tell the nurses he was mugged down a dark alley and can't remember anything else. And you can go home. But once you're there, you'll pack your bags, say your goodbyes and get the fuck out of this area.'

'Wh-What? Where would I go? This is my home,' Natalie whimpered.

'Not anymore it ain't.' Scarlet turned to face her, her grey-blue eyes harder than steel. 'The day you turned on me was the day you gave up any right to stay anywhere around here. Because this is Drew territory. So if I find out you haven't gone, if I lay eyes on you again for any reason' – her gaze bore into Natalie's terrified eyes – 'you'll be right back here. And things will finish in a very different way.'

Lifting her chin and feeling the ice of her ruling chip away one more piece of her heart, Scarlet turned away from her best friend for the last time.

CHAPTER SIXTY-TWO

Cath indicated to turn and waited as the traffic coming from the other way passed them by. She glanced sideways at her daughter. Scarlet's face looked drawn as she stared unseeing through the glass ahead. It was understandable, after all that had happened with Natalie the day before.

A gap cleared in the traffic and Cath turned, pulling the car into the long road that led to Lily's house. Next to her, Scarlet pushed her long raven hair back and rubbed her eyes tiredly.

'You look exhausted,' Cath said quietly. 'We could have missed this one, you know. Lily wouldn't have minded.'

Scarlet turned to her and raised an eyebrow in disbelief.

'We still could have missed it. She'd have understood, at least,' Cath corrected.

'Nah, I'm OK,' Scarlet replied, dismissing the notion.

Cath ran one hand back over her own hair, checking there were no flyaway strands. 'Who's minding the salon today? Sandra?'

'Yeah, she's in. It's not too busy today anyway, so it should be fine. I'll pop over later to check she's OK.'

'I still can't believe Natalie stole from you,' Cath replied, pursing her lips. 'I'm shocked actually. After all the years you two have been friends. You were like sisters as kids – inseparable.'

'People grow up. And the people they grow into aren't always who we expect.' Scarlet turned and stared out of the passenger window.

'I guess,' Cath replied sadly, glancing at Scarlet.

It was true, you never knew what to expect from a person. She'd never expected to see Scarlet enter the family business. She'd never expected that she'd be so hard and so fierce. And she also hadn't expected how strong and resilient and clever her little girl would turn out to be. She was so proud of the person Scarlet had become. So proud that sometimes it hurt.

Yes, people did change when they grew up. But not just then. People were capable of change at any time. People adapted to their surroundings and their situations as fluidly as a river bending round canyons. That was what made them human. That was what helped them survive even the toughest of life's challenges.

She bit her lip as they drew closer to the house. There was something she'd wanted to ask Scarlet for a while, and until now she hadn't quite worked up the courage. But now it was time.

'Scar…' she started.

'Yeah?' Scarlet continued looking out of the window.

'With Nat gone, you're going to need to hire someone else for the salon, aren't you?' she asked carefully.

'Yeah. I was thinking about that actually,' she replied.

'Yes?' Cath asked, her hopes rising. Had Scarlet perhaps been thinking the same thing that she had?

'I'm not going to hire a new manager; I'm going to promote Sandra. She's really good and she seems to have really taken to the place. She needs a bit of guidance but nothing she won't pick up quickly,' Scarlet replied.

Cath considered this. 'That's a good idea actually. She's a good girl. But then what about—'

'Ruby?' Scarlet cut her off. 'There's not much I can do about getting rid of her.' Her tone turned glum. 'But for now she's pulling her weight so I guess I shouldn't complain. Until she fucks things up in some colossal way, that is.'

'Actually, I think you should promote her too,' Cath stated.

Scarlet turned to her with a look of horror. 'You're joking?'

'No, I'm not.' Cath turned into Lily's road and began to slow down. 'Whatever your beef is with her, she did you a big favour in sniffing Nat out.'

'My *beef* is just the same as the rest of the family,' Scarlet replied indignantly. 'She's brought nothing but pain and destruction into our lives for years.'

Cath frowned and shook her head. 'No, that's not it. What's between you two runs deeper than that. But whatever it is, you need to figure it out. Because she's here to stay, Scar. It's different this time and you know it. Whatever the reason, she hasn't upped sticks, and she ain't fighting against us all like we're her own personal devils anymore. She's actually trying. And I think if you showed her that you see that, give her a little boost, that would go a really long way.'

Scarlet blew out a long breath and shook her head, but she didn't dismiss the idea. Cath pulled the car up onto Lily's drive and cut the engine. She undid her seat belt and turned towards her daughter, feeling a quiver of hope and fear flutter in her stomach as she finally approached the point of her conversation.

'Thing is though, you're still a person down. And I know that's making the juggle a lot harder.'

'I know. Don't worry, I'll put an ad out this week,' Scarlet said, hurrying to reassure her.

'What if you didn't have to?' Cath asked.

'Why, do you know someone?' Scarlet responded, looking over at her mother in interest.

'Yes,' Cath replied with a short laugh. 'Me!'

'Oh, Mum, don't worry about that. You really don't have to bother yourself with—'

'But that's just it, Scar,' Cath interrupted. 'It's not a bother. I actually *want* to.'

Scarlet searched her mother's face in confusion. 'Why?' she asked.

'Oh, Scarlet!' Cath shook her head. 'You know, since your dad went, I've been floating round that big house every day searching for something to do and I'm bored. Really, truly bored. I need a purpose. A reason to get up every day, you know?'

'You've got me,' Scarlet offered.

'I know, and darlin', you're everything to me. You're the reason I still breathe,' she said with feeling. 'But you're grown up now. You don't need me anymore, not really. Or at least, not in the same way.'

She sat back in her seat and sighed, staring over at Lily's front door. 'I was only twenty when I had you, you know. So young. And not that I'd change that,' she added quickly. 'But I threw myself into being a mum and a wife and that's all I've been ever since. Before that, though, I actually did a hairdressing apprenticeship. Did you know that?' she asked.

'No,' Scarlet replied, astonished. 'Christ, how could I not know that?'

'It was all over before it took off really. And I never talk about it much. Life before I married your dad is just one big hazy memory mostly. But I had so much fun back then, working with the girls and chatting with the clients. I loved it actually,' she admitted.

'So you really do want to work in the salon?' Scarlet asked gently.

'I do,' Cath replied. 'You know, I look at myself. I'm a widow with no career, next to no work experience, and other than you, nothing to really show. And the saddest part is, although I basically live the life of an old woman, I'm only thirty-eight.' She winced. 'I have so much life ahead of me still, and I can't just sit there rattling round the house doing nothing for the next fifty years. I need a job. I need a purpose.' She turned to Scarlet and looked her in the eyes. 'So please hire me? I know my old qualifications won't count – I'll need to go back to night school or something, but I could still be useful. I could help Sandra and Ruby; I could cover shifts when they can't be there. I can do a lot of things.'

Scarlet reached forward and grabbed Cath's hands. 'Mum,' she said, 'you don't have to sell me on it. The job's yours. Christ, the whole salon's yours if you want it,' she added with a laugh. 'I'm sorry, I hadn't realised you wanted in so badly.'

Cath's face lit up with happiness. 'Just the job will do,' she said with a small laugh. 'And thank you.' She squeezed Scarlet's hands. 'I appreciate that more than you know.'

'You never have to thank me for that, Mum,' Scarlet said. 'Come on, let's get inside. I wonder if Cillian's here yet.' She stepped out of the car and Cath followed. 'I do hope we're early. I wouldn't want to miss this for the world.'

'What are you talking about?' Cath asked with a frown.

'Oh, you'll see,' Scarlet answered with a low chuckle. 'You'll see.'

CHAPTER SIXTY-THREE

Lily glanced sideways at Cath with a narrowed gaze. Ever since they'd walked in, she and Scarlet had been acting strangely and exchanging what they obviously thought were private looks. What were they up to?

'Fancy a top-up?' Cath asked, reaching for her glass. Her eyes shot to the door and a fleeting look of worry crossed her face as a car drove past. Lily frowned. What on earth was going on with her sister-in-law today?

'Sure,' she replied, though Cath had already begun pouring. 'That's enough though – Christ, you trying to get me drunk?'

Cath laughed, a tad too brightly, then changed the subject. 'What are we doing with these peppers?' She stood next to Lily at the island where all the food was out, ready to be prepped, and tied the apron she'd just picked up behind her back.

'Slice them up, nice and thin. I want to stir fry them with some onion to put on top of the pork,' she answered, handing Cath a knife.

'Ooh, lovely,' Cath replied, grabbing a chopping board and pulling the peppers towards her. 'A Mediterranean twist.'

Lily picked up her own knife and began roughly chopping the potatoes she'd peeled earlier on.

'Come on then, drink up,' Cath urged, handing her the glass and taking a sip of her own wine with an encouraging smile.

Lily frowned and put the wine down, planting her hands on her hips and turning to face her sister-in-law. 'Cath, are *you* pissed?' she asked. 'Why are you so intent on me downing my wine?'

'No, I'm not, thank you very much!' Cath replied indignantly. 'It takes a bit more than one glass. And I was just thinking that you probably need a good drink or two after everything that's happened. You know, take the edge off, help you relax.'

'I don't need to relax; I need to stay on top form right now,' Lily replied, turning back to the potatoes. 'I'll have one drink, but I don't need to be downing them like they're the last few drops of water in the desert.' She watched Cath and Scarlet exchange glances again out of the corner of her eye as she chopped.

'Mum's right, you know,' Scarlet piped up. 'It wouldn't hurt to get a bit merry today. We've got some tough days coming up – we might as well relax while we can.'

'Drinking is the last thing we need to be doing,' Lily replied flatly. 'We need to keep our wits about us.'

There certainly were some tough days ahead. Grace was not someone who was going to be that easy to get rid of. She was a dangerous woman who would not take being made a fool of lightly. She'd killed her own husband for his betrayal, so she was hardly about to let a firm she had no love for get away with the stunt they'd pulled. She would be on the warpath, and they were going to have to deal with her – one way or another – if they hoped to ever be able to walk down a street without looking over their shoulders again.

There were a lot of fires to put out before they made it out the other side of all this yet. But that was OK. Putting out fires like this was what Lily was good at. And once they'd dealt with Grace, they could get back to dealing with everything else.

Her gaze rested on Scarlet. The police were still only a few steps behind, keen on her niece for Jasper's murder. Robert had said that there was nothing solid enough to stand up in court, but what if they pursued it anyway? What if they found something else? She pursed her lips and filed this away for later. Right now, the priority was to deal with Grace.

'I made the call to Arj by the way,' she said.

'And?' Scarlet asked, her attention sharp.

'And I told him to tell her we'll be waiting at the factory tonight, at ten, to talk to her.'

Scarlet nodded, her expression serious. 'Tonight? OK.'

Cath pulled a worried face. 'I hope you know what you're doing, Lily,' she said quietly.

'I do, don't worry.' Lily breathed in and sighed. 'We still have a way to go to deal with Grace, but I'm not even entertaining it until tonight. It's Sunday. And I don't give a shit who she is – she ain't getting in the way of our family lunch,' she said firmly.

'No, nobody gets away with doing that,' Scarlet said in a strange undertone.

Cath was taking a drink next to her and suddenly spat half of it out over the counter as she choked on what she'd been about to swallow.

'Jesus, Cath,' Lily admonished, handing her a tea towel. 'You OK? What is going *on* with you today?' She put her knife down and turned towards the pair of them, glancing at one and then the other in turn. 'Am I missing something here?'

The front door opened and Lily glanced over as Connor entered.

'Alright, Mum? Scar, Aunt Cath.' He nodded to them each in turn, walking over to give his mother a kiss on the cheek.

'Alright?' Scarlet replied, a strange combination of relief mixed with tension written on her face.

'Where's your brother?' Lily asked. 'He not with you?'

'Nah, he um…' Connor glanced at Scarlet with a curious gaze as if trying to work something out. 'We came in separate cars. He just pulled up though, so he'll be in in a minute.'

Lily watched as Scarlet's eyes widened and her smile became fixed. Connor glanced at his mother with what looked like guilt before he ducked off into the lounge. 'I'll see you in a bit.'

She felt Cath's arm brush against hers but thought nothing of it as she watched her son's retreating back. Shaking her head, she reached down for her knife and found it was suddenly missing. 'Oh, where's that gone?'

She glanced up and down the island at all the food waiting to be prepped but there was no sign of the knife she'd been using. Cath was focused on chopping the peppers, her head down and her eyes on the food. With a shrug, Lily reached down to open the knife drawer to grab another one, but as she pulled, there was an unexpected resistance. She glanced sideways and saw Cath's hip was pressed up against it.

'Cath?' she asked. But Cath appeared not to hear her.

She exhaled, trying to dispel some of her growing annoyance.

'Cath?' she repeated. She tried pulling the drawer again but Cath seemed to be pressing against it even harder. 'Jesus! Cath!' she shouted.

'Hm?' Cath turned to her with a bright fake smile.

'The drawer,' Lily replied, her tone laced deeply with irritated sarcasm. 'You're leaning against it.'

'Hmm,' Cath replied with a nod, her fixed smile not wavering.

'And I'm trying to get *in* to the drawer,' Lily replied, her sarcastic tone pitching dangerously low.

'And I can see that,' Cath replied in an overly friendly, understanding tone.

Lily's eyes flashed with frustration, and she bit down on her lip. 'I'm really not sure what's happening right now,' she said finally.

Cath's eyes darted around, stress showing behind her fake smile. 'The thing is,' she started slowly, 'about knives…'

'Alright, Mum?' Cillian's voice came through from the hallway.

'Oh God, here we go,' Cath muttered under her breath, looking down and putting her hand to the middle of her chest.

Lily's frown deepened, and for a moment she began to question the mental state of her sister-in-law. She *had* gone a bit off the rails after Ronan died – had even been carted off to a mental institution for several days, she'd been acting so off book. Was this some sort of second wave? Was the woman going crazy? She blinked, concern starting to replace the irritation she'd felt just moments before.

'Mum?' Cillian's voice broke through her thoughts.

'Hm?' she replied distractedly, before turning around to face him.

But as she turned, the behaviour of everyone around her over the last half hour suddenly made complete sense. Her gaze landed on the short smiling blonde standing next to Cillian, holding his hand, and her expression cooled to an icy stare.

'Mum, I'd like you to meet Billie, my girlfriend. Billie, this is my mum, Lily,' Cillian said proudly, not an ounce of caution in his brazen introduction.

The feel of Cath's arm brushing against hers shot back into Lily's mind. *She* had taken the knife. And had made damn sure Lily couldn't get her hands on another one before Cillian walked in. Which had been a wise choice. A very wise choice indeed.

CHAPTER SIXTY-FOUR

'What the *hell* do you think you're doing, bringing someone to Sunday lunch?' Lily roared, her temper reaching heights that even she hadn't known it could climb to.

They were in her study, Cath having hurriedly suggested they go and have a quick chat in private, before she could say a word to the girl he'd brought along with him.

'I brought her along because I damn well wanted to,' Cillian stated defiantly, pulling himself up to full height and standing over his mother, for once not flinching as her fury exploded.

'*Sunday* is for *family only*,' she growled, incensed that she'd had to point this well-known fact out – this *law* within their family. 'There is *one rule*,' she yelled, pointing her finger in his face. 'I don't care what you get up to in your spare time. I don't care if you fuck every whore from here to Timbuktu, from Monday to Saturday. But when it comes to *Sunday*,' she stressed, holding his gaze with hot blazing fury in her own, 'this is the one day of the week where we come together as a family, *just us*, Cillian. No one else. No one who ain't one of us. How long have you even known this girl?' she demanded.

'Couple of weeks,' he replied, nonplussed. 'But that don't matter. She's something special, and I want to bring her into my life properly. I wanted to bring her here today so she could meet *you*.'

'You could have brought her to meet me anywhere else at any other time,' she cried. 'If you wanted me to meet her, I'd have met her. But *not* at our *family* meal. I don't give a shit who she is, she could be Queen bloody Lizzie for all I care, she still wouldn't be welcome here today. *No* girlfriend has ever or will ever be welcome to join our family lunch. One day, Cillian, you'll find the love of your life and you'll marry her,' she continued with feeling. 'And on that day she'll be welcomed into our family, and she'll sit beside you at the table as we break bread and celebrate *being* this family. But until that day, you know damn well that the girls you and Connor date and fling away are not welcome here,' she said hotly, placing her balled fists on her hips as she glared up at her handsome son.

'Well,' he said, shrugging, 'I guess I'll have to marry her then.'

'Don't you fucking dare!' Lily exclaimed with furious horror. 'You can't marry a bird you've known two weeks!'

'Well, if you're saying I can't include someone who means a lot to me without marrying her...' Cillian shrugged again.

'Cillian,' Lily declared indignantly, 'you—'

'Where is she?' Suddenly, a deep, craggy voice came from the hallway. A voice that was all too familiar. 'Lily! Where are you?' The door opened and there Ray stood, concern and anger in his stubbornly set face.

'What the hell are *you* doing here?' Lily demanded.

Had the world suddenly turned upside down? she wondered. What was going on? Sundays used to be sacred in their household, a special day with rules that everyone respected. And now Cillian had turned up with a complete stranger, and Ray had bowled in unannounced like a bull in a china shop.

'Someone said you'd been collared by the FBI for stealing a painting. Is that true? Are you OK? What's happening?' His gaze travelled up and down Lily's body, his muscles slowly untensing as he realised she was unharmed. 'What happened? Who grassed you up? I'll find them, Lily. And I'll make them fucking pay.'

'No, you won't,' Lily shot back. She raised her hands to her face and rubbed, trying to make sense of all the craziness going on right now. 'Cillian, just go out to your aunt and get a drink. I'll deal with you in a minute.'

Cillian shot Ray a quick smile of thanks for taking the heat off himself, then ducked out without another word. He shut the door behind him, leaving Ray and Lily alone. For a long few moments, there was silence as they appraised each other. Eventually Ray walked slowly towards her.

'I had to come, Lil,' he said quietly with a shrug of resignation. 'You can tell me a hundred times that you never want to see my face again, but it will never stop me caring. It will never stop me watching your back, even from a distance. And these fuckers who grassed you up to the FBI, I *will* find them. And when I do…'

'No one grassed us up, Ray,' Lily answered tiredly. 'And we haven't had a collar from the FBI. We were working with them.' She went over to her drinks trolley and poured out two large whiskies. Handing one to Ray, she took a seat in one of the armchairs.

Ray sat down in the chair nearest to her and frowned. 'I don't understand. Why would you be working with them?'

She took a deep breath and sighed heavily. 'It's a long story, but it was all part of a job. We played them to get our hands on some reward money for a painting. Whoever told you all that has their wires crossed.'

'OK.' Ray stared at her, all sorts of emotions playing in his eyes. After a few seconds, he tore his gaze away and placed the whisky glass on the table next to him. 'It's like I said. I just had to make sure you were OK. I'll head off. I know it's your family Sunday thing.'

Lily watched him stand, her own emotions stirring at the sight of him and at his words. 'Wait,' she heard herself say.

Ray turned to look at her, a flash of hope in his eyes. Lily paused, unsure exactly what she wanted to say. She didn't want him to stay – he couldn't. But at the same time, she didn't want him to go either. He had always been there for her, no matter what. Even when she pushed him away. And despite how desperately she'd tried to ignore it, the truth was that Ruby wouldn't be here today if it hadn't been for his interference. She'd been headed down the darkest path of self-destruction possible. It would have only been a matter of time before Lily had received that dreaded call. But Ray had saved her.

For so long she'd been so angry. She'd felt betrayed. But after all they'd been through and now that her anger had begun to subside, she'd started to realise that she couldn't hate him for it forever.

She took a deep breath. 'I can't pretend that I'll ever fully accept what you did.' She exhaled slowly. 'But I do understand why you did it. I understand that sometimes good people do bad things for good reasons. And that this was one of those times.'

Ray opened his mouth to say something but then shut it again, seemingly unable to find the words. Lily moved closer to him, feeling the invisible magnetic pull that had drawn her to him for as long as she could remember.

'I'm still angry at you,' she admitted. 'But I don't want to be angry forever.' She stopped in front of him, close enough to feel the warmth coming from his body, but still she didn't reach out to touch him. 'I don't want to continue like this forever.'

'Neither do I,' he said in a husky voice, filled with feeling. He reached forward and grasped her arms with both hands, pulling her towards him. 'You're my one, Lily Drew. You always have been. And I'm not going anywhere. Whether you tell me to or not.'

He pulled her towards him and kissed her hungrily on the mouth. Part of Lily still wanted to push him away, to rally against him and thrive on the anger she still held inside. But a bigger part of her had missed him too much and never wanted to stop him again. She reached up and wrapped her arms around his neck.

Eventually they pulled apart and Ray looked down at her. 'I've missed you,' he said simply.

Lily nodded and touched his face. 'I've got to tie up some loose ends tonight to do with this painting, but I'll come over tomorrow. We can talk properly then.'

Ray nodded in response and grabbed her hand, putting it to his mouth to kiss her fingers. 'OK.'

They walked out together and Ray shouted his goodbyes to those all standing in the kitchen, who were busy pretending they hadn't all just been listening. He left, and Lily shut the door, touching her hand to her mouth, still feeling the tingle of his lips on hers. She'd missed him more than she'd admitted to herself, she realised.

As she wandered through to the kitchen, Ray was still very much on her mind, to the extent she'd momentarily forgotten that Cillian had decided to bring a stranger into their midst. But as her eyes rested on the girl, she bristled, her outrage flooding back.

Cath rushed forward with her wine, placing it in her hand and giving her a look that begged her to be reasonable. 'Here you go,' she said, her tone overly cheerful. 'Your wine. I've finished the potatoes and put them in to boil, so don't worry about those.'

Everyone else in the room remained tensely silent as they all waited to see what she was going to do. Lily looked at them all in turn. Connor looked terrified, even through his hard-man mask. Everyone else could be fooled by that, but not her. Not his mother. Scarlet had placed herself carefully to the side of the action zone, watching with an amused expression. The blonde girl was regarding her warily but not disrespectfully. She grudgingly gave her that. And Cillian was staring at her with brazen challenge. His brown eyes twinkled with dark promise, and no matter how intently she glared, his gaze didn't falter.

This defiance was new. In all their years, neither of her sons had stood up to her the way he had today. Not that they'd ever had much need to. She'd always been fair and had given them a very free rein, so when she *did* give an instruction, they understood it was for good reason. So the fact he'd stood his ground and gone against her the way he had today meant the girl really did mean something to him. And that was interesting. Interesting and dangerous.

She held his gaze and saw the firm resolution within. Things were changing in the Drew household. And she wasn't sure she liked it. But whether or not she did, there was little she could do to stop it. For the first time in their lives, she realised she was going to have to back down to Cillian. She could see that. Because he wasn't going to.

She stepped forward and looked the girl up and down with a hard, critical attitude. Turning away towards the kitchen, she put down her wine and picked up a punnet of mushrooms.

'Cillian, go and rearrange the table to include an extra place setting for your guest.' Her tone sharpened on the last word. 'And, Connor, you can find her a drink.' She pursed her lips and emptied the punnet onto the chopping board, picking up her knife, which had now miraculously reappeared.

Cath came to stand beside her as the tension broke and the younger generation started to chat between themselves. She pulled the carrots across the counter towards her.

'That was very big of you,' she said quietly.

'Sticks, not chunks,' Lily snapped back, letting her know she didn't want to talk about it. 'They're for crudités.'

Cath nodded, taking the hint as Lily had known she would. 'Lovely. You're making your famous garlic dip then?'

'I am,' she replied in a clipped tone.

'Good, good.'

Lily glanced sideways and Cath caught her eye, then they both turned back to the task at hand, chopping in companiable silence for a few minutes as the table was reset and Billie was asked questions by Connor and Scarlet in the lounge, where Scarlet had tactfully led them.

'You never know,' Cath said in a low voice, 'she might be allergic to garlic.'

They exchanged a loaded look and then suddenly the pair of them burst out into peals of shared laughter.

CHAPTER SIXTY-FIVE

Ruby descended the stairs and entered the kitchen, glancing through one of the windows by the front door in the hope that she might see her mother's car pulling up. The drive was still empty though, and she sighed as she made her way to the fridge. She grabbed a bottle of water from one of the neat rows her mother maintained, then closed the door, unscrewed the cap and took a long drink of the cool, refreshing liquid. She had arrived home from the salon just as everyone was leaving the family lunch, and her mother had left soon after, claiming there was some work that couldn't wait.

Lowering the bottle once her thirst was quenched, she looked around, wondering what she could do to pass the time. It was getting late, but that didn't necessarily mean Lily would be home any time soon. The firm kept her busy at all times of the day and night. It was something that had always bothered Ruby, her mother never being around. But despite her resentment, she understood why. Without Lily's hard work, the firm would have crumbled a long time ago and they as a family would be nowhere. Not that this had really benefitted her. She'd still ended up in all the lowest places.

As her mind wandered back to her old haunts, she felt the familiar pull. With a sigh, she tried to think about something else. It was a strange feeling that plagued her when she thought about heroin. It was like losing a loved one, as though she'd been dumped by the love of her life and was grieving for what they'd shared. Her heart was still there, though her body was not. But she could never go back. Not if she wanted to live. Ray had made sure she had no choice.

As she thought about Ray, her feelings of resentment began to bubble, but a small smugness rose up too. Her aunt Cath had told her about the roses, how Lily had angrily butchered the whole lot and ordered them to be dumped at his gate. She couldn't help but be pleased by this. And she also couldn't help but notice the raw loyalty her mother had shown her.

Ruby wandered to the window and leaned against the wall with crossed arms. Lily had always been loyal, had always been there for her even when she had treated her like absolute shit. Even when she'd pushed her away as hard as she could, she'd never let go. Over the years, Lily had never given up trying to help her, no matter how much Ruby had fought it. And even now, when she'd come home with nothing to offer, a jobless, angry, broken wreck, her mother had still stood staunchly by her side.

She'd dealt with Ash and cleared her debts. She'd given her a job despite everyone wanting nothing to do with her. She'd taken her back into the family home, and she'd even taken her side over Ray's, the man she had loved her entire life. And what's more, she never expected thanks. Nothing was ever a chore for Lily. Not when it came to her children. It was just who she was, and who she always would be.

Ruby wasn't blind to the fact that she went above and beyond compared to other mothers. She'd seen them over the years, watched some of her friends' mums. Some were OK, some were lazy and self-absorbed, some grudgingly did the odd favour then threw it back in their children's faces every time there was a disagreement. Some just downright didn't care. But yet she had somehow been blessed with Lily.

As she thought back over all Lily had done and sacrificed for her, and the heartache she'd put her through in return, she felt a trickle of shame. Lily hadn't just had the normal issues that came with a daughter – hormones and tantrums, fights over short skirts and heavy make-up, tears over stupid boys that weren't worth her time – she'd ended up with Ruby. She'd searched the streets night after night when Ruby had taken off for weeks at a time with no word. She'd dragged her out of drug dens, when she'd been too out of it to walk. She'd sat by her side in hospital time after time when she'd partied too hard for her body to handle, only for Ruby to disappear again the second she could.

Ruby closed her eyes as the toxicity of the whole situation overwhelmed her. She'd put Lily through all of that and for what? To what end? For the first time in her life, she suddenly felt incredibly guilty. Perhaps it was because this was the longest stretch of time she'd ever been completely clean, and because for the first time in years, her mind wasn't preoccupied with getting her next hit. Perhaps it was because she finally had the time and mental space to stand back and see the situation properly, for what it really was.

A tear formed and fell down her cheek, and she rubbed it away quickly, swallowing hard. It wasn't easy adjusting to this new life, to this *normal* way of living. But she was here and it wasn't going to change. But there were some things that needed to change. And she could see that now. The look of respect and belief Lily had given her earlier that day flashed through her mind.

She sniffed and turned back towards the hallway, making a decision. Picking up her boots, she shoved them on and went to find her jacket. She wasn't going to wait. She needed to talk to Lily now. She needed to tell her that she was sorry for all she'd done over the years and how much she appreciated that she was still around. She wasn't quite sure how she was going to word that yet – these sort of things didn't exactly come naturally to Ruby – but she could figure that out on the way over. The important thing was that her mother knew how she felt. She owed her that.

Ruby stepped out into the cold evening air and felt her heart lift. She owed her mother a lot, and tonight was the night she was going to finally begin repaying those many, many debts.

CHAPTER SIXTY-SIX

Grace pulled up outside the factory and stepped out of the car. It was now nearly eleven, meaning that Lily and Scarlet would be inside waiting. Her gaze travelled up the side of the building to the light that was on in one of the office windows. The blinds were shut, but she could make out the shadow of someone sitting at the desk. Her lip curled into an angry sneer. Which one of them it was she didn't really care. And whatever they had to say to her she didn't really care about either. After what they had done, they were past talking about anything. For what they had done, they were going to burn.

The two cars that had travelled with her came to a stop behind and her men got out to stand beside her. 'Seal all the doors,' she demanded. 'Make sure you check around the whole building. I don't want there to be any chance of escape.'

Two of her men nodded and set off one way while another headed in the opposite direction, all of them carrying strong metal chains and locks.

She turned to Duffy. 'Take the petrol barrels inside before we seal the front. Soak this floor, and make sure to douse the machinery. The quicker it goes up, the better.'

'Got it,' he replied quietly. 'Joe, Jason, come with me,' he said to the men next to him.

'Eric,' she called to the last man standing there. She pointed up at the brightly lit office window. 'Watch that window. If that shadow moves, even an inch, I want to know about it. Because whatever we have to do to make sure it happens, they need to still be in there when this place burns.'

A few minutes later, Grace stood back at a distance and watched with rising excitement as the fire quickly took hold and grew. As thick black smoke started to creep out of the cracks and crevices wherever it could find them, her mouth opened into a wide, ecstatic smile. Something about fire had always excited her, but to see it on a scale like this sent her heart racing.

Duffy came up behind her. 'Grace,' he said with a tentative note of warning. 'Grace, we should leave.'

'Shut up, Duffy,' she ordered, her eyes shining in the darkness as the flames crept out and up the sides of the burning building. 'I don't want to miss this.'

She wondered if the flames had reached them yet, up there, trapped in the office. She wondered whether they had screamed and fought against them, looking for a way out. She wondered if they'd managed to get downstairs only to realise that all possible escape routes had been blocked. Her smile grew wider as she pictured it, as she savoured the thought in her mind as one might savour the most cherished memories of the things they loved.

Finally, she wondered whether it would be the smoke or the fire itself that would kill them, as they realised in their last few seconds that they were going to die there, and that it had been her who'd ended their sad little lives.

The flames grew and climbed the walls, and then the ear-splitting sound of glass shattering cracked through the air like a gun as the windows all exploded outwards in a glittering, beautiful display of destruction.

CHAPTER SIXTY-SEVEN

One solitary tear rolled down Scarlet's cheek as she stood with her aunt in one of the flats down the road that belonged to one of their workers, watching the building burn. She couldn't quite believe Grace had actually done it. She'd threatened them, sure, but it was one thing making a threat and another entirely carrying it out. But Lily had known. Lily had been certain that the threat was real, and so they'd waited here, safely out of harm's way to see what she would do.

She raised her hand and wiped the tear away, not wanting to show weakness, even now. But as soon as she erased one tear, another fell, then another, and she found she couldn't stop them. It was just a building; bricks and mortar. But it was more than that too. That was the home of the firm, the hub of all their business dealings. It was the place her father had taken her to as a child, and where she had taken over the reins after his death. It held a hundred memories that she'd cherished having around her over the last few months as she'd struggled to come to terms with her loss.

She turned to Lily and saw the raw, haunted look on her aunt's face. Lily had lost everything tonight too.

Suddenly realising she was being watched, Lily turned towards her niece and quickly masked her pain. She took a deep breath. 'Pass me my phone.'

Scarlet shook her head. 'No,' she said. 'I'll do it.'

Lily conceded with a nod, and with a slight tremble of her hand, Scarlet picked up the phone. She dialled and then waited as it rang. It took a few rings, and as she stared down at the woman in the street transfixed by the flames, she wondered for a moment if she wouldn't answer at all. But eventually she looked down and answered.

There was a long silence as Grace waited for her to speak. Scarlet exhaled through her nose and swallowed as she carefully, and with difficulty, placed her deeper emotions aside.

'We're not in there, as you'd no doubt hoped,' she finally said, her tone as level as she could manage. 'But you have succeeded in destroying a family business that took decades to create.' She swallowed again as a lump rose in her throat.

'Then I guess I shall have to make sure my next attempt doesn't fail. You're on borrowed time now,' Grace said darkly down the line. 'I suggest you make the most of what little you have left.'

'You *could* kill us,' Scarlet countered, ready with a reply to the expected threat. 'If that would make you feel better. But doing that comes with several problems, now that we know what to expect.'

'Oh?' Grace replied. 'And what are those?'

'The first would be that we've left statements in various places with various people that will be sent straight to the police and the press if anything happens to us.'

Grace laughed down the line. 'Do you really expect me to believe that?' she asked.

'That's up to you, but it would definitely be a gamble not to, wouldn't it?' Scarlet shot back. She was met with silence. 'Those statements also mention the fact it was Duffy's car you used to kill Harry too, and where to start looking for it.' She glanced at Lily, wondering whether or not she should have used that bluff at all. They never had found any actual proof, and if they were wrong, Grace might assume they were bluffing about all of it.

'Well, well, well,' Grace hissed angrily after a short silence. 'Those are some sharp claws you have there, Scarlet. But what's to say…' she trailed off for a moment. 'I must ask, if that's not you shouting for help out the window, then who exactly is it?'

Scarlet and Lily squinted towards the burning building and both clocked what Grace was talking about at the same time. Lily gasped in horror as she recognised the telltale wild curly hair.

'Ruby!' she screamed.

She bolted for the door before Scarlet could even really register what was going on. As she did, her blood ran cold and a fist of ice grasped her heart. What was Ruby even doing there? They'd made sure the building was completely empty.

A dark chuckle sounded down the phone. 'Well,' Grace purred. 'It would seem I did repay your family after all. *That's* what you get for messing with someone like me, Miss Drew. A fact I doubt you'll forget any time soon.'

And with that the call clicked off and the woman in the street turned and walked away.

CHAPTER SIXTY-EIGHT

Lily beat at the door with both fists, trying to break it down but to no avail. They were solid fire doors, a health and safety necessity for a factory like theirs.

'Ruby!' she screamed, pulling back and looking up towards the window her daughter had been frantically calling for help from. She pulled her top up over her mouth and nose, straining to hear through the roar of the fire and to see through the thick plumes of black smoke, but she couldn't tell whether or not she was still there.

She ran at the door and tried shoulder barging it, but it stood firm. Smoke poured out through the cracks, and she could see the flames flickering through the holes where the windows had been either side, but still she fought. Back and forth she threw herself bodily, trying to get in. The chains holding the doors were too thick though – Grace had made sure of that.

Scarlet ran over, finally catching up. 'What do we do?' she yelled, the fire now so loud it was almost overpowering.

Something clanged and clunked inside, and Lily's fear intensified. The structure was giving way. And Ruby was still in there. She stared up at it, naked fear in her bearing. 'We…' She ran her hands up through her hair in despair. 'We need to get through one of the windows – we need to get in.'

Scarlet looked up through one of the windows, shielding her face from the burn of the raging hot inferno within. 'They're too high to climb in. And the fire's too strong,' she cried. 'We won't get two feet…'

'We have to try!' Lily screamed. 'Come on, help me! There has to be some water somewhere – think! I can douse myself, protect myself from the fire. And I'll climb up. I can do it if you help me.'

She geared herself up, ready to throw herself into the grasp of the flames, knowing it was insane but at the same time not able to give up. Her daughter was in there. Her flesh and blood. She had to protect her.

The sound of sirens began wailing in the distance, and for the first time ever, Lily was grateful to hear their cry.

'They'll have water – they'll get her out,' Scarlet said, hope and fear mingling in her voice. She began coughing as the smoke around them became overpowering. 'Lil, we can't stand here. Come back,' she begged, pulling at her aunt's arm.

'I can't. I *have* to get to her,' Lily sobbed, banging against the burning-hot door again with her arms, ignoring the pain it caused her. Her pain was nothing – she had to get Ruby out. She choked on the smoke and pulled her top up higher.

'Lil, they're here,' Scarlet said, her voice muffled through her own top. She pulled her again, harder, forcing her away from the door and through the thick smoke that now surrounded them. 'Lil, come on! You're no use to them or Ruby dead.'

The sense in Scarlet's words got through to her, and despite the ache to run in and save Ruby herself, she allowed her niece to pull her back. Firemen ran past with long thick hoses, immediately shooting water up at the burning building.

'Please.' She grasped at the arm of one of them as he passed. 'My daughter's in there – she's inside!'

'Where?' he asked, looking at her intently. 'Do you know where?'

'She was in the office on the top floor just above here,' Lily said. Her fear grew as she saw the look that crossed his face. A look of defeat before they'd even begun. 'She was at the window.'

Hope crossed his eyes and her own lifted along with it. 'Where? Show me,' he demanded. 'If she's been able to protect herself in that room, we might be alright.'

Lily hurried back to where she could see the office window through the smoke and peered up. But the window Ruby had been leaning out of crying for help no longer framed her wild red curls. Now, all that came out of that window were thick black curls of smoke.

CHAPTER SIXTY-NINE

Blue lights flashed around the scene in the weak morning light, though the detective inspector wouldn't have needed them to lead him to the burned-out shell. The smoke still rose steadily, despite the fact the fire had finally been put out hours before. As he approached, he looked up at it in amazement. Whoever had done it had made sure they did a thorough job. There was no chance of recovery – it would be a complete demolition job, that was for sure.

He whistled, taking in the blackened holes where windows had once been and the bare bones of one side where the wall had caved in. He ducked under the police tape, pulling his badge out as a uniformed officer ran over.

'It's OK, I'm the DI,' he said. 'Who's in charge?'

'Oh, no worries,' the officer replied with a note of relief. 'He's over there. He's been waiting for you.'

'Thanks.'

He approached the stout, miserable-looking man in charge of the scene and waited whilst he finished a call.

'Ah, you the DI?' the miserable officer asked.

'Yes…' he started.

'You took your time,' he complained. 'We've been here for hours.'

'I'm sure you've got things well in hand then,' he replied smoothly. 'I was held up with a double homicide. Been there all night and only just got the bodies off.'

'Oh, I see.' The officer in charge's tone softened slightly as he realised the other man hadn't been slacking. 'Here she is anyway.' He sighed. 'One casualty, structure is compromised, cause was petrol, stuff was thrown everywhere then lit from a small rag. Bit of it still intact – that's gone off with evidence. All the doors were chained shut.'

He frowned. 'Looks like I've got my work cut out for me,' he said quietly, staring up at the building once more. He'd already looked through the basic notes on his way over and it was an odd situation indeed. Whoever had done this had hell on their mind, and it was his job to work out who they were and why they'd gone to such lengths. 'I'm Jackson, by the way. Sergeant Paul Jackson,' the officer continued, holding out his hand.

He reached out and shook it. 'Richards,' he replied, looking up once more at the building with his bright green eyes. 'DI John Richards.'

A LETTER FROM EMMA

Dear readers,

For those of you who've started with this book, welcome to the Drews! I hope you enjoyed *Her Rival*, and if you'd like some backstory, check out *Her Revenge*, the first in this series. For those who've journeyed with me from the start, welcome back! I hope you've enjoyed watching the family grow and adapt in this book. If you would like to hear more about the series, sign up here. Your email address won't be shared and you can unsubscribe at any time.

www.bookouture.com/emma-tallon

It's been an interesting book for me to write, *Her Rival*. In particular, Scarlet's character. We've seen her grow tremendously from the beginning of the last book, and it's been really interesting plotting her journey, working out her struggles and seeing her fight her way through things. She's still so young and so new to the life, but she's made of stern stuff. I like her a lot.

Lily is someone I really enjoy writing. She's still my favourite character and someone I wish I knew in real life. She's also the character I first had in my head, before any of the rest of the family were created. She just popped up in my head one day about two years ago, demanding to have a series written about her – and here we are! I guess she really always does get what she wants.

You'll have noticed a couple of new characters have popped up in this one. Billie, Cillian's new flame, is going to be interesting to watch in the next book. The dynamic between her and Lily is something I'm greatly looking forward to writing. And of course the very handsome, green-eyed, DI John Richards. I can't *wait* to get stuck into that story! What will happen? Only time will tell…

I'll be back soon with more in the next instalment.

In the meantime, keep well and stay happy.

All my love,
Emma X

 emmatallonofficial

 EmmaEsj

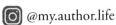 @my.author.life

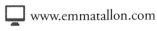 www.emmatallon.com

ACKNOWLEDGEMENTS

Big thanks to my wonderful readers. You make me smile and fill my heart with joy every time I read a review or get a message or comment, sharing your feelings about my stories or characters. Thank you for all your support through every book.

Thank you to all my amazing author friends who keep me sane throughout the writing process, especially Casey Kelleher and Angie Marsons. You two are very close to my heart, always.

I am forever grateful to my amazing editor and friend Helen Jenner. I couldn't wish for a better, nicer, funnier or more perfect editor. I feel genuinely blessed that I get to work with you. And you're never allowed to leave – this decree is now in a published book, so there's no going back. Emma's law!

And finally, special thanks to Helen Gracie, one of my oldest and dearest friends. Your unwavering support to me on all levels but especially my work has meant so much to me over the last few years. You are a wonderful person. Please never change a thing about who you are.

Printed in Great Britain
by Amazon

22939099R00192